A LIGHT *to* *My* PATH

Books by Lynn Austin

All She Ever Wanted
All Things New
Eve's Daughters
Hidden Places
Pilgrimage
A Proper Pursuit
Though Waters Roar
Until We Reach Home
While We're Far Apart
Wings of Refuge
A Woman's Place
Wonderland Creek

REFINERS FIRE

Candle in the Darkness
Fire by Night
A Light to My Path

CHRONICLES OF THE KINGS

Gods & Kings
Song of Redemption
The Strength of His Hand
Faith of My Father
Among the Gods

THE RESTORATION CHRONICLES

Return to Me

A LIGHT *to* *My* PATH

LYNN AUSTIN

BETHANYHOUSE
a division of Baker Publishing Group
Minneapolis, Minnesota

© 2004 by Lynn Austin

Published by Bethany House Publishers
11400 Hampshire Avenue South
Bloomington, Minnesota 55438
www.bethanyhouse.com

Bethany House Publishers is a division of
Baker Publishing Group, Grand Rapids, Michigan

This edition published 2014
ISBN 978-0-7642-1192-8

Printed in the United States of America

The Library of Congress has cataloged the original edition as follows:

Austin, Lynn N.
    A light to my path / by Lynn Austin.
        p. cm.—(Refiner's fire)
    ISBN 1–55661–444–6 (pbk.)
    1. South Carolina—History—Civil War, 1861–1865—Fiction. 2. African American women—Fiction. 3. Plantation life—Fiction. 4. Women slaves—Fiction. I. Title II. Series: Austin, Lynn N. Refiner's fire.
PS3551.U839L54 2004
813'.54—dc22   2004012913

Scripture quotations identified NIV are from the HOLY BIBLE, NEW INTERNATIONAL VERSION®. Copyright © 1973, 1978, 1984 by International Bible Society. Used by permission of Zondervan Publishing House. All rights reserved.

Cover design by Kirk DouPonce, DogEared Design

14 15 16 17 18 19 20   7 6 5 4 3 2 1

To Ken
with love.

Your word is a lamp to my feet
and a light for my path. . . . I have suffered much;
preserve my life, O Lord, according to your word.

Psalm 119:105, 107 NIV

Prologue

FULLER PLANTATION, SOUTH CAROLINA
NOVEMBER 1862

The only thing that was clear to Kitty in all the fussing and carrying on was that they needed to run. The Yankees were coming—thousands of them. The soldiers would steal everything they could find and burn Massa's plantation to the ground. They'd do unspeakable things to the women—white women like Missy Claire and even to slave women like Kitty. She and Missy had to flee again, just as they had fled from Massa's town house in Beaufort a year ago. The plantation was no longer safe.

"Better hurry, ma'am," the Confederate soldiers warned Missy Claire as they marched past the house. They didn't even pause for a drink of water or a bite to eat as they marched by on the double-quick. Two of the officers stopped just long enough to say, "The Yankees are coming. Six thousand of them have landed on the mainland at McKay's Point. That's only seven miles from Pocotaligo. We figure they're aiming to cut the rail line between Savannah and Charleston. I'd leave today if I were you, ma'am. Tomorrow morning at the latest."

"And be careful, ma'am," the second officer warned. "The Yanks have been stealing our slaves and arming them with guns. Nothing worse than a Negro with a gun in his hands." The soldiers tipped their hats and marched down the road toward Pocotaligo in their mismatched uniforms and worn-out boots and shaggy beards, leaving nothing but panic and a cloud of dust behind them.

They'd thrown the household into an uproar, filling it with so much fear that Kitty thought for sure it would overflow like a bucket. Missy Claire's face turned the color of pie dough, and she looked about to faint. Kitty made her sit down real quick in the nearest chair, and she grabbed a palmetto branch to fan her.

"Oh, Lord . . ." Missy Claire moaned. "Why is this happening to us again? Isn't it enough that the Yankees chased us from our home once before? Why have those cowards declared war on innocent women and children?"

Kitty waved the fan faster, moving it closer to Missy's face to help her breathe. "It'll be okay, Missy. Everything will be okay. . . ."

"No it won't!" she shouted. "Didn't you hear what they said? The Yanks are arming slaves! And once a Negro gets a gun in his hands, he'll murder us all in our beds!"

Her words gave Kitty the shivers. For a moment it was as if both of them had forgotten that Kitty was also a Negro. She'd been Missy's slave since they were children, but she'd never seen her this upset, even when they'd fled from Beaufort. Of course, back then they'd thought they would be returning to town in a day or two, once the Yankees were whipped. But that had been nearly a year ago. "Where we gonna run to this time, Missy Claire?" Kitty asked in a hushed voice.

"I don't know. They'll burn every plantation house in the area. . . . We'll have to pack up everything that we don't want to lose."

"Everything?" Kitty glanced around the drawing room. "There's so much, Missy! All of Massa Fuller's nice things. . . . How we gonna know what to take and what to leave?"

She could see that her mistress was getting control of herself again. Missy pushed the fan away from her face and rose her feet.

"We'll have to get all the other house slaves to help us. Now hurry! We'll pack as much as a wagon will hold, the most valuable things first—then leave the rest to God's mercy."

Kitty set to work as fast as she could, but it wasn't fast enough for Missy. She shoved Kitty backward and nearly knocked her down because she thought Kitty was packing one of the steamer trunks too slowly. When Kitty accidentally dropped the silver caddy, spilling the tableware, Missy grabbed hold of her hair and pulled. And when Kitty asked her who would take care of the house while they were gone, Missy Claire slapped her. "Don't bother me with your stupid questions, Kitty!" Missy wasn't usually this mean. She was scared, that's all.

"If only Roger were here," she kept saying as they went from room to room, trying to decide what to pack. The big house was crammed clear to the attic with Massa Fuller's things, passed down through his family for years and years. The paintings of all Massa's relations would fill an entire wagon all by themselves, and his books would fill a second one. Anyone could see that they would have to leave all his beautiful furniture behind—Massa's oak desk and his piano, the canopy beds and wardrobes and dressers, the walnut dining table that Delia polished with beeswax and turpentine until it gleamed like a mirror. There were closets full of table linens, feather beds and spreads; cupboards of fine porcelain, silver serving pieces and tableware. They couldn't possibly take it all. Those Yankees must be demons from hell if they would burn down such a fine old house and destroy all these beautiful things.

Kitty was upstairs packing Missy Claire's clothes when she heard the rumble of wagon wheels outside. She ran to the window, expecting to see soldiers and armed slaves coming with guns and torches. But the wagon that stopped out front was empty.

"Kitty!" Missy said as she hurried into the bedroom. "One of the field slaves finally brought a wagon up from the barn. Quit gaping out the window and start loading some of these things into it. I already told Delia to gather the baby's clothes."

Kitty scooped up two satchels and headed toward the stairs.

"Make sure you hurry right back," Missy Claire yelled. "None of your usual dawdling!"

Her words hurt more than a kick in the shins. Kitty never dawdled the way a lot of other slaves did. Maybe she daydreamed once in a while, but that was different from dawdling, wasn't it? Folks dawdled on purpose, but daydreaming was something you just couldn't help.

Kitty was still grumbling to herself about how unfair Missy was when she met Delia going down the stairs with a bundle of the baby's clothes. The little woman descended the stairs much slower than Kitty did, her joints painful with age. Kitty slowed her pace to match.

"What're you pouting about, honey?" Delia asked. "Mind you don't trip over that bottom lip of yours, hanging clear to the floor."

"Missy's been hollering at me all afternoon, Delia."

"Ain't just you, honey, that's for sure. Brr, it's chilly out here!" she said as she pushed open the door. Outside, the autumn sky was as raw and gray as a tombstone. "Can't be good for Massa's little baby to be dragging him all over creation this way," Delia said, shaking her head. "The Good Lord said that when Judgment Day finally comes, we're supposed to pray that our flight ain't coming in the wintertime."

Kitty looked at Delia in surprise. "Is this here the Judgment Day?"

"Seems like the Lord's judging some folks," Delia mumbled, nodding toward the wagon. "Never thought I'd see Massa's family riding in an old cotton wagon pulled by a team of mules."

Delia was right. The farm mules that had been hitched to the wagon were what poor folks drove around. But the Confederate soldiers had taken away all of Massa Fuller's horses a long time ago. Grady had stayed in the carriage house that day rather than watch them go. For as long as he'd been Massa Fuller's coachman, Grady had looked after those horses like they were his babies, same as Delia looked after Missy Claire's baby. He had to work as a field slave now that his horses were gone.

Kitty dropped her burdens onto the wagon bed. The driver stood near one of the mules' heads, adjusting its bridle. It took Kitty a moment to realize that the driver was Grady. He looked even thinner than the last time she'd seen him, and his clothes hung on him like rags. She longed to go to him and hold him in her arms, but when he looked up at her, his expression made her hesitate. It was almost as if he was holding her at arm's length.

But Delia didn't hesitate at all as she hobbled over to Grady and hugged him tightly. "Lord, Lord, honey! I hardly recognized you. You driving Missy Claire's wagon for her tomorrow?"

He shook his head. "I'm all through with being her slave," he said quietly. "Me and the others are stealing away to the woods tonight. Once we get to where the Yankees are, we'll all be free."

His words sent a tremor of fear through Kitty. "You can't run away, Grady! They'll send the dogs out after you if you run!"

"Who will? Ain't nobody left to chase us but the overseer. He can't catch all of us, can he?" He folded his arms across his chest and raised his chin. "You don't have to go with Missy Claire, you know. She can't make you go with her."

"What do you mean? She's our missy. We have to do what Missy says."

"No you don't," he said in a low, harsh voice. "We don't have to do nothing she says no more, now that the Yankees are coming. Y'all can come hide in the woods with us tonight . . . unless you think house slaves is too good to run off with field hands."

"Nobody's thinking that," Delia said.

"Then come with us," he urged.

Kitty gazed toward the south, the direction the Yankee soldiers would be coming from. The sky above the distant trees seemed a deeper shade of gray, as if darkened by smoke. "Missy says the Yankees ain't our friends," she told Grady. "She says they gonna have their way with all the women and—"

"Don't you know them white folks is lying?"

"Missy Claire don't lie! I been with her just as long as I can remember, and she—"

"Go on with your fancy white missy, then, if you're wanting to be her slave so bad." He spat on the ground near his feet, as if the words had left a bitter taste in his mouth.

Kitty gazed toward the woods again. It scared her to death to think about hiding in that terrible place. Snakes and spiders and alligators lived in those swamps, and the paddyrollers would chase after you with their baying dogs. When they caught you they would whip you until the blood ran. She remembered what had happened to her own parents, and she longed to run to Grady and beg him not to go. Kitty had seen the scars on his back from when they'd whipped him before.

Delia stood beside the wagon, not saying a word. But they all looked up a moment later when one of the second-floor windows slid open with a loud scrape. Missy Claire leaned out of it. "Kitty! Get back up here this minute!"

Kitty turned and ran straight into the house. Halfway up the stairs she realized that she hadn't said good-bye to Grady. She hurried to gather another load, but by the time she brought it down to the wagon it was too late. Grady was gone. She wondered if she would ever see him again.

Delia came down with two more satchels a moment later. She paused to catch her breath, leaning against the wagon.

"What are you gonna do, Delia?" Kitty whispered. "You gonna run off with Grady tonight and hide in the woods?"

"Never mind what I'm gonna do, honey. You got to be deciding for yourself what to do. Can't nobody tell you which way to go except the Lord."

"Decide? How?" Kitty had never made up her own mind before. She always did whatever Missy said and wasn't allowed to have any ideas or wishes of her own. Making up your mind was something you had to learn to do, like reading and writing—and she'd never learned those things either, only how to obey. "I don't know how to decide," she told Delia. Her words came out in a whisper, as if she were too scared to say them out loud.

"It ain't so hard," Delia said. "Just think of your life as a story. As if you're telling it around the fire someday to your children." Delia was a storyteller herself, well known among all the slaves in the area, so she knew a thing or two about spinning a yarn. She gave Kitty a minute to ponder the idea, then said, "Now, how are you wanting that story to end? What would be 'happy ever after' for you?"

Kitty didn't even have to think about it. The best ending would be to wind up in Grady's arms and finally hear him say that he loved her as much as she loved him. They would be together forever, with Grady driving Massa Fuller's carriage again and Kitty tending Missy Claire like she always had, and both of them knowing that Massa would never sell them apart.

But then Kitty remembered Grady's bitter words and she knew it was never going to happen: *"Can't nobody love you, girl, until you learn to love yourself. You obey that white woman like you were her dog—like you're dirt under her feet and she can walk all over you. Think a man can love dirt? Think a man wants a dog for his woman?"*

Kitty knew what he meant. Hadn't Missy lashed out at her just this morning, pulling Kitty's hair and slapping her? Grady said she needed to respect herself before he could respect her. But how was she supposed to do that? Would he admire her for disobeying Missy and running away?

"Now, are you seeing that ending?" Delia asked, interrupting Kitty's thoughts. She closed her eyes and imagined herself in Grady's arms.

"Yes, ma'am."

"What are you needing to do right now to get there? Beginning of that story has already been told. Can't change the 'once upon a time.' But you can be making up the middle part that will take you to the end."

Which path led to Grady? Kitty tried to picture herself running away with him, not answering Missy when she called, hiding in the woods until the wagon drove away. Then what? The only thing Kitty knew about disobeying white folks was that you got whipped for it. No, it was much easier to do what she'd always done—obey Missy, follow along behind the wagon, take care of her mistress and the new baby. But wasn't that what Grady got so mad at her for? For bending her back and thinking like a slave?

All of a sudden a scary thought shuddered right through Kitty, as if somebody had walked over her grave. How would she ever find Grady again if he ran away into the woods and Kitty went with Missy? What if she never saw him again?

"But, Delia," she said, "how will Grady and me ever find each other if he runs off and I don't?"

"Is that what you're worrying about?" Delia let out a big sigh. "Listen, honey. Maybe you'll find that boy again someday and maybe you won't. But first Grady has to find hisself. And so do you, child. So do you."

Everything went blurry as tears filled Kitty's eyes. "I don't know what that means. I don't know how to find myself," she said. "Can't you just tell me what to do, Delia?"

"Go back to the beginning," she said gently. "How'd you get to this day? If you know where you're starting from, and if you know where you're wanting to end up, then maybe you can find the path in between."

Kitty knew the beginning—of Grady's story as well as her own. She knew where they both had started out from. She wiped her tears and gazed toward the woods, remembering a time when her name had been Anna. . . .

Part One

❧

I cried out to God for help;
I cried out to God to hear me.
When I was in distress, I sought the Lord;
at night I stretched out untiring hands
and my soul refused to be comforted....
Has his unfailing love vanished forever?
Has his promise failed for all time?

Psalm 77:1–2, 8 NIV

1

Great Oak Plantation
South Carolina 1849

Anna stood on the cabin's top step, peering into the distance. It was no use. Even on her tiptoes she could see only the top of the Great Oak Tree. She was too small. And the carriage house blocked her view.

Behind her the other children squealed and giggled as they played in the muddy yard outside Slave Row. Last night's rain had pooled in shallow puddles, and her playmates had made a game out of squishing the mud between their fingers and toes and smearing it on their bare, brown skin.

Anna didn't want to play in the mud. And she didn't want to draw pictures in the dirt like she always did, either. She'd had the dream again last night, but it was growing as worn and faded as threadbare calico. If only she could touch the Great Oak Tree again and gaze at the vivid green woods beyond it, maybe she could keep the dream from fading altogether.

The tree seemed miles and miles away, up near the Big House where she was forbidden to go. Old Nellie had threatened to use the hickory switch on Anna if she went up there again. But Nellie was old and couldn't see very well. She'd gotten too tired and bent over to work in the rice fields with the other slaves, so now she took care of their children all day.

The Great Oak Tree's top branches swayed in the breeze, and they seemed to be waving to Anna. She suddenly decided that she didn't care if she got switched; she had to go. When Old Nellie carried one of the babies into the cabin, Anna saw her chance. She crept quietly away from the colorless slave yard, staying close to the row of weathered cabins, hoping no one would notice her. She turned up the driveway when she reached the carriage house, walking faster now that she was out of sight. Stones and crushed oyster shells dug into her bare feet; knots of buzzing flies warned her where the horse droppings were.

She reached the edge of the lawn at last and saw the tree up ahead, its massive trunk and spreading branches a dark silhouette against the blue sky. Pale silver moss entwined with the leaves and swayed gently in the breeze. Anna stepped off the driveway onto the warm, prickly grass and began to run.

The Great Oak Tree that gave the plantation its name stood on a rise overlooking the Edisto River, a sentry marker for ships that ferried the plantation's rice crop down to Charleston. Anna ran to it as if for shelter, resting her small palms against the bark. She felt dwarfed alongside it yet somehow very safe. She gazed up into the canopy of branches and leaves above her head, and the memories stirred.

Once there had been a tall, strong man she'd called Papa, a man she could run to for refuge. His voice was very deep and he sang to her sometimes, humming a tune that had no words. The oak's dark branches reminded her of his ebony arms, strong and muscular with corded sinews and tendons. Anna looked up at the outstretched limbs and remembered how Papa's arms had reached out to her, lifting her, carrying her.

She closed her eyes and listened to the swishing leaves and heard her mother's soothing whispers, the rustling of her skirts. Mama had been soft and sweet smelling, like the breeze that blew from the nearby flower beds. Whenever Anna had gazed into Mama's dark eyes she'd seen tenderness and love and a fierce protectiveness that made her feel very safe.

Then everything had changed.

One day the place where they lived and ate and slept was no longer surrounded by whitewashed walls but by trees—trees and bushes and tangled vines that were so tall and gnarled and thick they blotted out the sun. Anna remembered the sound of palmetto saplings brushing past her legs, rustling like her mother's voice: "Shh, Anna . . . shh. . . . You can't make a sound." Papa hummed his song very softly to her in that place.

Now Anna opened her eyes again, summoning the courage to peer into the distance beyond the Great Oak Tree, beyond the last swath of cut grass to where the woods began. She needed to soak up the lush green colors of the forest, memorizing them. But some deep fear kept her from ever venturing into that terrible place.

The woods she had lived in with Mama and Papa had been just like that distant forest—wet and green and sticky-hot, yet rich in the rainbow of colors she loved. There had been emerald blankets of thick moss coating the sides of the trees. Anna still remembered how fuzzy the moss felt beneath her hand. The trees wore long gray beards of Spanish moss.

Sometimes Papa carried her on his shoulders through the maze of green, his arms burdened with the quilt that held their bundled belongings. Sometimes Anna walked, following along behind Papa's creamy homespun shirt, the cloth dark with patches of sweat beneath his arms and down his back. The earth felt wet and soft under her feet, and tiny green frogs zigzagged across the path.

Papa carefully steered around the king snakes and rattlers that slithered across the trail or lay coiled in patches of dappled sunlight, but he hadn't been afraid. "They won't bother you none, if you don't bother them," he'd told her.

The sound of croaking, gulping frogs filled the thick air along with the harsh drones of cicadas and *whirrs* of insects. Anna swatted at the huge metallic-green dragonflies that swooped around her head. Mosquitoes and gnats and midges swarmed around her in a humming cloud, biting and stinging her arms and legs. Mama had tied a red bandana around Anna's head, just like the one she always wore, to keep the bugs out of her thick hair.

Once, as she rode on Papa's shoulders, they'd passed beneath an arch of tree branches and she'd felt cobwebs on her face. She looked up to see a huge spider, its outstretched legs as broad as her mother's hand. Anna had cried out in fright, and Papa had quickly dropped his bundle and swung her down from his shoulders, clapping his hand over her mouth to silence her. His movements had been swift and rough but his eyes were gentle and kind as he whispered, "Hush, now. Them spiders ain't gonna hurt you. They're big, but they don't mean you no harm. They're the Lord's creatures, too."

Papa and Mama walked a long, long time, it seemed, barely pausing to sleep or eat. Whenever Anna had grown hungry, Mama would pull a piece of corn bread or bits of smoked pork from the bag she carried, saying, "Thank you, Jesus, for this food" before they ate it. At dusk they sometimes saw white-tailed deer. Owls hooted in the darkness at night as Anna dozed on Papa's shoulders or in his arms.

They passed cypress trees with bell-shaped trunks that reminded Anna of hoopskirts. In places, the path grew so marshy that Papa's feet sank, and sometimes the path disappeared completely in the swamp. All that remained of it were tiny islands of trees surrounded by brackish water. Papa hopped from one island to the next until they grew too far apart, then waded through the knee-deep water. He put Anna high on his shoulders, and he unsheathed his knife, alert for alligators. He'd shown her one, floating in the water like a fallen log with only its eyes and snout peeking above the surface.

One day the narrow path ended beside a stretch of dark green grass. Papa had pulled Anna back as she'd started toward it. "You can't walk on that, Anna," he whispered. "That ain't grass, it's water. It won't hold you."

Anna didn't believe him. "Then why is that bird sitting on it? See?" she asked, pointing.

Papa shook his head. "He ain't sitting." He tossed a pebble at the bird, and as it launched itself into the air on graceful white wings, the bird's long, stick-like legs dangled for a moment. Then they curled beneath its body, hidden again, as they had been hidden beneath the water.

But as beautiful as the woods were, Anna recalled that journey with fear. Her family had been running from something. Anna didn't know where they were going or why, but her parents' faces wore looks of alarm and desperation. Mama would glance over her shoulder at each new sound, and Papa stopped to listen every now and then, wary and alert. "Lord Jesus, help us," he would murmur. "Shine your light on our path."

As the days passed, fear began building inside Anna, too, as she sensed her parents' tension, absorbing it. Even now, as she stood beneath the plantation's Great Oak Tree and gazed at the distant forest, that fear twisted inside her.

Their journey had ended in terror. One day Anna had heard a new sound in the distance, a harsh braying that made her skin prickle. Papa had stopped to listen as soon as he'd noticed the far-off barking, and his face turned gray with despair.

"No . . ." he groaned. "Oh, please, Lord Jesus . . . no . . ."

Mama clutched his arm. "What? What is it?"

"Dogs. They're tracking us with dogs." Papa scooped Anna into his arms and they began to run.

The barking drew closer. Along with it came the distant crack of gunfire. Bullets whizzed through the leaves around them like wasps. Papa ran and ran with Mama and Anna, never stopping, gasping for breath. They wove and ducked through the tangled woods and swamps, searching desperately for a place to hide. The dogs were much closer now, splashing through the water behind them. Shouts echoed through the woods, men's voices commanding them to halt. The men rode on horseback and Anna could hear hooves pounding down the trail, sloshing through the swamp, drawing nearer.

Papa ran and ran, but it was no use. The dogs had found them, and there was no place to hide in the gloomy swamp. The hounds raced through the woods, converging on them like a single, snarling beast, snapping at Papa's legs, tearing at Mama's skirts, forcing them to stop. Papa held Anna high above their reach, trying to kick the dogs away. But three white men suddenly broke through the woods on horseback, their guns aimed.

"Lord Jesus, help us!" Papa breathed.

Anna buried her face against Papa's chest as he lowered her into his arms, hugging her close to himself. She was afraid to look, afraid to cry out or make a sound. Then Mama screamed, and Anna felt her father's body lurch. He was trying to shield Anna and remain standing as the men clubbed him with their rifles. At last Papa staggered and fell, landing on his knees, still clutching Anna, covering her with his own body as men and dogs attacked. The rest of the dream turned into a nightmare that she couldn't—or wouldn't—remember.

"Anna! Get over here!"

She came out of her reverie to see Old Nellie beckoning to her from across the yard. "Anna? You hearing me? I said get on over here!" The old woman stood near the carriage house, as far as she dared to come.

Anna pressed her palms against the dark tree trunk one last time and braved a final, fleeting look at the distant forest. Then she turned and dashed across the grass toward Slave Row. Old Nellie had a hickory switch in her hand, and she caught Anna by the arm as she sped past and thrashed her bare legs all the way back to the cabin.

That night Anna lay alone in the darkness, clinging to the memories that the Great Oak Tree had awakened. She was no longer certain that the doomed flight through the swamps had been real—or that she'd ever really had a mama and papa. She drifted to sleep, longing for them to come to her again in her dreams, hoping that the dream would end differently this time.

2

RICHMOND, VIRGINIA 1853

"Get up, boy."

Grady opened his eyes. Gilbert stood over him, shaking the sleep from him. Was it morning? It seemed too dark, too quiet in the loft above the kitchen for it to be morning. He heard the faint drumbeat of rain on the roof.

"Get up," Gilbert repeated. "Massa Fletcher wants you."

The urgency in Gilbert's voice made Grady's heart pound faster, like the drumming rain. And there was something else that Grady couldn't quite place—something very wrong. The day had started out all wrong. Massa Fletcher's manservant never came up to the loft to wake him. Massa Fletcher never sent for Grady.

"But why? What's he want?" Grady asked. His movements felt sluggish, his limbs still heavy with sleep as he pulled on his trousers.

Gilbert opened his mouth as if to speak, then stopped. He quickly looked away but not before Grady saw Gilbert's chin tremble the way a woman's does when she's about to cry. "If you got shoes," Gilbert said hoarsely, "better put them on."

A sick feeling gripped Grady's stomach as he climbed down the ladder to the kitchen. He smelled ham frying and biscuits baking, but something was wrong here, too. Esther wasn't bustling around in her usual way, clanging pots and yelling at Luella. Instead, Esther stood beside the fireplace, her hands over her mouth as if she was trying to hold something terrible inside. Tears trailed down her broad face the same way the rain washed down the kitchen window. Esther's eyes never left Grady's face as he finished descending the ladder and slowly headed toward the door. He wanted to ask Esther what was the matter, but before he could speak she suddenly reached for him, pulling him into her arms, hugging the breath from him. Her body shook the way it did when Eli told one of his funny stories, but Esther wasn't laughing.

"Here, now!" Gilbert said. "Don't you do that, Esther. Don't, now." He pried her arms open, freeing Grady, then pushed him toward the door. The sick feeling in his belly tightened as he emerged into the cold rain. Then he froze at the sound of his mother's horrible, anguished cries.

"No . . . *no!*"

She was running toward him from the Big House wearing only her nightclothes, her eyes wild with fright. "*Please* don't take him. Please don't take my boy from me. *Please!*"

Eli ran right behind her, grabbing her and stopping her before she could reach Grady. "Mama!" he cried. He started toward her, but a white man Grady had never seen before lunged at him, gripping his arm and wrenching it painfully as he pulled him backward.

"Hey! Come back here, boy!"

Grady began to scream. It was what people did when they wanted to wake up from a nightmare—and that's surely what this was. He screamed and screamed, longing to wake up and see his mama bending over him, to hear Esther's familiar clamor downstairs in the kitchen. He would begin this day all over again, the way he always did, toting water and fetching wood for the kitchen fire, helping Eli with Massa Fletcher's horses. In the afternoon, when Missy Caroline finished her lessons in the Big House, they would play together in the backyard beneath the warm Virginia sun

But Grady didn't wake up. This wasn't a dream. He cried out for help as he twisted and kicked, desperate to free himself from the stranger's grip. He could hear his mama's cries above his own.

"*Please* don't send my boy away. I beg you, Massa! *Please!*"

A second white man gripped Grady's other arm and they dragged him down the brick walkway toward the street. Massa Fletcher stood near the wrought-iron gate, his arms folded across his chest. Rain darkened the shoulders of his overcoat and the brim of his hat as he calmly watched, deaf to Grady's screams and his mama's anguished cries.

"No! Don't take my boy! He's all I got! *Please,* Massa! *No!*"

Grady glimpsed Massa's cold, dark eyes for a moment and saw neither pity nor regret in them. Then the strangers dragged Grady out of the safety of the yard, propelling him toward a wagon filled with Negroes that was parked by the curb. One of the white men prodded the slaves with the butt of his whip, shouting at them to make room on the wagon. Then the two men lifted Grady like a sack of feed and tossed him onboard.

Grady struggled and fought for freedom as the damp bodies of strangers pressed all around him, holding him down. Rain soaked his clothes and ran down his face along with his tears. The wagon jolted and began to move.

"Mama!" he screamed.

"Don't you let them white folks hear you cry!" The hushed voice in Grady's ear was urgent, demanding. "Don't you ever give them that power over you."

But Grady couldn't have stopped crying even if he'd wanted to. "Mama! I want my mama!"

"Don't you let them know that," the man insisted. "That's how they keep us down, how they torment us. Show some pride, boy." The man gripped one of Grady's arms, but he continued to kick and squirm, desperate to break free.

"Hush, now . . . stop . . ." a woman's voice soothed. "Ain't doing no good to fight. You only hurt yourself if you're falling off this wagon, and then they're catching you anyways." Someone gripped his feet to keep him from kicking. The hands holding him all had shackles and chains attached to their wrists. The cold metal bumped against Grady as the wagon rumbled down the hill into downtown Richmond.

Grady was still fighting and struggling, sobbing in frustration and fear when the wagon finally drew to a halt. Every inch of his body ached, and his throat burned from screaming. The two white men climbed down from the wagon and began shouting at Grady and the others, prodding them like animals as they herded them into a fortress-like building. Dark faces peered out from behind barred windows. Grady heard the jangling, clanking sound of iron chains with every movement the captives made, scraping across the paving stones as they shuffled into the building, rattling from their wrists as they wiped the rain from their faces. Only young children like Grady had been left unshackled.

He needed to pray. Jesus would help him. Eli said Massa Jesus was always listening, always standing by ready to answer his prayers. "Please help me, Massa Jesus," he murmured. "Please, please help me!" He glanced around frantically, searching for help, waiting for Jesus to come. But one of the white men dragged him through the gate and slammed it shut.

Inside the fortress, his captors separated the men from the women and children, pushing them into two different jail cells. The big slave who had spoken to Grady in the wagon pulled him into the men's cage with him. The air seemed alive with defiance and anger while the white men were present, but as soon as the door slammed shut and they left, Grady felt his fellow captives' despair. The atmosphere was so thick with it that his insides writhed. He trembled uncontrollably. Why was this happening to him?

The cell was barren and unlit, the floor strewn with straw. The stench of filth filled every breath Grady took. Eli kept Massa's stables back home cleaner than this. Grady didn't want the filth to touch him, but there was no place to sit except the floor. As hours passed and he grew too weak with fear to stand any longer, he finally sank down, huddling with his knees drawn up to his chin, trembling. Each man seemed alone in the crowded room, unaware of the others, as if they not only were locked in this room but locked away inside themselves, as well.

Grady closed his eyes and tried to picture his mother's face. She was usually so happy, always humming or singing as she went about her work. But all he could remember was the terror he'd seen in her eyes that morning, the anguish he'd heard in her voice. He tried to recall the touch of her graceful hands as they soothed him, caressed him—but he couldn't. He felt an ache in the center of his chest.

Grady sat hunched on the floor for a very long time, wondering why he was here. Someone had made a terrible mistake. They'd realize it soon, and Eli or Gilbert or maybe even Massa Fletcher himself would drive the carriage downtown and make the jailers unlock the door. They would bring him back home to his mother. He bowed his head and prayed the way Eli had told him to. "Help me, Massa Jesus! Please, please get me out of this terrible place." He repeated the words over and over in his head, but the entire day passed, the rain continued to fall outside, and no help came.

As evening fell and the gloomy cell turned cold and shadowy, Grady smelled food and heard the white jailers' voices outside the door. As soon as his fellow prisoners heard the voices, a spark of hatred seemed to crackle through the air like lightning. Slumped shoulders stiffened with anger, and eyes that had been moist with sorrow a moment ago now froze with hatred. The hatred seemed to soak inside Grady until his blood turned to ice.

The big slave pulled Grady to his feet. He gripped Grady's face in one huge hand and raised it toward the ceiling. "You listen to Amos, boy. Hold your chin up, now. Don't you let them see you crying." The hard knot of grief in the center of Grady's chest swelled and grew, nurtured by the hatred all around him.

The jailers brought food to the other cell first. Grady heard the women clamoring and fighting for it, the children crying. Amos' hushed voice penetrated the men's cell, rallying them. "Don't be acting like animals," he ordered. "That's what they think we are. Show them we're men."

When their food came, the men divided it among themselves with no shoving or pushing. But they were forced to eat with their hands and to lap water from a trough like dogs. Amos offered Grady some food but he couldn't eat any of it, his stomach a cold, heavy lump of fear.

The cell grew dark, and the men lay down to sleep on the floor wherever they could find space. Grady sat with his arms wrapped around his knees and thought of his bed in the loft above the kitchen. He could cry all he wanted to now that it was dark and no one would see him. But he didn't think he had any tears left to shed. He had prayed all day, begging Massa Jesus for help. Why hadn't He answered?

Amos lay beside him, his hands cushioning his head. "Stop thinking about home, boy," he said. "You ain't going back."

Grady swallowed hard and spoke for the first time since morning. "W-why are we in jail?"

"You never heard of the slave auction?"

Grady shook his head, then realized that Amos couldn't see him in the dark. "No, sir."

"You're gonna be sold to a new owner. That's what they do with slaves—buy and sell us like cattle."

"My mama—" Grady began, but Amos cut off his words with an angry cry.

"Enough! You never gonna see your mama again, long as you live."

Grady pushed the heels of his hands into his eyes to hold back his tears.

"May as well know the truth, boy, so you won't keep hoping. You ain't never going home again, never seeing your mama. New massa gonna buy you and move you someplace else."

Grady managed to choke out a single word, "Why?"

Amos exhaled. "Maybe your old massa's needing the money, maybe

28

you done something wrong, maybe he's just tired of looking at you. He ain't needing a reason. You getting a new massa now. Find out soon enough if he be good or bad."

Grady lay down in the straw and covered his face to muffle his sobs. It couldn't be true. His mama would come looking for him and rescue him. She wouldn't leave him in this terrible place or let him be sold to a new master. Massa Jesus would show her where to come.

"Go to sleep," Amos said. His voice no longer sounded angry. "Only peace you ever gonna have in this life is when you're sleeping."

The words of a psalm Eli had taught him floated through Grady's mind: *I will both lay me down in peace, and sleep: for thou, Lord, makes me dwell in safety.* Eli had told him to recite those words whenever a thunderstorm or the wind scared him at night and he couldn't sleep. Eli had promised him that Massa Jesus would always be near, taking good care of him. *"Are you hiding them words in your heart?"* Eli would ask, and Grady would tap his own chest and say, *"They in there, Eli. They all hiding right down in there."* But Grady's heart felt very different in this godforsaken place, as if it were much too heavy to carry around in his chest. He lay awake for a long time listening to men snoring and women weeping. And for the first time in his life, Grady was afraid of tomorrow.

When he first awoke the next morning Grady didn't know where he was. Judging by the smell, he might have fallen asleep in the stable. He sat up and looked around. Pale bands of sunlight slanted through a high, barred window—and he remembered. Grady lay down again, buried his face in his folded arms, and wept.

After a breakfast of corn bread and pork rinds, the guards shoved Grady and the other men outside into an enclosed yard with high stone walls and a barred gate. A knot of men crowded around the gate, blocking the view of the street, but Grady could hear carriages and horses driving past. The incessant noise of scraping, rattling chains resounded in his ears, jingling like muted sleigh bells.

The rain had stopped. In the open patch of sky above Grady's head, gulls circled and screamed. The sun shone, but it seemed colder and dimmer than the sun he used to play beneath back home with his friend Caroline. He thought of her when a frail brown sparrow landed on top of the wall above him, pecking at the stones. *"That gal don't eat enough to keep a sparrow alive,"* Esther always used to say. Caroline was older than Grady but smaller, as fine-boned and delicate as a bird. For as far back as Grady could recall, they had played together in the backyard and pestered Eli with their endless questions.

Caroline had white skin like her father, Massa Fletcher. White skin like Grady's jailers. The color of a person's skin had never seemed important to Grady before, but he'd awakened yesterday to the realization that he was a Negro, a slave, like all the other dark-skinned people imprisoned with him. The men on the outside of the bars, the ones holding the keys, were white.

"God's eye is on the sparrow," Eli had told him. *"He knows if one of them be falling down."* Eli had always seemed so certain. But why hadn't God been watching over Grady yesterday when those men had grabbed him and locked him up in this place? Why hadn't He answered all Grady's pleas for help? Massa Jesus might still live back home with Eli and Caroline and Mama, but it didn't seem like He would ever come near a place like this. There were no words of Jesus hidden in Grady's heart here. The sparrow hopped along the top of the wall, then flew away. Grady's eyes filled with tears.

The big slave's voice came from behind Grady: "That's freedom, boy." Grady didn't turn around, unwilling to let Amos see his tears. "Freedom means flying away anytime you want, going wherever you want—just like that bird. Being free is all I think about, all the time. I'm just biding my time, and when the chance comes, I'll be flying away, too. In the meantime, you gotta plan for it, boy. Know where you gonna go and how you're getting there. Otherwise they catch you right away and whip you till you wish you was dead."

Grady had no idea what Amos was talking about. He'd barely known fear or uncertainty during all the years he'd lived above the kitchen with Mama and Eli and the others. He'd known that he wasn't allowed inside the Big House where Caroline lived, but until those white men had dragged him away against his will, until they'd locked him behind barred doors, Grady had never felt a lack of freedom.

The slaves' time in the exercise yard ended much too soon. The guards herded them back into the cell and left them there for another long night. Early the following morning, the jailers arrived and ordered them to strip to their underdrawers in preparation for the auction block. "Show them you aren't hiding any defects," a guard explained. Without a word, the other men began to undress. Grady hesitated.

"Do it, boy," Amos ordered.

Heat rushed to Grady's face as he fumbled with his buttons. He had never undressed in front of strangers before. He began to shiver, not from the cold but from shame at his nakedness. The big man poked his bare shoulder.

"You stand up tall and proud, you hear? This is the way God made you. You ain't needing to be ashamed. The white folks is the ones who ought to be ashamed."

Guards herded them out of the cell and marched them across the yard to the other building. Once inside, they ordered Grady and the others to stand on a raised platform above a huge crowd of spectators. Grady forced himself not to hunch his shoulders, not to cry, even though he saw white women and children staring up at him. One by one the white men shoved the other slaves to the front of the platform and auctioned them off to the highest bidder.

"Now, here's a healthy young buck," the auctioneer said when it was Grady's turn to go forward. He felt rage building inside him as he gazed into the distance above the heads of the spectators and bidders, refusing to look at their faces as they stared up at him.

"He looks well-fed, sturdy bones, good breeding," the auctioneer said. "About nine or ten years old, I'd say. Turn around, boy, and show us your back." Grady obeyed. "See there? Not a mark on him," the auctioneer said. "He knows how to mind. Turn around again and raise your arms, boy."

Grady had seen the other slaves lift their arms with their palms spread. He refused to make the gesture of surrender. He curled his hands into tight fists before raising them. Laughter rippled through the crowd.

"Well, now," the auctioneer chuckled, "you can see by the size of those fists that he's going to be a big, strong buck someday. Good breeding stock. Who'll start the bidding at forty dollars?"

Grady couldn't understand the auctioneer's babble as the spectators bid on him. He gazed straight ahead, unblinking, until the auctioneer shouted "Sold!" and Grady was pulled off the platform. Someone thrust his shirt and trousers into his hands, then marched him forward to meet his new master.

Mr. Edward Coop was a stern, shrewd-eyed man in his fifties, impeccably dressed in a dark, vested suit and starched white shirt. His graying brown hair was receding, making his long, narrow face appear even longer. A drooping mustache hid Coop's unsmiling mouth, and his gray eyes seemed cold and piercing as he examined Grady up close. Coop's Negro servant reached for a pair of manacles and tried to shackle Grady to the chain along with all the other slaves Coop had purchased, but Grady's wrists and ankles were slender enough to pull free.

"You won't run off, will you boy?" Coop demanded. "Know what happens if you do?"

Grady didn't reply. He had no idea what to say. Coop held a short riding crop in his hand, and before Grady could react, his new master raised his arm and whipped the leather across his bare shoulders with two quick slashes. The blows burned as if a hot poker had seared Grady's skin. The sudden violence and pain shocked him, but he forced himself not to cry, shuddering with the effort.

"Now you know," Coop said. "If you try to run off you'll get forty more when I catch you. And you better know I'll catch you."

The tears Grady swallowed seemed to travel to his chest where the knot of hatred swelled and burned. Added to what he felt for Massa Fletcher was a newly formed hatred for Edward Coop, a hatred that was quickly growing to include all white men. Because there was no doubt at all in Grady's mind that they were responsible for his pain and fear and grief. White men had done this to him. And he hated them all.

3

GREAT OAK PLANTATION
SOUTH CAROLINA 1853

It seemed to Anna that she was always hungry, all the time. She lived down on Slave Row like a wild barn cat, eating any crumbs that got tossed her way, staying in whichever dingy cabin she could sneak into at night, sleeping in any bed full of young ones that had room to spare. It was easier to find someone to curl up alongside in the wintertime than it was in the summer—as long as she was willing to be on the edge of the bed where the cold air came in and not snuggled down in the middle where it was nice and warm. And Anna was willing. She took whatever scraps of warmth she could find, dodging blows when she got in someone's way, scrabbling for enough food to quiet her empty stomach.

Every morning before the sun rose, the horn blew to wake everybody up. Folks would rise from their beds, weary in body and spirit, as if they hadn't slept at all. Nobody talked much as they made their way to the rice fields, their lean bodies moving like they always ached. Most of the time they'd go off singing, their voices slowly fading into the distance. But Anna knew by the sound of those songs that working in the rice fields was a hard, hard life. Folks called them songs, but they seemed more like groans to Anna, the way people moan in their sleep when they're having a bad dream.

It would be nearly dark before those grown-ups made their way home again. And they returned home bone tired, too—day after day, year after year. Theirs wasn't any kind of life, just a dreary existence, laboring and sleeping and laboring some more. And that was bound to be Anna's future, too, in another year or so. But for now she was still too young to go off to the rice fields, still young enough to be cared for by Old Nellie, even though Anna never needed much tending.

The spring morning had been warm the day Anna wandered into the carriage house and discovered the kittens. One of the cats had hidden a litter of them in the back corner behind an empty barrel. They were wild things, nearly as skittish as Anna was, but she petted those kittens every day until they got used to her. They brought pleasure and pain in one tiny bundle, their soft fur tickling her like feathers, their prickly claws raking like briars. They quickly became Anna's best friends, even if the sting of their claws did make her eyes water. Most of all, she loved the warmth of them, the life she felt in their purring, rumbling bellies.

One day when the kittens were old enough to leave their nest in the barn, Anna carried two of them down the long driveway and across the grassy yard to her favorite spot beneath the Great Oak Tree. She was sure to get a licking for wandering this far away, but Anna didn't care. She wanted to share her special place with her new friends. Together they played on the shady grass and climbed one of the tree's low hanging branches. Anna teased the kittens with a feathery strip of gray moss, watching them chase it in circles. Then, when both she and the kittens had played themselves out, Anna curled up beneath the huge tree with them and nodded off to sleep. A shrill voice startled her awake.

"You have kittens! Give me one!"

Anna opened her eyes to see a white girl hurrying toward her. The girl's eyes were as pale as water, and her pinkish-white skin made

Anna think of a newly plucked chicken. She'd watched the kitchen girls scald a bunch of chickens in hot water and pluck out all the feathers until they didn't look anything at all like the chickens that ran around the backyard. That's how this strange girl looked to her, barely resembling the real live, dark-skinned persons Anna lived with. She'd only seen the white folks who lived in the Big House from a distance, never this close. In fact, Anna had always run off whenever one of them came near, afraid that whatever had happened to make the rich, brown color fade from their skin would happen to her, too.

"I want a kitten," the pale girl insisted. "Give me one." Her voice was very loud, and as she walked toward Anna, something beneath her skirt made a rustling noise like a dog going after a rabbit in the bushes. Her hair was as ugly as the rest of her—straight as straw and as thin and colorless as smoke. She scared Anna half to death, and of course her kittens were just as scared as she was. They ran off and hid in the boxwood bushes at the edge of the garden. But Anna couldn't scramble to her feet fast enough to get away.

"Hey! Where did they go?" the girl asked, planting her hands on her hips. She was taller than Anna and a few years older. Anna could tell because the white girl had her two front teeth already, while Anna's were still growing in.

The girl stomped her foot. "Answer me! Where did the kittens go?"

"Y-you scared them away," Anna said.

"Well, go catch them and bring them back. I want to hold one."

No one had ever told Anna that she had to obey white people, but she knew. The girl was loud and bossy like the white overseer, and the look in her eyes was as sharp as knives.

"They'll scratch you," Anna warned. "Kittens have claws and they scratch." She held out her bare arms to show the claw-stripes, hoping the girl would change her mind. Anna didn't want to share her kittens.

The girl stuck out her chin. "They won't scratch *me*."

Her words made Anna curious. She wanted to see how this homely, white-skinned girl could tame those prickly kitten claws. Anna got down on all fours and crawled over to the boxwood where they had disappeared, meowing like a cat, trying to coax one of them out. The girl turned and skipped off shouting, "Mother! Mother come here. That little darkie has kittens and I want one."

Anna peered out from the bushes and saw a large white woman strolling across the lawn followed by Bertha, the Big House mammy. Bertha pushed a strange wicker chair with wheels and an umbrella on top, and riding inside was a fat little white girl with a round pink face.

"Don't shout, Claire," the large woman said. "Young ladies don't shout."

"That darkie has kittens," Claire said. "I saw a gray one and a striped one. I told the darkie I wanted one, but they ran under the bushes."

"It's just as well. They're wild animals, Claire. They probably carry all sorts of vermin and diseases. I don't want you anywhere near them."

"But I want one! I want to take one up to my room to keep!"

"Absolutely not. I won't have wild cats running around inside our house. They'll destroy the furniture and all the carpets."

All of a sudden it was as if an invisible animal had leaped on top of that girl and was tearing her limb from limb. She threw herself on the ground, kicking and wailing and making a terrible racket. "I want one! I want a kitten! I hate sleeping all alone in my room!" she wailed.

Anna had never seen such a fearsome sight, nor could she imagine what was wrong with the girl. But her mother didn't seem to notice anything wrong. "You know Mammy Bertha needs to sleep in baby Katie's room," she soothed.

"I hate Katie! I want Mammy with me, and if I can't have Mammy, then I want a kitten!"

"I'm sorry, but it's out of the question. They're nothing but mangy old barn cats. But if you stop fussing, maybe your father will buy a little dog for you the next time he goes to Charleston."

"No, *now*! I want a kitty now! Make that darkie catch one for me!"

The girl's angry red face was so terrifying that Anna got down on all fours again and began meowing and acting like a cat, trying to coax one of the kittens from its hiding place. Quick as can be, Claire's tears turned to giggles. Anna couldn't imagine how she could do that—switching from one to the other just as fast as you could blink.

"She's funny, Mama." Claire said. "She makes me laugh. I want the darkie to be my kitty."

"Oh, good heavens, Claire. She's just as filthy as those cats are. We can't have such a creature in our house."

The terrible wailing started up all over again, and Anna wanted to stay hidden in the bushes with the cats. Claire's mother must have known that the only way to stop the racket was to let her have her own way because that's what she finally did. And if Claire was going to make her mother choose between bringing a kitten into the house or bringing a darkie, Anna turned out to be the preferred choice.

"All right, Claire. All right. Stop fussing. Mammy can fix a blanket for the darkie on your bedroom floor. But first we'll have to find her kin. We can't have her crying for her mother in the middle of the night and waking everybody up." She bent down to speak to Anna, wrinkling her nose as if she'd smelled something sour. "You, there . . . come on out of the bushes and tell us your name."

"She's *Kitty*," Claire said before Anna could reply. "I'm going to call her Kitty because that's what she is—my very own kitty."

Anna crawled out from beneath the bush and saw that the angry red color was slowly fading from Missy Claire's face. Her mother turned to the nursemaid.

"Bertha, do you know who this darkie belongs to?"

"That one? She don't belong to nobody, Missus Goodman. Child's mama has been gone a long while back."

"All right then, come along," Missus Goodman said, but she didn't sound very happy about it. "We'll start by getting her cleaned up. She certainly can't come into the house all filthy. I won't have her bringing in fleas."

Anna scrambled to her feet, but Claire pushed her back down.

"Not on two legs. Kitties don't walk on two legs. And meow for me again."

She did what she was told, following Claire on her hands and knees, all the way across the grass to the yard outside the kitchen where the house slaves lived. Daisy and two other slaves had set up the laundry tubs and were busy washing clothes. Missus Goodman ordered them to scrub Anna, too. "I don't want her bringing fleas and lice into my house," she said. "And find her something decent to wear."

Anna had never had a bath in her life, as far as she could remember, and she didn't like it one bit—especially when they dumped water over her head to wash her hair. The harsh soap stung her eyes, and Daisy scrubbed her skin until Anna thought for sure all the color would come off. She really started to panic when she saw how black the water had turned. But when Daisy finally decided she was clean and hauled her out of the tub, Anna was glad to see that her skin was still as brown as it had always been. It felt good to be clean. For the first time in her life she didn't feel all itchy. Daisy dried her off.

"Here, put these on," she said. "We found you an old pair of Missy Claire's bloomers and a muslin shift she's outgrown."

"Come on, Kitty. Follow me," Missy Claire said in a sweet, sing-song voice. Anna crouched down on all fours and followed her through the back door and into the Big House, meowing every few steps. Missy Claire led the way up a tall staircase, and Anna had never seen so many steps before, much less climbed them on hands and knees. When she reached the top she thought for sure she'd climbed up to heaven as Missy led her into the most beautiful room Anna had ever seen, filled with sunlight and color. It was bigger than any of the cabins on Slave Row, and Missy had it all to herself! Missy slept in a high, curtained bed that was as soft as a bale of cotton.

The floors were made of wood, not dirt, and were covered with brightly colored rugs. Anna gazed around in wonder and saw a small horse made out of wood that had rockers on the bottom like Old

Nellie's rocking chair. Beside it was a little house, made to look like Massa's Big House, with tiny furniture inside the rooms. In the center of Missy's bedroom was a little table and four chairs that were just Anna's size, with beautiful, child-sized dishes at each place. Missy's dolls perched on two of the chairs, but they weren't at all like the cornshuck dolls Anna had played with on Slave Row. These dolls looked almost real with their beautifully curled hair and delicately painted faces and tiny hands. For a moment Anna forgot to meow as she tried to take it all in.

"Jump up on my bed," Missy ordered. She slept in a high, curtained bed that felt as soft as a bale of cotton. Missy climbed up beside Anna and began petting her head. At first Anna flinched because she wasn't used to being touched, but she quickly discovered how good it felt.

"Ooh, your hair feels funny, like a sheep," Missy said. "Now make that purring noise kitties make."

Anna was so happy she barely needed to be told. She curled up on that beautiful feather bed and purred like a contented kitten all on her own.

A week later, Missy Claire still wasn't bored with the game. Neither was Anna. She was quite content to pretend she was a cat and had even learned to answer to her new name, Kitty. Bertha put a blanket on the bedroom floor where Anna was supposed to sleep at night but after she and Missy were alone, Missy would sometimes let her jump up on the bed and sleep near her feet. Anna's knees were getting bruised from crawling all around on them, but she didn't care as long as Missy fed her and petted her. She would be a cat for the rest of her life and forget she'd ever been a little girl named Anna, if it meant living in the Big House from now on.

Every morning Mammy Bertha brought Missy Claire's breakfast up to her room on a tray, and Anna was allowed to eat the scraps when Claire was finished. Anna ate her evening meal outside in the kitchen with the other house slaves, and at first they weren't too friendly toward her. Cook made her feel about as welcome as a stray dog.

"Well, well! You sure moved up in the world, didn't you, now?" Cook said when Anna had been eating there about a week. From the way Cook stood with her head cocked to one side, Anna knew she wasn't too happy about it.

"Leave her alone," Mammy Bertha said softly. "She's just a child."

"Don't you be getting used to this," Cook warned. "That Missy Claire's a spoilt one. You'll be heading back down to them cabins just as soon as she gets tired of you."

"Leave her alone. She's Lucindy's girl, you know."

"You gonna be a kitten the rest of your life so you can stay?" Old Henry asked with a grin.

"That's my new name," Anna said. "I'm called Kitty now."

Henry laughed out loud. But later on, after dinner, Bertha took Anna aside. "They're right, you know. Better be making yourself useful if you don't want to be sent back down where you come from. Mind you, I could use some help with them two girls. And Missus Goodman's gonna have another baby, couple months from now. You keep Missy Claire and Missy Kate laughing at your antics, and maybe they let you stay. Otherwise, you be going back down to Slave Row."

"I don't want to work in the rice fields," Anna said.

"All right, then. Pay attention and work hard. That's the best way to make sure you're staying here. If Missy Claire takes a liking to you, maybe you can learn to be her chambermaid someday."

Anna paid attention to everything Mammy Bertha said and helped her every way she could. She emptied Missy Claire's chamber pot in the morning, fanned her when the afternoons grew hot, and swished away the flies while she ate her evening meal. If Missy got tired of her, Anna would go play with Missy Kate, turning somersaults, playing peek-a-boo, and doing anything else she could think of to keep the younger girl happy.

Meanwhile, Anna was starting to lose some of her scrawniness after eating in the kitchen every night. And the other house slaves were getting used to having her around, even Cook. There were a dozen or so house slaves and all their different shades of black skin fascinated Anna. She still thought white people's skin was sickly-looking, like the faded grass and pale worms you find when you move a stone. Old Henry's skin was the darkest of all, so black it almost looked blue—like the sky on a moonless night. Anna must have stared at him a little too long one day because he suddenly asked, "What you looking at me for?"

"B-because," Anna stammered, "I never seen anybody so dark. It's the most beautiful color ever. How'd you get skin like that?"

"Born with it, same as you."

"But it's not the same as me. It's not the same as anybody's. Daisy's skin is coppery brown, just like that kettle over there. And Cook's is like a plowed field. Mammy Bertha's is just the same color as ashes, and Mary's skin looks like molasses."

There were ripples of laughter all around the table, but Anna didn't know what had caused them. "How about your own skin, then?" Daisy asked, pointing to Anna. "What color are you?"

"Me? I'm like the crust on a fresh loaf of brown bread." The others laughed again. Anna still didn't know why. "We're all different colors, ain't we? Just like trees. Sometimes their bark is dark brown, sometimes lighter—just like our skin."

"You're wrong!" Cook said, frowning. She was the only one who hadn't laughed. "There's only two colors of skin—white and black. All the in-between ones is still black. And as far as the world's concerned, the only good color skin to have is white."

That was the first time Anna had heard anyone say it outright, but when she thought about it later, she knew Cook was right. People with white skin never did any work. They slept in soft beds and ate the very best food and had scores of black people to wait on them. Missus Goodman seemed terrified that Missy's milk-white skin would get dark, so she was always reminding her to use a parasol or wear a hat whenever she went outside. Anna couldn't understand why. Dark skin was much, much better—even if it did mean she had to work hard and sleep on the floor.

She was learning to do all kinds of things in the Big House—

helping Missy get dressed and undressed, filling and emptying her washbasin, running and fetching things for her or for Mammy Bertha. Anna had no time to play with her kittens anymore. And by the time they'd grown into cats, she had quite forgotten that her name had ever been Anna.

CHAPTER

4

RICHMOND, VIRGINIA 1853

A week after Grady had been sold at the auction, his new master, Edward Coop, came for him and all the other slaves he had purchased. Coop's manservant, William, carefully inspected the slaves' shackles to make sure they were secure before the guards unlocked the door. William was a stocky, fierce-looking Negro who showed no sympathy at all for his fellow slaves as he poked and prodded them into a column, walking two-abreast. He ignored one of the men who complained that his leg irons were too tight and were rubbing his skin raw, and it seemed to Grady that William sided with their white master more than with his fellow slaves, in spite of his inky skin.

William chained all of the slaves together except Grady and herded everyone out of the slave pen for the last time. Grady had gone all week without washing, and he felt grimy with sweat and filth. Mama had always kept him clean, making him wash his face and hands and scrub behind his ears every night before he went to bed. Once a week she would make him take a bath in the kitchen in the big tin tub. But even more than he hated the dirt, Grady hated that he reeked of fear.

He tried to look around as William and Massa Coop marched the slaves through the streets, hoping to see his mama or Eli coming to rescue him. But Coop forced them to shuffle along at such a brisk pace that Grady needed to watch his footing on the lumpy cobblestone streets just to keep up with everyone. His new master had purchased about fifty slaves, most of them men between the ages of twenty and forty. Grady was the only child. The women were all young and pretty, some still in their teens. They looked as terrified as Grady was.

He stuck close to Big Amos, who had also been bought by Massa Coop. But Amos' steps slowed when he saw that they were headed down to the docks at Rockett's Wharf. "This ain't good," he mumbled. "This ain't good at all."

Grady's stomach clenched in fear. "What's wrong?"

"He's gonna put us on a ship. That means we going a long ways away, not some plantation close by. If we was being sold around here, they'd make us walk."

The slave who was chained to Amos gave a tug to make him keep up. "I heard the guards talking yesterday," he said. "Massa Coop ain't buying us for hisself. He's a slave trader. Gonna sell us off in every port along the way, all down the coast, far as Florida and maybe New Orleans."

Amos swore. "Farther south we're sold, the harder it's gonna be to escape. Gotta go through too many slave states to get north again."

Grady didn't care about escaping to freedom, only about going home. But the farther they sailed from Richmond, the smaller the likelihood that he would ever see his home or his family again.

They turned a corner and Grady smelled the raw, fishy odor of the river. Sunlight reflected off the water, making him squint in the sudden brightness. Dozens of ships crowded the piers at Rockett's Wharf: steamboats with tall, black smokestacks, sailing vessels with masts and rigging, barges and keelboats and paddleboats. Well-dressed passengers ambled around the docks, preparing to board, saying good-bye to their loved ones: men in dark suits and hats, children dancing with excitement, women in brightly colored dresses, their stiff skirts flaring like bells. Families stood near their carriages and drays, waiting as house slaves shouldered trunks and carried satchels onboard. As Massa Coop herded Grady and the other slaves past, chains jangling and scraping, the white passengers took no more notice of them than they did of the sacks of grain and other cargo being loaded into the hold.

Panic swelled inside Grady at the thought of sailing far from home. He turned to look back at the city of Richmond, searching for St. John's steeple on Church Hill near his house, desperate for one last glimpse of the only home he'd ever known. But William gripped his arm and turned him around, marching him up the gangway onto the steamship. Grady tried to look over his shoulder, but before he could spot the familiar landmark nestled among the trees, he tripped over a coil of rope and fell facedown on the deck. William grabbed the back of his shirt and hauled him upright again, shoving him toward an open hatch with a steep set of stairs leading down into the bowels of the ship. Grady peered into the dark hole and felt as though they were shoving him into his grave.

Suddenly, the urge to fight back, to save himself, welled up inside him, out of control. *"No!"* he screamed. "No, help me! Somebody help me!" He ran to the ship's railing and clung to it, fighting with all his strength to keep from being sent below with the others. "Help me, Massa Jesus! Please help me!"

"Stop it, you little fool!" William hissed as he pried Grady's hands loose. "Don't make no trouble for me—or for yourself." He clamped his hand over Grady's mouth and carried him back to the hatch and down the stairs. Grady kicked and struggled all the way as William dragged him into a room in the hold with all the other slaves, men and women alike. He heard the door being bolted shut from the outside.

"Shut up!" William said as he dropped Grady to the floor.

He could feel the ship rocking gently. The room was dark and stuffy, the stench and despair even worse than it had been in the slave pen. Grady and the others were no longer human beings but trade goods being shipped to market like the bales of cotton, barrels of salted fish, and sacks of grain that had been loaded into the hold with them. His stomach ached with the injustice of it. Rage at his helplessness burned inside him until he thought it would consume him. When he looked around he saw the same anger mirrored on every man's face and heard the anguish he felt in the women's quiet, mournful weeping. Unable to stop himself, Grady closed his eyes and clenched his fists and roared with despair.

Without warning, William dealt Grady a blow to his stomach that knocked the wind out of him and sent him sprawling backward. Then William crouched over him as he gasped for breath and shook him like a rag doll.

"Now, you listen here, boy! If one of them white passengers up-stairs hears you carrying on this way, then both of us gonna get a whipping! You quit that hollering, you hear? If you don't, I'll tie you up and stick a rag in your mouth. That what you want? Huh? Is it?"

Grady managed to shake his head, battling panic at not being able to draw a full breath. The room whirled dizzily as William continued to shake him. Seconds before Grady thought he would pass out, Big Amos pried William's hands off.

"Okay, he's quiet now! Leave him alone!" Amos said. He'd had to drag the slave he was still shackled to across the room in order to defend Grady, and the man was not very happy about it.

"I gotta keep this boy quiet," William told Amos. "You mind your own business."

"If you kill him he'll be real quiet, won't he," Amos said with a growl. "Then Massa have your hide, too."

"Think you can make him mind any better?" William asked. He backed away a step, dusting off his hands.

"He won't make any more noise," Amos promised. He bent down to prop up Grady in a sitting position so he could breathe, then sank down beside him with a sigh, leaning his back against the hull. The slave he was shackled to had no choice but to sit down beside them.

"Leave us," Amos told William. The servant glared at them for a long moment, then shuffled away to begin unchaining the slaves.

At first Amos sat silently beside Grady, staring blindly ahead. But as Grady's breath returned to him and his gasps gradually gave way to quiet sobs, the big slave began to speak. His voice was so soft Grady had to strain to hear him.

"Every one of us knows exactly how you feel, boy. We'd like to start howling just like you done. But we already learned that it don't do no good. Ain't nobody taking pity on us, least of all them white folks upstairs. I been keeping all my anger inside for a long, long time now, storing it up for a better time. One of these days, soon as I get the chance, they gonna be real sorry they done this to me. Real sorry they sold me away from my wife and kids, because as soon as I escape, I'm gonna kill as many white men as I can get my hands on. Gonna kill their white women and children, too."

Grady heard the deadly rage in Amos' quiet voice and never doubted that he meant every word.

"You keep storing up that anger, boy. Let it burn inside you. Because there's gonna be some nights that are so dark and cold, you'll need that fire to stay alive."

As Amos recited his plans for revenge, the helplessness Grady felt slowly began to ease. He would get even, too. Someday he would make white people suffer the way he was suffering.

Soon they heard the rumbling, hissing sound of the steam boilers firing up, then the clamor of the anchor chain being raised. Grady wouldn't have known what those fearful sounds were if Amos hadn't explained each one to him in the same somber voice.

"They firing the boilers now—working up steam so we can shove off soon."

The whistle blasted and the ship began to move. Grady felt the motion like a vague dizziness until the rocking and swaying became more apparent. Water slapped against the hull behind him and vibrations from the screw propeller rumbled through the deck beneath him. He closed his eyes, fighting a new wave of panic as he pictured his mama and all the people he loved slipping farther and farther away. Amos said he would never see them again.

Who would he be without his family? How would he survive without his mama to hold him and tell him she loved him? Who would spend time with him the way Eli had, telling him stories and teaching him things, or give him special treats like Esther always did? Back home Grady had been surrounded by people who loved him, and their love told him who he was. Now they were gone. He was sailing far from home, and he felt as though he was losing himself as much as his family. But he wouldn't cry—and he wouldn't pray. He would let his unshed tears and his unanswered prayers turn to gall in his belly, fueling his rage.

By afternoon the sea had grown rough, the air in the hold stifling. Some of the others started to vomit. Grady might have, too, if there had been any food in his stomach to lose. Massa Coop had loaded plenty of smoked meat and cornmeal in the hold for them to eat. They would be well fed. But Grady shook his head when Amos offered him some.

"Won't do you no good to starve yourself, boy," he said.

Grady shrugged. "I ain't hungry." He swallowed painfully, his throat still sore from screaming earlier that morning. The slave who had been chained to Amos leaned toward Grady and spoke for the first time since they'd boarded.

"You're right, boy. May as well die now than die slowly down there."

A shiver passed through Grady. "Down where?" He hoped they weren't going to send him deeper into the bowels of this awful ship.

"Down south. They're taking us to the Deep South. Know what that means?"

Grady shook his head.

"Heat and fever and swamps and snakes. Hard, hard work chopping cotton, planting rice, or working in the sugar cane and hemp fields. Barely giving us enough food to stay alive. Whips flying across our backs all day long."

Grady looked up at Amos. "That true?"

He nodded silently, his face like stone.

Grady drew a deep breath, then let it out slowly. He wouldn't cry. He wouldn't. Snatches of scriptures that Eli had once taught him tried to float through his mind, but Grady angrily pushed them away. None of them were true. Massa Jesus didn't have His eye on Grady. He didn't love him. And for sure He wasn't here with him on this ship. Maybe Jesus wasn't strong enough to help him, or maybe He just didn't care. Either way, Grady was all finished with Massa Jesus. All the things Eli had taught him were a bunch of lies.

By evening the motion of the ship and the terrible smells in the airless hold had made Grady so nauseated that he began to vomit, too. There was nothing in his stomach to lose but he heaved over a bucket just the same, then lay curled up on the deck in misery between bouts of dizziness and vomiting. Amos tried to make him drink some water, but it wouldn't stay down. Grady couldn't remember ever feeling so sick. His head pounded and his insides ached until he felt so wretched he wanted to die.

He had no idea how many days and nights he spent that way. He was too sick to care. But eventually the ship docked in Wilmington, North Carolina, and Massa Coop came for his slaves. William, who had been locked in the hold with them all that time, fastened the shackles and chains onto everyone's wrists and ankles again before Coop finally opened the door to the hold.

As Grady went out the door, William grabbed his arm, squeezing it until it ached. "I ain't letting go of you," he said. "You open that big mouth of yours and I'll knock your teeth down your throat. Understand?"

Grady nodded. He was much too sick to holler, let alone try to run away. Coop led them ashore, marched them to a slave pen similar to the one in Richmond, and locked them inside. But at least there was fresh air and sunshine in this one. At least the terrible motion sickness would end.

It took two days on dry land for Grady to feel well enough to eat

His strength slowly returned. Massa Coop had added a few more slaves to the group and had sold several others to the white men who crowded around the gate of the slave pen every day, looking them over. Then they boarded another ship. Coop repeated this routine as they traveled down the coast, stopping in port cities like Charleston and Beaufort and Savannah, spending a few days in each one. Wealthy planters who were in the market for slaves would call on Coop, and he and William would escort them to the slave pen to make their selections.

On their last day in Savannah, Massa Coop sold Big Amos. It happened so quickly that Grady didn't even have a chance to say good-bye to his friend. One minute Amos stood near Grady in the yard, the next minute Massa Coop handed over the big slave to a new owner. Grady felt the loss like a blow to the stomach. But he held back his tears as he remembered Amos' words on the first day they'd met: *"Don't you let them white folks hear you cry! Don't you ever give them that power over you."*

As he watched Amos' new owner lead him and four other slaves away, Grady slowly became aware of Massa Coop and William eyeing him from the other side of the gate. "Come over here, boy," Coop finally said. Grady approached warily.

"Is he still sick?" Coop asked William.

"No, Massa. He's much better now. Back on his feed again."

"Good. Bring him inside."

Grady's heart pounded wildly against his ribs as he battled a new surge of fear. The guard unlocked the gate, and as soon as Grady walked through it, William planted his hand on his shoulder. The gate banged shut behind them. Grady gritted his teeth, determined not to let anyone know how terrified he felt. William never let go of him as they followed Massa Coop down the street to his hotel. A Negro porter held the lobby door open for Coop, but William steered Grady around the building to the servants' entrance in the rear, then up the back stairs.

Grady had no idea what was going to happen to him or why

Massa Coop wanted him. Facing the unknown filled him with such dread that he could scarcely breathe. William must have noticed his distress as they labored up the steps because he stopped and turned to him when they reached the door to Coop's hotel room.

"Ain't nothing to be afraid of," he said gruffly. "Long as you pay attention and do what you're told, ain't nothing bad gonna happen."

"I ain't afraid," Grady lied.

"Good." William knocked lightly on the door, then led the way inside. Massa Coop hadn't arrived yet.

Grady took a few steps into the room, then halted. He had never been in a place like this before, had never seen a canopied bed or curtained windows or a red plush armchair or a beautifully patterned carpet like the one on this floor. He'd lived in the loft above the kitchen with five other slaves all his life and had never been allowed inside the Big House where Caroline and her father lived. He wondered if those rooms had been as fine as this one.

"You know how to build a fire?"

Grady jumped at the sound of William's voice. William gestured to the fireplace where the coals smoldered.

"Well? Do you?" he asked when Grady didn't reply.

"Yes, sir," he replied, his voice squeaky with fear. He used to keep the kitchen fire going while Esther cooked, and he'd tended the fire in the scrub house whenever Luella did the wash.

"Then do it," William said.

Grady pulled two pieces of firewood from the box, then knelt by the hearth and carefully stoked the coals, blowing on them and rebuilding the fire the way Eli had taught him. By the time Massa Coop arrived, the flames blazed nicely, warming the room. William hurried to Massa's side as soon as he walked through the door, helping him with his coat and hat. Grady watched, scarcely able to breathe as Coop sank down in the red plush armchair by the fire, his long legs outstretched.

Grady dropped his gaze as Coop stared at him with his cold, penetrating eyes. "Come over here, boy," he finally said.

Grady edged closer on trembling legs. Coop pointed to his boots. "Pull them off for me."

Grady bent and lifted his master's foot. He tugged as hard as he dared, stumbling backward and nearly landing in the fire when the boot finally flew off.

"Anyone ever teach you how to polish boots?" Coop asked.

"Yes, sir," he said, recovering his balance again. Every night before he went to bed it had been his job to clean the mud and manure off Massa Fletcher's boots, then polish them until they shone.

"You a hard worker?" Coop asked as Grady pulled off the second boot. "Know how to do what you're told?"

"Yes, sir."

Coop snapped his fingers and William rushed over, holding open a cigar box. Coop fished out a cigar and waited for William to light it, his hard gaze never wavering from Grady's face. "I have it in mind to train you to help William in the slave pens," he finally said, blowing out smoke. "You can clean out the straw, empty the slops . . . help keep an eye on my property for me. If you prove to be trustworthy, things will go well for you. If not . . . don't expect me to give you a second chance."

It took Grady a moment to realize what Massa was saying. He wasn't going to be sold into a hard life on a cotton or rice plantation as he'd feared—at least for now. Instead, he would labor alongside William in slave pens and cargo holds like the ones he'd already experienced, coping as best he could with the stench and the seasickness and the despair. Grady wasn't sure which fate would be worse.

"Y-yes, sir," he remembered to say. "I mean, no, sir. I-I won't."

Coop took another pull on the cigar, then exhaled. "Good. Now get started on my boots."

William took Grady into the tiny servants' room and gave him boot blacking and a scrap of pigskin from Coop's trunk. "When you're done," William said, "take Massa's boots and set them alongside his bed." He leaned close to Grady and spoke so only he could hear. "And you better shine them boots like your life depends on it, boy—'cause it does."

William returned to their master. Grady could hear them talking softly in the next room while he polished. "Pour me a drink of whiskey, William."

"Yes, Massa."

Grady heard the clink of glass, the glugging sound of liquid being poured.

"Any more buyers coming tonight, Massa Coop?"

"No, we're all through for today. Two more are coming tomorrow, though. We'll leave for Jacksonville on Friday." The two men talked for a while longer while Grady worked. He had just finished the second boot, buffing it until his arm ached, when he heard William say, "I'll take your shirts and things down to the laundry now, Massa. That way they be nice and clean when you're ready to leave on Friday."

"You do that."

The door to the hallway opened, then closed behind William. Grady was alone with Coop. His heart pounded as he tiptoed into the room to put the boots beside the bed. He shot a quick, sideways glance at Massa Coop and saw him slumped in the armchair, whiskey glass in hand. His face was pink from the warmth of the fire, but his stern features were cold and unsmiling.

"Joe!" he called out suddenly. "Get over here and pour me another drink." His words sounded slurred.

Grady hesitated, looking around to see who else Coop could be talking to. They were alone in the room.

"Joe!" he shouted again. "What the devil's the matter with you? Why don't you come when I call you?"

Grady inched closer to the fire. "Y-you mean me, sir? My name is Grady."

Massa Coop rose up out of his chair and smacked Grady across the face. The blow was so sudden, so forceful it sent him stumbling backward,

"Don't you tell me what your name is!" Coop bellowed. "I'll call you anything I want to, you hear?"

White-hot anger blazed through Grady, not only because he'd been struck but because Coop was going to take away the only thing Grady had left—the name his mama had given him. "Yes, sir. I hear," he mumbled as he slowly backed away. "But my name is Grady."

He thought he had spoken too softly to be heard, but Coop shot out of his chair again and knocked him to the floor. Then Coop bent over him with the fireplace poker, beating him mercilessly with it. His wasn't a blind fury but a skillfully executed flogging, each blow planned so it wouldn't cause permanent injury, only agonizing pain and bruising. Whenever Grady raised his arms to shield his head, Coop would hit him in the gut. When he tried to shield his body, Coop struck his head. When he rolled over onto his stomach, Coop beat him across the back. All the while, Coop wore a twisted smile on his face, the first Grady had ever seen on him.

"What did you say your name was?" Coop asked as he hit him again.

"Joe . . ." he moaned. He wanted the beating to stop.

Coop grinned in triumph. "What did you say?"

"My name . . . is . . . Joe."

"That's right. And don't you forget it." Coop dealt a final blow to Grady's ribs and returned to his chair.

Grady didn't want to weep but the pain and humiliation were more than he could bear. He didn't know which was greater: his fear of this man or his hatred. He lay in a heap on the floor, too badly injured to move. Blood poured from his nose and from a split on his forehead. His left eye was rapidly swelling shut. Grady imagined plunging a knife into Coop's chest while he slept. He would do it someday. He would kill Coop and as many other white men as he could, just like Amos planned to do.

He was still curled on the floor, moaning, when William returned. "What happened, Massa?" he asked.

"The boy made a mistake," Coop said. "He misspoke. But he's never going to do it again, are you, Joe?"

Grady could barely speak. "No, sir."

"Want me to doctor him, Massa?" William asked. "Clean him up for you?"

"No. Pour me another drink, then take him back down to the pen. Let him lie in his own blood for a night."

GREAT OAK PLANTATION
SOUTH CAROLINA 1854

Kitty knelt on the floor of Missy Claire's room, gripping a pencil. She closed her eyes for a moment, picturing the outline and length of a horse's muzzle, the size and shape of its ears, then sketched what she remembered onto the paper spread out in front of her. Little Kate sat watching from her sister Claire's bed, her fat white legs dangling over the edge, kicking the feather mattress. "I know! It's a pony!" Kate said.

"Yep, that's right."

"Now draw a cat."

"But I ain't finished with the horse yet," Kitty said. "Don't you want me to give him a body and legs and a tail?"

"No, draw a cat," Kate insisted.

Kitty obeyed, even though she longed to finish the horse and then fill the page with flowers and trees and everything else she wanted to make. She loved to draw. Missy Claire had seen her sketching a picture in the dirt with a stick and had let her try using a real pencil and paper. Kitty had been entertaining Claire and her sister with drawings ever since.

Instead of finishing the horse, Kitty reluctantly chose a clean corner of the page to sketch the round head and pointed ears of a cat. She gave it eyes and a nose and whiskers, and was about to start drawing its body when Kate said, "Draw a bird."

"What kind of bird, Missy Kate?" While she waited for the answer, Kitty quickly gave the cat four legs and a skinny, pointed tail.

"Um . . . those skinny white birds with long legs that live down by the river."

Kitty smiled. She loved to draw herons with their slender bodies and graceful necks. But before she had a chance to begin, Missy Claire interrupted.

"No more pictures. Kitty is *my* slave and she's going to play dolls with *me* now." She snatched up the paper and shoved it into her sister's hands. Like all of Kitty's other drawings, this one wouldn't be hers to keep, either. Missy Claire needed to be entertained every minute, it seemed, and would quickly become bored with whatever game they were playing long before Kitty did. She had been living in the Big House with Missy for four seasons now, but trying to keep up with her made Kitty all tuckered out sometimes.

"Here's your picture, Katie," Claire said. "Now go away and play in your own room." She pointed to the door.

Missy Kate let out a loud wail. Kitty imagined an entire flock of white herons taking flight at the sound. Mammy Bertha scooped Kate off the bed and hustled her out of the room.

"We're going to play house," Missy Claire decided. "My dolls are coming for tea. You'll serve us, Kitty." Claire had two beautiful dolls with delicate porcelain faces and real hair. Kitty would watch her dress them in their lacy nightgowns or ruffled dresses, fastening rows of tiny buttons, and she longed to hold them and dress them—just once.

"Don't touch my doll!" Claire had shrieked the first—and only—time Kitty had ever dared to reach for one. "You'll break it!"

"Oh, please, Missy Claire," she'd begged. "I promise I'll be real careful. I ain't never gonna break your things."

"No. I don't want your filthy hands touching her."

Kitty had looked down at her hands. Her skin was dark, but it wasn't from dirt. Her hands were just as clean as Missy's were. But Kitty had learned that day that she would have to be content with keeping Missy company while she played with her dolls. Kitty could watch Missy move the tiny furniture in her beautiful dollhouse, but she could never touch it. She could laugh with Claire as she rode on her rocking horse, but she could never ride on it herself. Kitty had learned to accept the fact that Claire's white skin gave her these privileges; her own black skin denied them.

"Set the table for tea," Claire now commanded as her sister's cries faded in the distance. Kitty hurried to obey. The porcelain tea set was the only toy she was allowed to touch, and she loved the way the smooth, cool glass felt beneath her fingers. It was her job to set the table and serve tea to Claire and her two dolls; Kitty would never dare take a pretend sip from the little cups herself.

"Go tell Cook I want some cookies," Claire said. "I'll get my dollies dressed for the party."

"Yes, Missy Claire." Kitty had learned to always answer that way—and to hurry as quickly as she could whenever she went on an errand. Missy hated it when she dawdled. Kitty ran down the stairs, through the servants' door to the warming kitchen, then outside to the big kitchen to tell Cook what Missy wanted. The kitchen smelled like smoked pork roasting with onions, and like apples and cinnamon. Kitty drew a deep breath, inhaling the fragrant air. Her stomach rumbled with hunger.

"That Missy sure is a spoilt one," Cook said, shaking her head at Kitty's request. "She's thinking I ain't got nothing better to do than wait on her all day? Don't she know Massa's got company coming and I need to be fixing dinner?" But Cook wiped the sweat off her brow with a bandana and waddled over to retrieve the cookie tin. "Missy ever sharing any of these cookies with you?" she asked.

Kitty shrugged. "Sometimes . . . when she ain't wanting no more."

Cook placed three fat sugar cookies on a plate, then handed a fourth one to Kitty. "Eat it quick, and don't tell her I give it to you," she whispered.

Kitty grinned. "Yes, ma'am! Thank you, ma'am!" She skipped out of the kitchen, balancing the plate. As she followed the walkway to the house again, she was torn between eating her treasure slowly, savoring every bite, or gulping it down in one or two bites in order to hurry back, as she'd been told to do. She decided to eat óne bite slowly, making it last all the way to the house and up the stairs, then hide the rest of the cookie in her pocket for later.

When Kitty returned to the bedroom, swallowing her allotted bite, Claire was nowhere to be seen. It took Kitty a moment to realize that she had ducked behind the folding screen to use the "necessary." Claire would make her run back downstairs to empty it, next thing. White ladies were very lucky, Kitty thought. They never had to go all the way outside to use the privy the way menfolk and slaves did.

Kitty carried the plate over to the tea table while she waited. Missy had finished dressing her dolls and had seated them on two little chairs. But one of the dolls had slumped sideways and looked as though it was about to fall. Kitty reached to straighten it. The doll felt much lighter than Kitty had expected—and her hair looked so soft that she couldn't resist stroking it, just once.

"What are you doing!" Claire shrieked. "Don't touch her!"

Kitty whirled around in surprise. "But she was falling over, Missy Claire. I just sat her up again, and—"

Missy raced across the room and slapped Kitty's hand for daring to touch her doll, then she slapped Kitty's face—hard. Tears sprang to her eyes. Kitty had often seen Missy's mother strike the chambermaids that way, but Kitty had never been slapped herself.

"Get out! Get out! Get out!" Claire yelled, pointing to the door.

"I'm sorry, Missy Claire, but I thought—"

"You're very bad, and you can't play with me anymore!"

Tears rolled down Kitty's face as she hurried from the room, her cheek stinging. She didn't dare cry out loud, nor did she dare go off by herself to lick her wounds. Whenever Missy sent her away she was supposed to go find Mammy Bertha and help her tend Missy Kate or Missus Goodman's new girl-baby, Mary.

"What's the matter with you?" Bertha asked when she saw Kitty wiping her tears.

"Missy slapped me," she said, pouting. "Her doll was about to fall off the chair, and all I did was try and make it sit up again. She told me to get out."

From the way Mammy puckered her lips and shook her head, Kitty knew she wasn't going to get any sympathy from her. "Ain't Missy always telling you not to touch her things?"

"But it was going to fall. I thought—"

"You ain't supposed to be doing no thinking. Just do whatever the white folks say, and if they say never touch their things, then don't you dare touch them. Only job you have is obeying. You hear?"

"Yes, ma'am."

"Now turn off them tears and come help me fan Missy Kate so she can take a nap." Kitty lifted the skirt of her pinafore to dry her eyes, and the cookie she'd hoarded slid out of the pocket. She wasn't quick enough to catch it before it hit the floor, and it crumbled into pieces. Her tears started falling all over again. Bertha glared at Kitty as she dropped to her knees and scooped up the crumbs. "Are you stealing that cookie from Missy Claire?"

"No, ma'am. Cook give it to me, I swear. You can ask her yourself." Kitty stuffed the crumbs into her mouth. They tasted gritty with dust.

"You better believe I'm asking her . . . and you better not be spinning no lies."

"No, ma'am."

The long, hot day seemed to last forever. Late in the afternoon company arrived for dinner, just like Cook had said they would. Mammy Bertha said the guests were spending the night, and everyone had to be on their very best behavior—including Kitty. The two older girls, Claire and Kate, had to get scrubbed and brushed and dressed in their finest Sunday dresses, then they sat in the parlor and visited like proper young ladies. With all the fussing and showing off, Kitty didn't have a chance to eat anything all day except her one crumbled cookie. When the girls were finally in bed, Mammy Bertha told her she could go out to the kitchen and see if there was anything left over from dinner.

It was very late, but Kitty was surprised to see the kitchen all lit up. A big gathering of colored folks sat around the table, talking and eating roast pork and chicken and a bunch of other goodies from the white folks' dinner. Four strangers—the house slaves who had traveled along with the white guests—sat among the usual kitchen workers. Kitty fixed herself a plate of food, then sat on a stool near the door, listening to the news and gossip that the newcomers had brought.

"Delia, here, is a storyteller," the visiting coachman told them after a while. He gestured to a tiny gray-haired woman who was no taller than Kitty. "Delia's knowing all the old tales about our people before we was slaves," he said.

Everyone seemed real excited to hear Delia's stories, and they begged and begged her to tell one. The kitchen grew so quiet that Kitty was almost afraid to breathe. She sat forward in anticipation, watching the storyteller's every move. The little woman closed her eyes for a long moment, as if looking deep inside herself for the words.

"Back home where our people come from," Delia began, "folks call a storyteller like me a *griot*. We're the ones who're remembering the old ways and the old stories and passing them on to our children and to their children, so our past don't get lost. My mammy was a *griot*, and her mammy was one before her, so the stories I know go way, way back to a time that nobody alive can even remember no more—a time when all our people were free." She sighed as she said the last word, and it seemed to Kitty that it fluttered from the storyteller's mouth like a little bird and flew away.

"It's only in the telling of our story that we're ever gonna remember who we really are," Delia said. "And that's something we ought never ever to be forgetting." She gazed all around at her listeners, and her dark eyes rested for a moment on Kitty.

"We once lived in a land called the 'Mountain of Lions,'" Delia said, "in a tribe called the *Mende.* It's a big, rich land where every single person has black skin. Ain't no white-skinned people there at all, back in the beginning. And the whole land's belonging to us—all the forests and fields and rivers and hills is ours. We can hunt game and plant our own rice and build our own houses and live any way and anywhere we want to with no one but our own leaders telling us what to do. Long before the white men came, our people are learning how to trap the water and making it go wherever we want. We're making fields that we can flood and drain to grow our rice. Our women are weaving baskets out of sea grass for gathering up the crops and winnowing the rice. We're a peaceful people, living in our own villages with our own families all around us."

Kitty listened, fascinated, unable to imagine a land without white people. Delia's voice was as soothing as a cup of warm milk, and her small, wrinkled hands gestured gracefully as she talked.

"Then one day the white men come," she said. "They're seeing all that we have and how hard we're working, and they're deciding they want us for their slaves. So they come with their guns and chains, and they're stealing our people away, catching us in the woods and snatching us from our homes and away from our children. They're tying our people together with their big chains and forcing us to march a long, long ways. They ain't even caring that some folks are dying along the way of hunger or weariness or fear. No, them white men take all our captured people to a fortress on an island where we can't escape. They're putting us to work there, laboring to crush shells into lime. Our people are thinking life can't get no harder than this—but it does. Turns out we're just working to make lime while we're waiting for the ship to come. And, oh my! One day that slave ship surely does come.

"Seems like the white men just forgetting we're people, the way they're packing us down into the belly of that ship. They're making everybody lay down on hard wooden shelves, one row stacked up on top of the other, so there ain't even room to sit up. We're all packed in there so tight that nobody can move. The white men are filling up the whole ship with slaves that way. And it don't matter to them if folks is sick or needing to use the privy, it just have to run down on top of everybody. My Lord! There're folks dying of hunger and thirst and heat and grief every single day. That ship's tossing and rolling on the waves, and you can hear the sound of them waves pounding against the planks day and night. And also the sound of tears. Seem like the ocean's gonna overflow from all our tears.

"Takes a long, long time for that ship to sail to the white men's country. The full moon comes around twice, maybe even three times before we're finally landing here in the Low Country. The new land seems a lot like back home, but we ain't free no more in this new place. Rice we're growing ain't feeding our own families no more. Our husbands and children are getting sold away from us and moving someplace else. We have to work like animals for the white men, digging canals and ponds and growing rice for all of them because we're their slaves now. Our people ain't free no more. White men got guns, so they're capturing us and making us do all their work."

She leaned forward, her body tense, her eyes bright with tears. "But don't you ever forget that a long time ago, we was free. That's the way God created us. The way we're supposed to be—free."

When Delia finished, nobody moved. The room had grown so quiet that Kitty could hear her heart beating in her ears. This terrible story couldn't be true, could it? Missy Claire was old enough to read books aloud to her and Missy Kate, with stories of fairies and elves and animals that talked, but Kitty knew those stories weren't true. Could this one be?

"That story true?" she whispered, breaking the silence.

"Yes, it's true!" Delia said, slapping her palm on the table. "Every word I said is just as true as I'm sitting here. Black folks was born free and we was meant to live free. They stole that away from us. And now they're trying to make us forget that we ever was free. But don't you ever forget, honey. You remember who you are, and who your family is, and where you coming from."

That night Kitty dreamed that white men chased her through

the woods and captured her and locked her in a dark, fearsome place. When she awoke she felt as though she hadn't slept at all. The nightmare reminded her of the old dream she used to have when she was very small, and she wondered if she had once lived in the land where there were no white men. But no, Delia had said that story happened a long, long time ago. *"You remember who you are, who your family is, and where you coming from,"* Delia had said. But Kitty didn't know who her family was or where she'd come from. She couldn't remember.

Kitty was still thinking about all of these things the next morning as she opened Missy's bedroom curtains and saw the Great Oak Tree outside. She was certain that the tree was linked to her past, somehow—part of the dream she used to have when she was very small. But Kitty could no longer remember why the tree was important to her or what it meant. When she and Mammy Bertha were alone in the nursery, Kitty gathered the courage to ask about her past for the very first time.

"Mammy, did you ever know my mama and daddy?"

Bertha closed her eyes for a long moment. "Yes, child. I knowed your mama," she said softly. Mammy was usually very talkative and full of stories when they were alone, but she suddenly seemed sorrowful and afraid to talk.

"Well, where is she, Mammy Bertha? What happened to her?"

Mammy turned away. "We can't talk about it now," she said. "You come see me tonight, after Missy Claire's falling asleep."

Kitty thought the day would never end. Claire kept her hard at work until late that night, hauling hot water for her bath and brushing her hair, then making her stay and keep her company until she fell asleep. Every time Kitty sat up on her pallet beside the bed and looked to see if Claire had fallen asleep yet, Missy would glare down at her and say, "Why do you keep staring at me like that? Go to sleep!" But a mixture of dread and anticipation kept Kitty wide awake.

At last Claire slept, and Kitty managed to tiptoe from the room and look for Mammy Bertha. They found a quiet place to sit, outside on the steps of the warming kitchen, and Mammy told Kitty the truth.

"Your mama's named Lucindy, and she used to be one of Missus Goodman's chambermaids right here in the Big House," Mammy began. "She's a pretty gal like you, always sweet and cheerful to everybody. One day she fall in love with a man named George—your daddy. He's working as a slave for the preacher man and his wife, all the way over in town. Lucindy's meeting him while their massas go to church every Sunday, and pretty soon the two of them's falling in love. Everybody try and tell them it's gonna be hard for them to be together, but they decide to jump the broom anyways. Every Saturday night when his work's all done, your daddy George come walking all the way from town just to be with his wife. Then he's walking all the way back home again. His massa's a good man, though, and he's giving George a pass so he can come and go without the paddyrollers bothering him.

"Then one day your daddy's massa die, and in his will he's saying that George and all his other slaves can go free. Seems like a real good thing, being free—but it ain't. White folks hate to see Negroes going free even more than they hate us when we're slaves. They say free Negroes get uppity, and the whites are always worrying that the freedmen gonna give slaves the notion that we should all be free. So the white men pass a bunch of laws saying that free Negroes can't be living in town, and they can't own no property, and they can't be staying in any one place too long. If the freedmen break that law, the white folks throw them in jail and charge a big fine, then sell them back into slavery when they can't pay the fine. They're trying to drive all the free Negroes away from here—or else get them back as slaves again. Either way, they don't want freedmen like your daddy hanging around.

"So, poor George was free now, but he's wearing himself out trying to help your mama, especially after you was born. He gets himself a job on a steamboat in Charleston, loading wood and coal and such. He's working hard as he can so he can earn enough money to buy Lucindy. But even when he's saving up all his money, Massa Goodman ain't selling her. Poor George finally decides ain't nothing left to do but take his wife and child and run away. That's because your daddy's wanting your mama and you to be free, just like him.

"Everybody try and tell them they're making a big mistake. Things gonna go real bad for them if they's caught. 'Course they ain't listening. Your daddy's trusting Jesus to help him, and one night, he and Lucindy steal away. Soon as Massa Goodman find out that Lucindy's gone, he's calling the paddyrollers together and they're sending the dogs out after them. Your folks never even make it out of South Carolina, poor souls, before they was caught."

Kitty's dream came back to her, vivid and strong. She knew, then, that it had really happened. The dogs had come tearing at mama and papa's legs until they couldn't run anymore. Then the white men came on horseback with guns. But what was the end of that dream? She never could remember the end. Her mouth felt so dry she could barely speak.

"What happened after they was caught, Mammy?"

"Oh, child . . . you don't want to know," she said, shaking her head. "Some stories is best left untold."

Kitty shivered even though the night was warm. "I do want to know, Mammy Bertha. Please tell me."

Mammy sighed. She hesitated such a long time that Kitty was afraid she would never tell. When Mammy finally spoke, her voice was very soft. "They whipped your poor daddy and hanged him for a thief, right out there on the Great Oak Tree."

For a long moment Kitty couldn't breathe, couldn't swallow. That tree had always seemed like her friend, her place of refuge. Now she felt betrayed. The Great Oak Tree had helped them kill her papa. She closed her eyes at the thought of him hanging from its branches.

Bertha wiped her eyes with the corner of her apron. "Massa Goodman's saying your daddy stole his property when he's running off with your mama and you—which I suppose is true. They make all us slaves stand out there and watch so we'd learn what would happen to all of us if we try and run off. Whipped your mama, too, then they sell her to a slave trader. She's begging and pleading with Massa to sell you along with her instead of leaving you here all alone. You was still just a little thing, toddling all around. But Massa Goodman ain't listening." Bertha slipped her arm around Kitty's shoulder and pulled her close. "That's how you come to be all alone in the world."

Kitty slumped against Mammy Bertha and wept, pouring out years of loneliness and loss and a deep grief she hadn't known she'd had. She was sorry she had asked for the truth, sorry she knew. The Great Oak Tree would be an emblem of horror and death to her from now on, instead of comfort and refuge. And she would never be able to look at Massa Goodman the same way again, either. Why wouldn't he sell Lucindy to George? He had plenty of other slaves. It was Massa Goodman's fault that her father had died, his fault that her mother had been sold, leaving her all alone.

And Kitty knew she could never look at Claire the same way, either. Claire still lived with both of her parents. They gave her everything she needed or wanted. Kitty's parents had loved her, too, but they had been punished for trying to be free—trying to live the way all of the Negroes in Delia's story had once lived.

Mammy held Kitty tightly, rocking her. "It don't pay to be falling in love, child. Only leads to heartbreak if Massa's selling you or the man you love or taking your children away from you. I seen it happen over and over again too many times—way too many times. Slaves are put here on this earth to work, not to be loving somebody."

Kitty's tears gradually died away, but she stayed in Mammy's warm arms, needing to be held.

"I'll tell you something else," Mammy said after a while. "As hard as this here life is, folks have to be fools to try and run away. They say you can follow the North Star to freedom, but that land's way too far away from here. And the price you pay is much too high when you're caught. And folks is always caught. Them paddyrollers are the devil's own horsemen."

When Kitty finally left the comfort of Bertha's arms and returned to her pallet, nightmares filled her sleep. In the morning she carried her sadness and loss like a huge burden that she couldn't seem to lift from her shoulders. The grief Kitty felt didn't fade with time, either, but grew stronger each day, especially when she happened to glimpse the Great Oak Tree. And she couldn't avoid seeing it. The tree dominated the view from Missy's bedroom windows.

Massa Goodman's guests finally departed, leaving Missy Claire grumpy from all the excitement and Kitty exhausted from the extra work and restless nights. Tears she couldn't control filled her eyes at unexpected moments, and she could no longer find the energy to amuse Missy Claire and Missy Kate with her antics.

"What's wrong with you?" Claire demanded to know when she caught Kitty wiping her eyes one afternoon. Kitty should have known that it wasn't concern that had prompted the question, but irritation. Claire wanted her to snap out of it and be happy, again. Kitty should have known better, but she made the mistake of telling her the truth.

"Oh, Missy Claire, I can't help feeling sad when I think about my mama and papa. They're both gone, and now I ain't got no family."

"Why are you thinking about them? You're supposed to be playing with *me*, not pouting about people who aren't even here."

"But . . . but I can't help wishing I had a family like you do."

Claire's face went rigid with anger. "You don't want to be with me? You want to be with your own kind? Fine! Then I don't want you moping around here, either. Go back down to Slave Row where you came from."

Kitty's knees went weak with fear. "But my family ain't down on Slave Row, Missy. They—"

"Too bad. I don't want you in my house anymore. Get out."

"You don't mean that. Who's gonna play with you and—"

"I'd rather play alone than look at your stupid droopy face. Get out right now. Go live with all the other darkies since that's what you want."

"But Missy Claire, that ain't what I want." She dropped to her knees to beg. "Please! I got no family down there, and no place to sleep, or—"

"That's your problem, not mine. Go on, you heard me—get out!" Claire's voice had risen to an angry shout, and Mammy Bertha hurried into the room with the baby in her arms.

"Hey, now. What's all this shouting about, Missy Claire?"

"I'm sending Kitty back down to live with all the other darkies. I don't want her up here anymore."

"No, please!" Kitty begged. "I promise I'll be happy again. I promise!"

"Well, it's too late," Claire said. She smiled, as if pleased with the power she wielded. "Daisy will be my maid from now on. And I don't want Kitty to help you, either, Mammy. She's a crybaby, and I don't want her in my house."

Mammy gripped Kitty's arm with her free hand and pulled her to her feet, then steered her out of the room. Claire slammed the door behind her. "You heard what Missy say. You best be doing what you're told, girl."

"But, Mammy—"

Bertha shook her head. "Go on, now." She turned her back on Kitty and shuffled away to the nursery. Mammy couldn't help her. Neither could any of the other house slaves. There was nothing Kitty could do but obey.

She cried all the way down to Slave Row, barely able to see where she was going through her tears. Nor did she know what to do once she got there. It was early in the afternoon, and the other slaves hadn't come home from the fields yet. The yard was deserted except for three small children digging in the dirt. Kitty found Old Nellie in her cabin, fanning four little babies who were sleeping crossways on the bed.

"What do you want? What's wrong with you?" Nellie asked when she saw Kitty's tear-streaked face.

"Missy Claire send me away. She don't want me working for her up in the Big House no more."

"What'd you do wrong?"

"Nothing! She said I was moping around and she didn't want to be playing with me no more."

"If you're crying and carrying on like that, I can see why. I don't want you around here, either. Got enough crying babies to take care of."

Kitty struggled to get a hold of herself, drying her tears and drawing a deep breath. She knew that slaves were never allowed to be idle, and that she would have to find some kind of work to do to if she wanted to avoid being sent into the rice fields. "I been helping Mammy Bertha take care of the white children up in the Big House," she said hopefully. "I can help you, too, if you want."

"Ain't up to me where you work, and you know it. I'll let you help me today, but you're big enough to work the rice fields tomorrow. I reckon that's where they gonna send you."

Kitty's eyes filled with tears. "I got no place to live, Nellie. I got no family down here."

The old woman eyed her silently for a moment. "Your name's Anna, ain't it?"

It took Kitty a moment to remember that it was. She hadn't been called by that name in a year. "That's the name my mama, Lucindy, gave me," she said. "But Missy Claire's been calling me Kitty."

Nellie shrugged. "Don't make no difference to me what you're called. Here, you fan these little ones for a while," she said, handing Kitty the palm branch. "I could use a little rest."

Kitty worked as hard as she could for the rest of the day, hoping Old Nellie would put in a good word for her and that she'd be allowed to help her again tomorrow. When the other slaves came in from the fields at dusk and gathered around for their rations, the black foreman noticed Kitty right away.

"Where'd you come from?" he demanded. He was a huge, towering man with a scowling face. His massive arms and shoulders seemed to burst out of his homespun shirt. Kitty was so afraid of him she couldn't reply.

"She been working up at the Big House," Old Nellie said. "She been sent down."

"What'd you do wrong?"

"N-nothing!" she stammered. "Missy Claire got mad 'cause she said I was moping. That's all, I swear!"

"Guess you have to work like the rest of us now," he said with a grunt.

Kitty ate the meager supper she'd been given and went to bed hungry. Nellie gave her a threadbare blanket and she slept on the dirt floor of the cabin with mice scurrying around her all night. The horn blew in the morning, just as the sky was growing light, and the foreman himself took Kitty out to the rice fields and assigned her a row of plants to hoe. The two girls she labored alongside had once played with her in Old Nellie's yard, but they seemed much older than Kitty and already worn out from hard work. Kitty's lack of experience with a hoe didn't matter; she was expected to keep up with the others as they worked their way down the rows, making sure she didn't overlook any weeds or accidentally chop a rice plant. Blisters had formed on her hands by noontime and had begun to bleed and ooze long before dusk. Kitty felt the sting of the lash, falling harder and more often across her shoulders as the day wore on, punishment for making a mistake or failing to keep up.

But as each day merged with the next, it wasn't the hunger or fatigue or constant fear that made Kitty's life unbearable—it was the drab hopelessness of her new surroundings. Everything seemed devoid of color: the dingy cabin, the dirt floor, the slaves' faded clothes and lifeless faces, their dusty bodies aching with toil. She wasn't allowed to gaze up at the blue sky and white clouds or off into the distance at the green forest; only down at the dirt, at the endless row that must be hoed, her view a monotony of rice plants and weeds. At night she curled up on the cabin floor, too exhausted for nightmares, let alone dreams.

By Sunday afternoon, her only day of rest, Kitty felt close to despair. She decided she would rather jump into the river and drown than face a lifetime of such hopeless labor. She left the barren slave yard and walked to the edge of the plantation yard, intending to cross the broad swath of green grass and just keep on walking—down to the pier, off the end of it, and into the water. But as she neared the Great Oak Tree, Kitty saw Missy Claire and Missy Kate seated on a blanket beneath it, playing with their dolls. They were alone. If Daisy had taken Kitty's place as Claire's chambermaid, she was nowhere to be seen.

Kitty dropped down on her hands and knees and crawled across the lawn toward the girls, meowing loudly. When she reached the tree, Kitty rubbed against Claire, purring, trying to smile as she fought desperate tears. More than a year had passed since the summer day when Missy had adopted Kitty, and she hoped Claire would remember.

At last she stole a glance at her face. Claire was trying not to smile, but Kitty could tell she was amused by her performance. She took hope.

"Of course, some folks would rather have a dog," Kitty said, forcing a wide grin across her face. She pretended to be a puppy, barking, sitting up on her haunches to beg, her tongue lolling happily. Missy Kate began to giggle.

Kitty hated what she was doing, but she had nothing to lose. The alternative was so much worse. She would never survive as a field slave, especially when fall arrived and the rice had to be cut and threshed and winnowed. The foreman would expect her to do as much work as the adults, day after day, and anything less would mean a whipping. Her life was little more than an animal existence as it was. It was better to live as Missy Claire's house pet than to die as a beast of burden from overwork and slow starvation.

"Woof! Woof!" Kitty repeated bravely, trying not to think of the dogs that had attacked her parents.

"No, I think I'd rather have a kitty-cat," Claire said with a smug smile. Kitty dropped down on all fours and meowed. Claire laughed. "Come on then, Kitty. Time to go inside."

Kitty knew she should feel ashamed and degraded. But as she made her way inside the Big House, still crawling on all fours, she felt only relief.

CHAPTER

6

JACKSONVILLE, FLORIDA 1853

"Hey, Joe! Massa Coop's calling for you."

Grady set down the bucket of slops and slowly turned to face William. It was the first time Massa had sent for Grady since the night of the beating two weeks ago. Dread shivered through him. "He's wanting me?" he asked.

"That's what he said."

Grady drew a deep breath. "You know what for?"

A look that might have been pity flickered briefly across William's face, then disappeared in a scowl. "Bunch of rich planters coming to Massa's hotel room. You gonna help me wait on everybody. That's the reason Massa Coop buy you."

Grady's stomach rolled as if he stood on the deck of a ship in tossing seas. The bruises he'd received from his beating were gradually healing but still visible against his light brown skin, fading from deep purple to greenish black. The pain was slowly fading, as well, but he still felt a dull, throbbing ache whenever he moved. He'd been confined to slave pens and ships' holds during the past two weeks as Massa Coop had traveled down the coast from Georgia to Florida, selling some slaves, buying others. It had been Grady's job to clean up after everyone, emptying the slop buckets, shoveling straw, scrubbing filth from the decks. He worked as hard as he could, but the pens and holds where the slaves were kept were nearly impossible to keep clean.

"I brought a bucket of clean water and soap," William said, pointing to where he'd left them near the gate. "Massa says for you to wash first, before the others do. He says to make sure you don't stink. And he send some clean clothes."

Grady glanced around at the crowded yard, then closed his eyes. As much as he longed to get washed and change out of his bloody clothes, the thought of stripping in the open air in front of men and women alike filled him with angry humiliation.

"Better get moving," William said, pushing him toward the bucket. "Massa's customers be coming soon." If William felt any pity at all for Grady, he didn't show it. In fact, he seemed relieved to have another slave sharing his own plight, sharing a portion of their master's abuse.

"What do I have to do?" Grady asked as he removed his shirt. William glanced at his bruised body, then looked away.

"You got two jobs from now on: serving Massa Coop and his customers, and taking care of his slaves down here in the pens and on the ships."

"Like I been doing?" Grady asked. He splashed water on his face and wet his hair, then worked the soap into a lather.

William exhaled. Grady couldn't tell if it was from anger or impatience. "There's more to it than what you been doing. You listen carefully to every word I tell you, now—you hear?"

Grady nodded, unsure if the tremor that shuddered through him was from the cold water or from the warning that he heard in William's tone.

"Every minute of every day," William said, "day and night, it's our job to watch and make sure nobody ever escape. Gotta keep their chains on, locked up tight all the time, hand and foot, so nobody's getting away. They been known to try and jump out the portholes when we're sailing or jump overboard near the shore when we're getting on and off. They won't try it if they all chained together, but sometimes one of them works his shackles loose when we ain't looking, and that's when they escape."

Grady quickly washed his chest and arms, then slipped into the shirt William handed him. It was well-used and a size too large, but clean.

"Some of these folks is pretty desperate," William continued in a low voice. "They try anything. There was one woman Massa bought who had to leave her young one behind. She wouldn't eat nothing for days and days, and she got so skinny the shackles wouldn't stay on. One day, when the boat was way out to sea, she jump overboard and drown herself." He paused, biting his lip. Then he said quietly, "Massa beat us near to death for that. He says we supposed to watch and listen in the slave pen and tell him what we see and hear, find out who's planning to escape."

Grady shook his head in disbelief. "Is that what you do? Spy on all the others and then tell Massa?"

"That's right! And you better be doing it, too, if you know what's good for you. Didn't I just tell you? If one of them tries to escape, we're paying the price whether we hear them planning it or not."

"How can you spy like that? You ain't white—you're a slave just like the rest of us."

"Remember that beating Massa gave you?" William jabbed his finger into Grady's still-tender ribs. "That was nothing. Believe me, after Massa strings you up and gives you forty lashes, you'll be telling him every word folks say. My body's already marked." He turned and lifted his shirt so Grady could see the wide lumps of ugly scar tissue that crisscrossed his back. "Massa can't sell me for much, so he don't care if he whips me or not. Once a slave's back is scarred, white folks figure he's a runaway or a thief and they won't buy him. My life ain't worth nothing . . . and Massa's gonna do the same thing to you if you ain't careful."

Grady stopped washing, frozen in horror by what he was hearing. William motioned impatiently for him to continue. "Massa Coop loves to beat us Negroes," he said. "Only time he ever laugh out loud is when he's winning at poker or whipping somebody."

Grady swallowed, remembering Coop's grinning face the night he'd beaten him.

"In fact," William said, "he like to whip us so much that some folks bring their slaves to Massa Coop to be punished. They don't even have to pay him for it. And he'll make you watch so you'll know what you're in for if you ain't careful." For a brief moment the fierce expression William always wore vanished, replaced by a look of dread. Then he frowned again. "Listen good, Joe. Make sure you never give him a reason to whip you."

"That ain't my real name," Grady said. "Don't call me Joe; call me—"

"No, sir! You think I want a beating? From now on your name is Joe. Don't even be thinking about that old name. And your last name is Coop, just like Massa's."

Grady repeated the hated name to himself: Joe Coop. That wasn't who he was. He was Grady Fletcher, not Joe Coop. "Was William your real name?" he asked. "The name your mama gave you?"

"It's my name now."

Grady dropped his trousers and quickly changed into the clean pair of pants William had given him.

"Make sure you wash your old clothes tomorrow and always keep a clean set to change into," William warned. "Massa can't stand it if we smell bad. Up to us to make sure none of his slaves smell bad or is dirty or wearing rags. He can get more money for them if they look nice. One thing for sure, you'll always be well fed. You'll never go hungry like a lot of slaves do."

When Grady finished with the wash water, William hefted the bucket and carried it across the pen to where three frightened teen-aged girls stood huddled together. Coop had purchased them shortly after he'd bought Grady, and they had traveled from port to port without being offered for sale. "Here's some soap and water," William told them. "Wash your hair and fix yourselves up nice." He rejoined Grady at the gate and signaled for the guard to unlock it.

"Massa gonna sell them girls tonight?" Grady asked.

William shook his head. "He's saving them for the brothels in New Orleans."

"What's that?"

"You're too young to understand," he said with a wave of his hand. "Maybe it's better that you don't."

Grady hurried down the street to Coop's hotel with William, grateful to be away from the stench of the slave pen for a while. The streets were full of life, with horses and carriages rumbling past and street vendors hawking their wares. Gentlemen in frock coats and ladies in flowered hats crowded the sidewalks. William pulled Grady off the wooden walkways and into the gutter whenever a white person passed.

Grady longed to savor his momentary freedom, but he couldn't. Fear and dread pounded through him at the prospect of facing Edward Coop again. He finally summoned the courage to ask William what was ahead.

"Massa gonna want me to shine his shoes again?"

"Probably. But that ain't all. Massa's inviting all the rich white men to come to his hotel room and we're supposed to serve them drinks, maybe fan them if it's hot, sometimes give them food. Just help them with whatever they're needing. You got to act smart, stay alert, and be ready to jump the second Massa asks you to do something." He glanced at Grady as if to see if he was listening. "And if you're pouring them a drink, make sure you don't be filling that glass too full. I done that one time and a gentleman spilt it down his shirt. Massa whipped me good for it."

Grady nodded, but he wondered how he would manage to pour drinks at all with trembling hands.

"Later on," William continued, "we'll be coming downstairs to the pens so the customers can look over all the slaves. Massa likes to sell the best ones this way, by private sale. When he gets home to New Orleans, he'll sell all the ones that's left over at the auction."

Grady had heard of the city of New Orleans, but he had no idea where it was or how far it was from his home in Richmond. "Is that where we're gonna live? New Orleans?" he asked.

William shook his head impatiently. "We don't live anywhere. Massa Coop's just stopping home for a little while to see his family and wait till winter's over. Then he's setting sail again. That's what he's doing most of the year—traveling from city to city, buying and selling slaves. That's Massa Coop's job. There's certain cities he's going to all the time, like Richmond and Jacksonville. The white men can read in the newspaper that he's coming and what kind of stock he has for sale, and they're all coming around to buy what they need."

Too soon they reached the hotel, a beautiful three-story brick building with shuttered windows. William halted outside and turned to grip Grady's shoulders. "Pay attention, now! You do any little thing wrong to hurt Massa's business, he'll make you real sorry. Understand?"

Grady drew a shaky breath and nodded.

For the next several hours, he circulated the crowded hotel room, passing out cigars and pouring drinks, careful not to accidentally brush against anyone or trip over the men's feet as they lounged around. The room grew very warm. William warned Grady not to let any of the gentlemen get overheated—he should offer to take their coats and cool them with a palmetto fan. His own discomfort didn't matter. He didn't dare rest for a moment or take a sip of water to ease his own thirst. And when his hands became slippery with sweat he had to make sure that he wiped them dry so he wouldn't spill anything and earn a beating.

Throughout the long evening he felt Massa Coop's eyes on him, watching for a lapse or a mistake, waiting to pounce. By the time the long evening was over and Grady was safely locked in the slave pen again for the night, far away from Coop, his shoulders ached with tension. His stomach felt like a tightened fist.

"You did okay," William told him. He offered Grady a sandwich left over from their gentlemen guests. "Just do the same every night."

Grady ate it, but a short time later when he recalled his unrelenting fear and the despair he'd seen in the eyes of the slaves who had been sold that night, he ran to the nearest slop bucket and heaved his dinner. William had said that Massa Coop bought and sold slaves for most of the year. Grady would be doing this work from now on—helping Coop tear lives apart.

When his nausea passed, Grady lay down on the straw and closed his eyes, weeping quietly in the night.

The slave mart in New Orleans looked much the same as all the others Grady had seen in cities and towns along the coast: a small gated yard surrounded by locked buildings where the slaves slept at night. Customers arrived in a steady stream each day to examine Coop's slaves, and by the end of the week the pen was nearly empty. A large white woman in a bright red gown and hair the color of dandelions had purchased a half-dozen of the prettiest young women. Grady overheard Coop telling her that he had picked them just for her customers.

Grady had lost all track of time since leaving his home in Richmond, but he knew that several months must have passed. Summer had been nearly over when he'd left home, and now he heard Massa Coop say he would celebrate the Christmas season here in New Orleans with his family. When all of his remaining slaves had been sold at auction and the pen was empty, Coop took Grady and William home with him to his town house.

"Gonna have us a little rest now," William said with a sigh as they settled into the slaves' quarters above the washhouse. "Ain't nothing much for us to do till we leave with Massa again in a few weeks." Grady nodded, but after months of hard work and constant watchfulness, he couldn't comprehend the notion of rest.

Massa's house was tall and narrow and elegant. Decorative

balconies hung from the brick structure in the front and rear. It stood very close to the street and to the houses on either side of it, with only a small gated courtyard at the back. Coop's town slaves, who lived in simple rooms above the outbuildings, treated Grady kindly, and he found himself wishing he could stay. He and William shared a room with a slave named Beau, whose only job, it seemed, was to play the fiddle. He performed at fancy gatherings in Massa's town house, and Coop hired him out for other peoples' parties and dances when he wasn't needed.

Beau was slender and wiry, no taller than Grady, and as spirited as the lively tunes he played. Grady knew by Beau's wooly gray hair and plentiful wrinkles that he was no longer young, but he was so full of energy—toes tapping, fingers dancing across the strings—that he might have been Grady's age. Grady had a great deal of free time while they stayed in New Orleans, and he spent most of it with Beau, watching him practice the fiddle, memorizing all the tunes that flowed out of his instrument so effortlessly.

"Wanna learn?" Beau asked him one day as they sat outside on the washhouse steps. "I could teach you." Grady was afraid to believe it.

"I . . . I don't know. I never made no music before."

"Well, it ain't that hard if you put your mind to it," Beau said with a grin. "Seems to me you're a bright boy. William says you learn fast. Wanna try?" He offered the fiddle to Grady, and he accepted it carefully, using both hands.

"Okay . . . thanks."

Beau gave him his first lesson that day, then loaned him an older fiddle to practice on in his spare time. "This used to belong to one of Massa's other slaves," Beau said, "but he ain't around no more. It's an old fiddle, but it still plays okay. Try it."

Grady spent all of his days practicing, sometimes stopping only late at night when the others wanted to sleep. He grew to love the feel of the warm, smooth wood beneath his chin and the way the notes vibrated through him as he played. It seemed as though his fingers had always known where to sit on the strings and just how firmly to press to make the notes sing. The bow felt at home in his right hand, and his arm felt designed to lift the bow and glide it against the strings with just the right pressure and speed. Beau taught him where to put his fingers to make each note, and once Grady got a melody in his head, he would patiently pick out the notes, one by one, and string them together to repeat the song.

Playing the fiddle was immensely satisfying—like eating a full, rich meal—and it helped soothe all of Grady's pent-up anger and frustration. As the weeks passed he worried, sometimes, that he was no longer storing up his rage the way Amos had told him to do. But it seemed impossible to be anything but happy as he sat beside the ever-cheerful Beau and made music.

"You sure do learn fast," Beau told him. "Before long you be playing as good as me." Grady doubted it was true, but the compliment brought a rare smile to his lips.

Grady barely saw Massa Coop during all the weeks they stayed in New Orleans, and the knot of fear that had rested in his stomach since the night Coop had beaten him slowly began to uncoil. But one winter afternoon as Grady sat alone on the washhouse steps, fiddling a tune, he looked up to see Coop standing in the courtyard a few yards away, watching and listening. Grady halted mid-song. His arms went limp and fell to his sides, still clutching the fiddle and bow.

"No, keep playing," Coop ordered.

Grady obeyed, his hands trembling and slick with sweat. Fear made his rhythm clumsy, the notes scratchy and out-of-tune. He glanced up and saw Coop listening, his hands on his hips, his expression unreadable. Then as quickly as he'd appeared, Coop vanished into the house again.

"We're sailing tomorrow," William told him a week later. "Massa say for you to bring the fiddle."

Grady stared in disbelief. He had never imagined that he'd be allowed to play in the overcrowded ship's hold and slave pens, certain that there'd be no time to continue practicing with endless work to be done. Why would Coop make such a kind offer? Grady longed to ask William why he was being granted this privilege, but he was afraid Coop would change his mind if he did. "Where're we going?" he asked instead.

"Where do you think," William said angrily. "Back for more slaves. This is what Massa does for a living. Some folks trade cotton or tobacco, our massa trades slaves."

The long journey around Florida by steamship, then up the coast to Virginia took a few weeks. They stopped in dozens of ports along the way to refuel or change ships, but since Coop hadn't purchased any slaves yet, Grady had plenty of time to practice his fiddle. Sometimes he would hear a new tune while he attended Coop in the ship's salon or in one of the many hotel lounges they visited. Grady would hum it over and over in his mind, memorizing it, then he would try to pick out the melody on his fiddle when he returned to his quarters. He was becoming quite good, and he knew it. But sometimes he would catch William watching him with an expression on his face that Grady couldn't quite read. It wasn't jealousy or disapproval—it was as if William knew something that Grady didn't.

"What's wrong?" Grady asked him one night. "Why're you always looking at me that way when I play?"

"No reason," he said with a shrug.

"This bothering you? Want me to stop playing?"

"No. I'm used to it." William's frown deepened. "The slave Massa Coop had before you played that fiddle, too."

A shudder passed through Grady when he saw the grim expression on William's face. "What happened to him? Massa sell him?" Grady asked. Their eyes met for a moment before William looked away.

"Reason he's gone ain't got nothing to do with playing the fiddle," he finally said.

Grady found no comfort in his answer. William's uneasiness made him afraid—and certain that he was hiding something. "Why didn't he take this with him?" Grady asked, holding up the instrument.

"That fiddle belongs to Massa Coop, not him. Now quit asking me questions."

One afternoon as their ship steamed into yet another port, Grady looked out of the porthole in Massa Coop's cabin and saw the familiar steeple of St. John's church pointing above the trees. The stately capitol building came into view on the hill, then he recognized Tredegar's Iron Works sprawled near the shore. They were landing in Richmond. He was home.

Tears blurred Grady's vision, but he quickly blinked them away, unwilling to miss a thing. He heard William gathering all Massa's belongings together and setting the bags near the cabin door, and Grady knew he should be helping. But he couldn't tear himself away from the view. Maybe Mama or Eli or someone he knew would be waiting for him at the dock. Maybe he'd be allowed to go home and see them tonight and tell them all the things he'd seen and done. Wouldn't they be surprised to hear him play the fiddle?

"What're you staring out that window for?" William asked. "There's work to be done."

Grady scrambled to help with the luggage, eager to be ashore all the sooner. It seemed to take forever for the ship to ease close to the dock at Rockett's Wharf, longer still for the gangway to be secured so the passengers could disembark. Grady stood at the rail, longing to race over to Broad Street and run up the hill toward the church. He had ridden that way in the carriage with Eli dozens of times, and he knew exactly which street to turn down in order to get home. He could picture Caroline's Big House on the corner, Eli's garden and the stables behind it, the loft above the kitchen where he used to live. He ached to set foot on shore and run. But as the first passengers began to disembark, he slowly became aware that William was eyeing him, studying him carefully as if trying to read Grady's thoughts.

"This is where you come from, ain't it," William said slowly. "Richmond, Virginia."

Grady didn't answer. Suddenly William dropped Massa's suitcases to the deck and gripped Grady's arm.

"Don't do it, boy!" he said in a low, angry voice. "Don't be a fool!"

Tears filled Grady's eyes in spite of all his efforts to stop them. It was impossible not to think of his mama or to long for home. He was so close, only a few dozen blocks away.

"You carry the bags," William ordered. He hefted a third satchel in his left hand so he could keep his grip on Grady's arm with his right hand.

Grady bent to lift the heavy suitcases and strained to carry them. By the time they went ashore, hailed a carriage, and loaded everything on board, Grady's arms ached from his burdens—and from William's grip. He saw William whisper something to Coop, and Massa ordered the driver to go to the slave pen, first, instead of the hotel. William led Grady inside and locked him there for the night—in the same pen where his long imprisonment had begun. William went to the hotel with Massa.

Coop spent a month in Richmond, purchasing slaves, but Grady remained locked behind bars the entire time. Little by little, the cage filled with angry, bewildered, despairing people. Their stories matched his own—they'd been cruelly ripped from their homes and their families and left to wonder what would become of them, or if they'd ever see their loved ones again. Every time Coop locked a new slave inside the pen with Grady, it brought back his own pain and the memory of the terrible day he'd been torn away from his mama. Grady knew exactly what lay ahead for all of these people, and the knowledge made him sick at heart. William had brought the fiddle to him, but Grady wouldn't allow himself the comfort of playing it. His rage slowly swelled and grew as if it were a living thing, planted inside him. The knowledge that he would have to bear a lifetime of watching his fellow slaves being bought and sold filled him with despair. He couldn't live this way. But Grady was a slave, and there was no hope of ever being set free from this life until the day he died.

When Massa Coop finally sailed from Richmond with his load of human cargo, Grady couldn't look back at the city that had once been his home.

❧

That afternoon, Massa Coop stood in the center of the hold beside Grady and William, surveying his cargo. "It seems like it's getting harder and harder to find first-rate slaves these days," Coop said. "We'll have to fix up this bunch, William. Get Joe to help you so he learns how to do it."

"Yes, Massa."

"What's he making us do now?" Grady asked after Coop had left.

William gestured to a middle-aged, gray-bearded man slumped against the bulkhead. "See him? He's looking too old. Massa can't get a good price if folks think his working days is about over. Get a bucket of water and some soap. His whiskers are gonna have to come off."

Grady spent the next few hours, while on route to their first port, helping William shave beards and mustaches off all the men whose whiskers had turned gray. Then they rounded up all the men and women with gray threads in their hair so William could give them short haircuts. He showed Grady how to brush boot blacking through their hair, afterwards, to dye it black. Few of these slaves knew their real age, so William instructed them how to answer if a buyer asked how old they were, always making them as young as he dared. Helping Coop get rich through this deception made Grady heartsick.

"Get your fiddle tuned up and ready, Joe," Coop ordered when they reached their first port. "You're going to do some playing for me."

Grady obeyed, taking the fiddle out of the case and tuning the strings for the first time in weeks. He wondered if Coop planned to hire him out for parties the way he'd hired out Beau in New Orleans, or if Grady would have to perform in Coop's hotel room while the planters drank bourbon. He hoped he'd be hired out. Better to fiddle for white folks than help Coop sell slaves, even if Coop would be keeping all the money Grady earned. But instead of taking Grady to the hotel, Coop led him down to the slave pen and locked him inside with all the others.

"All right, play something lively," Massa Coop ordered. "William, get these Negroes on their feet. I want them singing and dancing and looking happier than this by the time my customers arrive or you'll all feel my wrath. Every one of you."

Grady stood frozen in shock as he watched Coop stride away, unable to believe what he'd been asked to do.

"You heard him. Start playing," William told Grady.

"I don't want—"

"Did anyone ask if you want to?" William said fiercely. "Massa knows you can play, and by heaven you'll play! He ain't whipped anyone in a good long while, and he's just itching for a reason to. I'm making sure it ain't me—and you better make sure it ain't you. Now, play!" William turned to the other slaves, gesturing angrily. "Rest of you gonna start dancing and looking happy, if you don't want a beating."

Grady wanted to smash the instrument against the wall. It had been his sole source of joy and pleasure, but Coop had suddenly turned it into a means of torture. He felt duped—conned into learning to fiddle and blinded to the true reason why. But now that Coop knew he could play, Grady didn't dare refuse, whether he felt like it or not.

He lifted the instrument with shaking hands and played one of the first tunes Beau had ever taught him, hating the sound of the bow as it grated against the strings, hating the feel of the fiddle beneath his chin, hating what Coop was forcing him to do. This was what the slave before him must have done. Grady finally understood the grim knowledge he had read on William's face as he'd practiced all those months.

All that day, Grady had no choice but to play song after song, repeating his small repertoire of tunes over and over while the slaves danced, until all of Massa's customers had come and gone. By the time Grady finished the afternoon's work, his entire body was shaking with rage. But even then his work wasn't finished. He was forced to swallow his anger and accompany William to Coop's hotel where their massa spent a long evening playing poker with three other gentlemen. It was very late, the stars shining in a midnight sky, when the poker game ended and Grady walked back to the slave pen with William for the night.

"Why didn't you warn me?" Grady demanded, finally giving voice to his rage. "You knew he was gonna make me play for them—you knew! Why'd you let me practice and learn how if—"

"Shut up!" William gave Grady a shove, knocking him off the sidewalk into the street. "If Massa ever find out I warned you not to learn that fiddle, he'd whip us both. Don't you understand that yet? Don't you understand that one wrong move and our life ain't worth a nickel? Just shut up and do whatever he says! Don't matter what you want, and it don't matter what I want."

"I hate this life," Grady mumbled.

"Well, nobody's asking your opinion."

The slave pen was several blocks from the hotel, but William seemed to know the way by heart, weaving through the maze of back lanes and warehouses near the docks. No one guarded them, and although they passed a few carriages and pedestrians, no one seemed to notice the pair of slaves walking freely through the streets.

"Ever think about running away?" Grady asked quietly. "Be easy enough to do, with you knowing your way around all these cities like you do."

William glared at him, then looked away. "Ain't worth taking a chance."

Grady saw the slave pen ahead and all his pent-up frustration swelled inside him again. "I hate Massa Coop! I hate working for him this way! You and me are helping them filthy white men when we ought to be helping our own. Must be something I can do to make Massa sell me along with the rest."

"Don't be a fool," William spat. "This is a good life compared to field work on a plantation. We're getting plenty of food, wearing decent clothes, the work ain't that hard. As long as we're careful and nobody try to escape, we'll be fine."

"But I can't stand this anymore! And now, making me play the fiddle . . ." His throat choked with rage. "How can you live this way?"

"Being sold is worse. Why do you think these folks is always so upset about being sold South? Talk to the ones that come off the plantations, sometime. Ask them what that life is like. Then you'll know how good you have it."

"This ain't a good life. I don't want to be working for Massa Coop no more. I know he'll whip me if I try and run, but maybe if I make him mad enough he'll sell me afterwards."

William halted and spun Grady around to face him. Fear filled his eyes. "Don't you do that! Don't you ever be doing that! He won't sell you, boy. He spent all this time training you, and he won't ever forgive you if you betray his trust and try and run off. He'll whip you until you die!"

A chill ran through Grady, but he pushed his fear aside. "I don't believe it. He paid good money for me, and I know how much Massa hates losing his money."

"No, sir! You came cheap because you're so young. You had no skills before Massa's teaching you. He ain't selling you, boy, so get it out of your head."

"There must be some way to get free . . ." Grady mumbled.

William gripped his shoulders, shaking him. "You want to know what happened to the slave Massa have before you? Massa killed him! He whipped him to death because he try and run off!"

Grady battled a surge of nausea. It was easy to imagine Coop being carried away in such an act of violence, a grin of triumph on his face. But as shocking as the truth was, Grady's stomach rolled with hopelessness, not fear.

"That's why I don't try and run," William said. "I seen what Massa done to him. He made me stand right there and watch him die."

90

William shoved Grady forward again, and they walked the last dozen yards to the pen in silence. A guard dozed on a chair near the gate. William woke him up and asked to be locked inside.

"What was his name?" Grady asked as they settled down to sleep in the inky darkness.

"Huh?" William asked gruffly. "Whose name?"

"The slave Massa Coop had before me. The one who played the fiddle." The man Coop had killed.

"Joe," William said hoarsely. "His name was Joe . . . same as you."

CHAPTER

7

CHARLESTON, SOUTH CAROLINA 1857

"I never rode on a boat before," Kitty said with a nervous laugh. She felt giddy with excitement and more than a little scared as the steamer chugged down the Edisto River toward Charleston. All the familiar sights of Great Oak Plantation—the only home Kitty had ever known—disappeared as the ship rounded a bend. "The floor sure is wobbly, ain't it, Missy Claire?"

"It's called a deck, not a floor," Missy replied. She seemed bored with their journey to Charleston and impatient to arrive. But, then, Missy had been to the city before; Kitty hadn't.

Kitty leaned over the rail as far as she dared and peered down. The gray water looked angry and bottomless. The boat bobbed up and down, rocking like a runaway wagon. The motion made her stomach feel queasy. She closed her eyes for a moment until the feeling passed.

"I think I like riding in a carriage a lot better," she said.

Missy made a face. "Don't be such a baby. A steamboat will get us there much faster." She strode away from Kitty as if she was tired of her and joined a group of white people standing at the stern.

Kitty decided to watch the scenery drift past along the shore and ignore the churning river. They passed through thick, green woods, buzzing with insects. Then the woods gave way to marshes and creeks, where alligators drifted like fallen logs and herons and other waterfowl waded near the bank. Every now and then they passed a plantation, the rice and cotton crops newly harvested. As Kitty gradually grew used to the motion of the ship and the churning water, she began to relax, enjoying the chance to rest and do nothing. It was the first rest she'd had after the week-long flurry of packing.

Missy Claire and her family made the trip to their town house in Charleston twice a year—during the hottest summer days to enjoy the city's sea breezes, and again in the winter when the city's social season was in full swing. Kitty and the other house slaves had to pack everything the family would need into hatboxes, satchels, steamer trunks, and bureaus with handles that could be easily transported. Massa Goodman even had a clever traveling desk that folded all up with his important papers still inside, so he could carry it back and forth between Charleston and the plantation. Twice a year, Kitty had helped the other servants get ready, but she had always stayed behind at the plantation. This year, Kitty had finally been promoted from mammy's helper to chambermaid, and she'd been allowed to make the journey for the first time.

"Your mama, Lucindy, was a chambermaid, too," Mammy Bertha told Kitty. "Missus Goodman only wants pretty gals up in the Big House where white folks might see them. It's lucky you're real pretty, like your mama."

"Yours is a very important job," Missy's mother had warned when Kitty's training had begun, "so no more of your silliness. We'll see if you can learn to behave properly and wait on a lady."

That's what Claire was, now—a lady. She'd had five birthday parties since Kitty had lived with her in the Big House, and at fifteen, Claire was old enough to dress like a grown-up in long-sleeved dresses and hoop skirts, old enough to wear her pale brown hair pinned up on her head. Her figure had changed, too—to that of a woman. Kitty envied her, but Missy had pointed to Kitty's tiny bosom one morning and said, "You'll have a woman's figure, too, in a year or two."

One of Missus Goodman's maids was teaching Kitty how to dress Missy's hair. She had to be careful and not pull too hard when combing out the snarls or Missy would slap her. But Kitty loved colorful things, and she loved choosing the perfect hair ribbon or jeweled comb to make Missy look pretty.

She had been brushing Missy's hair last night before bed when Missus Goodman came into the room to talk to Claire. "This is your first winter season as a young lady," she'd said, "so it will be a very important one for you. You're old enough to begin courting a husband, and that's what you must think about during all the parties and dinners and balls and receptions you'll attend. These are golden opportunities to be seen by the right sort of people and to make a favorable impression. Your future depends on it."

Kitty had wanted to ask Missy Claire how she felt about being paraded all around Charleston like an item for sale, and how she felt about getting married and going off to live with a husband. They used to talk and giggle about all sorts of things back when Missy would let Kitty climb on her bed and sleep down by her feet. But Claire behaved very differently now that she was all grown up. It was as if she and Kitty had never laughed and played together at all or pretended that Kitty was a cat. She was Claire's slave, not her friend. If she dawdled or made a mistake or did something to displease Missy, she would earn a smack and a reprimand, just like any other slave.

Missy Claire had grown too old for dolls and games, too sophisticated to have a slave play with her and entertain her. Kitty dusted and cleaned Missy's room, emptied her slops, made her bed, mended and brushed and cared for her clothes. Meanwhile, Missy Claire studied lessons with a governess every day, reading and writing and studying history, arithmetic, and French. She was also learning the womanly arts of needlework and watercolors. Kitty loved to gaze at the beautiful strands of wool in Missy's sewing basket, a rainbow of soft colors that Missy would stitch into pretty designs. But Kitty was never happier than on those days when she hauled Missy's easel and watercolors outside for her and stood beside her to fan away the bugs while Missy tried to paint the Great Oak Tree or a river scene.

Missy Claire was not a very good artist. She couldn't seem to judge shapes and sizes and colors the way that Kitty could, and she lacked the patience to practice until she got better. The first time Claire had tossed her paintbrush onto the ground in frustration, Kitty had scooped it right up.

"It ain't so bad, Missy Claire. All you need to do is add a little more color here . . . and here. . . ." She had dabbed paint on to the picture as if it was the most natural thing in the world to clean up Missy's pictures the way she cleaned up everything else for her. And from that very first time, Kitty had fallen in love with the feel of the paintbrush as it slid across the page, leaving a trail of color.

Missy let Kitty fix all her pictures, after that. And the tutor praised Missy's work, never guessing that an ignorant slave had painted most of it. Kitty didn't care. When she found a half-used folio of paper that Claire had thrown into the trash, she felt as though she'd discovered gold. "Can I have this old paper, Missy Claire?" she begged. "Please . . . please?"

"I don't care," she said with a shrug. Then, in a rare moment of kindness, she added, "Here . . . you may as well have a pencil, too." Kitty carried the treasures all around with her, sketching late at night when her work was all done. She longed to sketch the scenes she was seeing from the riverboat, but her satchel of belongings had been stowed below with the rest of the luggage. She had to be content to soak it all in, hoping that she could remember and recapture the scenes someday.

A few hours later, dozens of fishing boats and heavier river traffic told Kitty that they were approaching the city. By the time they finally docked in Charleston, her heart pounded so wildly with excitement she was afraid it might burst. She wished she had a hundred eyes so she could look at a hundred things in a hundred directions at once. Everything seemed to move faster in Charleston, as if the days and nights had speeded up. Everything was louder, too, and there was more of everything—more ships, more houses, more people, and certainly more horses and carriages than Kitty had ever seen in her life. She followed Missy off the ship and down the pier, gazing all around, trying to take it all in.

"Stop dawdling," Claire ordered, "or we'll leave you behind."

"Sorry, Missy Claire." But she couldn't help gawking. There was so much to see in Charleston.

A carriage arrived to meet them, and Missy Claire and her family climbed onboard. Massa Goodman had hired a wagon to transport their luggage, and Kitty watched as slave porters unloaded all their goods from the ship, hauling the cargo down the pier on their backs. She and the dozen other servants who had come from the plantation rode on the wagon with the luggage, sitting on top of it as they bumped down the lumpy cobblestones. So many carriages and horses jammed the streets that Kitty wondered how they would ever make any progress. She savored her first impressions of Charleston, inhaling the scent of tobacco and horses and a bakery.

The buildings downtown looked enormous to her: mountainous structures of brick and tabby and glass, with church steeples so tall she had to tilt her head way back to see the tops. They passed stately public buildings with pillars and statues and fancy carving, and tiny green parks with palmetto trees and neat flower beds. Best of all, Kitty saw color everywhere she looked—on the ladies' dresses and flowered hats, on the canvas awnings that shaded the shops, on the brightly lettered signs that hung above the storefronts. She couldn't read any of the signs, but most of them had pictures painted on them to show what was sold inside.

The traffic gradually thinned as they left the downtown area and drove through residential streets. The houses looked as big as Missy's plantation house, but instead of being surrounded by fields and trees and grass, the city houses were crowded close together on small patches of land. One row of homes was painted a rainbow of colors with contrasting shutters and trim Kitty itched to get out her paper and pencil—better still, Missy's box of watercolors—and try to capture all of these wonderful sights.

The wagon finally reached the Goodmans' town house and drove around to the courtyard at the rear. The house sat at the very edge of the city, overlooking the water, with broad piazzas that wrapped around the front and side of the house to catch the ocean breezes. The bay across the street looked bigger and wider than any river Kitty had ever seen. She longed to explore the mansion from top to bottom, but there wasn't time. She had to follow Missy's luggage upstairs to her bedroom and unpack all Missy's things so she could get settled into her room. It was late at night before Kitty even saw her own quarters.

The slaves slept dormitory-style in a long, drab, two-story building behind the house. The kitchen and washhouse were downstairs, the slaves' rooms upstairs. Bessie, her husband, Alfred, and a third slave stayed year-round to take care of the house. The remainder of the slaves—a dozen or more—traveled with the Goodmans from the plantation each time: the butler, cook, footmen, parlor maids, scullery maids, and chambermaids like Kitty.

The room Kitty shared with three other chambermaids had little more than a fireplace, a shuttered window, and two wooden beds. By the end of that long first day, Kitty was so tired from the fresh air, the excitement, and all the hard work, that she climbed in beside her bedmate and fell sound asleep.

Missy Claire spent the first few days that they were in Charleston shopping. She begged her mother to bring Kitty along with them. "She has a good eye for pretty things, Mother," Missy Claire insisted. "And she always knows which colors go best together." Kitty gladly followed Claire and Missus Goodman from one store to the next as they bought hats, shoes, jewelry, combs, and ribbons for Missy's hair, and bolts of colorful fabric for new dresses. Charleston had a store for anything you wanted to buy, and Kitty shopped until her feet ached, savoring every minute of it. She loved choosing beautiful things for Missy, even if she would never wear any of them herself.

One afternoon, Missy Claire and her mother stopped for refreshments at a tearoom. Kitty stayed outside with Alfred, the coachman, riding beside him high on the driver's seat. As they drove around the block, looking for a place to park the carriage, Kitty heard a strange jangling sound like broken bells. Trudging toward her from a side street was a long line of slaves, all chained together in two long rows. Shackles bound their wrists and feet, and they were forced to shuffle awkwardly, barely able to walk as the short, heavy chains that were fastened to their ankles dragged across the cobblestones. The slaves walked with their heads down, their backs bowed, passing through a gated entrance and into a grim building made of tabby.

"Is that a jail?" she asked Alfred.

"No, it's the slave mart." He spoke in a hushed voice, as if they were driving through a cemetery. He suddenly seemed in a big hurry to drive past the building, and he didn't relax again until they had turned the corner.

"What's a slave mart?" Kitty asked. She spoke as softly as he had.

"Them slaves is for sale," he said with a sigh. "White folks are buying and selling them in that building, just like they buy and sell other things."

Kitty had seen the endless variety of goods in the stores in Charleston, but she had never imagined that there would be a store for slaves, too. All of the slaves she knew had been born on Great Oak Plantation, starting out as little babies, just as she had. But Bertha said that Kitty's mama had been sold after she'd tried to run away. Kitty tugged on Alfred's sleeve to get his attention.

"If Massa Goodman was to sell one of us," she asked, "would we go to a store like that, do you think?"

"I reckon so. Why?"

"He sold my mama when I was a little girl. Think she might still be in there?"

"No, they don't stay there very long," he said gruffly. "Slave trader comes along and buys her, he could be taking her anywhere. . . . That's just the way it is."

"Oh."

Kitty had no choice but to accept this sad truth and give up the notion of ever seeing her mama again. It had seemed to her like such a long, long way to Charleston from the plantation, and she knew from the pictures in some of Missy Claire's books that the world was an even bigger place than she could ever imagine. No telling where her mama went after she was sold.

For the next few minutes, Alfred was too busy maneuvering through the traffic and searching for a place to park the carriage to talk to Kitty. When he finally found a place within sight of the tearoom, he pulled the carriage to a stop, hitched the horses to the post, then climbed back up on the seat beside her to wait. A chilly breeze blew from the nearby river and Kitty hugged her shawl tightly around her, wishing she had white skin so she could sit inside the carriage, out of the wind—or better still, sit at a table inside the cozy tearoom.

"If you work real hard and do whatever Massa say," Alfred said softly, "you never have to worry about being sold."

Kitty was a little surprised to learn that he'd been thinking about the slave mart all this time—but then, so had she.

"I don't even remember what my mama looked like," she said.

Alfred gazed silently into the distance and nodded, his face somber. Kitty wondered if her own face looked as sad as his did. Then, worried that it did—and that Missy might see her—she forced all thoughts of her mother from her mind and tried to smile as she watched the door of the tearoom for her mistress.

⁂

"May I be excused from this luncheon, Mother? Please?" Missy Claire begged a few days later. "I don't feel well. I have cramps."

Kitty thought her mistress's pale skin did look whiter than usual as she lay burrowed in her bed beneath the rumpled comforter. Missus Goodman pondered the request for a moment, and Kitty found herself hoping that she would give in and excuse Claire. Kitty was just as exhausted as Missy was from the endless round of social gatherings and parties. But unlike her mistress, Kitty wasn't allowed to remain in bed until noon after a late night out, no matter how ill she felt.

Ever since they'd arrived in Charleston, Missy Claire had been attending countless dinners and teas and dances. Last night she'd gone to a lavish ball at the Citadel, where she had waltzed with so many young cadets that Kitty had to pull off Missy's slippers and massage her aching feet. They'd driven home late at night beneath twinkling stars and gaslights, with carriages full of other partygoers rumbling past.

As Missy's chambermaid, Kitty was required to attend every function with her, waiting nearby in case Missy required assistance for any reason, perhaps repairing Missy's hair or her gown, if needed. The slaves often gathered together to socialize with each other while they waited, sometimes having quiet little parties of their own. Kitty was aware of several romances flourishing between her fellow servants, and she'd even seen couples kissing in the shadows and climbing into their masters' empty carriages. But she was much too shy to make friends with any of the other slaves. Instead, she was content to watch Missy Claire and the other white folks from afar, smelling the food, listening to the distant music and laughter. She accepted her life the way it was. Her skin was black. Parties and balls and tables piled with luscious food were for white people.

So was sleeping until noon as Missy had done. Kitty watched, waiting for her orders as Claire's mother stood appraising her daughter. "No, your father really wants you at this dinner today, Claire," she finally replied. "Roger Fuller is a friend of his, and the Fullers are one of our state's leading families."

"I don't care," Missy groaned, pulling the covers over her head.

"Well, you should care. Mr. Fuller has an enormous cotton plantation near Pocotaligo and a lovely town house in Beaufort."

"Is he as rich as Father?" Claire asked from beneath the sheets.

"No," Missus Goodman replied with a sly smile, "I believe Mr. Fuller is even wealthier. He has two sons, and all three men are here in town because the older son is thinking of attending the Citadel."

"Then he's too young to hunt for a wife," Claire mumbled. "I'll have dinner with them next year."

Missus Goodman strode across the room and jerked the covers all the way down to the bottom of the bed. "Roger Fuller's wife died six months ago. That makes *three* eligible gentlemen, Claire, all coming to our home for dinner today. Surely you can manage to impress one of them with your charm? Few families are wealthier than the Fullers." She turned toward Kitty, gesturing to the heavily draped windows. "Open those curtains and get to work, girl. You have a little over an hour to make Claire presentable."

Missy groaned. "But what about my cramps?"

"Take some laudanum."

"I took laudanum last night, Mother. That's why I still feel so groggy."

"Then maybe a cup of warm milk will help. Kitty!" Missus Goodman shouted. "Don't just stand there, move! Make her beautiful!"

"Yes, ma'am." Kitty quickly opened the drapes, then grabbed the pitcher and ran downstairs to fetch warm water for Missy's washbasin. After Missy's sponge bath, Kitty began the arduous task of dressing her in layer after layer of clothes—chemise, drawers, corset, stockings, hoops, crinolines and petticoats. She helped Missy into one of her beautiful new gowns, spending long minutes fastening the endless rows of fussy hooks and eyes. Then the delicate job of fixing Missy's hair began. It was spider-web thin and difficult to style. It also tangled easily, and knowing the mood Missy was in today, Kitty braced herself for the inevitable slaps she would receive for hurting her. By the time the Fullers' carriage arrived, the only remaining task was to help Claire choose her jewelry and accessories—parasol, handkerchief, hat, purse, cloak and reticule. Kitty was thankful that the dinner was being held here in the Goodmans' home and the accessories would be kept to a minimum. Missy Claire had been known to take hours to make these final choices.

"Stay close by, Kitty," Missy ordered as she prepared to sweep down the stairs to greet her guests. "I may need you."

"Yes, Missy Claire." Kitty tried to sound willing and cheerful, but she groaned inside at the thought of standing rigidly in place for the next two or three hours while her mistress dined on the multi-course meal. She found a spot in the hallway outside the dining room and watched the waiters carry in platters of food—oysters, broiled fish, buttery potatoes and vegetables, glazed ham. Everything looked delicious, but it was the aroma of roast turkey and gravy that made Kitty's mouth water. She closed her eyes and imagined pouring creamy golden gravy over Cook's buttermilk biscuits. Kitty's stomach rumbled at the thought.

Hours passed, and Missy Claire left more food on her plate than she ate, pushing it around delicately with her fork while she chatted. Kitty watched the waiter whisk Claire's still-laden plate away after the meal and longed to snatch it from his hand and eat the leftovers. She would have a chance to taste the remnants of the meal later, in the kitchen, but that could be hours from now, when Missy was in bed.

Kitty decided to study the dinner guests to help take her mind off her hunger. She was surprised to see how young Mr. Fuller's two sons were—no older than Missy Claire. Surely they wouldn't be making marriage arrangements at their age, would they? And Mr. Fuller looked too old for Missy, nearly the same age as her father. Mr. Fuller had an interesting face, though, with a broad forehead, pointed chin, and a brush-like mustache. His pale eyes were deep-set and a little too far apart, but he looked very kind. Kitty would have loved to sketch him.

By the time dessert was served, Kitty's back and legs ached. She wondered how long she'd been standing. It felt like days. She was running out of ways to distract herself, and decided to inch closer so she could eavesdrop on the dinner conversation.

"What did you think of the Dred Scott case?" she heard Mr. Fuller ask.

Massa Goodman smiled broadly. "I think Chief Justice Taney and the Supreme Court made an excellent decision." He turned to Fuller's younger son who was stifling a yawn and said, "You young men may not realize, now, how important their ruling was, but you'll appreciate it in the future."

"What was it all about, Father?" the older son asked.

Fuller pushed his half-finished dessert away and pulled his coffee cup closer. "A slave named Dred Scott sued the court for his freedom, claiming that he had lived on free soil in the Missouri Territory for several years. The Supreme Court denied his claim, saying that since the Negro race is so far inferior to ours, they have no rights. Therefore, the court was not bound to consider the issue of Negro rights. Scott will remain a slave."

"Of course, we knew that Negroes were inferior to us all along," Massa Goodman added. "Anyone who works with them knows that they are. Without us, the entire race would be unable to fend for themselves. Slavery has helped Negroes learn a measure of civilized behavior, but by no means will they ever be equal to whites. We're doing them a favor by teaching them skills and giving them food and clothing. They would never survive on their own."

His words made Kitty want to shrink very small and hide somewhere. But as she fought the urge to disappear in shame, she saw Missy Claire beckoning to her from across the room. Kitty felt as though all eyes were on her as she tiptoed into the room and leaned close so Missy could whisper in her ear.

"I don't feel well. Fetch me a cup of warm milk from the kitchen."

Kitty hurried outside to the kitchen, relieved for the chance to flee from the conversation and the humiliating stares. She found Bessie and Cook and some of the other house slaves seated around the pine table, eating the remnants of the meal they'd worked so hard to prepare. In the middle of them all, sat the little old storyteller named Delia, who had visited along with the Fullers once before.

"Excuse me," Kitty said. Her voice sounded louder than she'd planned. The conversation stopped as everyone looked up at her. "Missy Claire's needing a cup of warm milk," she said meekly.

"Missy Claire's spoilt rotten," Cook grumbled as she labored to her feet. "Five-course meal ain't enough for her?"

Kitty didn't reply. She couldn't take her eyes off the storyteller. "Excuse me," she said again, "but I once heard you telling about a land with all black people. You said they had villages and families and everything else without no white folks helping them. Is that true?"

"It's true," Delia replied. "And don't you ever forget it, honey."

"But I heard them talking at dinner just now, and Massa says we'd never be able to get by without white folks. Don't he know about that land?"

"Oh, he knows all right," Delia replied. "He has to lie about it because he also knows that they stole us away from there and forced us to be their slaves."

Kitty still couldn't forget the shame she'd felt at Massa's words. "He's saying we ain't as good as white folks are. He says we're an inferior race."

"Lies!" Delia banged her fist on the table making the plates jump. "We're no different than they are! We're all God's children, no matter what color skin we have. Don't you know we all come from the same mother and father—from Adam and Eve?"

"N-no, ma'am."

"Don't you go to church? Didn't anyone ever teach you the Gospel, honey?" Something about the little woman's gaze seemed to hold Kitty captive, against her will. She was sorry she had ever asked the question in the first place, sorry she had eavesdropped on Massa's conversation.

"No, ma'am," she replied, taking a step backward. "Missy Claire and them go to church every Sunday, but they say religion ain't for colored folks. She say we don't have souls."

Delia exhaled and closed her eyes briefly. But when she spoke to Kitty her voice was kind. "You have a heart and a soul and a mind just like your missy. There ain't no difference at all between the two of you."

Her words shocked Kitty. She quickly glanced around at the others, worried that she might get into trouble for listening to Delia's outrageous ideas. "But there is a difference," Kitty said. "Missy can read and write, and her daddy owns a plantation and a house in town—"

"That don't matter one bit," Delia said, interrupting. "Underneath our skin, we're all the same. And we *ain't* inferior. The white folks believe it, and they want us to believe it, but it ain't true."

Kitty shook her head as if she could shake off Delia's words. They couldn't be true. If she was the same as Claire on the inside, then why did Claire eat rich food, wear beautiful clothes, and sleep in a feather bed? Why did Kitty have to empty Claire's slops and sleep on cornshucks and do whatever Claire said, no matter how much she hated it? No, it couldn't be true. She was Missy's slave. There must be a good reason why. She glanced at the pan of milk warming on the coals. She wanted to grab it and run.

"Listen to me, honey," Delia said. She stood and walked around the table toward her. The tiny woman had the commanding presence of a loaded cannon, aimed straight at Kitty. She paid attention.

"I'm going to tell you another true story," Delia began. "Long time ago, God made the first man and woman, Adam and Eve. They lived with God, as His children, but one day they sinned and God had to send them away. This old world's been filled with suffering ever since that day. And wouldn't you know, the first two children ever born couldn't get along with each other? The one boy starts fighting with the other one and acting jealous, and the next thing you know, he's killing his own brother. Been like that ever since—brother fighting against brother, hating and killing each other. Right now our white brothers and sisters is hating their black-skinned brothers and sisters, and they're forcing us to be their slaves. But God's gonna put a stop to it. Oh yes. He's gonna help us get free from them white folks one of these days."

"Hush, now!" Bessie said sharply.

Her husband, Alfred, scrambled to his feet as if ready to run somewhere. "Better watch what you say, Delia," he whispered.

Kitty glanced around and saw a frightened look on everyone's face.

"Lord Jesus is gonna set us all free," Delia repeated firmly. "He loves all His children, black and white. In Jesus' eyes, honey, you and me ain't no different from our massa. Just the color of our skin's different, that's all."

"Then why does God let them treat us this way?" Cook asked. The others around the table tried to shush her but she said, "No, hear me, now. If God's loving us all the same, why don't He help us? Why's He standing back and watching us suffer? Don't tell me He loves us, Delia. God loves the white folk. He's their God, not ours."

"You're wrong," Delia said. "God's skin ain't no color at all. And Jesus knows what it's like to suffer the way we do. He felt the lash on His back, same as us. If we pray and believe, then in His own time, in His own way, the Lord Jesus is gonna help us."

The memory of her daddy's voice suddenly came to Kitty. She remembered him murmuring softly, *"Help us, Lord Jesus.... Help us...."* as if he were talking to someone.

"Who's Jesus?" Kitty asked. Everyone stared at her. "When I was little, my papa used to ask him for help all the time," she explained.

Delia smiled. "Jesus is God's Son, come down to earth to save us. Your papa surely must have known Him, if he called on Him for help."

"I guess Jesus didn't hear him," Kitty said, "because he never did come to help us. The white men came, instead, with dogs and guns. They hung my papa on the Great Oak Tree and sold my mama to a slave trader."

She hadn't meant to blurt out her story but the words had flown out of her mouth before she could stop them. The kitchen fell so utterly silent that Kitty could hear the milk hissing in the pan. She saw tears in Delia's eyes. But when Kitty felt them welling up in her own, she forced them back, knowing she must never let Missy see her cry.

"Plenty of things I don't understand," Delia said. "But the moment the breath left your papa's body, he was in paradise with Jesus, and all his suffering was over. They can kill his body, but his soul belongs to God, and no one can ever snatch it away. Devil may try

106

and separate us from God, and when bad things happen he's telling us God don't love us and can't hear our cries. But—"

"Then why didn't Jesus help her folks get away?" Cook asked as she poured the warm milk into a cup.

Delia sighed. "We ain't gonna know this side of heaven. But those white men will have to face God's judgment someday and answer for what they did to her mama and papa." She seemed about to say more, but Kitty interrupted.

"Excuse me, but Missy's waiting for her milk. She hates it when I dawdle."

"God loves you, honey," Delia said softly. Kitty froze at the intensity of her stare. The little woman's words frightened her, yet there was a power in them that Kitty couldn't resist. "You're His child," Delia insisted. "You and your missy are both the same to Him."

"That can't be," Kitty whispered. She wanted to believe it but couldn't. There were no stores in Charleston that sold white people, all chained together. She carefully took the cup of milk from Cook's hand and hurried past Delia and into the house.

BEAUFORT, SOUTH CAROLINA 1857

Grady stood beside Massa Coop's chair, fanning him with a palmetto branch. His arms ached, and his eyes burned and watered from the strong cigars that the men were smoking. Massa had spent the past three hours in this private salon in the bay-front inn in Beaufort, drinking and gambling with a group of wealthy planters, but he showed no signs of quitting. Grady was so tired he could scarcely stand, much less wave his arms. It was past midnight and he longed for sleep, his feet burning with fatigue, but he didn't dare complain.

"Pour me another drink, Joe," Coop growled.

Grady quickly laid aside the fan and picked up the bottle of bourbon. He poured slowly and carefully, not daring to spill a single drop. Massa Coop took a sip then nodded to his opponents across the table.

"Want him to fill yours, Fuller?"

Grady hurried around the table with the bottle, ready to pour. But Mr. Fuller covered his empty glass with one hand. "No more for me, thanks."

"You sure?" Coop asked. "How about you, Jackson?"

Mr. Jackson shook his head as he shuffled the cards. "I'm good."

Grady had traveled with the slave trader for four years, growing taller and stronger each year. Like William, he'd become familiar with all of the hotels in all of the port cities that they visited regularly, from Charleston to Savannah to Jacksonville, all the way to New Orleans and back to Richmond again. And Grady's hatred for Massa Coop—for all white men—had grown stronger each year, as well.

He'd attended enough poker games with Coop over the years to know that his master was losing badly tonight—and he hated to lose. The pile of money that Coop had started out with had grown steadily smaller, while Mr. Fuller's pile, across the table, had grown steadily larger. Now only three men remained. The others had all gone home when their money ran out. But Coop would stay to the bitter end, trying to win at least some of his money back. And if he didn't, he would vent his anger on one of his slaves—most likely Grady.

"I'll see you and raise you fifty dollars," Fuller said. He was an elegantly dressed gentleman in his mid-thirties, a wealthy planter who sometimes purchased slaves from Coop. His wavy hair and eyebrows were the color of wet sand, his bristly mustache a darker shade of brown. His heart-shaped face had a wide brow that narrowed to a pointy chin. He seemed to be a shrewd gambler, yet there was a gentleness in his features, even after a night of drinking, that Massa Coop's face never wore even when he was sober. Fuller's pale blue eyes, bloodshot from too much bourbon and cigar smoke, still looked kind.

Coop counted his remaining coins and cursed. "I don't have fifty. Hey, Joe. Who's left in the slave pen to barter with? Any females?"

"Yes, Massa Coop. There's a few." Grady had a sudden, desperate idea. He bent close to Coop's ear so that the other two men couldn't hear what he said. "But you know them gals is worth more than fifty dollars each. How about betting me? Save you the bother of going out to the pen. Looks like you got a good hand." Grady had no idea if the cards in Coop's hand were good ones or not. He waited, holding his breath, while his master decided.

"All right," Coop said after a moment. "Tell you what, Fuller. I'm going to wager my boy, Joe. He's worth at least fifty dollars. Plays the fiddle, too."

Grady watched Fuller's face, not daring to hope. When Fuller began shaking his head, Grady felt a stab of disappointment.

"Sorry. I don't need any more slaves."

"Sell him to somebody else, then," Coop grunted. "He'll fetch twice that, easily. Besides, you don't have to worry about getting stuck with him because you can't beat my hand."

Mr. Fuller studied the cards in his own hand again then met Coop's gaze. "All right," he said, smiling slightly. "I'll call."

Coop grinned as he spread out his cards. "Full house. Queens and nines."

Fuller paused for a long moment, then laid down his own cards. "Sorry, Coop. Royal flush."

Massa Coop's smile faded. He paled slightly, and when the color did return, his face turned as red as the hearts and diamonds that dotted his cards. He'd lost. Grady had encouraged his master to bet everything, and he'd lost.

Grady could scarcely breathe. His gaze darted from one man to the other, watching their expressions, afraid to hope that Mr. Fuller was going to be his new master. Fuller had said he didn't want another slave, and Grady knew that if Fuller refused to accept him in payment, Grady would have to go home with Coop and bear the brunt of his rage.

Coop stood abruptly, upsetting his chair. Grady's skin prickled with terror. He quickly bent to straighten the chair.

"Good night, Fuller," Coop said coldly. "It's been a pleasure." He staggered to the door and jerked it open. Grady scooped up the bourbon bottle, ready to follow him to his hotel room, but Coop whirled around and pushed Grady backward, nearly knocking him down.

"Stay here, you stupid fool! You belong to him now!" Coop stomped out of the salon.

Grady's heart pounded loudly in his ears. He was free from Coop!

But what if William was right and life with a new master turned out to be even worse? Grady had watched Coop gamble and lose; now he wondered if he had just lost the biggest gamble of his life.

Mr. Fuller broke into a smile after Coop left. "I guess this was my lucky night," he said to Mr. Jackson. Grady watched his new master warily. Fuller's movements were graceful and unhurried. He pulled out a drawstring bag and scooped all his money into it while the other man gathered up the cards. Fuller had none of the mean-eyed edginess of Coop, who'd always been coiled like a rattlesnake, ready to strike. "I can't recall ever having a run of luck like this one," Fuller said as he pulled the drawstrings closed.

Mr. Jackson chuckled. "I'll say. Looks like you even got yourself a new slave."

Fuller made a face. "I'd sooner have the fifty dollars. What am I supposed to do with him? You want to buy him? I'll let you have him for thirty."

"No thanks, I'm broke," Jackson said, shaking his head. "But don't worry, Coop will probably show up in the morning when he's sober and offer to buy him back."

Grady's hope abruptly died. Jackson was right; Coop would never sell him.

Fuller stood, stretching his arms over his head and yawning. He was very tall and lean. "I suppose you're right," he said, lifting his jacket from the back of his chair. "I just hope Coop comes early. I'm heading back to the plantation tomorrow."

Jackson smiled wryly. "If I were you, I'd make Coop pay you more than fifty dollars. Didn't he say the boy was worth twice that? Give the dirty so-and-so a taste of his own medicine for once. Drive as hard of a bargain as he always does."

"You mean out trade a slave trader? That'll be the day!" Fuller laughed. "I've dealt with Coop before."

"You beat him at poker tonight."

Fuller smiled. "Yes, I guess I did." He ambled over to the door where Grady stood and examined him for the first time. Grady dropped his gaze. If he'd learned anything at all in his years with Massa Coop, it was never to look a white person in the eye.

"What did Coop say your name was?" Fuller asked.

Grady wondered if his new master was trying to trick him, or if he really didn't remember that Coop had called him Joe. He decided that even if it was a trap, even if Fuller beat Grady the way Coop had, it would be worth it for the brief moment that he'd reclaimed his dignity, his identity. They could never take away his real name.

"My name is Grady," he said. The words came out more forcefully than he'd planned. He saw from the corner of his eye that his new master looked taken aback.

"Scrappy little beggar, aren't you?"

Grady stared at his feet, fighting the urge to lift his chin in pride. "No, sir," he said meekly.

"Very well. Come with me, Grady."

He felt a sliver of hope, the first he could recall feeling in four years. He followed Mr. Fuller out of the smoky salon, out of the hotel and down the front steps to the street. As soon as he stepped outside, the hot, humid air clung to Grady's skin like a wet cloth. The city of Beaufort seemed peaceful at this late hour, the tree-lined streets nearly deserted. Fuller found his coach parked outside the hotel and woke the old, gray-haired driver who sat dozing on the seat.

"You ride up there with Jesse," Fuller told Grady. The old slave wore a question on his face as he appraised him. "I won him in a poker game," Fuller said, smiling slightly. He seemed proud of it. "Let's go home."

Grady felt as though he'd been set free as they drove through the streets of Beaufort to Fuller's house. He inhaled the humid night air, savoring the exhilaration of riding high on the carriage seat with the warm river breeze in his face, the sense of release in being somewhere new after years of smoky hotel rooms, crowded slave pens, and the dark holds of ships. Most of all, he reveled in his freedom from Coop. He would no longer have to live in suspense every minute of his life, terrified of doing something wrong and angering a master who looked for any excuse to punish him.

They drove away from the center of town, down a tree-lined street that followed the curve of the bay. Large, stately homes loomed in the darkness, adorned with porches and pillars. When the carriage turned up a side street, away from the water, the oak trees formed a canopy overhead, with dangling, silvery moss waving gently in the moonlight. Grady wondered if the city of Beaufort had always been this pretty or if it only seemed that way now that he was free from Coop.

Much too soon, they pulled to a halt at the front steps of Fuller's house, a large, two-story home with graceful white pillars and wrap-around piazzas. Grady looked up at the elegant façade with its wide porches and rustling, moss-draped oak trees, and his stomach tightened. His freedom from Coop would never last. Fuller didn't want another slave. He'd already offered to sell him to Mr. Jackson for thirty dollars. Besides, Grady was worth far too much to Coop for him to let him go for a mere fifty-dollar bet. Hadn't William always insisted that Coop would never sell either one of them?

Mr. Jackson had been right. Massa would come here tomorrow morning with cash. He would offer to buy Grady back, and of course Fuller would agree. By noon, Grady would be lying in the hold of a steamship heading to Savannah, bruised and bleeding at the very least, his punishment for encouraging Coop to place that last bet. The knowledge that Coop had beaten his last slave to death made Grady sick with fear.

As soon as the carriage halted, he scrambled down from his seat beside the driver and opened the carriage door for his new master. He watched Massa Fuller step out, tipsy with drink. He didn't look like the kind of master who would beat a slave to death. If only Grady could stay with him.

"Better lock the boy up for the night," Fuller told Jesse, "so he doesn't run off."

"I won't run off, Massa, I swear," Grady said.

Fuller's eyes narrowed. "Is that so?"

"I won't! Only please don't sell me back to Massa Coop tomorrow! Please!" Grady dropped to his knees in front of Fuller, desperate enough to beg for his life. He didn't care if this white man saw his tears. "I'll do anything you want, Massa. But *please* don't make me go back to him!"

Fuller frowned slightly. Then he turned away and climbed the front steps, striding across the porch, and disappeared into the house. Grady slumped to the ground, weeping with rage and humiliation. He had groveled and belittled himself for nothing. He should have known that a white man would never show pity.

"Come on, boy. It's late." The coachman motioned for him to climb on board for the short drive around back to the carriage house. Grady obeyed, the last of his strength and hope gone. As soon as they reached the stable, Jesse sent Grady up to the hayloft and took away the ladder.

"You'd probably break both legs if you try and jump down," Jesse said. "Maybe break that scrawny neck of yours, too."

Grady examined every inch of the windowless loft, searching for a way to escape, while the coachman finished bedding down the horses. He saw none. The old man must have heard him pacing around because he came to the opening with a lantern and peered up at Grady.

"Massa Fuller's treating us okay," he said gently. "If you mind what he say, and work hard, you ain't got nothing to worry about."

Grady remembered William telling him the same thing about Massa Coop. He had learned differently.

Then Jesse snuffed out the lantern, plunging Grady into darkness. He had no choice but to lay down in the hay and try to sleep. He wished he could pray, wished he still believed in Eli's Jesus and the promise of help. He closed his eyes, exhausted. The familiar smells and soft snorts of the animals made him dream of Eli, dreaming that he was home in Richmond again. But fear of what would happen tomorrow made for a restless night.

114

Grady awoke to bright sunshine and the oppressive heat and humidity of a July morning in South Carolina. Jesse was hard at work in the stable below him, getting the carriage and horses ready to go. He let Grady down from the loft and offered him some breakfast, but Grady was too frightened to eat. Every time he heard horses and carriage wheels outside on the busy street he held his breath, waiting to see if they stopped, waiting for Massa Coop to appear and reclaim him.

Just when Grady thought he might be sick from the anxiety, one of the house slaves came outside to announce that Massa Fuller was ready to leave. Jesse pulled the carriage up to the door, and Grady helped load Massa's baggage onboard, silently begging everyone to hurry. He spent another two hours sweating in terror as Jesse drove Massa Fuller all around Beaufort on errands, with Grady seated high on the driver's seat where Coop couldn't fail to see him. Grady wondered if Fuller was going to deliver him to Coop's hotel or perhaps to the docks. But at last Jesse steered the carriage away from the bay and out of the city. The farther they traveled from town, the freer Grady felt from Coop. Maybe he really was safe! He stared at the passing countryside without seeing it, his vision blurred by tears of relief.

After a while they reached the Coosaw River, and Jesse told him they would have to wait for the Beaufort ferry to take them across to the mainland. Once they were on the other side, Grady finally began to gaze around at the scenery. He'd lived in the city of Richmond until Coop had bought him, and the only sights he'd seen since then were slave pens, hotel rooms, city docks, and ships' holds. Now that he was out in the countryside for the first time in his life, he couldn't get enough of it.

The road, paved with crushed oyster shells, crackled beneath their wagon wheels and sometimes ran parallel to a set of railroad tracks, visible through the trees. It meandered through forests of tall pine trees, moss-draped oaks, and dense underbrush. Then the scenery changed, the forest giving way to a maze of marshy creeks, swamps, and inlets. Grady gazed up at the blue sky and feathery clouds and felt as free as the birds circling overhead. The air smelled of pine and salt marsh.

As the miles lengthened, they passed more and more stately plantation homes with acres of cultivated rice and cotton fields. Grady saw hundreds of slaves laboring beneath the blazing sun, their backs bent, and wondered if he would soon be joining them.

The old driver had barely spoken a word to Grady, but he seemed kind enough. The gentle way he handled Massa Fuller's horses reminded Grady of his friend Eli, back home in Richmond, only Jesse looked much older than Eli. Grady thought of all the gray heads that he'd been forced to disguise with boot blacking, and he wondered what had become of all those poor old souls.

Later that afternoon they reached the Fuller Plantation. Flower gardens and moss-draped oak trees surrounded the imposing brick house, making Grady's new home seem immeasurably peaceful and serene after his years of hectic city life. He couldn't believe that slaving on a plantation would be any worse than slaving for Massa Coop.

"Get Massa's bags," Jesse said as the carriage pulled to a halt in the yard. Grady scrambled to do what he was told, jumping down the moment the wheels stopped rolling. Several servants hurried out of the house to greet Massa Fuller, led by a short, muscular Negro who was obviously in charge of all the others. Fuller climbed from the carriage looking hot and tired and rumpled.

"Welcome home, Massa Fuller," the head slave said, smiling broadly.

"Thank you, Martin. It's good to be home. How are things?"

"They fine, sir. Everything's running smoothly while you gone."

"Very good."

Grady studied the house servants' faces as they hurried to help with the luggage. Having experienced terror every day when he belonged to Coop, Grady could easily spot fear in other slaves. But while Fuller's slaves seemed eager to please him, and wary of the butler, Martin, no one cowered in dread the way Grady had been forced to do.

The front door opened again and two white teenagers ran outside, followed by a tiny, wrinkled slave in a calico dress. Grady guessed that she was their mammy. Gray curls poked from beneath the kerchief on her head as she chased after them, scolding them.

"John! Ellis! You come back here! Don't you be pestering your daddy, now. He had a long, hot trip."

They ignored her, running to Massa Fuller and shouting, "Father! You're finally home! We've been waiting all day."

He patted their shoulders and grinned. The younger boy was about Grady's age, the other a year or two older. Grady watched the reunion from a distance, then quickly looked down at his feet, avoiding eye contact when Fuller's younger son suddenly turned to stare at him.

"Who's that boy, Father?"

"That's a new slave I acquired in town."

"He's a *slave*?"

"Yes, of course he is."

"But he doesn't look very black."

"Look at his hair," the older boy said. "Can't you see he's got kinky Negro hair?"

Grady felt them studying him for a moment longer, then the younger boy asked, "Did you bring us anything, Father?"

Fuller laughed. "Yes, of course—in that bag. Fetch it here." They forgot all about Grady as Massa Fuller opened the satchel and pulled out sweets and books and a new set of dominoes. The affection between father and sons seemed genuine as the three of them walked toward the house together.

"What are you wanting us to do with the new boy, Massa Fuller?" the head servant asked.

Fuller glanced back at Grady as he climbed the front steps. "Find out what he can do and put him to work." He disappeared into the Big House with his sons.

Martin strode over to Grady with a slight swagger in his step. Grady quickly took his measure and felt an instant dislike for the

Negro butler. Their master had entrusted him with a great deal of power, and he looked as though he enjoyed flaunting it, feeling superior. He would likely take sides with the white folks rather than with his fellow slaves, just as William had done.

"You do anything useful, boy?" Martin asked.

"Yes, sir."

"Well?" he said impatiently. "Speak up! What kind of work did you do for your last massa?"

For a moment Grady could only recall his fear. "I . . . um . . . I shined his boots and waited on him when he's eating, poured his drinks—I done whatever he ask." The butler looked unimpressed, as if waiting to hear more. "And I was helping take care of his other slaves, cleaning up and stuff," Grady added.

"That all?"

"I-I play the fiddle. . . ."

Martin gave a short, derisive laugh. "That's what I thought—you're useless. Massa Fuller ain't needing another boot boy or manservant. Guess it's gonna be the cotton fields for you. You're sturdy enough. Wait here and someone will take you down to find the overseer." He turned to go.

Grady felt desperate. He didn't think he would survive the hard, hot work in the cotton fields with the lash falling across his back all day. "Wait!" he shouted. "Back h—" He stopped himself from saying "home" just in time. "Back when I was living with my first massa, I was helping take care of his horses, feeding them and rubbing them down and everything. I know how to grease a carriage wheel and oil the harnesses, too."

Jesse still hadn't driven the carriage away so Grady reached out to stroke the big gelding's flank. The horse's back stood taller than Grady's head.

"You ain't afraid of horses?" Jesse asked, looking down at him from the high seat.

"No, sir. Eli taught me how to talk to them to make them calm and all. They do anything I tell them. Ain't none of them ever kicking me, neither." He stepped up to the horse's head and rubbed his neck to make friends.

Jesse turned in the driver's seat to face Martin. "I could use some more help," he said. "Them other two stable boys you give me is useless."

Martin crossed his arms, confronting Grady. "Tell me something, boy. Why'd that first massa get rid of you if you was so good with horses?"

After four years with Coop, Grady knew what the best answer to that question always was. "Massa's needing the money," he said. "Had to sell a whole bunch of us."

Martin took his time answering. "All right, Jesse. Take him, then," he finally said. "But don't you be thinking about running off, boy. The swamps around here are chock full of 'gators and snakes. They'll be eating you in one bite." He strode up the front steps and into the house.

Grady knew he had just been granted an enormous favor. He looked up at Jesse, wondering why, not daring to ask. "Thank you," he said hoarsely.

"Yeah, well, I'm expecting you to help me, you know," Jesse said gruffly. He twitched the reins and the carriage started forward. Grady jogged alongside as Jesse drove slowly down the long drive to the stable, mindful of raising too much dust.

"I will help you! I'm telling the truth about them horses," Grady said. "You'll see. I been mucking straw out of slave pens for a long time, and I can shovel out a stable, too."

He offered Jesse a hand as the old man climbed down from the driver's seat, and the two of them set to work. Grady felt very much at home among the familiar sounds and smells of the carriage house. They rubbed the horses down, fed and watered them, then cleaned the mud and dust off the carriage. It seemed to Grady that a hundred years had passed since last night's poker game—with a hundred years' worth of worry and anxiety to go along with it. He only hoped that this wasn't a dream.

When they finished, Jesse sank onto a wooden chair near the stable door. "Come here, boy," he said, motioning to him. Grady set aside the rag he was using to polish the brass carriage fixtures and obeyed. Jesse studied him for a long moment. "Your old massa come to see Massa Fuller this morning," he said quietly. "He try to buy you back."

Grady stared. He opened his mouth to speak but nothing came out. For some reason, his heart began pounding so hard it was as if he faced Massa Coop, not Jesse.

"The man offer Massa Fuller a lot of money," Jesse continued. "Said he'd trade you for any other slave if Massa want—even a pretty slave gal. Got all heated up when Massa Fuller refuse to sell you." He nodded, as if to emphasize the truth of his words, then added, "Just thought you'd be wanting to know."

Grady sank down on a bale of hay, weak-kneed. He felt breathless and queasy, as if he'd been pulled out of deep water and narrowly escaped drowning. Why had Massa Fuller done it? If he didn't need another slave, why hadn't he sold him back to Coop? As hard as Grady tried, he couldn't think of a sensible reason. He understood injustice and cruelty, but not undeserved kindness.

Before Grady's strength had a chance to return, the stable door opened and the little gray-haired mammy appeared in the doorway. She stood for a moment, watching them.

"What you needing, Delia?" Jesse asked when he saw her.

"Where'd this new boy come from?" she asked.

"Massa Fuller say he won him in a poker game."

"Who from?"

"Nobody round here. Fella was a slave trader, passing through on business, I guess."

"Is that so?" she asked Grady.

"Yes, ma'am."

"My name's Delia," she said. "What's yours?"

"Grady." It felt good to say his real name.

"You been slaving for a 'soul trader' all your life?" she asked as she took a few steps toward him.

120

Something in her voice and in her eyes made it hard for Grady to answer, hard to hold back his tears. She was looking at him with an expression of pity and understanding—and he was still overwhelmed by the unexplained mercy his new master had shown. He swallowed the lump in his throat and waited until he was sure he could speak in a steady voice.

"No, ma'am. I belong to Massa Fletcher back in Richmond, Virginia, first of all. He sell me to Massa Coop about four years ago. I been traveling all over with him ever since, while he's buying and selling slaves."

He glanced up and saw compassion in her eyes, something he hadn't seen in a very long time. He quickly looked away. No one had shown any concern for him at all in a long, long time.

"You got room for him to sleep in here with you, Jesse?" she asked.

"I dunno. Why?"

"Because I was thinking he could stay with me if you don't have a place. I can send him back to help you in the daytime."

"Take him, Delia. I don't care none."

Grady wondered what she wanted him for, and he realized that he was afraid to trust anyone. Massa Coop had made him come to his room every night and wait on him for every little thing, until Grady was so tired he wanted to drop. Coop had scrutinized his every move, too, waiting for him to make the smallest mistake so he'd have an excuse to beat him.

"Go on, take him," Jesse said again. "We all done working for now."

Delia motioned for Grady to follow her. She was a small woman, her head barely reaching his chin, but she looked strong and sturdily built. She walked so briskly he had to hurry to keep up as she led him out of the stable and across the yard to a tiny cabin that looked as though it might have been a shed at one time. It was neat and clean inside, but very hot, even with the windows open. The two rooms were simply furnished with a brick fireplace, shelves of dishes and crocks, and a table with two chairs in one room, a rope bed with a cornshuck mattress in the other. Delia left him standing in the middle of the first room while she bustled around, closing the door, drawing shut the scraps of muslin that served as curtains, talking all the while.

"I been working here on the Fuller place all my life," she said, "and I seen a lot of slaves coming and going, bought and sold. But I never did see one taken from his home as young as you. Did you have to leave your mama?"

Grady nodded, staring straight ahead at the whitewashed wall. He would not cry. But it upset him to realize that the memory of his mother's face seemed faded and blurred after all this time, and he could no longer recall it clearly. But he did remember her gentle hands, and how she would hold him tightly in her arms. He hunched his shoulders and folded his arms across his chest, shivering as if he was cold. But the coldness he felt was deep inside him, not in the stifling cabin.

Delia rested her hand on his arm, startling him. When he looked at her he saw tears in her eyes. "It's a hard thing for a boy as young as you to be leaving his mama, especially to go and live with a soul trader."

"Yes, ma'am." He swallowed.

"We're all alone, Grady," she said softly. "No one's gonna see you cry." She opened her arms to him.

Grady went to her and she pulled him close, holding him tightly, rocking him. How long had it been since anyone had held him this way? Esther had been the last person to hug him—on that last terrible morning. He'd been pushed and jammed into slave pens and ships' holds, poked and prodded and beaten, but never held. The warmth of Delia's body, the softness of her, slowly melted the hard lump of hatred in his chest. And as it melted into grief, he began to cry.

"You go ahead and cry for all the times you couldn't, honey," she said.

Grady wept for the terror, for the pain and unfairness of the beatings. He cried for all the anguish he'd seen, the families who'd been cruelly torn apart, as he'd been torn from his family. He cried for the memory of green grass beneath his bare feet back home in Richmond; for his friend Caroline, with skin as white as the blossoms on the magnolia tree they'd climbed. He cried for the cold rain that had soaked him on the day he'd been snatched away, and for the coldness in Massa Fletcher's face as he'd watched him go. Most of all, Grady cried for his mother, the beloved face he could no longer clearly recall.

"No one's ever gonna know about this but you and me, Grady," Delia murmured. She rubbed his back to soothe him. He remembered his mama doing the same thing, and he sobbed.

A long time later, Grady's tears were finally spent. He realized that he was sitting on the rope bed beside Delia, her warm arms still wrapped tightly around him. "Tell me about your home, Grady. Tell me what you remember."

He began to talk, and a flood of memories poured out—haltingly at first, then with the words tumbling all over each other. "I use to live in the kitchen behind the Big House with Esther and Eli and the others. I never been inside the Big House, but Mama was always staying there and taking care of Missy Caroline because Missy's mama was sick all the time. Mama love me more than Missy Caroline, but she can't let Missy know that or Missy be feeling bad. Mama said I had beautiful brown skin, but Missy's skin's ugly, with no color in it at all, so we have to be extra nice to her to make up for it. Esther and Eli and all the others was taking good care of me when Mama can't. They're always working hard, but Eli says he don't mind because he's serving the Lord. And Massa Fletcher's never yelling or beating anybody. . . ." He swallowed hard, remembering Massa Coop.

"Missy Caroline was my best friend. We use to play in the yard every day and climb that old magnolia tree and talk to Eli while he's working. Missy do her lessons every morning and I do my chores, but then we played when we was all finished. Sometimes we use to sit on Eli's lap and he'd tell stories about Massa Jesus—"

Grady stopped abruptly, the memory sharp and painful. Eli had said that Jesus was always with him, taking good care of him, but it wasn't true.

"Bless you, child," Delia murmured, "you didn't know what slavery's all about, did you?" She sighed, then added, "I reckon you know now."

"Massa Fletcher sold me for no reason!" His mother's face may have faded, but Grady clearly recalled Massa Fletcher's face and the way he stood in the rain with his arms folded. "He sold me for no reason at all!"

"There's a reason, honey. There's always a reason—just something you ain't knowing about."

Grady drew a shuddering breath. "The wagon carry me to the auction house and Amos say to forget about home. He say I ain't never going back again, never gonna see my mama."

"It's the truth, Grady. I know it's hard, but it's the truth. You're a long, long way from Virginia. Once folks is sold, ain't no way back."

Grady's tears began falling again. Delia had made him relive that terrible day, and now he relived the loss, as well, the feeling of being all alone in a world that was so large, so uncaring.

"Was Eli your daddy, Grady?" she asked softly.

The question surprised him. "No ... Eli is Esther's husband."

"Did you know your daddy?"

"I don't have one. I asked Mama one time why Caroline has a daddy and I don't. She say slaves don't have daddies."

"Now, you know that can't be true," Delia said. "The only baby born on this earth without a flesh-and-bone daddy was the Lord Jesus—and you sure ain't Him."

Grady stiffened at the name. Eli had told him that Jesus had God for His daddy instead of having a daddy here on earth. But Grady didn't want to think about Massa Jesus anymore.

"What color skin did your mama have?" Delia asked. "Dark as mine or light as yours?"

"Like yours." He remembered now. Mama's skin was a rich, warm brown, as dark and smooth as the molasses cookies Esther used to bake.

He was struggling to bring his mother's face into focus when Delia said, "Your daddy's a white man."

The words stunned Grady like a slap in the face. He twisted out of her arms shouting, "That's a lie!"

He hated white men—all of them. They had carried him away and locked him in a filthy cell and made him stand on the auction block without his clothes. Massa Coop was a white man, and he had beaten Grady unmercifully. White men bought and sold Negroes, stealing them from their homes and their families without an ounce of compassion for them. The only white man he'd known back home in Richmond was Massa Fletcher, and Grady hated him most of all. He was *not* his father!

"Maybe Gilbert's my daddy or . . . or somebody else," he said with cold fury, "but he sure ain't no white man!"

"It happens all the time," Delia said matter-of-factly. "Truth is, most black gals are a whole lot prettier than white women. Massa sees a beautiful Negro gal and he can't resist. He don't have to. She's his slave, so he can do whatever he wants."

Grady knew that his mama was beautiful, more beautiful than the slave women Coop used to sell to the brothels in New Orleans. Grady had learned what brothels were. He knew very well what Delia was saying. He felt heat rush to his face, but he was too angry, too outraged to speak.

"I may not look it now," Delia continued, "but I used to be pretty, long time ago. Plantation had a white overseer and he decide he can use me that way anytime he wants. I had me a little girl baby from that white man. She's as light-skinned as you are, honey. Could pass for white if you didn't hear her calling me Mama. Massa Fuller was just a baby himself, back then, so they brought me up to the Big House and I nursed him alongside my own baby. The two of them just as white as each other. Couldn't tell no difference."

Grady didn't want to hear this, didn't want to think about this. He glanced around the tiny cabin but saw only one bed. "Your daughter living here with you?" he asked.

"No, she's gone now," Delia said sadly. "Her grave is up in the cemetery with all the other slaves who've gone to be with Jesus. My little girl only five years old when she left me. I see you climbing down from that carriage today, and you're reminding me of her. Her skin's just as light as yours."

"That don't mean I had a white daddy," he said angrily.

"Ain't nothing to be ashamed of."

"But it ain't true!" Only one white man lived in that house in Richmond. Mama had cried and pleaded with him as they'd dragged Grady away, and he hadn't even cared.

Delia tried to pull Grady into her arms again, but he twisted away. He stood, fists clenched, his body rigid with hatred. She touched his arm. "Listen, Grady—"

"I ain't got nothing to do with no white man!" he yelled. "Don't you ever say that to me again!"

FULLER PLANTATION, SOUTH CAROLINA 1860

Delia stood in the tiny cabin behind Grady, watching him preen in front of the mirror. "You the vainest man I ever did meet," she told him. "Handsomest one, too. But I suppose you already know that."

He grinned at her in the mirror as their eyes met, but she didn't distract him from his primping for very long. He took his time washing, shaving, brushing his neatly trimmed hair. During the three years Delia had known him, Grady had grown into a tall, well-built young man, muscular and solid from his hard work in the stables with Jesse. Dressed in livery and sitting high atop the driver's seat of Massa's carriage, Grady was a sight to behold. That was his job now—coachman for Massa Fuller.

Delia still felt a stab of grief when she recalled the morning Grady had come running up to the Big House to fetch her, his face pale with shock. "Better come quick, Delia. Jesse fell down, and I can't get him on his feet."

She and the butler, Martin, had both hurried down to the stable where they found the old coachman lying in an awkward heap. Massa Fuller had sent for a doctor, but there wasn't anything he could do. Jesse had broken his hip, and his old bones were just too brittle to mend properly. Grady had grown very close to Jesse in the years they had worked together, and he took the news harder than any of them did.

"They can't just let him lay here and die, like he's worn out and useless!" Grady had shouted. "He's a human being!"

Delia had tried to soothe him. "Honey, there ain't nothing the doctor can do."

"There has to be!"

"Jesse's going home to be with the Lord. Can't you see he ain't afraid?"

"Lot of good believing in the Lord ever done him," Grady said as he stomped out of the carriage house.

Delia had let him go. Grady never would listen to a single word about God. She'd tried and tried for the last three years, talking to him at night in the cabin they shared, inviting him to the slaves' worship services—but he refused to listen. She knew from what he'd told her about his family in Richmond that he'd been raised to know the Lord. But everything that had happened to him in the years since had turned him bitter. As soon as Delia mentioned God, Grady would light out of there like the paddyrollers were after him.

He had helped Delia take care of Jesse as tenderly as a son with his father, but the poor old soul never did recover. Two days before Jesse died, Massa Fuller came out to the carriage house to ask him which of the stable hands should replace him as coachman.

Grady had spoken up before Jesse had a chance to reply.

"I can do it, Massa Fuller. Tell him, Jesse. Tell him I can handle them horses and drive his coach better than anybody."

Jesse nodded. "He's young but he knows how to handle a team of horses. And he works harder than all them other stable hands put together, even if he is the youngest."

"He knows how to act around white folk, too," Delia added. Grady had a lot of natural dignity and poise for one so young. Besides, he was nice-looking and very light-skinned—qualities that the white folk wanted in slaves who were seen in public. Massa Fuller had made Grady his coachman.

They'd buried Jesse in the slave cemetery, right beside Delia's daughter's grave. Grady's grief was so great that he barely spoke a word for days. Delia had tried to console him with the promise of heaven, but he hadn't wanted to hear it. Now, in the months since Jesse's funeral, Grady had worked hard and had quickly earned Massa Fuller's trust as his driver.

"Where you off to tonight?" Delia asked as Grady put away his shaving things. "I didn't think Massa Fuller was going anywhere tonight."

"He ain't. But he give me the night off. I'm going over to the Emerson place to see a gal I know over there."

Delia's smile faded. She shook her head. "I'm starting to hear stories about you, through the grapevine. I ain't liking what I hear."

"What'd you hear?"

"That while Massa Fuller's been looking for a wife, you been playing around with all the slave gals everywhere you're driving him."

She hated to scold, but Delia worried about him. He was running from the Lord, no doubt about it, and heading down the wrong path. Hard things happened when you tried to run from God. She had loved Grady since the first day he'd arrived—a gift from the Lord, she knew. God had taken one child from her, and now He'd given her another one. She prayed for Grady every morning and every night—and in between times, too, when he needed it. Now she was very worried about him.

"I hear that while Massa Fuller's courting some lady inside the Big House," she continued, "you're taking your time, rubbing down his horses out in the stable yard where everyone can watch you. Pretty soon all the kitchen gals and parlormaids start finding excuses to sashay out and see if you want a drink of water or maybe a bite of corn bread. You lean against the hitching post and smile as you dish out your sweet talk, and the gals soak it up like rain on dry ground. Folks say that when you come driving up, it's like setting a dish of honey out on the table and waiting for the flies to come buzzing."

Grady tried to suppress a grin but couldn't. "Nothing wrong with that, is there?"

"I hear you got a gal on every plantation, and half a dozen more in Beaufort that's all in love with you. Problem is, they're all thinking you're in love with them."

"That ain't my fault," he said with a shrug. "I ain't making any promises."

"You're taking advantage of them, honey, and that's wrong. The Bible says—"

"Hold it." Grady held up both hands to silence her. "None of your God-talk, Delia. You know how I feel about that."

But Delia knew that Grady's soul was at stake. She stood in the doorway, blocking the only way out of the cabin. "I know you don't want to hear it, honey, but tonight I'm gonna tell you anyway. A man ain't supposed to be with a gal that way unless they's married. If you ain't, then all your fooling around is a sin in the Lord's eyes."

Grady's dark eyes flashed with anger. "What good's it gonna do me to fall in love and get married, huh? My life ain't my own, you know that. Ain't no way I can ever choose a wife and be with her for the rest of my life. This here's a white man's world, and slaves don't get to choose. My life belongs to Massa Fuller."

"You're wrong. Your life belongs to God. He's the One you'd better be obeying."

"God never did me any favors, so why should I obey Him? No, sir! I'm gonna make the most of this sorry life, and if I can scrape up a little loving on Massa's travels, then I'll do it. Never know what tomorrow's gonna bring. Gals don't have to say yes to me. I ain't forcing no one to give me hugs and kisses."

"You gonna marry this girl you're seeing tonight?"

Grady made a face, as if she'd asked a ridiculous question.

"Then what you're planning on doing with her is wrong."

He folded his arms across his chest. "I don't care, Delia."

"You know what I think? I think you're afraid to be getting close to anyone. Afraid if you love people, they'll be ripped away from you again."

"I got good reason to be afraid—they might be! First my family, now Jesse . . . You know they never would of let Jesse die if he'd been a white man."

"Don't matter if our skin is white or black—our day to die is in the Lord's hands. And white or black, we're always taking a risk when we love people. There's always a chance of losing them. But you can't go through life without love, Grady. Life just ain't worth living without love."

He held up his hands in partial surrender. "Look, I'm just having a little fun. That's all."

Delia could see that he was holding back his temper, reluctant to argue with her. She didn't want to argue, either, but she loved Grady too much to keep quiet.

"Fun? You think that's all it is—just *fun*? Then you're no better than an animal. That's what white folks are thinking about us anyway, ain't it? That we got no more feelings or morals than animals do? Go on! You go right on out there, now, and prove them right." She stood aside, pointing to the door.

He looked chastened, but not repentant. "Don't nag me, Delia. I got me a night off, the only time that belongs to me and not to Massa. Ain't nobody gonna tell me what to do with it." He squeezed past her and through the door.

"God's gonna punish you for making slave babies all over the county," she yelled after him. "Don't you care that you're condemning your children to be slaves?"

Grady halted, glancing all around as if worried that someone might have overheard her shouts. He turned to her, anger flushing his face. "I ain't condemning them to slavery," he said in a harsh voice, "the white folks are. And as far as God is concerned, He's a white man's God. I ain't got nothing to do with Him."

Delia grabbed his sleeve to stop him from striding away. "What happens when a slave runs off?" she asked. "Don't his master do everything in his power to find him and bring him back? You belong to God, Grady."

"No I don't! I already told you—"

"Don't try and tell me otherwise," she interrupted, "because I know you do. Your mama and all them other good folks taught you all about Him, didn't they? And God's gonna chase you down and hound your steps until He gets you back. Not because you're His slave, but because you're His son. God will get you—"

"He already has! He sold me to a slave trader for no reason. I didn't do anything to deserve that. Now leave me alone!" He pried her fingers off and left.

Delia let him go. But as she watched him stride down the road, her heart ached for him. "I know he's running from you, Lord," she murmured. "But please bring him back soon. . . ."

Grady's anger propelled him down the road at a brisk pace. He was fond of Delia, but tonight she'd gone too far. She wasn't his boss. She had no right to try and tell him what to do. Sometimes she reminded him of Eli with all her Jesus talk, and Grady didn't want to be reminded.

The Emerson plantation was about four miles away. It would take him more than an hour to walk there, even at the rate he was moving. The moonless night was as dark as his mood. Grady hoped that his temper would cool down by the time he arrived, but Delia's words were still racing around in his mind like riled hornets as he turned down the path to Slave Row and walked toward the girl's cabin. She stood on the steps, waiting for him, leaning seductively against the doorframe. To make matters worse, he'd forgotten her name.

"Hey, Grady. I thought you'd never get here. What took you so long?"

"Don't matter. I'm here now, sugar."

He slipped his arms around her and began kissing her neck. What was her name? She didn't seem to notice his lapse as she responded eagerly to his kisses.

"Let's go inside," she whispered a few minutes later.

Grady followed her into the darkened cabin, determined to forget his argument with Delia and allow more pleasant sensations to carry him away. But the accusation that he was condemning his children to be slaves still haunted him. If this girl ever did get pregnant, Grady's child would belong to Mr. Emerson. Grady was helping white men like Emerson and Fletcher and Coop enslave his race.

He stopped kissing her. His arms fell to his sides.

"What's wrong, Grady?"

"Listen . . . um . . ." He fumbled for her name. "I ain't feeling so good. I must have eaten something that didn't agree with me. Can we . . . um . . . finish this later?"

"I guess so." Even in the darkness he saw her confusion and disappointment. "You sure you're okay?"

"Maybe some air will help." He hurried from the cabin and slumped down on the step outside. She followed him, sitting down beside him, leaning against him. She was a pretty girl, and it shamed Grady to realize that not only didn't he know her name, he didn't know anything about her. The only feelings he had for her were physical. He silently cursed Delia for telling him he was no better than an animal.

"You walked such a long way to get here," she said softly. "Be a real shame if you can't enjoy the evening."

But Grady knew that he wouldn't enjoy it. Delia had ruined it for him. He didn't know what to do. There seemed to be a lot of activity on the Row tonight, knots of young people talking and flirting with each other, mothers chasing their little ones off to bed, older men chewing tobacco and swapping stories. Folks were glancing his way, seeing the girl twined all around him the way she was, and it embarrassed him. But he didn't want to hide inside the cabin with her, either.

"Maybe I better go on home," he mumbled.

"Aw, come on, Grady. I went through a lot of trouble to get all my work done—and to make sure we'd have this cabin all to ourselves tonight."

"I know. I'm sorry—" Her name still eluded him. He pried her arms from around his shoulders and moved away from her.

"What's wrong? Don't you love me no more?" she asked.

Grady sighed. He couldn't force himself to lie. "You know we can't get married or anything. We belong to two different masters. Don't you think we better be calling this whole thing off before it's too late?"

"What?" she shouted. "Too late? We—"

"Shh . . . listen," he said as her shouts drew stares. "You'd be happier if you fell for someone around here, on your own plantation. Don't you think?"

She planted her hands on his chest, shoving him backward as she began to shout. "You no-good two-timer! You found someone else didn't you? They warned me about you—sweet-talking all the girls to get your own way. You never cared about me at all, did you?"

Grady saw people peering out of their cabins, staring at him. "Is everything all right, Rosie?" a man across the row asked. Rosie stood, hands on her hips.

"Yeah, it will be just fine when *he's* gone. Get out of here, Grady! Go on back to whatever hole you crawled out of!"

He took his time walking home, unwilling to let Delia know she'd ruined his night off. He stopped to sit on a fallen log beside the road for a long time, gazing up at the stars that were barely visible through the leaves, listening to the quiet murmurs of the night forest. Then he moved on. He was half a mile from home, still thinking about Rosie, thinking he'd been a fool to throw away a night of fun, when he heard dogs barking. Grady froze, listening. No one around here owned dogs. His heart began to race at the sounds of horse hooves, baying bloodhounds, muted laughter. They were coming toward him.

The paddyrollers.

Grady had left home in such a hurry after arguing with Delia that he'd forgotten to ask Massa Fuller for a pass. The paddyrollers would demand to see one. Before he could decide what to do, four horsemen rounded a bend in the darkened road. Two dogs trotted alongside them. Without thinking, Grady plunged into the woods to hide.

"Hey! Stop right there!" one of the men shouted. A second one fired his shotgun over Grady's head.

Grady ran through the woods in a blind panic, branches whipping against his face, brush and leaves rustling beneath his crashing feet. He hadn't done anything wrong, but there was no telling what the paddyrollers would do to a slave who couldn't show them a pass.

A shotgun boomed behind him again, echoing through the woods. "You want to die, boy?"

The dogs quickly caught up to him, barking and lunging at his legs. Grady realized it was useless. He cursed himself for getting caught, for running into the woods in the first place and making the men suspicious. He might have been able to talk his way out of trouble if he'd stayed on the road. Now he looked guilty—and acted guilty, too. He stopped and turned to face them, leaning against a tree, panting.

The four paddyrollers were young, not much older than Grady was. As they dismounted and walked toward him he could tell that they'd been drinking. Two of them grabbed his arms, pinning them to his sides. Grady let himself go limp. It would be useless to struggle.

"Where's your pass, boy?"

He stared at the ground, forcing himself to act subservient. "I don't need one, sir. Massa Fuller trusts me."

"You were running off, weren't you?"

"No, sir. Massa's plantation is just down the road half a mile. I was heading that way."

"Then why'd you run from us, boy?"

Before Grady could reply, one of the men lifted his rifle butt and punched him in the stomach with it. Grady hadn't seen it coming and he doubled over in pain, the breath knocked out of him.

"Guess we'd better teach this boy a lesson for trying to escape."

Before Grady could recover, the men spun him around and ripped his shirt down to his waist, then wrapped his arms around the tree, tying his hands. Panic filled him. They were going to whip him. He tried to fight back but there were too many of them. His hands were bound too tightly.

"Wait! I ain't a runaway!" he said. "Go ask Massa Fuller. He'll tell you I have the night off. I'm his coachman. I forgot my pass. Please!"

They paid no attention to him, laughing and hooting as they discussed whose turn it was to deliver the punishment. Rage consumed Grady as he struggled against his bonds, the same helpless rage he'd felt the day they'd carried him from his home, the same rage he'd felt every time Coop had beaten him. Crazed, helpless rage.

"You have no right! I ain't done nothing wrong!"

The whip cracked through the night air and Grady felt the first stroke of pain. He made up his mind that he wouldn't cry out, wouldn't give them that satisfaction, just as Amos had counseled him to do that first night. But each blow of the whip brought an agony of white-hot fire that blazed through him. He grew to dread the sound of the lash as it sliced through the air, anticipating the pain, waiting that long second before it struck. He could feel the skin on his back being ripped into shreds, the lash landing on flesh, then raw muscle, then bone. Long, slow minutes passed. The torture went on and on until Grady couldn't help crying out in agony.

"Stop!" he begged. "I ain't done nothing wrong!" He writhed against the tree, trying to dodge the next blow. *"Stop!"*

"Hey, maybe that's enough," Grady heard one of them say.

"What do you care?" There was more drunken laughter, another stroke of the whip.

"I think he's telling the truth about being Fuller's coachman. I think I remember seeing him driving Mr. Fuller all around."

136

"So what? He doesn't have a pass. He deserves a whipping for that." The lash struck again.

Grady's knees buckled and he slid down the tree, scraping his chest and face on the bark. Shock and pain had made him so weak he was about to pass out. He felt his own warm blood soaking the back of his trousers.

"Okay, but maybe that's enough," one of the men said. "We showed him."

"Yeah, better not kill him or Fuller will make us pay for him."

"Since when are you two Negro-lovers?"

Grady lay slumped and quivering, waiting for the next blow, trying to brace for it. His back was a sheet of fire. But instead of the whip, he felt someone fumbling with the rope around his hands, untying him. Grady wanted to sink all the way to the ground, but two of them grabbed his arms again and pulled him to his feet, tying his hands behind his back. He could barely stand, but they mounted their horses and forced him to walk ahead of them, tethered by the rope.

A few minutes later, they emerged from the woods and started down the road. The bully with the whip laughed as he cracked it over Grady's head every now and then, but it didn't make contact. As weak as Grady was with shock and loss of blood, he knew an anger that was powerful enough to commit murder. If his hands weren't bound, if he had the weapons instead of these white boys, he would kill all four of them without an ounce of remorse. Again, he thought of Amos and his vow to get even. Grady would do the same, even if it cost him his life. He'd seen these boys' faces. He would find out where they lived, and he would kill every last one of them along with their families. He comforted himself with these thoughts for the half-mile walk home. The prospect of revenge kept his mind off his staggering weakness and pain.

Martin appeared at the front door of the Big House as soon as the paddyrollers' horses tromped into the yard. The butler quickly appraised the scene and his eyes went wide. Grady was surprised when a look of pity flickered across Martin's face, but fear swiftly replaced it.

"This boy belong to your Master?" one of the men behind Grady asked.

"Yes, sir," Martin replied. He couldn't seem to move from the doorway.

"We were on patrol tonight, and we caught him down the road a ways, trying to run off. He didn't have a pass, so we punished him and brought him back."

"Tell them I ain't no runaway," Grady said in a tight voice. Martin knew Massa had given him the night off. He knew Grady was seeing a girl, not escaping. Grady glared up at Martin, daring him to tell the truth. But Martin seemed too scared to defend him. The four men were white, Martin wasn't.

"You wanna talk to Massa Fuller?" Martin asked. But before they could reply, Fuller himself appeared in the doorway.

"What's going on, Martin? Who's here?" He squinted into the darkness. "Grady, is that you?"

"We were on patrol tonight, Mr. Fuller," one of the men said. Grady recognized the voice of the man who'd whipped him. "We caught your boy running off. He couldn't show us a pass."

"I wasn't running."

"What happened to his shirt? What'd you do to him?" Fuller demanded.

"We needed to teach him a little lesson."

"You had no right!" Fuller shouted.

"Well, when we catch a runaway it's important to set an example for the others," one of the men said, but he sounded less sure of himself, now that he faced Fuller's wrath.

"Even if he had been escaping—which I doubt," Fuller said, "it's up to me to punish him, not you. He belongs to me, and you have no right to damage my property."

"We're real sorry, sir. Guess we got a little carried away."

"You can't be too careful these days, Mr. Fuller. Slaves have been getting all kinds of crazy ideas into their heads ever since John Brown tried to start that slave rebellion up at Harper's Ferry."

"If he's permanently injured, I'll expect compensation," Fuller said coldly. "Good night, gentlemen."

Grady felt the rope go slack as they dropped it, leaving his hands tied. Fuller waited in the doorway until the sound of hoof beats faded down the driveway. "Turn around," he finally said. Grady obeyed. Fuller was silent for a long moment. "We'd better wake Delia up," he told Martin. "Go fetch a bottle of brandy and some hot water. And bring that jar of salve I bought in Beaufort."

"Yes, Massa."

Fuller descended the porch steps and untied Grady's hands himself. Grady swayed, unsure how much longer he could stand. He was surprised when Fuller gently propped one of Grady's arms around his own shoulders to help support him. They walked down to Delia's cabin that way—Grady stumbling, Massa Fuller half-carrying him. By the time they reached the door, dark patches of Grady's blood stained Massa's trousers and white shirt. Delia's face blanched when she saw them.

"What happened?"

"A gang of patrollers got carried away. It seems Grady forgot to ask me for a pass tonight."

"Oh, Lord . . . oh, Lord," she murmured. Grady wondered if she was going to faint alongside him. He felt light-headed, the pain so agonizing that his legs collapsed beneath him as soon as Massa Fuller steered him to his bed.

"Martin is coming with some brandy and salve," Fuller told Delia. "If you need anything else, let me know." Then he left.

"Oh, Lord . . . What'd they do to you, honey?" Delia's voice quavered with tears.

Grady didn't answer. He didn't know which was greater, his pain or his rage. He turned away from her and lay facedown on his bed.

"Why'd you have to fight against the Lord?" she murmured. "Don't you know He'll always have the last word?"

"What are you talking about?" Grady shouted. "I didn't do anything wrong! Why doesn't God punish the men who did this to me?" He punched the wall beside his bed with his last reserve of strength, then struggled to breathe as anger threatened to suffocate him.

"Someday I'll get even! I swear, by all that I am . . . I'll make them pay for this! I saw their faces! I'll find them and pay them back in full!"

Delia laid her hand on his head and stroked his hair. "I worry about you, honey. You're storing up so much hatred in your heart. Don't you know that hating somebody is like drinking poison and expecting the other person to die?"

"They're the ones who taught me to hate. Step by step, lesson after lesson. And they've been excellent teachers! How can I help hating them when they don't even think I'm human?"

"Vengeance belongs to God. It's up to Him to pay back the guilty ones."

"But He never does! I've been suffering all my life, and the white men who've caused it are all going free. Don't be talking to me about God's justice, Delia. Don't be talking to me about God at all!"

"How do you think your mama and those good folks who raised you would feel if they knew you turned your back on God?"

"He turned His back on *me*! Every time I ask for help, He's turning His back."

"Grady, instead of using God to get what you want, maybe God wants to use you to get what He wants. Yes, you was sold. But maybe God has a reason you don't know about yet."

"What reason would He have for letting them do this to me tonight? Huh? If He's such a powerful God, why didn't He stop them? Why's he letting them torture me for no reason at all?"

Before Delia could answer, there was a knock on the door. Grady kept his face turned toward the wall as she let Martin in.

"They done him pretty bad, didn't they?" Martin murmured. "He gonna be okay, Delia?"

"Lord willing. It ain't these wounds I'm worried about, though."

"What do you mean?"

"Never mind. What's all this? What'd you bring me?"

"Massa sent some brandy, and there's warm water and clean rags. Massa just bought this here salve in town. Suppose to be pretty good. I be glad to help you, Delia."

"I know. But I don't think I'll be needing any help. Thanks, Martin."

"I'll come back in the morning and check on him."

A moment later the door closed. Grady tensed, dreading the first touch of Delia's washcloth on his back almost as much as he had dreaded the next crack of the whip. She sat down on the edge of his bed.

"You know the story of Joseph in the Bible?" she asked. "His brothers sell him into slavery, far from home. Then his massa's wife accuse him of something he didn't do and they send him to prison. He suffer a long, long time—for no reason. Joseph don't want to be no slave. He don't want to be laying in no jail. Years pass, and he keep asking God for help—and it never come. But God use all that Joseph's going through to make him strong. Then one day, God raise Joseph up again, so he can save all his brothers. God give him back all he lost and more."

Grady knew the story. It had been one of Eli's favorites because the hero was a slave. Eli used to tell him the same thing—that God used slavery to change Joseph into a leader. Grady had loved listening to Eli, had loved Eli like a father, but he would probably never see the old man again. Tears filled Grady's eyes as grief piled on top of the pain and rage he already felt. He heard Delia dipping a cloth into water, wringing it out. He gritted his teeth.

"God answers our prayers in the way that's best for us, honey," she said. "Having faith means trusting that whatever happens is God's will. He's right beside you in every trial you go through. And He was with you tonight. The Lord could have saved you, just like He could have saved Joseph. But God wanted Joseph to save all his brothers. Ever think that maybe the Lord's preparing you to save your black brothers and sisters?"

141

Grady didn't reply. He didn't want to listen to what Delia was saying. He didn't want to think about Eli or Joseph or God or anyone else.

The next moment he got his wish. As Delia laid a warm cloth on his back, his unwelcome thoughts vanished in a wave of searing pain.

CHAPTER

10

CHARLESTON, SOUTH CAROLINA
JULY 1860

Grady sat on the carriage seat, gazing at the enormous crowd that filled the city plaza and the side streets all around it. Red, white, and blue bunting draped a raised platform where a brass band played and a group of white men gave speeches. They were going to elect another president of the United States in the fall, and Massa Fuller was so worried about it that he'd made Grady drive him all the way to Charleston so he could hear all these speeches and meet with other worried plantation owners. Grady had overheard Massa talking about "that slave lover, Abraham Lincoln," and how they had to stop him from becoming president.

"We must fight to keep our way of life," one of today's speakers had shouted from the platform, "our right to live as we please." Grady knew what he really meant: the right to keep slaves.

The July day felt as hot as a blacksmith's forge, the humid air suffocating. The side street where Grady had parked the carriage offered little shade. He climbed down from the driver's seat and fastened the reins to the hitching rail, then glanced around for a shadier place to stand. A small group of slaves had gathered beneath a tree, nearby, laughing and visiting with each other while they waited for their masters, but Grady didn't feel like joining them. He wanted to get as far away from the music as he possibly could, away from the bitter memories it evoked. But he didn't dare stray too far from his horses.

He stepped behind the carriage and stretched his arms, gently easing the soreness from his neck and shoulders. His back was still stiff and barely healed from the whipping, the new skin tight and tender to the touch, especially where his shirt rubbed against it. The lash wounds had festered in spite of Delia's best efforts, and Grady had been feverish for several days before his back finally began to heal. Only in the last week or so had he been strong enough to drive again.

A sudden movement caught his eye. Grady saw a slender young slave woman climb down from her carriage and cross the street behind him, heading toward the sparse shelter of a gardenia bush. He watched her, admiring the sway of her hips, the tilt of her head, the way her shapely body moved when she walked. Even dressed in worn homespun, she walked as gracefully as the fancy white ladies did in their silk gowns and jewels. Something about her seemed familiar to Grady, although he was sure he'd never seen her before. He watched her and slowly realized what it was. His mother had moved that way, like water flowing between rocks or branches swaying in the breeze.

The woman sat down on a low stone wall with her back to Grady and reached into her apron pocket to pull out something. He couldn't see what it was. He moved closer and discovered that she was unfolding a piece of paper. She spread it out on her lap and began to write on it with a stubby pencil. The sight of a slave with paper and pencil was so unusual that he edged closer until he was practically peering over her shoulder. To his surprise, she wasn't writing words at all, she was drawing a picture.

"What're you doing?" he asked.

The woman jumped and her pencil fell to the ground. She clutched her chest as if to keep her heart from escaping.

"Sorry," Grady said. He quickly stooped to retrieve the pencil. "Sorry. I didn't mean to scare you."

"That's okay." She smiled uncertainly as he handed it back to her. She was very pretty, with wide, dark eyes and a slender, oval-shaped face. He found himself at a loss for words.

"My massa's over at the rally, listening to the speeches," he finally said, shoving his hands in his pockets. "There ain't much to do except stand around and wait, is there?"

"I know. My missy ain't needing me, either, so I thought I'd try and draw that church over there. It's real pretty, ain't it?"

Grady shrugged. "I guess so. Mind if I watch you?"

"I don't care." Her voice was as soft as cotton.

He sat down on the wall beside her, careful to leave a space between them so he wouldn't frighten her again. He was curious about the paper and pencil—white folks were usually too suspicious of literate slaves to allow them to have such things. He was about to ask her where she got them and if her mistress knew about them, but he decided it was none of his business. He watched in fascination as the church took shape on the page, the pillars and windows and towering steeple as perfectly proportioned as the real one in front of him.

"My name's Grady. What's yours?" he asked.

She took a long moment to answer, totally absorbed in adding the tree that shaded the front of the church. "Kitty," she replied absently.

He made a face in disgust. She was much too pretty to have such a stupid name, an animal's name. She should be called something lovely and graceful. His mother's name was Tessie, and it seemed to fit the elegant way she tossed her head with laughter or swished her skirts when she walked. Grady was a little awed by this woman, who not only reminded him of his mother, but who could bring a tree to life on paper before his eyes. She was no ordinary slave.

"You making that picture for a reason?" he asked.

"Nope, just for me. I like to draw. I wish I had some paint, though. See the way the sun's shining on them stones? Makes them look like they're made of gold, don't you think?"

Grady hadn't noticed the color, before, but she was right, the glow of golden sunlight on the beige stones was very beautiful. "Yeah, I guess it does," he said. He wondered if she noticed colors and itched to paint things the same way he used to hear a new melody and itch to play it on his fiddle. He gazed into the distance and felt a sudden surge of anger at white men for destroying his enjoyment of music.

"What's wrong?" she asked. "Why'd your face turn mad all of a sudden?"

She had stopped drawing to study him. "Nothing," he said. "Just thinking about something else. Where'd you learn to draw?"

"Nowhere. My missy used to take painting lessons but she hated them. She was always letting me paint the pictures for her, and everybody's thinking they were hers." Kitty laughed as if the deception was very funny. It made Grady mad.

"That's typical. Slaves do all the work and the white folks take all the credit."

"Oh, it don't matter," she said with a wave of her hand. The gesture was so lovely that he wished she would do it again. "I like fixing Missy's paintings. She give me all her leftover paper, too."

Grady wondered what was wrong with him. By now he'd usually be sweet-talking a woman this pretty, trying to make her fall in love with him so he could steal a few kisses. Was it the memory of Delia's words and the fear of God's punishment that stopped him? Or was he still just too angry after what had happened to him to be able to smile and flirt and sweet-talk the way he used to?

"There. What do you think?" she asked, holding up the picture.

"It's really good. If you had white skin you could be a famous artist." She didn't seem to hear him. She was staring intently at his face, studying him.

"What? Why're you staring at me like that?" he asked.

"Can I draw you?" she asked with a shy smile.

"Why?"

"I like the lines of your face. You have such a proud jaw." She traced his chin with her finger. It was a tender gesture but not at all flirtatious. "And your eyes—they're like lumps of charcoal with the fire deep inside them."

"Go ahead, I don't care," he said with a shrug. She unnerved him, but he determined not to show it. He'd never posed for a picture before and didn't know quite how to do it. He folded his arms stiffly across his chest, waiting while she turned the paper over to the blank side. She studied him again for a long moment, then began to sketch. It made him uneasy the way she kept looking up at him, looking down, looking up again, the pencil scratching across the page. She had delicate hands, the bones as fragile as a bird's.

A long time seemed to pass. Neither of them spoke. Grady heard music in the distance again, drums pounding and the blare of a brass band as they played another song. He recognized the tune—"Dixie's Land." He'd played it on the fiddle before. He wished he could run from the music, and from the image it brought to mind of his fellow slaves being forced to dance as he fiddled.

"There. Want to see?" Kitty asked with a tentative smile. She didn't seem to know how pretty she really was. All of the good-looking girls that Grady knew weren't afraid to flaunt their beauty and take advantage of it, flirting with every boy in sight. But Kitty had an innocence that was as unusual as she was.

"Here." She turned the picture around and handed it to him.

Grady drew a harsh breath. He recognized the likeness immediately—the stern, unsmiling features, the haughty, squared jaw. But it wasn't his own face that he saw on the stark, white paper—it was Massa Fletcher's. The face he hated. Kitty had drawn Grady with his arms folded, a frown on his face—the same pose, the same expression Massa Fletcher had worn on the day he'd sold Grady. For a long moment, he couldn't seem to breathe.

Delia had tried to tell him that his father was a white man, but Grady had refused to accept the truth, refused to acknowledge the resemblance he saw in the mirror every day. But as he stared at the portrait Kitty had drawn, he could no longer deny the bitter truth.

His father was Massa Fletcher. His father had sold him—his own son—to a slave trader.

"What's wrong? Don't you like it? Please don't be mad. I-I'm sorry." She pulled it out of his hand and hid it against her bosom. "I'll tear it up."

"No, don't. It ain't your fault." He hadn't meant to upset her. He reached to stop her from destroying the portrait and saw that his hand was shaking. "The picture is very good . . . but . . ."

"What? Tell me."

"It reminds me of . . . of my father."

"Would you like to keep it?" She held out the drawing again, uncertainly. "I wish I could remember what my daddy looked like."

"No!" he shouted. "I don't want to remember him! I hate him!"

His voice made her jump. She drew back. Grady glanced around and saw other people turning to stare at him. He scrambled to his feet. He wanted to run, but no matter how far he went, he would never escape the truth.

"Look, Kitty. I'm sorry. I—" He couldn't finish. Grady strode toward his carriage without looking back.

❧

"Ouch! Stop brushing so hard!" Missy Claire said.

"Sorry, Missy. But I'm afraid if I don't pull your hair tight, it'll all be falling down again." Missy's thin hair was difficult to fix, and Kitty knew she was running out of time. She'd already heard a carriage pull to a stop out front and voices in the foyer as Missy's gentleman caller came to the door. Missus Goodman would be rushing into the bedroom any minute, hollering for Kitty to hurry up.

She slid the last hair comb into place and gave Missy the hand mirror so she could see the back. "No, I don't want to wear those ivory hair combs," Claire said. "They don't match my reticule. Take them out."

"But if I take them out, Missy Claire, your hair's gonna all fall down for sure. You don't want that, do you? Then I'll have to start all over again, and it sounds like your gentleman friend's already here."

Claire reached up and yanked out the combs. "Don't argue with me. Do it again."

"Yes, Missy."

Kitty wasn't surprised when Missy's mama hurried into the room a few minutes later. And she knew before Missus Goodman said a single word that she was going to get the blame for making Missy late.

"Kitty! What on earth is taking you so long? Quit dawdling and finish Claire's hair. Roger Fuller is here, and we mustn't keep him waiting."

"Yes, ma'am. I'm hurrying, ma'am." Kitty swallowed her frustration and drew the brush through Claire's hair.

"Ouch! Not so hard!" Missy complained.

"I need to have a word with you alone, Claire." Missus Goodman sat down in the slipper chair, her expression serious. Kitty continued her task, knowing that she really didn't need to leave the room, in spite of Missus Goodman's words. White people talked in front of their slaves all the time as if they were blind or deaf or weren't even there.

"Everyone knows that Roger Fuller is looking for a wife," Missy's mother began. "There has been a wild scramble among the eligible ladies to catch his eye these past few months. Your father and I have been talking, and we've decided that you should be his next wife."

"Isn't he a little old for me, Mother? His son Ellis is eighteen, the same age as I am."

"That doesn't matter. I've been told by a very knowledgeable source that Roger is quite interested in you. In fact, you're one of the reasons he's been hanging around Charleston this summer instead of returning to Beaufort. He thinks you're beautiful."

Claire smiled at her own reflection in the mirror. "Really? He said that?"

"Yes, dear, he did. Now, your father and I agree that you would do well to marry a man who is already so well established in life.

Younger men can be careless with their money, gambling it away or chasing loose women. They can be stingy, too. Roger Fuller may be a little older than you are, but he's settled and secure. He runs his business interests very wisely and is highly respected all across South Carolina. I know that he was quite generous to his first wife. She was always dressed in the latest fashions and had the best of everything money could buy. You'll be set for life, Claire."

Missy Claire gazed into the distance, smiling faintly, as if already picturing herself in rubies and silks. Kitty knew how hard Missy had been chasing for a wealthy husband these past three years. Kitty had seen a lot of suitors come and go, but this was the first time she'd ever heard Missy's parents say that they'd made up their minds.

"In that case, I'll be so charming he'll want to marry me before Christmas," Claire said with a smile.

"Good girl." Missus Goodman patted Missy's shoulder and rose to her feet. "Hurry down now, dear. You don't want to keep Roger waiting."

Kitty quickly finished Missy's hair, then followed her downstairs to the drawing room. She watched Missy from a discreet distance, curious to see this man she had suddenly decided to marry. Mr. Fuller was elegantly dressed but not especially handsome—his skin and hair, like Missy's, were much too pale. His face looked very kind, though. Kitty had seen him here before; he had visited the Goodman home on several occasions.

When she was certain that Claire no longer needed her, Kitty crept through the servants' door and hurried outside to the kitchen for her own dinner. She was crossing the yard when she happened to notice Mr. Fuller's carriage and team of horses parked nearby. Tending them was a young slave dressed in livery, a man she was certain she had seen before, too. She paused to watch him and realized that he was the young man whose portrait she had drawn on the day of the political rally.

His skin was the lightest shade of brown Kitty had ever seen on a slave, like a buttermilk hotcake that was baked just right. Up close, his eyes had been as dark and rich as blackstrap molasses. No, darker—like charcoal. She recalled the fire blazing in them, like hot embers. She'd hung the picture she had drawn of him on the wall beside her bed, although she didn't know why. And now, here he was.

He looked up and saw her, too. "Hey, you're Kitty—the girl who draws pictures—aren't you?"

"Yes," she replied, surprised that he'd remembered. "I know you told me your name the last time, but I forgot it. I'm sorry."

"That's okay. It's Grady." He was very handsome, and as strong and solid as the horses he drove. Just watching him saunter across the yard toward her made Kitty's knees feel like bacon melting and curling in a frying pan.

"I ran off kind of sudden the last time," he said. "Want to try again?"

"T-try what?"

"Talking. You know, getting acquainted with each other."

"Sure. Okay." Why was her heart beating so strangely? Maybe it was because nobody had ever looked at her the way he was looking at her, like she was a fancy cake and he was licking his chops, ready to dig in. Kitty didn't get to meet many male slaves her own age. White folk usually chose older men for their house servants, sending the younger, stronger slaves like Grady out to work in the fields all day.

"You work here?" Grady asked, gesturing to the town house.

"I'm Missy Claire's chambermaid," she replied, proud of her position as a house servant. "You must've come here with Mr. Fuller, the man who's courting my missy."

"I'm his coachman."

Kitty was impressed. Coachman was an important position. "You look awful young for a driver."

"I'm good at what I do." He studied her for a long moment and his smile broadened. "You know what? I been driving Massa Fuller all over the place, from Beaufort to Charleston and back again, but you're the prettiest chambermaid I ever did see."

Kitty had no idea what to say. The melting sensation that had started with her knees seemed to be spreading all through her. As much as she enjoyed these exciting new feelings, they were much too sudden and overwhelming. She needed to break the hold this stranger had over her.

"Y-you want to come in the kitchen and get a bite to eat with me?" she asked, trying to regain her balance. She barely recognized her own voice.

"No. I'd rather sit out here and look at you." Grady smiled, as if he knew exactly how handsome he was. His self-confidence unnerved her.

"Well, I need to eat a quick bite," she said. "Then I have to go back inside in case Missy needs me."

He looked disappointed. "Will I see you later?"

Kitty didn't know how to answer. *Yes* sounded like a promise and *no* like she was mad at him or something. "I-I don't know. . . ." She gave him a weak smile and fled into the kitchen.

Before long, Massa Fuller and Missy Claire were courting all the time, and Kitty bumped into Grady nearly every day. It seemed like everywhere she and Missy Claire went, Grady and Massa Fuller were there, too. While their owners attended political rallies, receptions, dinner parties, and the theater, Kitty and Grady spent a lot of time waiting. And it seemed like every chance that he got, Grady would try to sit close to her and look into her eyes and say sweet things to her. As much as Kitty enjoyed the attention, it still made her uneasy. She wasn't sure how to react, so she carried her paper and pencil everywhere, quickly sketching something before he could distract her with his sweet talk. He liked to watch her draw. And he also liked to fuss over his horses—brushing them, rubbing them down, making sure their harnesses weren't rubbing or their legs getting sore. One Sunday morning, while Kitty and Grady waited outside the white folks' church, she decided to sketch one of Grady's horses.

"Hey, that's Blaze," he said, peering over her shoulder. "You drew that patch of white on his forehead perfectly."

"You like them horses a lot, don't you? And they like you, too. I can tell."

Grady reached up to rub Blaze's neck, then patted his shoulder affectionately. "They're my babies . . . ain't you?"

"Must be nice driving all around, seeing new things. Missy and me travel from the plantation to Charleston and back, twice a year, but I ain't seeing much else."

"I saw all of the world that I ever want to see before Massa Fuller bought me." Grady's smile vanished and his face went rigid. He was suddenly angry, his mood changing as swiftly as it had on the first day she'd met him. Kitty was never sure what would spark his anger, why some topics would touch off a fire inside him like a match to straw. Rage would shudder through him until he looked as though he might burst into flames.

"Your massa gonna marry Missy Claire?" she asked, trying to change the subject.

"He ain't telling me his plans. Why?"

"Missy's wanting to marry him real bad. She and her mama say he has a lot of money and a nice big house."

"Maybe I should warn Massa that she's chasing after his money."

"Please don't do that! You'll get me in trouble and—"

He rested his hand on her shoulder. "I was joking, Kitty."

"I really didn't mean to make Missy sound so greedy. I been with her since we was little girls, and she's really very nice. Sometimes she gives me things when she's done with them, and—"

"Don't defend her. And you shouldn't have to be content with her leftovers. You ought to be the lady of the house, with servants waiting on you. You're the prettiest girl in South Carolina." Grady smiled. He lifted his hand from her shoulder and stroked his fingers down her cheek. "Lots of gals in this city, but . . . umm um . . . you're the prettiest one."

Kitty shivered at his touch. Nobody in the whole world had ever told her she was pretty. Then the sound of the church organ drifted through the open windows, breaking the spell. The service was nearly over. Kitty stood, putting her sketch away, and backed out of Grady's reach. As she waited for her mistress to emerge from the church, Kitty wasn't sure which frightened her more: Grady's unpredictable anger or his attempts to get close to her.

She saw him again a few days later, when he and Mr. Fuller came to Missy Claire's house for dinner. The party lasted until late at night, and though part of Kitty longed to go outside and talk to Grady, part of her was grateful when Missy Claire insisted that she stay near the dining room. After dinner, the men retired to Massa Goodman's study for drinks and the ladies went outside to the piazza for air. Missy signaled to Kitty.

"Go down to the kitchen and fetch me a cup of mint tea. My stomach is all aflutter tonight."

"Yes, Missy." Kitty had noticed the way Mr. Fuller hovered close to Missy, gazing into her eyes and whispering things to her. If Missy felt the same way Kitty did when Grady stood real close and whispered things, it was no wonder she needed tea for her stomach.

Outside, the backyard was so bright that Kitty could see her faint shadow. A full moon shone overhead, luminous and golden, lighting up the feathery clouds that surrounded it. She wandered toward the side yard so she could see it better through the trees. A moment later, Grady appeared by her side.

"I was hoping I'd see you tonight," he whispered. "Where've you been all day?"

"Look at that!" she said, pointing to the sky. "Did you ever see such a beautiful moon? It looks like it's made of gold, and the clouds are all made of silver. I love this time of night, don't you? When the sky is deep, deep blue—almost purple?"

He laughed. "You're always showing me colors and things I never would of noticed otherwise."

"That's because you're always looking down, Grady. You're gonna miss a lot of pretty things that way."

"Kitty?"

She turned to face him. He rested his hands on her shoulders, drawing her closer. Grady's hands were large and strong and warm. They felt good caressing her. She loved the way he smelled, like leather and horses and soap. She looked up into his eyes—darker than the sky—and saw the moon reflected in them. He stood so close she could feel the warmth of his body, but for once she didn't want to back away. He was going to kiss her. And she wanted him to.

"Kitty!" Missy Claire shouted.

Kitty stepped out of Grady's arms and whirled around. Missy stood on the porch above her, leaning over the railing.

"What are you doing out there, you stupid girl? I told you to hurry back!"

"I'm really sorry, Missy. I was just getting the tea, like you said, when I saw the moon and—"

"You weren't supposed to stop and gaze at the moon! Can't you do even the simplest thing right?"

"I'm sorry, Missy. I guess I didn't think—"

"You never think! I swear there isn't a brain in your head. Now, fetch my tea and get back in here!"

"Yes, Missy Claire. I'm fetching it."

Grady followed her as she hurried across the yard to the kitchen. "I hate white people," he murmured.

"Don't say that. Missy sounds mad but she don't mean it. She needs me."

"That's because she'd be helpless without you. You do all her dirty work."

Kitty glanced at him, and the rage she saw in his eyes frightened her. For the first time she realized that the common thread to all of his angry outbursts was his hatred of white people.

"You needing something?" Cook asked as they entered the kitchen. She sat at the table with Bessie and Albert.

"Don't get up," Kitty said. "I can fetch it." She quickly found a tray, a cup and saucer, and the teapot. Her fingers trembled as she crumbled mint leaves into the pot. She had to hurry. Grady watched her from the doorway, his arms folded. "Besides," Kitty told him. "Missy's right. It was stupid of me to forget what I come out for."

"You're not stupid, Kitty. Just because the white folks can force us to do what they say, it don't mean they can force us to believe all their lies. You're just as good as any white woman. She's wrong to be talking to you that way all the time."

Kitty paused to look up at him. "Why are you so angry?"

"I had a massa just like her, once. Treated me like I was an animal."

"That don't mean you have to hate all white people."

"If you'd traveled with that slave trader and seen what I've seen, you'd hate them all, too. They rip our families apart and beat us to death, and they don't even care!"

Kitty thought of her parents as she poured boiling water from the kettle. For a brief moment, she understood Grady's rage. Then she pushed her anger and grief aside, determined to never think of that tragedy again. Sorrow would only make her life with Missy Claire much worse.

"Mr. Fuller don't treat you bad, does he?" she asked Grady.

"No. But he thinks of me as his property, not a human being."

"We are their property, Grady."

He stalked out of the kitchen, banging the door behind him.

"What's wrong with him?" Cook asked.

"I don't know." Kitty didn't understand Grady at all. Why couldn't he accept things the way they were instead of getting so angry? It didn't change anything to get mad. She glanced around the yard on her way back to the house, but she didn't see Grady. Then she hurried inside as quickly as she could without spilling the tea.

❧

Every time Grady made up his mind to forget about Kitty he would run into her again, and his resolve would drain away like water into sand. The way she accepted her white missy's abuse made him so angry he wanted to walk away and never look back. But then he would recall the night he'd almost kissed Kitty beneath the full moon, and he could hardly wait to see her again.

Kitty was different from all the other girls he'd been with—prettier, certainly—but something more. She was smart and alive and always seeing color and beauty in a world that Grady only saw as gray. She had a childlike quality, an innocence that touched his heart. Yet the way she defended her missy made him furious. He wanted to shake her, convince her to hold up her head in pride and stop making excuses for her. Why didn't Kitty hate Missy's guts the way he hated Coop and Fletcher and Fuller? Grady would help her see the truth. He would teach her to have pride in herself, to know she was just as good as any white woman. Slaves might have to play dumb in front of white people and act subservient, but inside, they were free to store up all the hatred they wanted to, just like Amos had taught him.

Grady saw Kitty often over the next few weeks, and they spent a lot of time talking as they waited for their masters. Grady was used to winning a woman's affections very quickly and had never had trouble persuading a gal to sneak off behind the bushes with him. But Kitty was as skittish as a newborn colt. He'd been forced to pursue her more slowly than he'd ever pursued a woman before—and there had been no more opportunities for romance, like on the night of the full moon. Then, as the weeks passed and his master continued to court Kitty's mistress, Grady realized that something else had been missing lately.

"How come I never see you drawing no more?" he asked as they sat side by side on the Goodmans' back steps.

Kitty smiled her shy, embarrassed smile. "I finally ran out of paper. I made it last as long as I could. My pictures kept getting smaller and smaller," she said with a little laugh, gesturing to show how tiny her pictures had become. "But I just can't squeeze any more of them onto the pages. There ain't even a tiny little corner left."

"Does your missy know you're all out of paper? Would she buy you some more?"

"Oh, she ain't drawing pictures now that she's chasing a husband. Only reason she give me paper the last time was because she's throwing it out. I found it in the trash."

"Ask her for some more, Kitty."

She shook her head. "I can't do that." He saw fear in the slump of her shoulders and downcast eyes. It made him furious. He wanted to yell at her, but he held his tongue, knowing it wouldn't do any good. He would only scare her away.

"Well, if you ain't gonna be drawing no more pictures," he finally said, "do you think I could have one to keep? One you don't want no more?"

"Why?"

"I never did see a slave who could draw like you do. Please? Just one?"

She seemed confused by the request, then her eyes suddenly brightened. "I know which one I can give you," she said, leaping to her feet. "I'll be right back."

"Wait!" Grady hurried toward the slaves' quarters behind her. "I'll come with you. I'd like to see your room. I bet you got pictures hanging all over your walls, don't you?" He rested his hand on the small of her back and she nearly jumped out of her skin.

"I don't have nothing on my walls. I share the room with three other girls. You'd better stay here."

He waited at the foot of the stairs, angry that Kitty always shied away from him. There were plenty of other girls he could be chasing here in Charleston. Why was he wasting his time with her?

When she came back with the picture, he remembered why. Kitty was unlike any girl he'd ever met. She'd brought him the drawing of his favorite horse, Blaze.

"Here. Now I better go and see if Missy needs me," she said. "Good night, Grady."

When he parked the carriage in front of Massa's hotel later that night, Grady pulled the drawing out of his pocket. "Can I show you

158

something, Massa Fuller?" he asked as he opened the door for him. He handed Fuller the picture Kitty had drawn.

"This looks like my horse. This is Blaze. Where did you get this?"

"Missy Goodman's chambermaid drew it. She likes to draw but she's all out of paper. I was wondering if there's some extra work I could be doing to make a little money on the side. . . . I'd like to buy her some more paper."

Fuller smiled knowingly. "Are you sweet on her, Grady?"

"You know me, Massa. I got a gal on every plantation. But look how good that is. Shame she can't be drawing any more, ain't it?"

"Does Claire know her girl can do this?" he asked, handing back the drawing. "Why doesn't she ask Claire?"

"Kitty's a real shy gal, Massa. Afraid of her own shadow. Missy gave her this paper and a pencil, but Kitty would never dare ask for more. She won't ask for nothing for herself." Even as he explained the reason, it made Grady mad. He was asking his master for a favor. Begging him. Kitty had no backbone at all.

Fuller stared into the distance for a long moment, as if in thought. "I believe there's a stationer's shop down the block from Institute Hall," he finally said. "After you drive me there for my meeting tomorrow, why don't you buy your girlfriend some paper." He reached into his pocket and pulled out a handful of loose change, spilling it into Grady's hand. Grady had never held money in his life. He had no idea how much he'd been given or how much paper it would buy.

"Thanks, Massa Fuller. Can I do something to repay you?"

Fuller grinned. "Well, I wouldn't mind if word of this little favor got back to Miss Goodman. I'm very interested in impressing her, you know."

"I'll be sure and tell her chambermaid, Massa Fuller. I'll tell her it come from you. Thanks, Massa Fuller."

"Good luck with your own romance."

Grady couldn't wait to give Kitty the paper. Several days passed before he saw her again, and then it was at a fancy party at some white man's house. Grady and Massa Fuller got there first; the Goodman family arrived later in their own carriage with Albert driving. Kitty had to follow her missy inside, but Grady managed to whisper to her on the steps, "Come back outside when you can. I have something for you."

He had to stand around forever, waiting for her. Then, late in the evening she finally slipped outside for a moment. Kitty stared in disbelief when he handed her the sheaf of paper. "For . . . *me*? All of this?"

"Yeah. So you can draw some more pictures."

She hugged the paper to her bosom and wept.

"Hey . . . Hey, don't cry. You'll get the paper all wrinkly." Grady held her gently in his arms, unsure how she would react to his touch. She accepted his comfort for a long moment before pulling away, staring from Grady to the paper and back again as if afraid to believe him, afraid the treasure might disappear.

"Where'd you get this?"

"I showed Massa Fuller that picture you drew of his horse and he let me buy it for you."

"Thank you, Grady! Thank you! Nobody ever did such a nice thing for me before." She went into his arms willingly, hugging him tightly. Grady had hugged dozens of women before, but never one as fragile and vulnerable as Kitty. He was almost afraid to hug her too hard in return. But he hadn't held a girl since his disastrous date with Rosie, the night he'd been whipped, and Kitty felt good in his arms, warm and soft in all the right places. Much too soon, she pulled away again.

"I'm gonna draw my first picture right now."

She sat down on the carriage step beneath a street lamp and carefully tore one of the pages into four pieces, conserving it. Grady watched. She was drawing a face, a woman's face, and it soon became clear that it was a picture of Missy Claire.

"Why're you drawing her?" he asked, frowning.

"You'll see."

That's all she would say When she finished, they stood side by side in the shadow of Grady's carriage and waited for the dinner party to end. Kitty seemed so happy she nearly glowed. "Thank you, Grady. You made me so happy tonight."

"I can see that." He took her face in his hands. She had amazing eyes, the same color as chestnuts. He noticed colors in things now. Kitty had taught him that. He bent his head toward hers and kissed her. She responded so shyly and hesitantly, at first, that Grady soon realized she'd never been kissed before. He slowed down, enjoying her delight as she relaxed in his arms and returned his kisses.

Much too soon, the dinner party ended. The front door opened, and Massa Fuller emerged from the house with Missy Claire on his arm. The Goodmans were right behind them. Grady ran around to open the carriage door for Massa Fuller, while the Goodmans' driver climbed down to help his owners. But before Massa Fuller had a chance to climb inside, Kitty hurried over to him.

"Thank you for buying me the paper," she said. "I made this for you." She gave him the drawing of Claire.

Grady was furious. Why was she thanking an ignorant white man who didn't even care two cents about her? Buying the paper had been Grady's idea. He was the one who had to lower himself to ask for the money. Kitty was always doing that, always bowing down and kissing the white folks' feet. It made him sick.

"What is that?" Claire asked, leaning out of her carriage window. "What did she give you, Roger?"

Fuller held the picture out to her. "It's a drawing of you, Claire. Look, it's an excellent likeness."

Missy Claire waved it away. "Yes, her little sketches always were amusing. Good night, Roger."

Massa Fuller climbed into his own carriage. He was still staring at the picture in amazement as Grady closed the door. Grady was so angry he had to resist the urge to flog the horses into a wild gallop all the way down Meeting Street to the hotel.

⚜

Kitty sat on the driver's seat beside Albert, hugging her new sheaf of paper. She had never felt happier in her life, not only because she had drawing paper again, but also because Grady had kissed her. She had never been kissed before, never even been held by a man, and she was sorry that the night had ended so soon. His kisses stirred up feelings inside her that she'd never felt before, and she wished she could have kissed him all night.

"You been hanging around with Massa Fuller's coachman an awful lot," Albert said as if reading her thoughts. He gave her a long, hard look before turning his attention back to the road. "I seen him kissing you," he added.

Kitty's face felt very warm. "Please don't tell Missy Claire," she whispered.

"You better watch yourself with him, girl. What's his name?"

"Grady Fuller."

"I been asking around about him. Some of them others say he has a girlfriend on every plantation from Beaufort to Charleston. His massa's been courting all the white ladies, trying to find his self a wife, and meanwhile, that boy's been loving up all their young slave gals. I hear he's promising to marry at least a dozen gals by now. He promising you?"

"No ..." But her face felt as if she was sitting in front of a blazing fireplace.

"Massa Fuller's a gentleman. He won't make no promises till he makes up his mind. But that young rascal boy of his is just taking advantage of silly young gals like you. He's cocky as a rooster, and he's collecting a whole yard full of hens. Mind he don't play you for a fool."

Was that why Grady had given her the paper? So that she'd fall into his arms? She remembered how willingly she'd kissed him—in fact her mouth was still tender from the crush of his lips and the stubble on his chin. She was glad Albert couldn't see her flushed face in the dark.

"Thanks for telling me," she mumbled.

"Yeah . . . well, watch you don't get your heart broke," he said.

The next time she ran into Grady, Kitty wasn't so quick to fall into his arms or follow him into the shadows. He finally grew impatient with her for fending off his advances. "What's wrong with you tonight, girl? Why're you giving me the cold shoulder?"

"I'm very happy you gave me the paper, Grady. I'm real thankful for it. . . ."

"But . . . what? What's the matter?"

She stared at the ground, embarrassed. "I hear I ain't the only gal who's been falling for your sugar."

He lifted her chin so she had to face him. "How do I know who you're seeing when I ain't here?" he asked.

"Nobody—I ain't seeing nobody." Kitty wanted to stay angry and pull away, but he had a hold over her that she didn't understand.

He tilted his head to one side and grinned. "You expect me to believe that? You expect me to believe that the most beautiful gal in South Carolina ain't got a dozen boyfriends? Uh uh. I ain't believing that for one minute."

"It's true. You're the only one, Grady. But from what I hear, there's a whole hen house full of girls clucking around your feet."

"Who's feeding you all them stories?" The sudden rage in his eyes sent a chill of fear down her spine. Something inside Grady was like a wild animal, untamed and barely under his control. At times Kitty longed to soothe away the loss and the pain that she saw in his dark eyes. But then the anger would flare, as it did now, and she knew that she needed to run before she got hurt.

"Is it true?" she managed to say. "Can you look me in the eye and tell me you ain't sweet-talking a dozen other girls?"

"What's so great about being the only one?" he asked, hiding his fury behind a smile. "It don't matter to me if I'm the only man in your life."

"Then all those things you said about me being the prettiest gal in the state—they was all lies?"

His smug grin faltered. "They weren't lies. You are the prettiest one," he said, and for just a moment, it was as if a mask had come off. The cocky, self-assured man melted away and she saw the real Grady, underneath. He was telling the truth.

Kitty didn't know what to make of that. She had no experience with men, no knowledge on which to base her decisions, only Albert's warning to be careful—and a deep, inner fear of being hurt. Her parents had fallen in love and it had led to sorrow.

"I have to go," she said. "Missy might need me." Walking away from him took more effort than Kitty would have ever guessed, starved as she was for love and affection. But Albert said Grady was playing her for a fool, and she didn't want any part of that.

Grady watched her go, flatly refusing to run after her and beg. From now on he would stay far away from her. Let her sit by herself and sketch, if that's what she wanted. What did he care? But he had told himself the same thing countless times before, and each time he'd been drawn back to her like a horse galloping the last mile home.

He cared about what Kitty thought of him. She hadn't been just like all the others to him, another gal to win, another heart to conquer. She was different. It bothered him that she drew back in fear every time he allowed his anger to leak out. And it seemed like every time he was with her, something always made him angry—ever since the first day they'd met and she'd drawn his picture. He knew that he kept scaring her away, and he hated to see himself in her reaction, to glimpse himself the way she saw him—angry, bitter, filled with hatred.

Something was going on in his heart that Grady didn't understand at all, something he didn't want to happen. Maybe he was afraid to get close, just like Delia said—but that was a good thing. He certainly wasn't going to limit himself to only one girl for the rest of his life. The only reason he'd pursued Kitty as long as he had was because Massa Fuller hadn't been covering as much territory as he used to cover. This was the longest either of them had ever courted one woman. Well, maybe Massa Fuller was ready to limit himself, but Grady sure wasn't, even if Kitty was the prettiest gal around. He was glad that she had walked away before she touched something deep inside him.

So why did Grady feel such a loss at the thought of never seeing her again? Why did it hurt so much to watch her walk away? Was it just his pride, his desire to win Kitty's heart as he'd won all the others? To make matters worse, he kept running into Kitty all the time. He wished Massa Fuller would go back to the plantation or to Beaufort and stay away from Charleston for good. Grady decided to ask him about it when they reached their hotel that night.

"We going back home to Beaufort soon, Massa?"

"Yes. As a matter of fact, we're leaving next week."

Grady sighed. Good. He wouldn't have to see Kitty anymore. He could forget all about her, and once she was out of sight, any feelings he had toward her would quickly fade.

"But we'll be returning right after the election," Massa Fuller added.

"Returning to Charleston? When's that election, Massa?"

"In November." Fuller smiled slightly. "I've asked Claire Goodman to be my wife. We're getting married this Christmas."

The announcement upset Grady, but he didn't know why. "That's wonderful, Massa Fuller," he said with a phony grin. "Congratulations."

"Thank you."

Grady watched Massa Fuller disappear into the Charleston Hotel, then drove the carriage around the block to the livery stable for the night. Did a chambermaid move to a new plantation with her mistress when she got married? He hoped not. He hoped so.

Grady wanted to punch somebody.

11

CHARLESTON, SOUTH CAROLINA
DECEMBER 1860

Grady pulled the horses to a halt in front of Institute Hall in down-town Charleston. He and Massa Fuller were back in the city again, staying at the Charleston Hotel after a short trip home to Beaufort. Every day, for more than a month, Grady had been waiting outside the hall while Massa attended meetings all day, then he'd drive Massa to see Missy Claire nearly every night. From what Grady had overheard, he knew that Massa thought the wrong man, Abraham Lincoln, had just been elected president. The white men were so angry about it that they'd been meeting here at Institute Hall ever since the election.

"Can I ask you a question, Massa Fuller?" Grady said as he opened the carriage door for him. "I hear everybody talking about 'secession,' and I'm wondering what that means."

Massa Fuller frowned. "The United States began as a union of free, independent states," he said. "We're deciding whether or not South Carolina should leave that union—secede from it—now that the federal government no longer represents our interests. If secession passes, and I pray that it will, South Carolina will be an independent commonwealth once again." Massa's frown deepened, but Grady didn't think he was mad at him for asking; it was the subject itself that seemed to anger him. Another white man, who had stepped from his own carriage at the same time as Fuller, joined the conversation.

"It's everyone's prayer, Roger. The Union has fallen into the hands of northern fanatics. It's no longer a partnership. When the majority starts oppressing the minority, it's time to fight back."

"Hear! Hear!" a third man added.

Grady wondered if they would feel the same way if the Negro minority decided to fight back against their oppressors.

"By the way, Roger, congratulations on your engagement," the first man said. He pumped Massa Fuller's hand vigorously. "My wife and I are looking forward to your wedding next week."

"I daresay I'm looking forward to it, too," Fuller replied, laughing. Grady watched them all disappear into the building. He would park the carriage somewhere and settle back for another long day of waiting, then another long evening at the Goodmans' house, trying to avoid Kitty. It wasn't difficult to do. With Missy Claire's wedding to prepare for, neither Kitty nor any of the other slaves had a free moment to spare.

All of Charleston seemed to be in an uproar over secession, but Grady knew that the fuss was really about slavery. Above all else, Massa and the other planters would fight for the right to keep their slaves. There was even talk of war. Grady had driven Massa Fuller to a haberdasher's shop and watched through the front window as a tailor measured him for a new uniform. While they'd been home in Beaufort, Massa Fuller had been made a captain in the Beaufort Volunteer Artillery.

Grady was waiting for his master outside the hall a few days later, when several men burst through the doors, shouting, "Freedom! Secession has passed!" Within minutes the excitement spread throughout downtown Charleston. Shops closed, church bells rang, and by the time Massa Fuller emerged with the other men, all wreathed in smiles, artillery had begun to boom, rattling windows all over the city.

"What's going on, Massa?" Grady asked. "There a war starting?"

"We've signed the Ordinance of Secession. South Carolina has become the first state ever to secede from the Union."

Grady forced a smile and said, "That's good news, Massa. That's what you been wanting, ain't it?"

"Yes, it certainly is."

"Where'd you like me to take you now?" he asked as he loosened the reins from the hitching post.

"Let's stop at that haberdasher's and see if my uniform is ready."

"I seen an awful lot of people putting on uniforms lately. There gonna be a war?"

"I doubt it. We joined the Union voluntarily, and we're entitled to leave it voluntarily. But it doesn't hurt to be prepared. Our state's militia laws require all men my age to serve for three months every year. As soon as I return to Beaufort, my artillery unit is going to begin drilling." Massa seemed too excited to stand still, much less climb into the carriage for the slow drive through the clogged streets.

"Looks like them shops is all closing early today to celebrate," Grady said as he surveyed the bustling streets around Institute Hall. "We better be hurrying to that tailor shop before it closes, too."

"I'm getting married tomorrow!" Fuller shouted above the clanging bells of the neighboring church. "From now on Claire and I will celebrate our anniversary and our independence at the same time."

❦

Grady rose very early the next morning to decorate the carriage with holly and evergreen boughs the way Massa wanted. He braided ribbons in the horses' manes and tails, and fixed feather plumes to their harnesses. Then he drove a very nervous-looking Massa and his two sons to the church. Missy Claire arrived in her carriage a short time later, and Grady saw Kitty, briefly, as she helped her mistress into the church. But he quickly lost sight of her as hundreds of guests began arriving in their carriages. He didn't get to see the wedding as he waited outside the church with the other drivers.

When it was over, Massa came down the steps with Missy Claire on his arm. Church bells rang, and guests showered the couple with rice as Grady helped them into the carriage for the drive back to Missy Claire's house. He would have to remember not to call her Missy Claire anymore. She was Missus Fuller now.

The December day turned out to be sunny and unusually warm, so while the white folks gathered for a celebration in the Goodmans' second-floor ballroom, Grady and all the guests' drivers and slaves were treated to a much smaller party outside in the yard. The jib windows of the Big House had been flung open, and some of the slaves danced to the lively music that drifted down from the wedding reception. Grady didn't see any gals his age that he wanted to dance with. And he didn't have to worry about bumping into Kitty, since the Goodmans' slaves were busy cooking and serving food to hundreds of people.

As Grady wandered restlessly around the yard later that afternoon, the Negro musicians came outside for a break. One of them laid his fiddle and bow on a bench right in front of Grady, then left to fill a plate with food. Grady picked up the instrument. The heft and balance of it felt immediately familiar, and it stirred a longing in him that he hadn't known was there. Without thinking, he placed the fiddle beneath his chin—then quickly lowered it again. How many years had it been since he'd played? At least three. Unable to resist, he lifted it into place again, and drew the bow across the strings. The sound vibrated pleasantly through him. He smiled without realizing it and played a quick scale.

The instrument was out of tune, probably from all the lively playing its owner had done. Grady reached for the tuning pegs, turning them to adjust the strings, testing the pitches with the bow until the notes sounded in tune. Then he played a simple melody, his fingers remembering exactly where to go, how firmly to press down. It was as if he had played mere days ago, not years.

"You got good pitch," a voice behind him said. "You play a lot?"

Grady turned and saw the man who owned the fiddle. "I used to. I ain't played in a long time." He offered the instrument back to him but the man shook his head, balancing a plate and a glass of cider in his hands.

"No, go ahead, let's hear you play something else."

"I don't remember how to no more," Grady mumbled.

"You tuned up them strings like you still remembered."

Grady hesitated. Part of him longed to play, to allow the music to flow through him again like a healing balm, the way it had when he'd first learned from Beau in New Orleans. But another part of him couldn't forget what he'd been forced to do in the years that had followed. He never wanted to play again.

"No, thanks," he mumbled. He laid the fiddle down on the bench where he'd found it.

"Ever hear this tune?" the fiddler asked as he set down his plate. He lifted the instrument and played a slow, beautiful tune that Grady had never heard before. Without realizing it, he studied where the man placed his fingers, learning the tune as if he intended to play it himself. By the third verse, Grady had memorized it. He slowly became aware that the conversations all around him had quieted as the other slaves listened, too.

"You know that song?" the man asked when he finished. Grady shook his head. "It's called 'Amazing Grace' but I call it the slave trader's song. Man who wrote it was captain of a slave ship."

Grady tensed. His face must have shown his revulsion because the man touched his arm with the bow, as if to soothe him.

"No, no. He gave up the slaving business when he found Jesus," the fiddler explained with a grin. "He wrote that song afterwards. Said that Jesus had saved him and forgiven him and gave him a brand-new life. The last verse says we're gonna have ten thousand years to sing praises to Jesus in heaven. I like to think I'll be playing my fiddle up there, too, don't you?"

"I got nothing to do with Jesus," Grady said coldly. He strode off to find another glass of cider.

Kitty came outside through the servants' door in time to see Grady stride away from one of the musicians, an angry look on his face. Even on this happy occasion, he seemed unable to relax and have fun. She shook her head and hurried over to the table of food, determined to eat and enjoy herself for a few moments. She had just filled her plate and was looking for a place to sit, when she heard Grady's voice behind her.

"I'm surprised your missy let you come to the party."

Kitty glanced up at him, then quickly looked away. It was so hard to see Grady and not recall what it had been like to be kissed by him. So hard not to wish he would kiss her again. "I been very busy," she said. "This is the biggest day of Missy's life. She's needing me more than ever."

"I figured you'd defend her."

Kitty let his comment go by. She found a place to sit on an empty bench and began eating. There was room for Grady to sit beside her, but he remained standing. "Ain't you gonna eat something?" she asked.

"I already did." He shifted nervously in place, stuffing his hands into his pockets, then pulling them out a moment later. "Massa said we're going back to Beaufort real soon," he finally said. "You coming, too?"

"Yes. Missy's bringing me with her."

"You ain't looking very happy about it. What's wrong?"

Kitty forced a smile. If Grady noticed that she was unhappy, then Missy Claire would notice, too. She mustn't be gloomy. "Nothing's wrong. I never been away from home before, that's all. Going to live in a new house and a new town is a little scary. Only places I ever lived is on Great Oak Plantation or here in Charleston."

"You got family you leaving behind?"

"No. I got lots of friends, like Mammy Bertha and Cook and

Bessie, but I ain't got no family. What's it like where you and your massa live?"

"I don't know. I never been allowed inside the plantation house. Or the town house in Beaufort, either." His anger flared momentarily, but Kitty saw him carefully bank it. "I don't notice colors and things like you always do," he said with a shrug. "But it's quiet and peaceful there. Lots of pretty things for you to draw, I guess. The town of Beaufort ain't nearly as big and noisy as Charleston. I'll be glad to be gone from here."

He glanced up at the open windows as the musicians started playing again in the upstairs ballroom. The music seemed to make Grady uneasy for some reason.

"Are the other slaves nice?" Kitty asked.

"Huh?"

"The other slaves where your massa lives. Are they nice?"

"I guess so."

Kitty ate a bite of pork, wondering how many girlfriends Grady had back home and if they would get along with her. She knew it would make him mad if she asked about other girls her age. "Well, at least I'll know one person there," she said.

"Yeah. Your missy."

She knew by his bitter tone that he was still angry with her. But before she could reply, one of the parlormaids came to the back door, calling to her.

"Kitty! Missy Claire's wanting you to come right away."

Kitty set her half-finished plate aside and hurried to obey.

"See you later," Grady mumbled.

⸙

BEAUFORT, SOUTH CAROLINA
DECEMBER 1860

Delia watched in alarm as Massa Fuller's carriage drew to a halt in front of the town house. "Better come quick," she shouted to all the other slaves. "Massa's come home early, and he brought his new bride." She didn't know which to do first: rush outside and greet her new missus, hurry into the front parlor to pull the dust sheets off the furniture, or run upstairs and finish getting the bedrooms ready. She decided on the parlor, telling Martin to go greet them and Minnie to hurry upstairs.

Massa Fuller led his new bride into the room just as Delia stuffed the last sheet out of sight. She had to hide her shock at how young the girl was. She could be Massa's daughter, not his wife. White folks certainly were peculiar.

"Claire darling, this is Delia," Massa Fuller said. "She was my mammy when I was small, and now she and Martin supervise the house slaves for me, both here in town and out at the plantation."

Delia kept her eyes lowered in respect. "Welcome, Missus Fuller. We real happy to have you here. I'm sorry if we ain't quite ready, but we ain't expecting y'all until next week."

"I know," Massa said, "but there have been some unexpected developments in Charleston. We're on military alert."

"That don't sound good, Massa. And it look like you wearing a new uniform, too. We starting a war or something?"

"Let's hope not. We ordered all U.S. troops to leave South Carolina after we seceded, but they've refused to surrender Fort Sumter in Charleston harbor. I've returned to my command with the Beaufort Artillery just in case there's a showdown."

Delia shook her head in sympathy. "That sure ain't a very nice way to celebrate your wedding, Massa."

"Claire understands, don't you, dear," he said, smiling at her. She quickly returned his smile. But Delia noticed that Missus Fuller had been studying the room, eyeing all of Massa's fine furniture and paintings as if adding up how much they were all worth. She was quite pretty for a white girl, but it was an icy beauty, like a clear, crisp winter day, without the softness or warmth of spring. Massa's first wife had been much the same.

"Show her around, Delia," Massa said. "And Claire brought her

173

chambermaid along, too. See if you can find someplace for the girl to sleep."

"Yes, Massa Fuller."

He left the house again in a big hurry and drove away in the carriage as Delia began conducting Missus Fuller on a tour of the downstairs. This town house wasn't nearly as large as Massa's plantation house, but it seemed to take forever because the new missus had to examine every valuable item in every room. When they were ready to go upstairs, Delia noticed the new chambermaid standing in the back hallway, looking as wide-eyed as a frightened child. She had come in through the rear servants' door and seemed afraid to move from there without permission. The girl looked familiar to Delia, but before she even had a chance to ask her name, Missus Fuller began yelling at her.

"Don't just stand there, Kitty, get upstairs and start unpacking my things. Must you be told everything? Don't you have a brain in your head?"

"Sorry, Missy. I ain't knowing my way around yet, and—"

"Then ask someone! You have a tongue, don't you?"

"It's the big room on the right at the top of the stairs," Delia said quickly. "You'll see all the suitcases and trunks in there." Kitty scampered up the stairs ahead of them like the devil was chasing her. Delia glanced at Massa's new wife and wondered if maybe she was.

By the time Delia had a chance to sit down and eat her own dinner in the kitchen that evening, she'd already had her fill of her new mistress. The Lord was surely going to have to work a miracle in Delia's heart before she could love that woman. Of course Missus Fuller was all sugar-sweet when Massa was around, but as soon as he was out of earshot it was another story. And she had run that poor little chambermaid of hers ragged.

"How you doing, honey?" Delia asked when Kitty was finally allowed to join her in the kitchen. "You ain't had time to sit down and eat a bite of food all day, have you?"

"That's okay. I know Missy's wanting to get settled in right away."

Something about Kitty's smile seemed forced. She'd worn it bravely all afternoon, even when her mistress had been sharp with her.

"You sit down now, and let me fix you a plate," Delia said. "Then maybe me and you can get better acquainted."

"You don't have to wait on me. I can—"

"I know you can," she said as she steered Kitty to a seat. "But serving you is my way of serving Jesus."

"You're that storyteller, aren't you?" Kitty said. "You came to visit Massa Goodman's house a couple of times. You told us all about that land where everybody had black skin."

Delia nodded. "I thought I'd seen you before. I remember you saying how you lost your folks when you was just a little girl."

For the first time all day, Kitty's smile faded. She nodded, then tried to hide her sorrow by biting into the biscuit Delia had placed in front of her. She lowered her head as if expecting a beating.

"Did you have to leave any other loved ones behind when your missy got married?" Delia asked.

"I never had no loved ones," Kitty said softly. "I can't really recall my mama and papa. Only reason I know what happen to them is because Mammy Bertha told me."

"There ain't nobody else, honey?" Delia asked in amazement.

"I have Missy Claire. She's been like family to me since I was just a little girl. That's when I first started working up at the Big House and being her slave."

Delia had heard the way Missy Claire treated her—and how Kitty responded, poor child. Delia thought she understood, now, why the Lord had brought this girl to her. "God love you," she murmured. "Pretty soon we'll all be just like family to you around here. Minnie and Jim stay here in Beaufort all year round to take care of Massa's town house. And you met Faye, the cook, didn't you? And Martin? He acts bossy sometimes, but don't pay him no mind. Martin, Faye, and me always go back and forth to the plantation whenever Massa goes. You will, too, I guess."

When the back door opened a moment later and Grady strode

into the room, Kitty jumped. Delia saw something unspoken pass between them as they greeted each other, but she couldn't tell what it was. She wondered if he had tried to sweet-talk Kitty the way he had so many others. Then Grady crossed the room to sweep Delia into his arms for a hug.

"I missed you, Delia."

"Me too, honey. Welcome home. You went driving off so fast this afternoon I didn't even get a chance to say hello."

He kissed her forehead, then sank down at the table across from Kitty. "I know. Massa needed to run over to the arsenal right away."

"Guess I don't need to ask if you're hungry, do I," Delia said. She hurried to fix him a plate. She could tell by their strained small talk that something had gone on between Grady and Kitty. There was a history there. Delia hoped he hadn't hurt her. Kitty seemed very innocent and naïve, not at all like Grady's usual conquests.

Delia decided to find out as soon as Kitty went back into the house and she and Grady were alone. "I'm gonna ask you a question, Grady, and I want a straight answer. What's between you and the new girl, Kitty?"

"Nothing. We got to know each other while Massa Fuller was courting her missy. Ain't nothing between us."

She studied him for a long moment, trying to see if he was telling the truth. He avoided her gaze, shoveling sweet potatoes into his mouth like it was his last meal. "That ain't like you, Grady. Kitty is a real pretty gal."

"Yeah, well . . . I can't be respecting a gal who lets herself be treated the way she does."

"What's she supposed to do? Tell her missy off?"

"I know we have to talk like slaves to their faces," Grady said, getting angry. "But when Kitty ain't with Missy she's the same way, always defending her, won't say nothing bad about her."

"I suppose you want her to hate Missus Fuller the way you hate all white people?"

176

"They're our enemies, Delia, but she don't see that. She thinks Missy's her friend."

"Jesus says we're supposed to love our enemies, turn the other cheek."

"Kitty ain't doing it for Jesus," he said pushing his plate away. "She don't respect herself at all. She's always fawning all over that white woman, taking her abuse."

"Let me tell you something," Delia began. Grady held up his hands.

"I don't want to hear no Jesus talk."

"I know. I ain't gonna talk about the Lord. But, Grady, do you remember what it's like to be loved? How your mama and them other folks loved you before you was sold? Well, ain't nobody ever told Kitty they love her. Think about that."

Grady met her gaze for a moment, then looked away.

"The only scraps of affection she ever got was from Missy Claire," Delia continued, "and you know that white woman ain't loving any slave. Nobody in the whole world loves that poor gal. No telling what you and me would be like if nobody ever loved us."

The angry lines on Grady's face softened, and Delia knew she had reached him. "Thanks for dinner," he said. He stood and kissed Delia's cheek, then headed outside to the stable.

BEAUFORT, SOUTH CAROLINA
FEBRUARY 1861

Cold rain soaked right through Kitty's dress as she ran outside from the town house to the kitchen. Inside, the kitchen's steamy warmth smelled of coffee and wood smoke. Faye, the cook, looked so comfortable sitting near the fire with Delia and Grady that Kitty hated to disturb her.

"Missy Claire and her mama would like some tea," she said, out of breath. At home Kitty would have fixed the tray herself, but she didn't know her way around Faye's kitchen yet.

"They wanting something to eat, too?" Faye asked as she rose to her feet.

"I-I don't know," Kitty stammered. "I'll go back and ask."

Delia stopped her before she could open the door. "Wait a minute, honey. Don't go running out in the cold again. We'll fix a little something and if they don't want it, they don't have to eat it." She got up to help Faye with the tea tray.

Kitty had only known Delia for a few months, but she had already grown very fond of the little woman. She didn't always understand everything Delia said, especially when she started talking about Jesus. But Delia always watched out for Kitty, making sure she had enough to eat and a chance to sit down for a moment's rest. When Kitty had first seen Grady hugging her, she had thought Delia was his mother. Then she remembered his story about being sold from his home and forced to live with a slave trader.

"Seems like Missus Fuller's mama is just as mean as Missy is," Grady mumbled. "Why is she ordering everybody around all the time? What's she doing here, anyway? When's she going on back to Charleston?"

Kitty glanced nervously out the window, worried that Missus Goodman might have followed her outside and overheard him. She often did that back home—listening in on the servants' conversations to see what they were up to. "Poor Missy was feeling a little lonely and homesick," Kitty said, "so her mama come for a visit. Missy don't know anybody here in Beaufort, and Massa Fuller's gone so much."

"Poor Missy . . ." Grady repeated, mimicking her.

"Where'd Massa Fuller run off to this time?" Faye asked as she filled the teapot with water.

"He took the train down to Alabama," Grady said. "They're starting a new government down there with all them other states that seceded."

"Can they do that?" Delia asked.

Grady shrugged. "I guess so, because that's what they're doing. Massa told me we was starting the new year in a brand-new country. And you know why, don't you? Just so they can keep us all slaves."

Kitty didn't understand it all, but she'd overheard enough conversations in the Big House to know that all the white folks were afraid that a war was about to start. She thanked Faye and Delia for the tray when it was ready, then hurried back into the house.

Missy and her mother sat by the fireplace in the front parlor. Martin had built a fire for them earlier to help take the chill off the winter afternoon. Kitty set the tray on the table between them, idly listening to their conversation as she arranged the cups and poured the tea.

"You'll need to start looking for a wet nurse," she heard Missus Goodman tell Missy. "It may not be long before you start your own family, and every woman needs a black mammy to nurse her babies for her. Believe me, that's not something a proper lady ever wants to do."

"Could you send Mammy Bertha to me?" Claire asked.

"Heavens, Claire, she's much too old. She suckled you and your sisters when you were small. Doesn't Roger have any house slaves who might be in a family way?"

"Not that I know of. His house slaves all seem a lot older than ours. The head woman, Delia, is older than Mammy Bertha. I think Minnie and Faye are, too."

Kitty stood to one side as the ladies sipped their tea, waiting to be excused. Should she just slip away or would that make Missy angry? Kitty decided to stay.

"You don't really want to bring a field slave up to the house," Missus Goodman said. "They're much too coarse and rough."

"And they're too dark," Missy added. "The ones with jet-black skin frighten me."

"What about your girl, Kitty?"

She heard her name but didn't dare react unless it was a command. She stood perfectly still with her eyes downcast, pretending she couldn't hear.

"Kitty isn't even married," Missy said with a little laugh.

"Slaves don't marry, Claire. We don't hold weddings for cows and horses, do we? Well, there's no such thing as marriages for slaves, either."

Kitty thought of Bessie and Albert back in Charleston. They seemed like husband and wife. They even called each other that. So did Minnie and Jim here in Beaufort.

"Slaves don't have the same feelings we do," Missus Goodman continued. "They're simple creatures. And they live with anybody and everybody down on Slave Row without ever bothering to get married. Part of an owner's job is to direct their breeding in order to produce the best possible stock. I'm sure Roger does it all the time.

That's how owners produce the next generation of slaves. It saves a lot of money, too. Negroes can be expensive if you have to buy them off the auction block, but if you breed them yourself you can replenish your stock and sell all the extra ones at a profit."

"I'm glad that's Roger's job and not mine," Missy said with a shiver.

"Well, it will be your job if you want a wet nurse for your baby. If you want milk, you have to send your cow to a bull to be freshened. We get a wet nurse the same way."

"Mother, please."

"Well, it's the same thing. Slaves aren't like us, Claire. You're always forgetting that. Kitty is your property, and if you want her to be your child's nurse then she'll need to be bred so she'll have a baby before you do."

Kitty had only a vague idea what they were talking about. Their words sounded frightening—and embarrassing—to her.

"Is that what you did with Mammy Bertha?" Claire asked.

"Of course. Bertha always bred quickly, too. She made a fine nurse."

"Where did all her babies go? I don't recall any black babies running around the house when Katie and Mary were little."

"Of course not. You don't think I'd allow them in my house, do you? Slave babies are raised down on Slave Row. Kitty, come here," she ordered suddenly.

Kitty jumped to attention, hurrying over to stand by the tea table. "Yes, ma'am? You want me to pour more tea?"

"Not now. Look, you're comfortable with her, aren't you, Claire?" Missus Goodman asked, pointing to Kitty.

"Of course. Kitty's been my slave for years—you know that."

"Then she's obviously the best choice. But you'd better arrange to have her bred soon."

Claire's cheeks flushed pink with embarrassment. "How do I go about that? Choosing the . . . you know, her partner?"

"It's simply a matter of seeing who's available and then making the best selection. Roger's butler seems suitable. What's his name?"

"You mean Martin? I'd feel funny asking him."

"You don't ask, Claire, you command. You're the lady of the house. You simply give orders and your slaves are expected to obey them. And you must punish them severely if they don't. You have a right to breed any of your slaves that way, any time you want to."

"This is very . . . distasteful."

"Oh, for goodness' sake! Stop reading emotions into this that aren't there. Negroes aren't like us. Look at her! And unless you want some slave up in your nursery who's as black as soot and just as filthy, you'd better take care of this matter soon."

"All right," Claire said with a sigh. "When I meet with Delia and Martin tomorrow morning to plan the meals and so on, I'll talk to him."

Missus Goodman turned to Kitty again, her face stern. "Listen to me, girl. It's an honor to be chosen as Claire's wet nurse. That job is even more important than being her chambermaid. You'll be entrusted with your mistress's children. But in order to get that job, you'll have to do whatever Claire says. If she tells you to sleep with Martin, you'll do it. Do you hear?"

"Yes, ma'am. I-I like babies."

Kitty didn't know Martin very well, and he scared her. She couldn't imagine sleeping in a bed with him—or doing whatever it was that people did there. But she was even more frightened of Missus Goodman. If having a baby was important to her and Missy, then Kitty would have to do whatever she was told.

Kitty thought about the conversation she'd overheard for the rest of the day. Gradually, the idea of taking care of Missy's little babies—and of having a baby of her own—began to excite her. She had helped Mammy Bertha take care of Missy Kate and Missy Mary when they were babies, and she always enjoyed snuggling them in her arms, making them giggle, even rocking them to sleep sometimes. Kitty convinced herself to think about all those good things—and to push aside the shame she felt at the thought of sleeping with Martin.

When she saw Delia alone in the warming kitchen that night,

Kitty decided to tell her about the new job. She had learned to trust Delia these past few months, and knew she could confide in her. Delia would understand Kitty's fear and embarrassment—and ignorance—of making a baby.

"I'm getting a new job, Delia," she said shyly. "Missy's going to let me be a wet nurse."

"A wet nurse!" Delia's eyes widened. She leaned close to lay her hand on Kitty's stomach. "You got a baby growing in there, honey?"

"No, not yet. Missy says I have to sleep with Martin first."

"*What?*" Grady shouted.

Kitty whirled around and was horrified to see him standing in the doorway.

"I-it's a very important job," she hurried to explain. "If I have a baby, then I can take care of Missy's baby when she and Massa Fuller have one."

Her words seemed to infuriate Grady even more. He strode into the room, his face rigid with anger. "It ain't right! She can't make you do that!"

"Yes, she can," Delia said grimly. "Old Missus Fuller done it to me, only she didn't pick another slave. The white overseer was already taking advantage of me. Wasn't nothing I could do about it, either. I had his baby just a few months before Massa Roger was born. That's how come I could be his mammy."

"But it's wrong!" Grady shouted. "We have to put a stop to this!"

"No, wait. It's okay," Kitty said. She had to pretend that everything was fine, that she wanted to be a wet nurse. She didn't want to get into trouble with her mistress. "Missy's mama says they're always doing it this way."

"Do you know anything at all about how babies are made?" Delia asked her.

Kitty's face felt warm with shame. "I know Missy Claire married Massa. Now they sleep together and . . . and they want a new baby."

"That's right," Delia said. "Missy and Massa Fuller got married. You ain't married, Kitty."

"Missus Goodman says colored folks don't get married. She says there ain't no weddings for cows and horses, and there ain't none for slaves, either."

Grady scooped a tin cup off the table and threw it, shouting, "Missus Goodman is *wrong!*" It bounced against the wall with a crash.

Fear tingled through Kitty. She glanced at the door, worried that Missus Goodman would hear the commotion and storm into the kitchen to punish them.

"Grady, calm down," Delia said.

"Don't tell me to calm down!" he shouted. "My mother went through the same thing! My first massa . . ." He couldn't finish.

"I know, honey, but you're scaring her." Delia turned to Kitty again. "Slaves certainly do get married. We call it 'jumping the broom.' It's the same thing as the white folks' weddings, with a preacher and everything. But slave or not, the Bible says it's wrong to be making a baby with a man unless you're married to him in the sight of God."

"I have to do what Missy says, don't I?" Kitty was so scared she could barely hold back her tears. She never should have told Delia. Now she and Grady were both upset, and Kitty was going to get into trouble for it.

"Please don't say anything," she begged. "Missy will get mad at me if I don't obey her, and she'll send me away to work in the rice fields again."

Delia pulled Kitty into her arms. "Don't worry, honey. I'll talk to Massa Roger for you. He's a good, God-fearing man. I know he won't allow this."

"He ain't home," Grady said. "And he ain't coming home until next week."

"Do you know how soon your Missy's planning this?" Delia asked.

Kitty squirmed out of Delia's arms and inched toward the door. She didn't want to say another word. She'd said too much already. "I need to go back upstairs. Missy will be looking for me."

"Wait," Delia said, stopping her. "I know you want to obey your mistress, but what she's planning on doing ain't right. You don't have any feelings for Martin. You don't want to be sleeping with him, do you?"

"No, but—"

"Then it's wrong for Missy to try and use you this way, just so she can get what she wants. Making babies is a God-given blessing when a man and woman love each other, when they're married to each other. It's wrong for Missy or anyone else to choose a man for you and force you to have a baby with him. Do you understand?"

Tears rolled down Kitty's cheeks. "I guess so, but—"

"Then please tell me when Missy's planning to do this. You won't get into trouble, I promise."

Kitty hesitated, unsure what to do. Grady looked angry enough to beat the truth out of her if she didn't tell. She decided to trust Delia. "Missy says she's going to talk to Martin tomorrow morning."

"We can't let this happen to her!" Grady shouted. "We're people, not animals! They can't be treating us this way! We have to hide her, Delia. Or help her run away."

"No!" Kitty cried out. "Terrible things happen if you try and run. They always catch you and—" She couldn't say the words. "I don't mind having a baby if that's what Missy wants. It don't matter." She tried to leave again, but Delia stopped her.

"Yes, it certainly does matter," she said. "Grady's right. We need to stop this, but running away ain't the answer. Maybe I can talk to Martin, and—"

"I'll marry her," Grady said.

Delia frowned. "How's that going to help?"

Grady reached for Kitty's hand, holding it gently in both of his. "You and me, Kitty—we'll jump the broom, okay?"

"Why are you offering?" Delia asked him.

Grady drew a deep breath. "When I worked for that slave trader I had to watch white folks mistreating slaves every single day for four years. And I had to help them do it. I hated it, Delia, and I swore I ain't gonna stand by and let them mistreat us no more. If I can stop this from happening to Kitty, I will. Missy can't be forcing her to sleep with Martin or anyone else if she's my wife. But I won't take advantage of her. We won't make a baby."

"But Missy says I have to have a baby before she does or—"

"No! We ain't helping the white people get one more slave! Listen, Delia. They won't ever know that she's my wife in name only. We'll get even with them. This is how we'll fight back. Someday when Kitty falls in love, she'll be free to be a real wife to someone because we won't . . ." His voice trailed off. "I won't touch her, Delia. I swear."

Delia studied him for a long moment. "You know you can't be running all around with other girls no more if you supposed to be married."

"I know. Will you help me do this, Delia?"

Kitty pulled her hand free from Grady's. She was very surprised that he'd promised to give up all his other girlfriends for her, but Missy would be furious if she and Grady didn't have a baby. "Please, I have to do what Missy says," she begged.

"You will, honey," Delia said. "Except that Grady wants to marry you. Wouldn't you rather be living with him than Martin?"

Kitty had often wished that Grady would take her in his arms again and kiss her the way he once had. She envied the closeness she saw between Missy Claire and Massa Fuller. "Yes, I guess so. But Missy Claire says—"

"I'll talk to Missy Claire," Delia said. "Don't you be worrying about a thing. She won't ever know what we talked about, I promise."

❧

Delia felt torn. It seemed like a crime to keep that poor girl so beaten down she had no self-respect at all. But if Delia taught Kitty to respect herself, then the abuse she suffered at her mistress's hands would become torture. It would probably break Kitty's heart to discover that the woman she thought cared for her was really mistreating her. Kitty had nobody else in the world to love, and the truth might even destroy her. Delia had tried to tell her about God's love, but so far her words had been met with true incomprehension.

At the same time, Grady's offer to marry Kitty had given Delia great hope for him. Even if his motives were revenge and the desire to fight back, he seemed to care about someone other than himself. Maybe this was the Lord's way of reaching Grady, to get him settled down and married. Maybe having a wife and babies to love would help crowd out the hatred. Because there was no doubt in Delia's mind that Grady would never be able to resist loving a girl as pretty as Kitty.

Delia didn't sleep much that night as she tried to sort out what the Lord was trying to do. And to make matters worse, this whole nasty business had stirred up memories of the abuse she had suffered. The Lord had helped her to forgive, in time. He'd given her a beautiful baby girl—a child who wasn't to blame for her father's crime. Hating was a poison, she'd learned, and God had worked everything out in the end. But even though the Lord had healed Delia's heart, it didn't stop the pain and sorrow from being stirred up all over again like coals of a fire when she saw another innocent slave girl about to be abused the same way.

Delia felt as though she'd lost a week's worth of sleep instead of one night's as she met with Missus Fuller and Martin in the morning room the next day. They met this way every day to discuss how the household would be run, what meals would be served, which guests were expected, and all the other tasks that needed to be done around the house. But after what Kitty had confided, Delia had a hard time feeling the respect she knew she should have for her mistress. She'd only known the new Missus Fuller for a short time, but she already wondered why Massa Roger had ever chosen to marry such a selfish, spoiled woman.

She'd prayed all night, hoping that Kitty had misunderstood; hoping that it was Missus Goodman's idea, not Missy Claire's, and that Missy would never carry out such a plan to mistreat her lifelong friend. Delia barely heard all of the other orders for the day as she continued to pray, asking the Lord to spare Kitty the abuse Delia herself had once suffered. But when the meeting was finished she heard Missy say, "You're excused, Delia. Martin, stay for a moment longer. I need to have a word with you."

Delia hadn't truly believed anyone could be so cruel until that moment. The injustice made her angry enough to tell a lie. God forgive her, but she would do it—not for revenge, but for Kitty's sake.

"Missus Fuller, there's something else I need to be asking you before I go," she said. "It's about your chambermaid, Kitty."

"Yes, what about her?"

Delia forced a big smile. "She's telling me all about how you're gonna give her the job of wet nurse, and she's real happy to have such a fine job. I was a wet nurse for Massa Roger when he was just a tiny baby and I know what a fine thing it is to be trusted with Massa's little baby that way. Kitty's real proud that you're asking her, ma'am."

"Then what's the problem?"

"She's afraid to tell you this, ma'am . . . but she's having someone else in mind to be the daddy of her baby."

Missus Fuller frowned as if the idea was ridiculous. "Oh, really? Who's that?"

"Massa's coachman, ma'am. His name's Grady. He's a strong, healthy young boy, and I know he can be making a whole bunch of slave babies with her if you give him a chance. Massa Fuller thinks the world of Grady, too, don't he, Martin?"

The butler looked at Delia warily, as if unsure where this conversation was headed. "That's true enough, ma'am," he finally said. "Grady's been working real hard for Massa all the years he's owning him."

"Grady's wanting to be with Kitty, too," Delia added. "They can be making babies in no time at all."

It pleased Delia to see that Missy Claire was blushing. The color showed up plain as day on her white face. Missy should feel embarrassed for what she was forcing her slaves to do. Delia only hoped she hadn't gone too far and made Claire angry by being so blunt.

"Fine. Kitty can be with the coachman," Claire said. "Is that all, Delia?"

"Then they have your permission to jump the broom?"

"To what?"

"That's the slave folks' ceremony for getting married. Massa Fuller always allows us to jump the broom as long as we ask him first. He knows his slaves are happier and they're working harder if they're getting married and having families of their own. Kitty and Grady will be needing your permission, since Massa ain't here. But once they jump the broom, I'm sure they'll do what you want them to do right away."

Missy's cheeks were so bright it was as if she had stood uncovered in the sun too long. She seemed very eager to end this discussion. "Fine. Have your little broom ceremony or whatever you call it," she said with a wave of her hand, "as long as it doesn't interfere with Kitty's work. Tell the two of them this won't change any of their other duties."

"Thank you, ma'am."

As Delia left the room, she heard Missy say, "Never mind, Martin. You're excused."

<hr>

Grady stood alone in Massa's rear courtyard, staring blindly at the puddles that dotted the brick pavement. The wind blew through the tree branches overhead, showering Grady with drops of cold water. It had finally stopped raining, but the night was cloudy and moonless. He and Kitty would have to jump the broom by lantern light.

He had wanted to get their phony wedding over with quickly, with no fussing at all. But Massa had returned home earlier than expected and insisted on throwing a regular party for Grady and his bride. Massa told them to wait until Saturday night, the end of a long workday, so the slaves could stay up late and have the following day free.

"Invite all your friends," he'd insisted. "Faye can roast some pork and we'll buy a keg of cider." Massa Fuller even promised to come outside with his wife to watch.

"You sure picked a gloomy night to get married, young man."

Grady turned to face a tall white man dressed in black. He was wearing a preacher's collar. "I'm Reverend John Howard, and I'm here to perform the ceremony," he said with a smile. "Delia tells me you're the lucky groom."

"That's right. I am." This wedding was getting out of hand as far as Grady was concerned. He certainly hadn't wanted no preacher-man to come—and a white preacher, at that. "Where's Delia?" he asked harshly. The preacher's smile faded.

"She and the others are setting up the buffet table in the wash-house in case it starts raining again."

"Excuse me. I need to have a word with her."

"Now what?" Delia said when Grady pulled her aside. "You ain't having second thoughts, are you?"

"What's he doing here?" Grady asked, gesturing to the minister with a tilt of his head. "I don't want no preacher at this thing. He ain't supposed to be part of this. We was just gonna jump the broom, plain and simple."

"Oh no, you don't," Delia said. "I ain't letting you two set up housekeeping together unless you're married in the sight of God. Reverend Howard's here to make sure everything's legal."

"I already told you, I ain't touching Kitty. Don't you trust me?"

Delia shook her head. "No, sir. You're only human, Grady. But that ain't why I asked him here. The other slaves are gonna know if it's fake. So will Massa Fuller. We ain't fooling him or anybody else. I'm doing this to protect Kitty from her missy, because she's gonna get good and mad when you and Kitty don't have a baby on time. We got to make sure she don't give Kitty away to another man."

"I still don't see why we need a preacher."

"He ain't here for you, he's here for Kitty. That gal deserves to have a real wedding with a real man of God. He's gonna write everything down in his record book: On this date Massa Fuller's coachman, Grady, and Missus Fuller's chambermaid, Kitty, was legally married in the sight of God. Amen."

Grady stormed across the courtyard and up to his room above

the stable to let his temper cool. The room, which used to be Jesse's, looked different already with Kitty's bundle of clothing and other belongings setting in the corner. Jim had built a new bed for the two of them, and it took up a lot more space in the room than Grady's old one had. He'd moved his old bed downstairs to an empty corner of the stable. No one would know that he crept down there every night to sleep.

Grady lit a lantern so Kitty could find her way upstairs in the dark later on, and he noticed her pile of drawings lying on top of her other belongings. He picked up the pages and rifled through them, shaking his head at the simple beauty of her work. How did she capture the grace of a tree or a bird or a face in just a few simple lines the way she did? It bothered him to see that she still crowded dozens of pictures onto one page in order to save paper, filling both the back and the front. Didn't she have anyone she could trust to buy her some more paper once it ran out? Grady knew the answer to that question.

He sighed and put the pictures back where he'd found them. Delia was right; no telling what Missus Fuller would do if she found out Kitty was deceiving her. He supposed he could put up with a white preacher and a little Jesus-talk for Kitty's sake.

When everything was ready, Kitty came down from her old bedroom to stand beside Grady in the courtyard. She wore one of the only two dresses she owned, but she had removed her work apron for the occasion. She looked scared to death. When Grady took her hand in his it felt as cold as spring water. He felt angry, not scared—furious with all these white people for making this sham marriage necessary. He barely paid attention to the minister as he made Grady promise to love Kitty all of his life and she promised to love him in return. Instead, he silently raged at the injustice that forced them to do this.

Massa Fuller and his wife had come out to watch, standing off to one side, away from all the slaves. Grady was aware of Missus Fuller's sharp eyes on them, so when Reverend Howard said, "You may kiss your bride,"he kissed Kitty with more than enough passion to be convincing. They were legally married.

Next thing Grady knew, Martin and Delia were standing in front of him and Kitty, holding up an old broomstick. "Time to jump the broom," Delia said. "Whoever lands first is gonna be head of the house."

Grady put his arm around Kitty's waist so she wouldn't trip over the handle—but he made sure he landed first. "Kiss her again!" Jim shouted, and all the slaves began banging pots and clapping their hands until he did.

The night was cold and raw, and as soon as Massa Fuller had offered his congratulations, he and his wife went back inside the house. Grady was relieved when they took the white minister with them. Everyone else crowded into the washhouse where Faye and the others had prepared a table full of food. Jim had built a fire. The party grew noisy as people ate and drank their fill. Everyone seemed happy for them, offering Grady and Kitty their wishes for a long, happy marriage. He felt a little ashamed for deceiving them, but Delia had insisted that no one but the three of them should ever know the truth.

When the food was gone and the night had grown late, the guests all began clapping and cheering and banging pots, refusing to stop until Grady carried his bride into the stable and up the stairs to their room. The guests stood outside in the courtyard below his window, continuing their racket as Grady snuffed out the lantern. He and Kitty sat side by side on the bed until the wild cheers finally subsided below them.

"It's dark in here," Kitty whispered.

"Yeah. There's no moon tonight. . . . Are you okay? Want me to build a fire?"

"No." She exhaled as if she'd been holding her breath all night. "I sure hope Missy don't find out that the only reason we done this was to make her mad. You didn't tell nobody, did you?"

"Of course not. But that ain't the only reason, you know." It was hard for Grady to admit the truth, especially to himself. "I did it so you wouldn't get hurt. I like you, Kitty. We're . . . we're friends, ain't we?"

"Yeah. We are."

"Kitty," he began, then stopped. He hated calling her by that name, an animal's name, especially after Missy Claire had tried to breed her like one, saying she had no more feelings than a horse or cow. "Is Kitty your real name or is it short for Kate or Katherine or something?"

"Missy Claire named me Kitty the first day I came to live in the Big House. Her mama wouldn't let her have a real cat, so she pretended I was her kitten."

"*What!*"

"Shh . . . It don't matter, Grady," she said, squeezing his hand. "I had fun being a cat. After a while the name just stuck to me, I guess."

He clenched his jaw, wanting to murder Missus Fuller. "What was your name before that?" he asked when he could speak.

"Why are you so angry? How come talking about names makes you so mad?"

He drew a deep breath, then exhaled, trying to calm himself. "My mama named me Grady. *That's* my name—the one *she* gave me. When the slave trader bought me he changed it to Joe. It was his way of having control over me. You have a lot of power over somebody if you can change who he is. See this scar on my forehead? I made the mistake once of telling him my name was Grady, not Joe. He beat me with a fireplace poker for it. But my name ain't Joe. It's Grady."

She touched his forehead lightly, then looked away.

"Don't give that white lady power over who you are. She has no right to be changing your name and . . . and turning you into an animal. Only a mama who knows you and loves you has the right to name you."

She was quiet for a moment, then said, "My mama called me Anna."

"Anna," he repeated. "That's beautiful. Just like you are. From now on I'm going to call you Anna, too."

"Please don't do that. Missy's gonna get real mad if she hears you calling me that."

"She won't hear me. Besides, that's what this is all about," he said, gesturing to the room. "That's why we jumped the broom."

"Because you want to make Missy mad?"

"No. I want to stop her from hurting you. I just wish . . ."

"What?"

"I wish you wouldn't be letting her treat you the way she does. I wish you could see that it's wrong and . . . and that you'd want to fight back as much as I do. You deserve better."

"It don't matter to me, Grady. I learned a long time ago that it don't do any good to be getting mad at Missy. I'm still her slave. That ain't never going to change. This is just the way Missy is. She can't help it."

"See? That's what I mean. You don't even realize what she's doing to you."

"But I'm happy, Grady. Are you?"

"How can I possibly be happy when my life ain't my own? When I'm somebody's slave? Their property?"

"You get angry so fast, and it seems like for no reason at all, sometimes. I don't want to be mad all the time like you are. I can't be living that way. Tell you the truth, you scare me a little. I think you could get mad enough to hurt somebody."

Grady gently wrapped his arm around her shoulders and pulled her close. "Don't be scared of me, Anna. I'd never hurt you."

"I been with Missy a long time. I know that even when she's acting angry, she don't really mean it. But I think you do mean it."

He released her again. "If I'm angry, it's because we were meant to be free and we ain't."

"Does getting mad change anything? Does it make you free?"

"It helps me, okay? Your way of dealing with it is to shrug it off. Getting mad is my way."

194

"How does hating white people help?"

"It's their own fault if I hate them! They taught me how. My first master was my own father—and he sold me! The second one used to beat me just because he enjoyed it. He was always trying to break my will, pounding all the hope right out of me. Then there were the four white boys who lived near Massa's plantation. You want to see what they done to me? For no reason?" He lifted his shirt and turned so Kitty could see his back. Her icy fingers caressed his skin as she felt the lumpy scars.

"I'm so sorry," she whispered.

"Why are you sorry? You didn't do it!" He pulled his shirt down again and stood up to tuck it in.

"That ain't what I meant, Grady. I'm sorry you been treated so bad. I never had it as bad as you, or maybe I'd be angry, too."

"But you *have* been treated badly. I wish I could make you understand that. Missy ain't your friend. What she wanted to force you to do with Martin was just as bad, just as degrading as what them four white boys done to me."

Kitty closed her eyes. Grady was afraid she was going to cry. When she opened them again she said, "Then I'm glad that you saved me, Grady. Thank you."

Her words defused his anger. He stood, looking down at her, then bent and took her face in his hands. He kissed her gently.

"Good night, Anna," he whispered.

Grady longed to stay with her. But he refused to give the white folks what they wanted, even if it meant giving up what he wanted. He left his wife sitting on the bed in the dark and hurried downstairs to sleep, alone.

13

CHARLESTON, SOUTH CAROLINA
APRIL 1861

The room was still dark when the first cannon fired. The explosion jolted Kitty awake and for a moment she forgot where she was. She sat up on her pallet, her heart thudding, and saw bright flashes of light outside the window. Then she remembered saying good-bye to Delia and Grady, and leaving Beaufort to travel back to Massa Goodman's Charleston town house with Missy. A moment later, Kitty heard three more explosions. The floor trembled and the windows rattled with every boom.

"Kitty!" Missy Claire called in a frightened voice. "Light the lamps! Hurry!"

Kitty scrambled to obey. This was why Missy had insisted that Kitty sleep on the floor of her room all night instead of out back in the slaves' quarters. She saw Missy sitting upright in the big feather bed, clutching the covers to her bosom.

"Fetch my robe and shoes," she said. "I want to go out on the piazza and see what's going on."

Kitty put on her own shawl and went outside to stand beside Missy on the third-floor porch. They both shivered in the early dawn air. Out in the harbor in front of them, the horizon glowed like a sheet of orange flame. Battery after battery of heavy guns pounded Fort Sumter with a rumbling, thundering noise that never ceased. Kitty could see cannon fire pouring into the distant fort from three sides.

Massa Goodman joined them a moment later, wrapping one arm around his daughter's shoulders as they stared into the distance. "Well, it has begun," he said grimly. "The war is on."

Kitty had stood here with Missy and her father last evening and heard him explain the coming battle. Rebel forces were stationed on Morris Island and James Island on their right, at Castle Pinkney and Fort Ripley in front of them, and at Mount Pleasant and Sullivan's Island on their left. Fort Sumter was nearly surrounded as all these batteries aimed their cannons at it, demanding surrender by four o'clock in the morning on April 12. Missy's new husband was out in the middle of it all, stationed with the Beaufort Artillery at a place called Fort Stevens on Morris Island. His sons were among the cadets from the Citadel who manned guns in White Point Gardens, just down the street from the house. They would fire on any warships that sailed past the batteries and into the harbor to bombard the city.

As the cannonading continued, dense smoke filled the horizon, shielding everything from view, at times, except flashes of fire. Kitty thought that the dull gray color of the sky and the water and the smoke was a good color to paint death and destruction. It was the color of tombstones. Only the brilliant speckles of red and orange from exploding shells and flames relieved the gloom.

Eventually she went back inside with Missy to help her dress. But Missy wouldn't eat, worried as she was about her husband. The bombardment went on and on, until it seemed to Kitty that the whole city of Charleston shook like an earthquake.

Later that morning, Massa Goodman's friends and family members began to arrive, gathering on the piazzas to watch the battle out in the harbor. They talked in quiet, grave voices, as if at a funeral. On the streets below, masses of people crowded along the promenade to watch. They'd done the same thing last evening as they'd waited for the battle to begin. Now it had, and spectators packed every rooftop and piazza and street along the waterfront.

Hours passed as the deafening noise continued. Kitty could see streaks of flame and smoke shooting out from the fort as Union soldiers returned fire on the ring of batteries surrounding them. The air was thick with the smell of gunpowder and smoke. Missy Claire's sisters and aunts and cousins huddled together, weeping for all their loved ones who were taking part in the battle.

"I can't bear this terrible waiting," one of her cousins moaned. "If only we would hear some news."

"I wish Roger had never left Beaufort," Missy wept. "Why did he have to come here to fight?"

Kitty had heard Massa Roger explain the reason to Missy when they were still home in Beaufort. "The U.S. government is trying to send a ship to resupply Fort Sumter," he'd said. "The Rebels ordered them to abandon the fort or face hostile fire." Massa's artillery unit had been needed to help force the Yankees to surrender.

But Delia had offered a different explanation. "The Lord's hearing our prayers," she'd told the slaves as they'd gathered in the kitchen in Beaufort. "That's what this is all about, not some silly old fort. There's a bunch of good Christian folks up north who been working hard to set us all free. The slave owners here in South Carolina know that, and they all fighting to keep us slaves."

Kitty missed Delia. She missed Grady, too. They hadn't been allowed to come to Charleston. As she stood on the piazza of the Goodmans' town house, Kitty didn't think that the little fort out in the harbor looked like it was worth fighting for. She listened to the rolling boom of artillery fire and the women weeping, and she wondered how it would all end. Was all this noise and fear necessary just so Missy and the others could keep their slaves?

"I can't watch anymore," Missy said. But she stayed anyway, twisting her handkerchief in her hands.

"Can I get you anything, Missy Claire?" Kitty asked.

"No! This is all your fault!"

Kitty knew she didn't mean it. Missy Claire was just upset because Massa Fuller was out there where all the shooting was going on. Kitty wondered what it would be like if Grady was fighting in a war, being shot at this way. What if she didn't know if he were dead or alive—or if she would ever see him again? The thought upset her. Even though they'd only been married a short time, even though it wasn't a real marriage like Missy Claire's, she still cared about Grady. And she believed that he cared for her, too. He'd given up all his other girlfriends just for her. That meant something, didn't it?

"Why can't the North just leave us alone instead of trying to interfere with our way of life?" Missy said. "It's none of their business if you're my slave," she told Kitty.

"Save your breath," Missy's cousin said, comforting her. "Slaves are too stupid to even understand what we're talking about."

"I'm not so sure about that," another cousin said. "I saw a bunch of our slaves whispering together this morning. I think they're just biding their time, waiting to start an uprising. They may act stupid, but they hate us, you know."

"No, they don't."

But Kitty knew at least one slave who did. Grady hated white folks enough to murder them all in their beds.

Missus Goodman joined the little group to try to comfort Missy. "Maybe you should go inside and lie down, Claire."

"That won't help. I can still hear the battle. Oh, why didn't Roger take an exemption, like Father did? He owns more than twenty slaves. He didn't have to be drafted."

"You're just going to get yourself all worked up for nothing," Missus Goodman said.

"It's hardly *nothing*, Mother. If Roger dies, then *I'll* have nothing. Everything will go to his son, Ellis, instead of to me. Not only that, but I'll have to be in mourning for at least a year. I won't be able to remarry for ages."

A prickle of fear shuddered through Kitty at her words. If Massa

Fuller died, Grady would belong to one owner and she to another. They would be torn apart, just as her parents had been. Like Missy Claire, Kitty began to fear for Massa's life, too.

"As soon as this ends, you'd better hurry up and have a son," Mrs. Goodman told Missy. "He won't be Roger's firstborn, but at least he'll be entitled to a portion of his estate."

"I'm doing the best I can, Mother."

A while later, Massa Goodman pulled out his pocket watch. "Well, it's been going on for twelve hours now," he announced, "and there's still no sign of a surrender."

"Maybe there's no one alive over there to raise the flag," one of the men said. "We've been pouring thousands of rounds of ammunition into the place."

"No, they're still firing back," another gentleman said. "Here, see for yourself." He offered his opera glasses to Massa Goodman for a better look.

"Yes, it looks like the Yankees are pounding Fort Moultrie at the moment. I wonder how much longer this will go on."

Kitty wondered, too. She was tired of standing outside on the piazza, tired of the noise and the smoke and the fear. She wanted Massa to come back safely so she could go home to Beaufort. The thought startled her. Was Beaufort her home? She had lived there for only a few months—how had it become home to her already? Kitty knew the answer: Grady and Delia were there.

Just before dinner, a messenger finally arrived with some news. "There have been no injuries at any of our batteries on Morris and Sullivan's Islands," he announced. A cheer went up from the little group. "Fort Stevens was hit several times, but there was no damage and no casualties. That means Roger is fine."

Missy's knees went weak with relief. She fell into her mother's arms in a swoon. Kitty ran inside to fetch the smelling salts.

By six o'clock it had begun to rain, and everyone moved indoors. It was still storming at bedtime, the wind whipping tree branches against the house and lashing rain against the windows. But the terrible bombardment never let up. Missy ordered Kitty to remain with her for the night, sleeping on the floor beside the bed again, in case she was needed. Kitty curled up with a blanket, but she didn't sleep. At dawn, a full day after the first cannon had fired, the battle still raged.

The storm had cleared away much of the smoke, and the sky was so brilliantly blue it made Kitty's chest ache. One of Massa Goodman's relatives set up a telescope on the piazza, and the men took turns gazing through it, describing what they saw to the anxious ladies.

"Sumter's on fire. There's a lot of black smoke, and I think I see flames. . . . Yes, I definitely see flames."

The ladies cheered delicately and clapped their hands.

"Looks like three or four Union ships are anchored out there beyond the bar, but they don't seem inclined to join the battle."

"That's because they know we'll blow them out of the water if they come within range."

Massa Goodman was peering through the telescope after lunch when Kitty heard him exclaim, "Look! They've taken down the Stars and Stripes! They're flying the white flag!"

"No! Are you sure?"

"Yes! Yes! See for yourself!"

Kitty's heart pounded with excitement and hope. Maybe now all this terrible worrying would end. Massa would come back, and they could all return home to Beaufort. Missy would have a baby, and maybe Grady would change his mind and give Kitty one, too.

The bombardment slowed to a halt. Then silence. The terrible shooting had finally stopped. The hush seemed eerie after a day and a half of thunderous noise. Everyone waited for the smoke to clear.

"The white flag is definitely flying," Massa Goodman said. "And I can see a ship of truce heading toward the fort."

It was over. As soon as Missy Claire received the news that there had been no fatalities on either side, she went to her room, lay down on her bed, and wept. Church bells pealed all over the city, and the cadets in White Point Gardens sent up a seven-gun salute, one for each state in the new Confederacy. Massa Goodman and all the other gentlemen hurried to the docks, boarding any ship they could find to sail out to the victorious batteries to celebrate.

When Kitty went outside to the kitchen for dinner, she found the mood among the slaves quiet and subdued. "What do you think all this excitement means?" she asked them.

Albert the coachman sighed. "It means we're all gonna be slaves a while longer," he said.

On Sunday afternoon, just as Kitty was leaving the house with Missy Claire to watch the cadets' dress parade at White Point Gardens, a carriage pulled to a halt in front of the house. Massa Fuller stepped out, his face dirty, his nice new uniform smudged with soot. Kitty felt as relieved to see him as her mistress did. Claire ran into his arms.

"Thank God you're safe, Roger. And thank God it's over."

"Yes, but I'm afraid it has only begun, Claire. There's likely to be a full-scale war now."

His words sent a tremor of fear through Kitty. She thought she understood now what a war was all about—bombs falling and guns shooting, the endless waiting and uncertainty and fear. The past few days had been frightening enough for all of them. She didn't want to think about an entire future spent that way.

"But at least we won the first battle," Massa Roger said, smiling. "God willing, we'll win all the rest of them, too."

"Come inside," Missy Claire said, leading him up the front steps. "How long can you stay?"

"My artillery unit has been ordered back to Beaufort. We're leaving tomorrow morning."

Kitty could have danced with joy. But Massa's next words filled her with dread.

"Claire, I know it's lonely for you in Beaufort, especially since I'm away so often. I'll understand if you would like to stay here in Charleston with your family."

Kitty held her breath, waiting for Missy to decide, hoping she wouldn't choose to stay. Kitty would have to stay here in Charleston with her.

"I want to be with you, Roger," Missy finally said.

Kitty closed her eyes in relief. She was going home—home to Grady and Delia. When she opened them again, she felt tears in her eyes. She quickly excused herself, so Missy wouldn't notice, and ran upstairs to start packing for the trip.

❈

BEAUFORT, SOUTH CAROLINA
JUNE 1861

Kitty balanced Missy Claire's breakfast tray in one hand so she could knock softly on her bedroom door with the other. As soon as she heard Missy mumble something, she went inside.

"I brought you some break—"

"Take it away!" Missy shouted. "I don't even want to smell food!" She leaned over the side of the bed, holding both hands over her mouth as if she was about to be sick.

Kitty quickly retreated, closing the door behind her. She stood in the hallway for a moment, wondering what to do, then set the tray down on the hall table and slipped back into the room without it. "You needing the basin, Missy Claire?"

"No . . . there's nothing in my stomach." She lay back against the pillows again, her face pale. Kitty picked up a folding fan and waved it to cool her.

"Is that better, Missy?"

"I don't think I can help out at the hospital today," she said weakly. "I don't feel very well."

"Should I tell them 'never mind' about getting your carriage ready?"

Missy nodded. The two of them had been going downtown to a warehouse on the wharf every day this week, working with the other women of Beaufort to organize a small two-room hospital. It would be used, if necessary, for injured soldiers who were from outside the Beaufort area. Soldiers from town would be nursed in their own homes, of course. Kitty had enjoyed working alongside her mistress and the other slaves, and she was disappointed that they weren't going today. But she was also very worried about Missy. She had been feeling sick and miserable for the past two days, but she'd never wanted to stay in bed before.

"I think I better go fetch Delia, Missy Claire. She would know which doctor Massa Fuller would send for if he was home."

Missy waved her hand in dismissal as if too sick to reply, and Kitty ran downstairs to find Delia. "Missy hasn't eaten much at all for the past few days," she explained as the older woman slowly plodded up the steps with her. "This morning she didn't even want to smell the food, and she's too sick to get out of bed. Should we send for the doctor?"

Delia glanced at the breakfast tray as she paused in the upstairs hallway to catch her breath. "Well, let's see . . ." She led the way into the room, leaving the door open.

"Shut the door!" Missy yelled. "That bacon smells nauseating!"

Kitty quickly pushed the door closed, then picked up the fan again to chase the smell away from Missy's nose.

Delia stood beside the bed, looking down at her. "I can fetch the doctor for you if you want me to, Missus Fuller, but I think I know what he's gonna say."

"What?"

"Well, first he's gonna ask when's the last time you had the 'curse of women.'"

Missy's cheeks flushed bright pink. Kitty fanned harder.

"Then he's gonna ask if you're feeling a little tender up on top when Kitty pulls the corset laces tight."

Missy nodded slightly.

"Well, I ain't no doctor," Delia said, "but it looks to me like you're gonna have a baby, Missus Fuller."

She groaned. "How long will I feel this way? I can't even bear the thought of food."

"The sickness usually goes away in two or three months. I can fix you some tea that might help. So will a little plain toast. Shall I go fetch you a tray?"

"Fine. As long as you don't bring me any food with a strong smell."

Kitty was relieved to know that her mistress's illness wasn't something serious like measles or ague. She wondered why Missy didn't look any happier. "That's real good news, ain't it, Missy?" she said after Delia left. "I know you been wanting to give Massa Fuller a baby. Maybe now you will."

Missy groaned and pulled the covers up to her chin. "I didn't know that having a baby was going to make me feel this awful."

Kitty smiled to try and cheer her up, but Missy returned the look with an angry glare. "And what about you? You should be feeling just as miserable as I do by now. Why haven't you and that stupid coachman of yours made a baby yet?"

A jolt of fear shot through Kitty. She had been so afraid this would happen, so afraid that Missy would get mad. She wished Delia would hurry back and help her explain things. But there was no sign of Delia. "I-I don't know why, Missy Claire. I'm sorry—"

"Sorry doesn't help. What am I going to do about a wet nurse? You were supposed to have a baby before I did."

"I-I know, Missy. But getting upset is only gonna make you feel worse. Let me get Delia. She'll know how to help."

"Never mind about Delia." Missy struggled to sit up in bed. "Now, you listen to me, girl. You'd better do what you're told in the next few weeks or I'll have to find someone else to replace you. Do you want to go back to the rice fields?"

"No, ma'am."

"Well, if you don't have a baby soon, that's exactly where you're going. You're worthless to me without a baby. If you aren't going to be my wet nurse, then I'll fetch one from Great Oak Plantation and I'll send you back there."

It was not an idle threat. Kitty knew that Missy Claire would do it. Why had Kitty ever agreed to deceive her? The worst thing she could have possibly done was to make Missy angry. Now she was going to separate her and Grady and send her away from the home and the people she'd grown to love.

Kitty worried about what to do for the rest of the day. Missy yelled at her for every little thing and glared angrily at her every time she walked into the room, reminding Kitty of her dilemma. "I shouldn't have trusted you," Missy growled as Kitty brushed her hair. "I should have known it would be a mistake to rely on you."

Late that afternoon, Grady returned home with Massa Fuller for the first time in nearly a week. But Kitty had no opportunity to talk to him alone or even to ask Delia what to do. She worried and worried, picturing the drab slaves' cabins back at Great Oak Plantation, remembering the rice fields and the sting of the overseer's lash, and imagining life without Grady. By the time she returned to her own room to go to sleep, Kitty knew what she needed to do. She lit a candle and sat down on the bed, waiting for Grady to come upstairs to get his blankets.

"Where have you and Massa been running off to every day?" she asked before he could go back downstairs for the night. "You're hardly ever home these days."

"I know," he said wearily. "Now that the war has started, all the white folks are acting crazy."

"What does Massa do all day?"

Grady sighed and sank down on a wooden crate. "Him and all the other white men are getting a regiment together called the Ninth South Carolina volunteers to try and protect the seacoast. They're worried that the Yankees are gonna come with a bunch of warships and try and take Beaufort."

"You think the Yankees are gonna come here?"

"I don't know," he said with a shrug. "But Massa and the others are building two big forts to try and stop them."

"Here in town? Over on the Point?"

He shook his head. "Give me your pencil and I'll show you."

Kitty brought him the pencil and a scrap of paper, then crouched beside him as he drew a rough map.

"Beaufort and Port Royal are inland from the ocean, on a bay. The Rebels are building Fort Walker over here on Hilton Head Island, and Fort Beauregard across from it on St. Helena Island to guard the entrance into the bay. The Yankees are gonna have to sail right between the two forts to get to Beaufort."

"Missy Claire said Massa's been going down to the Green on the Point every day. She said we was gonna go over sometime and watch him drilling all the soldiers."

"Yeah, we been going over there, too," Grady said with another sigh. "There's a whole bunch of new soldiers that are needing to be trained, so they're using the Green. They're camping over there and everything. When the forts are done, most of the soldiers will be sent there. The rest will guard the railroad between Charleston and Savannah. The town of Pocotaligo is on that railroad line, halfway between the two cities. It's only eighteen miles from here."

"And you been driving Massa to all these places?" she asked.

"Yeah. And then standing around in the heat all day, waiting for him. Here . . ." Grady handed her the paper and pencil, then stood and stretched. "I drew real lightly so you could erase it again."

She watched him unbutton his shirt and hang it on the peg where he kept his clothes. He usually undressed in the dark but Kitty had left the candle burning as they'd talked. When he turned his back, she saw the mass of ugly scars crisscrossing his beautiful brown skin. She longed to smooth them away, to make his skin whole again, and to erase the memory of that night. As long as the scars were there to remind him, she knew that Grady was never going to erase the hatred he felt, either.

She laid down the paper and went to him, embracing him from behind, resting her cheek against his shoulder. She felt the June sunshine in the sweaty warmth of his body and inhaled his scent of leather and horses.

"Hey, now. What's the hug for?" he asked.

"I missed you, Grady." Delia had told her that making a baby wasn't wrong if she was married. She and Grady were.

He turned and pulled her close, wrapping her tightly in his arms, laying his cheek against her hair. She felt the strength in his arms and shoulders, and knew she was safe.

"Anna . . ." he whispered.

She savored his embrace for a long moment, then lifted her face for his kiss. She saw the longing in his eyes, but he pried her arms from around his waist and stepped back.

"Don't," he said.

"Why not?"

"Because I want you . . . and I won't be able to stop with one kiss."

"I don't want you to stop," she said, embracing him again. "We're married, Grady. We love each other. It's okay."

He pulled her close again and kissed her. At first he was gentle and tender with her. But Kitty felt his growing passion, and a glow of warmth spread through her like candle wax melting beneath a flame. It was the most wonderful feeling she ever had. She never wanted his kisses to end.

But they did. Grady stopped suddenly. She felt a shiver pass all the way through him. He pushed her away again.

"I need to go."

He turned his back on her and rummaged quickly through his belongings, as if eager to flee. Kitty felt a terrible loss. She had made up her mind to entice him tonight because she was afraid of Missy's punishment, but everything had changed once he'd started kissing her. She loved him. And she wanted desperately for him to love her in return. He was only a few feet away from her, but as he hurried toward the door, she never felt more alone in her life. Kitty covered her face and wept.

Grady paused in the doorway. "Anna, please don't cry. I'm sorry . . . I wish things could be different. But they can't."

Kitty cried harder still. She hadn't wept this way since the day she'd learned about her parents. She couldn't make herself stop.

Grady came back and held her gently. She could feel him restraining the desire he'd shown a moment ago, as if trying to halt a galloping horse. "Don't cry . . . please."

"I don't understand," she sobbed. "We're man and wife. We've been married for four months. I want to be with you, Grady."

"I know, Anna, but we can't. I'm sorry . . . I need to go." He released her and turned to leave.

Kitty felt a wave of panic as she remembered Missy's threats. She and Grady were going to be torn apart forever, just like her parents had been.

"Grady, wait! Missy's gonna separate us if we don't have a baby!"

He froze in the doorway, then slowly turned to face her. "Is that what this is all about?"

"Missy found out she's gonna have a baby, and she said she's gonna send me back to Great Oak Plantation if we don't have one, too."

He closed his eyes. When he opened them again, Kitty saw shock and sorrow and anger all mingled together on his face. "You started this tonight because *she's* wanting you to?" he asked.

"Grady, listen—"

"I guess that makes me a pretty big fool. I thought you really cared."

"I do care! I love you, Grady."

"No, Anna. First you have to love yourself. Then you'll be able to love somebody else."

"What do you mean? What makes you think I don't?"

"Because if you had any self-respect at all, you wouldn't be wanting to do everything Missy Claire's telling you to do."

"But she's gonna send me away!"

"Maybe that ain't such a bad thing. Maybe if you got away from her, you'd start seeing things more clearly."

"Don't you love me, Grady?"

The surprise and sadness faded from his eyes. The only thing left was anger. "Can't nobody love you, girl, until you learn to love yourself. You obey that white woman like you were her dog—like you're dirt under her feet and she can walk all over you. Think a man can love dirt? Think a man wants a dog for his woman?"

"Grady, wait! Come back!" But he slammed the door on his way out, and his footsteps thundered down the stairs. A moment later the stable door slammed, too. Kitty lay down on the bed and sobbed.

A long while later she heard the stairs creaking as someone slowly ascended them. She looked up, hoping to see Grady coming back to apologize, but when the door opened, it was Delia.

"Grady asked me to come," she said. "He told me what happened."

"I love him, Delia."

She sat down on the bed where Kitty lay and gently stroked her hair. "Are you sure, honey? Because Grady told me you was worried about Missy Claire being mad at you."

"She's gonna send me back to Great Oak Plantation if I don't have a baby."

"No, she won't. She might be needing to find another slave for a wet nurse, but she won't be sending you away. She depends on you. You said it yourself, time and time again—Missy's acting mad but she don't really mean it. She's feeling poorly right now, that's all."

"But I do love Grady. I think about him all the time when he's away. And when he kisses me I . . . I don't ever want him to stop. You said it wasn't wrong to make a baby if we're married and if I loved him. I do love him, Delia. And I can tell by the way he kisses me that he loves me, too."

"Honey, you need to forget about loving Grady."

"But he's my husband. Why are you telling me to forget him?"

"The only thing you're gonna get from Grady is your heart broke. I love that boy like he was my own, but he can't love anybody back."

"What do you mean? Why not?"

"He got his own heart broken when he was a little boy, snatched away from a mama who loved him. He traveled with that soul trader for four years and saw folks ripped away from their loved ones every day, bought and sold like cattle. Now he's scared to love you, scared he might lose you, too—and he's got a right to be scared. Slaves are getting torn apart from their husbands and wives all the time."

That was exactly what Missy had threatened to do. Kitty remembered her own parents again and shivered.

"Besides, Grady's heart is too filled with hate to make any room for love," Delia continued. "He's gonna have to get rid of it all, first. But the way things been going—him getting whipped by those paddyrollers and all—the hate just keeps getting worse and worse."

"How can I help him?"

"The only one who can help him is Jesus, and right now Grady's mad at Him, too."

"Why's he mad at Jesus?"

"People are always thinking they can use the Lord to get their own way—all they have to do is pray and God's gonna take away all their suffering and give them whatever they ask for. But it don't work that way. God's doing His business, and it's up to us to be serving Him, not the other way around."

"Then why do people pray at all? My papa asked Jesus to help him escape with me when I was just a little girl. But Jesus didn't help us."

"Praying ain't about asking for your own way. It's all about talking things over with God, just like you and me are talking things over. In the end, you have to be trusting the Lord to do what's best."

"So the Lord thought it was best that my papa died and my mama was sold?"

Delia slowly shook her head. "I don't know, honey. I just don't know. The hardest thing of all to understand is why a loving God keeps letting us suffer. That's what Grady's always wrestling with, too. I don't know what to tell him because I don't know all the answers myself. I seen my share of suffering, believe me. But there's two things I do know for sure. One is that God loves us—you, me, Grady, and even the white folks. And the second thing is that God's always in control of everything that happens. When bad things come our way and it starts looking like He don't love us, all I can say is that maybe we ain't knowing everything He knows."

Kitty's tears started falling again. "I still don't understand."

"Remember what you told me about the fighting up in Charleston? How you was standing on that porch, not able to see what's going on? This here's the same thing. We're standing in the smoke, hearing the noise all around us, and we don't know what God's doing because we can't see things as clearly as He sees them. But He's gonna make everything turn out okay when the smoke clears. When it does, God's gonna be the winner and all our suffering here on earth is gonna finally make sense. We're gonna look in Jesus' face and say, 'O Lord, it was worth it all.'"

"What should I do about Missy Claire? She's real mad at me, Delia. I can tell."

"She'll get over it. Sooner or later she'll figure out that she can't be snapping her fingers and making somebody have a baby just because she wants them to."

"And what about Grady?"

"Don't be tempting that poor boy no more, honey. He's already carrying around a load that's much too big for his shoulders."

Kitty began to cry again as soon as she was alone. If only Grady were here to hold her in the darkness. If only they could have a baby like Missy wanted them to. Maybe then this terrible dread Kitty felt would finally go away.

14

BEAUFORT, SOUTH CAROLINA
NOVEMBER 1861

The fall Sunday had started out so perfectly, Kitty thought. The weather was sunny and clear, Massa Fuller and Grady were home after being gone for a week, and Missy Claire's morning sickness had finally passed—and with it, her threats and crabby moods. Kitty helped Missy get dressed in one of her newly altered dresses, and she and Massa Fuller went to church together to pray with the other white folks about the war. Kitty sat outside on the carriage seat beside Grady, listening to the distant organ music and sketching the pretty white church with its graceful steeple. As Grady watched her, they talked quietly, the way they used to talk in Charleston. Kitty felt happier than she had in many months.

Then the white folks began streaming from the church, their faces grim, their voices grave and subdued. The seed of fear that had first taken root in Kitty's stomach at the battle for Fort Sumter sprouted anew. She could tell by the way the white folks acted that things were about to change again. The war must have worsened. The happiness she felt was about to vanish.

"Pay attention to what they say at lunch," Grady whispered to her on the drive home. He'd been trying to follow the war's progress, eavesdropping on Massa's conversations as he drove him around Beaufort or out to the fort. He wanted Delia and Kitty to do the same, to remember every detail they heard about the battles that had been fought and who had won them.

"It's important that the Union wins," Grady had told them at breakfast this morning.

"But that means that Massa Fuller and his sons have to lose," Delia replied.

"Yes," Grady said, "but if they lose, there's a chance we'll all go free."

Delia shook her head. "Much as I want to be free," she said sadly, "you know I been raising Massa and his boys since they was tiny babies. I don't want to see any of them hurt."

"They started this war," Grady said stubbornly. "They knew what they were getting into."

Massa Fuller invited another soldier home for dinner after church, so Kitty had a chance to hear some of the news. They ate in the big dining room, even though there were only three people at the huge table. Kitty helped Martin serve the food, then stood aside, listening.

"Tell us what you know for certain, Lawrence," Massa Fuller said as he cut into a slice of ham. "We've heard all the rumors."

"For certain? The Union armada sailed from Hampton Roads with more than sixty vessels," he said.

"Sixty," Massa repeated. "Warships, I presume?"

"Yes, and troop ships." He reached for another biscuit. "We don't know which city they plan to attack, of course. Charleston . . . Savannah . . . perhaps even Beaufort. So we must all remain on the alert."

Massa Fuller nodded. "They announced in church this morning that we should be prepared to evacuate the town on a moment's notice, if necessary."

Kitty wondered how they could sit here eating so calmly as they discussed the possibility of an enemy attack. Sixty warships sounded like a lot to her. She must remember the number so she could tell Grady later.

"Reverend Walker said they would ring the church bells tomorrow at noon," Missy added. "He told us that with Union troops approaching, we need to gather in our homes for prayer."

"I hate having my family so scattered," Massa said.

"Where are your two boys, Roger? They're not old enough to fight yet, are they?"

"My older son, Ellis, is. He joined a South Carolina regiment and was sent north to Virginia. He fought in the Battle of Manassas last July, in fact, and now he's part of our defense forces up there. My other son, John, is still a cadet at the Citadel in Charleston."

"You're from Charleston aren't you, Mrs. Fuller?" Lawrence asked.

"My father has a town house there, but also a plantation on the Edisto River."

"I assume you'll go to Charleston if you have to evacuate?"

"I don't think it will be necessary for her to go that far," Massa Fuller said before Missy could answer. "Not in her delicate condition. I thought perhaps you could go to my plantation for a few days, dear," he said, turning to Missy. "I'm sure it won't be for long—a week at the most."

"Then why go away at all?" she asked.

Massa exchanged a quick, worried glance with his guest. "Well, we're quite certain that the forts will remain secure," Lawrence explained, "but one of our fears is that a warship might slip past them and sail up the Beaufort River to bombard the town from offshore."

Kitty recalled the horrific bombing of Fort Sumter, and the thought of all those flaming shells falling from the sky onto Beaufort made her want to pack up and run right now. From the expression she saw on Missy's face, she knew her mistress felt the same way.

"The evacuation is only a safety precaution," Massa said. "Everyone expects to return once the Yankees are chased away."

Missy smiled uncertainly. "I'm not sure what to pack, in that case."

"Not much, dear," Fuller said. "Some personal belongings and any small valuables. The furniture and silver and so forth can remain here. Jim and Minnie and the others will look after things."

"Unfortunately, our most valuable resources can't be moved out of harm's way," Lawrence said, "our land, our field slaves, our crops. And since they can't be moved, our way of life depends on protecting them at all costs."

When the dinner was finished, Massa Fuller signaled to his butler. "We'll have our coffee now, Martin."

"Sorry, sir. But I don't think we got any more."

"Yes, I'm sorry, Roger," Missy said, "but supplies have been very difficult to get since the Union blockade began."

"I'll see that you get some coffee," Lawrence said. "I have connections."

"You may bring us our dessert now, Kitty," Missy said. "And kindly clear the table."

Kitty quickly gathered their dishes and hurried downstairs with them to the warming kitchen. When she returned to the dining room with dessert a few minutes later, another uniformed gentleman had joined them. His arrival raised the level of fear and tension in the room, as if the newcomer had poured turpentine on a comfortably blazing fire.

"I'm so sorry to disturb your dinner," Kitty heard him say, "but I'm afraid the message is rather urgent. Both of you gentlemen are needed at once. We just received confirmation that the Union fleet has sailed past Charleston and is heading farther south as we speak."

"Coming here?" Missy asked with a look of alarm.

"I'm afraid it is a very real possibility," the gentleman said. "We're warning the citizens in Beaufort and the surrounding Sea Islands to be prepared to evacuate their homes and plantations on short notice."

The beautiful, flawless day shattered completely. The horror of Fort Sumter that Kitty had witnessed from afar was about to be unleashed on her and on the people she loved. She wanted to run now, not wait.

Massa Fuller was already on his feet. He came around the table to help Missy Claire with her chair. "Lawrence and I are going to have to leave for the fort at once," he told her. "You understand, don't you, dear? The servants will take good care of you. You'll be fine. There's nothing to worry about, I assure you."

"If you have any type of sailing vessel," the newcomer added, "and any Negroes you can spare, kindly bring them. We're assembling a flotilla at Seaside Plantation on St. Helena Island to evacuate our soldiers from Fort Beauregard, if it becomes necessary."

"Yes, of course. I'll take Martin and Jim with me," Massa told Missy Claire. "I'll leave Grady here to drive you to the plantation."

"And what if the fort falls?" she asked. "Will you join me at the plantation?"

He frowned as he shook his head. "If we're forced to retreat, our unit will be reassigned to the mainland to protect the Charleston & Savannah Railroad. I'm sorry, Claire, but I'm afraid that I'm committed to this war until it's over."

Kitty followed Massa Fuller outside as he collected Martin and Jim, and gave instructions to the rest of his slaves before leaving. "You must be prepared to get my wife out of Beaufort if the battle starts," he told them. "I'm confident that it will only be for a short while. Once we've chased away the Yanks like we did at Sumter, you can all return. Minnie, I know you'll take care of things here while we're away. Grady, I'm trusting you to drive your mistress to safety. You know the way home to the plantation. Take good care of her, Delia. You too, Kitty."

His words eased some of the sick feeling in Kitty's stomach. At least her own little family would remain together. But as she watched Missy Claire and Minnie saying tearful good-byes to their husbands, Kitty couldn't help wondering about her future with Grady.

She was in the warming kitchen, fixing Missy's breakfast tray the next day when sounds of distant artillery fire echoed through Beaufort for the first time. "I know what that is," she told the others. "It's cannons. That's just what it sounded like when the battle at Fort Sumter started."

Missy was already out of bed by the time Kitty reached her room. "I don't know what to pack," she said. "You have to help me." She looked as frightened and forlorn as a small child. She stood in the center of the room in her bare feet, her arms folded around her middle as if trying to shield her unborn baby from harm. In an instant, Kitty's heart went out to her mistress. She quickly forgot all the times Missy had been mean to her, forgot all about Missy's threats to send her back to Slave Row, and silently vowed to do whatever she could to protect Missy and her baby.

"Of course I'll help you, Missy. You sit down now, and eat a little something for that baby's sake. I'll bet he's hungry even if you ain't. You leave all the packing to me."

She steered Claire back into bed and settled the breakfast tray on her lap, then glanced around the room at all of Missy's things, wondering where to begin.

"Roger said to take only the essentials," Missy said. She sounded dazed. Her usual sharp tone and demanding manner had vanished, turning her into an altogether different person. For some reason, this woman frightened Kitty even more than the real Claire did.

"Yes, ma'am. Which carriage are we taking? I can pack your big steamer trunk or a bunch of smaller satchels, but I need to know how much room there's gonna be."

Missy shook her head, staring blindly at the window across the room as if trying to see the distant warships through the drawn curtains. Kitty went to her side and placed the fork in her icy fingers. "Here, you better eat them eggs before they get cold. I'll go down and ask Grady which carriage we're taking."

He wasn't in the kitchen or in the yard. Kitty hurried into the stable, thinking he might be with his horses. "Grady?" she called out.

"Up here," he replied.

She hurried up the steep steps to their room and saw him carefully removing all of Kitty's pictures from the walls. He'd asked her if he could have them right after they had jumped the broom, and he'd pinned them up on all the walls himself.

"What are you doing?" she asked.

"Packing. I ain't leaving these behind."

He turned his back to remove another one, and the tenderness with which he handled it—the fact that he'd thought to pack them at all—left her speechless. For a moment she forgot why she had come.

"You needing something?" he asked.

"I need to know which carriage we're taking if we have to leave Beaufort. I need to know how much of Missy's stuff it can carry."

"It's up to her. We'll take whichever rig she orders me to take."

Kitty could tell by the set of his jaw that he was angry about something. She was afraid to ask what it was. "I think you'd better decide, Grady. Missy ain't herself. The sound of them guns this morning scared her half to death."

"They've stopped now."

Kitty was surprised to realize that they had. She wondered what it meant. "Even so, Missy's real worried about Massa Fuller. And her baby."

"Good. Let the white folks be worrying about *their* loved ones for once." He turned to remove the last picture, then silently straightened them into a neat pile, aligning all the edges.

"Can't you just tell me which carriage we're taking?" she asked.

He didn't reply. His stubbornness frustrated her.

"Then I'll decide," she said quietly. "We'll take the biggest one, okay?"

He answered her question with a shrug. Kitty sighed and hurried back to the house.

She and Delia were packing the last of Missy's things into her steamer trunk later that morning when the church bells began to toll. "Does that mean something?" Delia asked with alarm. Kitty remembered what Missy had said yesterday after church.

"It must be noon. Everybody's supposed to stop and pray for their families at noon."

Missy collapsed into the slipper chair as the bells continued to toll. Tears brimmed in her eyes, then rolled down her pale face. "What am I going to do if something happens to Roger? Oh, God, I'm so alone! I wish this would end!"

Delia knelt on the floor in front of the chair and took Missy's hand in both of hers. "You want me to pray with you, honey?"

"No!" she said, pushing Delia's hands away. "If it weren't for you Negroes, we wouldn't be in this mess!"

Kitty froze, fearing Delia's reaction. But it wasn't at all what she expected. As the little woman pulled herself to her feet again, the compassion in her eyes was genuine. "I know this is a hard, hard time for you, Missus Fuller. Me and Kitty better just go away now and let you talk to the Lord by yourself."

"I want Kitty to stay," Missy said. "She'll sleep in here with me tonight. She can fix herself a pallet on the floor."

A messenger came to the door a while later and told Missy that the fleet of Yankee warships had indeed massed at the entrance to Port Royal Sound. Everyone's fear had become a reality. The warships weren't going to attack Charleston or Savannah, but the port of Beaufort, halfway between the two cities. Confederate forces at Fort Walker and Fort Beauregard were preparing to fight to protect their city.

For Kitty, the hardest part was waiting. After a night of restless sleep, listening for the battle to begin, she awoke to the sound of distant skirmishing. But once again, the guns fell silent a short time later. "I wonder what they're waiting for?" Delia said at breakfast. "They gonna fight or ain't they?"

"Maybe the Yanks are waiting for more ships to arrive," Grady said.

Kitty stayed by Missy Claire's side for another long day and night, the distant guns ominously silent. On Wednesday a storm struck, and Kitty imagined the Yankee ships being forced to ride it out, tossing like toy boats on the darkened sea. The rain was still falling in sheets that afternoon when she and Missy heard crowds cheering and drums beating a few blocks away in downtown Beaufort. "Go see what happened," Missy ordered.

Kitty wrapped a shawl around her shoulders and ran outside into the cold rain. She was soaked and shivering by the time she returned home with the news.

"It's a whole bunch of fresh soldiers," she told Missy through chattering teeth. "They come all the way down from Columbia to help out at Fort Beauregard. Somebody said that a thousand volunteers came up from Savannah, too, during the night. Massa Fuller gonna have plenty of help now, don't you worry."

Missy smiled for the first time in days. "God is answering our prayers," she said. "Those Yankees will turn and run just like they did at Manassas." Even so, Kitty had trouble sleeping that night, her stomach twisting like a dishrag as she imagined bombs falling on the town.

The storm ended during the night, and a brilliant sun dawned on Thursday morning. Kitty halted on her way outside to the kitchen for Missy's breakfast, dazzled by millions of tiny rainbows of color and light that sparkled from all the water droplets. She was still savoring the beautiful sight when she heard the first explosions. This time they didn't stop. The long-awaited battle for Beaufort had begun. Massa Fuller's town house was farther away from the forts than Massa Goodman's house had been from Fort Sumter, and there was no view of the fighting this time, but the rumble of battle was unmistakable. Kitty turned around and ran straight upstairs to her mistress.

"Oh, God," Missy moaned. "Oh, God, they aren't going to stop this time, are they? It's going to be a terrible battle and . . . and Roger is in the middle of it all."

Kitty slid open the jib window and they went outside together to stand on the upstairs piazza, gazing toward the harbor. The only thing they could see through the moss-draped tree branches was a billowing cloud of smoke, rising in the distance. When the cannonading grew to a continual roar, all of Beaufort's church bells began to ring. Missy stood frozen in place, her face pale with fear, her hands resting protectively against her stomach.

"I think we'd better leave Beaufort now, Missy Claire," Kitty said.

"You're right," she whispered. But she didn't move. Kitty had to take her arm and lead her gently into the house.

Kitty's hands shook so badly as she helped Missy get dressed and fixed her hair that she could barely fumble through her tasks. All she could think about was getting out of town before enemy warships sailed past the forts and bombarded Massa's house. It was only two blocks from the waterfront. Once the enemy got past the forts, the city was unprotected.

Grady drove the carriage around to the front of the house. Kitty and Minnie had to help him carry Missy's heavy steamer trunk downstairs since there were no other male slaves to help him. The horses capered skittishly as they waited, frightened by the clamoring church bells and deafening bombardment. Grady stood by their heads, petting and soothing them as Kitty and Delia helped Missy Claire get settled inside the carriage. Kitty climbed in to sit beside her—something she'd never done. Neither of them looked back as they drove away.

They headed west out of town, then north across the island on the shell road. It seemed to Kitty that hours passed before the thundering explosions finally faded into the distance behind them. Refugees jammed the roads, all desperate to flee the now-deserted town. Missy's carriage joined a huge exodus of people, rich and poor, white and slave. They drove all manner of vehicles, some rode on horseback, many traveled by foot. With all the able-bodied men fighting at the forts, the refugees were mostly women, children, and elderly men. Like Missy, they had to depend on their slaves to get them to safety.

Progress was fearfully slow, but when the carriage halted altogether and remained stalled for several long minutes, Missy grew upset. "Get out and see what the delay is," she said. "I'm tired and uncomfortable and I need to lie down and rest."

Kitty's knees felt wobbly as she climbed out. Delia, Faye, and Grady stood beside the carriage, talking. "What are we stopping for?" she asked them.

"The Coosaw River is up ahead," Grady said. "We have to wait for the ferry to take us across to mainland."

"How long will that take?"

He shrugged. "Awful lot of people waiting. Missy's gonna have to wait her turn." He glanced back at the carriage, then motioned to Delia and Kitty to lean closer. "Listen, I've been talking to some of the others," he whispered. "I think we should sneak off and hide in the woods until the Yankees come."

"But we can't desert Missy!" Kitty said. "Massa's trusting us to keep her safe."

"Shh . . . There's plenty of other white folks to look after her," Grady said. "I want my freedom."

"You can't run off!" Kitty said. "You'll get caught!"

Grady gestured to the waiting crowd. "Look around you. There's only women and old men left. They ain't gonna go chasing us through the woods."

Delia rested her hand on Grady's arm. "I want my freedom, too, honey. But this ain't the time or place. We ain't off the island, yet. If Massa and them others chase the Yankees away, he'll come looking for you next. You'll be trapped, with no place to go. It ain't worth the risk."

Grady was still arguing with Delia when it was finally Missy's turn to be ferried across the river. Kitty could feel the heat of his anger as she stood beside him onboard the ship, watching the mainland draw nearer. He was as tense as a wild animal, ready to bolt. She hoped Missy wouldn't notice.

Hundreds of armed Confederate soldiers guarded the ferry dock on the other side. Kitty shuddered at the sight of them. But maybe Grady would change his mind now about running off.

Soon after their carriage got underway again, they passed through the town of Pocotaligo. More Confederate soldiers were stationed there to guard the railway line. "We're almost home," Kitty said aloud, still worried about Grady.

"How do you know where we are?" Missy said. "You've never been to Roger's plantation before."

"I know, Missy Claire. But Delia and Faye told me that it wasn't far from that town we just passed—where the railroad station is."

Missy had never been to her new husband's plantation either, but as they drove up the long, shaded driveway and glimpsed it from afar, Kitty could tell by the astonished look on Missy's face that it was even more splendid than she had imagined. The imposing two-story brick mansion was covered with ivy and shaded by moss-draped oak trees and palms. Kitty had thought that the Big House at Great Oak Plantation was huge, but this house was even larger and grander than that one. Flower gardens and broad green lawns surrounded the house, creating such a peaceful scene—as if the war didn't even exist.

"That sure is a pretty house," Kitty said. Her fingers itched to get out her paper and pencil and sketch it. Missy seemed too stunned to reply.

Several slaves hurried outside to unload Missy's trunk and other belongings as soon as Grady pulled the carriage to a halt. Kitty followed behind her dazed mistress as Delia led them on a tour through the seemingly endless maze of rooms.

"The Fuller family just keeps adding onto this house over the years," Delia explained. "That's why it's all spread out. They used to have a lot of company staying here back when Massa's folks were alive . . . and before his first missus died. Massa Roger and his father both loved it out here. They done so much of their business from here that they added one whole wing just for all the gentlemen who come calling."

Kitty wandered through room after room with the two women, gazing at all the beautiful furniture and books and dishes. But it was the oil paintings that fascinated her the most—landscapes and sailing ships and dozens of portraits of Massa's relations. She could have stared at them for hours, but there wasn't time. Missy wanted to rest after the long drive, so Kitty had to help her get settled first.

Later that night, Delia took Kitty outside to a neat row of white-washed cabins, hidden behind the Big House, where she and the other house servants lived.

"That don't look like enough slave cabins for a plantation this big," Kitty said.

"This ain't all of them," Delia replied. "The field slaves is all living someplace else, out of sight. That way, Massa never have to lay eyes on the poor souls and see all the suffering that's making him rich." Delia gestured to the last cabin in the row. "Those two rooms is where Grady and me been living ever since he come here," she said.

Kitty paused outside the door. "Are Grady and me still supposed to be married to each other?" she asked Delia.

"You are married," she said. "Can't change things now or Missy's sure to find out. Suppose one of them scrub maids or serving girls accidentally says something? No, you're gonna have to share my bed and Grady can sleep in the other room, like he always done."

It seemed unfair to Kitty that the three of them had to crowd into two tiny rooms while Missy Claire lived all alone in a house that would hold dozens of people. But Kitty was safe from the cannon fire here. She was living with the two people she'd grown to love most in the world. For now, that was all that mattered.

Three days later, Massa Fuller arrived at the plantation on horseback. He looked so exhausted and dejected that he seemed to have aged ten years. "The Yanks were too strong for us," Kitty heard him tell Missy Claire. "We had to evacuate both of the forts and ferry all our men across the river to the mainland." He was clearly shaken.

Missy reached for his hand. "Thank God you're safe, Roger. But what's going to happen now?"

He sighed wearily. "The Yankees control Beaufort, Port Royal Island, and all of the neighboring Sea Islands. They're probably not leaving anytime soon. But at least you're behind Confederate lines. You'll be safe here."

"How long can you stay with me? I'm all alone out here, and I'm so frightened for you."

"I can't stay. I just came to make sure you were okay and to have a word with Walt Browning, my overseer." He hesitated as if weighing whether or not to say more. Missy noticed.

"What's the matter?"

He sighed again. "When all of the Sea Island plantations were evacuated, the owners had to leave thousands of their field slaves behind. Some of us are worried that the Yanks might arm them and turn them loose against us. I came to tell Browning to keep a close eye on my slaves." He paused, then said quietly, "Martin and Jim both ran away to the Yanks."

Kitty dreaded telling Grady the news later that night. But he had seen Massa Fuller arrive, and both he and Delia wanted to know what he'd said. Grady exploded with anger when Kitty told him that all the slaves on the Sea Islands were now in Yankee hands.

"See that? I should have run off, too! I'd be a free man right now!" he said.

Delia tried her best to calm him, but it was no use.

"Never again!" he vowed. "I don't care what you say, next time I have a chance to be free, I'm going!"

Kitty watched him storm out of the door into the night and knew that a day would come when he wouldn't return. Someday, Grady was going to walk out of that door and out of her life forever.

15

FULLER PLANTATION, SOUTH CAROLINA
FEBRUARY 1862

On a cold, foggy winter morning, a small company of Confederate soldiers marched up the road to Massa Fuller's door. "Oh, God," Missy breathed when she saw them. "Not Roger . . . please . . ."

Kitty helped her mistress from her chair by the morning room fireplace, then ran to fetch a shawl for each of them. The new butler, Lewis, hurried to answer the door, but Kitty knew that Missy would want to go outside and talk to the soldiers herself. Her baby was due to be born any day, and she was so ungainly that she had to lean on Kitty's arm wherever she went. She was also so irritable and short-tempered that Kitty sometimes wondered if chopping cotton down on Slave Row would be an easier job than working for Missy Claire.

"Good afternoon, Mrs. Fuller," one of the soldiers said, sweeping off his hat, "I'm Captain Randolph. Sorry to trouble you, ma'am, but we've come for your horses."

"My horses?"

"Yes, I'm afraid that the army needs them. I have a letter here from your husband, Colonel Fuller, authorizing us to requisition them."

"You must be mistaken. My husband is a captain, not a colonel."

"He received a field promotion, ma'am." He removed a folded paper from his jacket as he spoke and handed it to Missy Claire. "You'll be allowed to keep your farm mules for now," the captain continued as Missy looked over the letter. "Your crops are very important to our cause, of course."

Missy refolded the letter when she finished reading it. "Go fetch your husband," she told Kitty.

"Yes, ma'am." Kitty dreaded telling Grady. She knew how much he loved those horses. Now that he wasn't driving Massa Fuller everywhere, he spent most of his time down in the stables taking care of them.

The fog seemed to muffle all the usual barnyard sounds and blur the outlines of the buildings as Kitty hurried down to the carriage house. The familiar landscape appeared alien and strange, like a scene drawn with a worn pencil, then smudged.

The brick stables and adjoining carriage house were neat and clean inside, pungent with the aroma of horses. The first time Grady had brought her here, Kitty had been surprised to see how beautiful both buildings were. The fancy woodwork that decorated the stalls was nearly as elegant as the woodwork up in the Big House. Grady said that before the war Massa Fuller liked to bring all of his gentlemen friends and visitors down here and show off his fine horses and carriages.

She found Grady leading Blaze from his stall to the corral behind the stable. "Missy wants to see you right away," she said breathlessly.

"She needing a carriage?" he asked as he turned the horse loose.

Kitty shook her head, unwilling to say more. But as soon as Grady walked through the stable door and saw the soldiers in front of the Big House, he slowed his steps.

"What's going on, Anna?"

She hated being the one to tell him. But maybe it would be better if he heard it from her instead of Missy Claire. He didn't dare show any emotion in front of Missy. "The soldiers are needing more horses," she said. "Massa Fuller say to take his."

Grady halted, his expression a mixture of shock and pain. "How many? Which ones?"

"I don't know. They gave Missy a letter from Massa Fuller, but I don't know what it said."

He started walking again, but his feet seemed to drag as he approached the waiting soldiers.

"Captain Randolph is requisitioning our horses for the Confederate cause," Missy told him when he reached the house. "You will escort his men down to the stables and help them with whatever they need."

Grady didn't move. He stood with his head lowered, powerless. Kitty could only imagine the emotions he must be feeling as he faced this terrible loss. "Which horses, ma'am?" he asked.

"All of them."

Grady closed his eyes. When he opened them a moment later, they smoldered with anger. "Excuse me, ma'am," he said in a tight voice, "but how you gonna send to town for a doctor when your time comes if you ain't got any horses?"

Missy drew a harsh breath. "How dare you!" she cried.

It would have been inappropriate for a white person to mention her condition in front of strangers, but for a mere slave to do so was scandalous. Kitty knew that the only reason Grady had spoken was because he loved his horses. He was desperate to save even one of them, if he could—most likely Blaze. But he had stirred up Missy's temper in the process, and Kitty cringed, waiting for the explosion that was sure to follow.

"There are no longer any doctors in town," the captain said quickly. "The Confederacy needed them, too."

"Show these men to the stable," Missy said coldly.

Kitty stayed with her mistress, aware of the tension and anger building inside Missy like a brewing storm. But Missy remained sweetly polite to Captain Randolph, who had stayed behind to chat with her while the rest of the men accompanied Grady.

"Any news of the war, Captain?" she asked. "I'm afraid I'm rather isolated out here. It's nearly impossible to hear the latest news."

Kitty listened intently, waiting for his reply. She and her fellow slaves knew even less about the war than Missy did. At least Missy saw an occasional newspaper and received letters from Massa Fuller and from her family in Charleston. But Missy never said a word to anyone about what they contained.

"Well, ma'am, I'm sorry to say that Nashville, Tennessee, just fell into enemy hands a few days ago. That's the first Confederate state capitol we've lost. But we're confident that we can win it back come springtime."

It seemed to take a long time, but the soldiers finally emerged from the stable, leading all twelve of Massa's magnificent horses by their bridles. Kitty recognized Grady's favorite horse, Blaze, but there was no sign of Grady. He had stayed in the carriage house so he wouldn't have to watch them go.

"Thank you, ma'am. Much obliged," Captain Randolph said as he and his men took their leave.

Kitty shivered in the cool winter air. She wore only a thin shawl and was eager to return to her seat by the fireplace. Missy must be feeling the chill, too. But even after the men marched away, Missy didn't move from the steps. "Go fetch your husband again," she said. The angry way she spat out the word *husband* made Kitty afraid.

She couldn't find him, at first. She wandered through the stable, calling his name until he finally emerged through the door to the corral, his face grief-stricken. "Missy's asking for you again," Kitty said. "Better come right away."

Neither of them spoke as they walked back to where Missy stood on the front steps with Lewis beside her. Anger radiated from Grady like a bonfire. He halted in front of Missy with his head lowered, not uttering a word, not daring to look at her. But Kitty stole a glance at her mistress, and her heart began to race when she saw the suppressed rage on Missy's face, too.

"Your boldness in mentioning my condition will be punished with forty lashes," Missy said.

"No!" Kitty cried. She swayed as her legs went weak with horror. She tried to drop to her knees to beg Missy not to whip Grady but he gripped her arm and held her up.

"Don't," he whispered.

"This morning's incident also reminded me that you have failed to do the work that was required of you," Missy continued. "Your wife was supposed to have a baby. Now it's too late. Not only have you failed to produce a child, but it also seems that I no longer have need of a coachman. Since your work up here is finished, Lewis will take you down to Mr. Browning, the overseer. After you've been punished with forty lashes, Mr. Browning will make certain that you carry your weight as a field slave."

Missy started to go inside, then turned back. "Oh, and from now on you will live on Slave Row, not with Kitty."

Grady turned and strode away without waiting for Lewis.

Kitty was so stunned she couldn't speak. She'd long been afraid that she would be punished for not having a baby, but she never dreamed Missy would punish Grady or send him away. During these past four months, he and Delia and Kitty had become a family in the little cabin they shared. Now Missy was ripping that family apart, just like Massa Goodman had torn her first family apart.

Kitty followed Missy inside, numbed with grief and shocked by Missy's cruelty. She had done some mean things over the years, but this time Missy's actions were indefensible. Kitty imagined the lash tearing across Grady's scarred back, and for the first time, she understood his bottomless anger. He had married Kitty in order to rescue her, and now he was going to suffer for his kindness. Kitty fell to her knees in front of her mistress, clinging to her skirts.

"Please don't whip Grady! Please, Missy Claire! It ain't his fault that—"

"Be quiet!" Missy said, smacking Kitty on the side of her head. "If you say one more word, I'll put the lash to both of you. Now get up!"

Kitty struggled to her feet, weeping uncontrollably. "Whip me, then. Not Grady!"

"I said stop that! Do you want me to tell Mr. Browning to give your husband ten extra lashes?"

Kitty forced herself to be quiet for Grady's sake. But tears blurred her vision as she helped Missy to the morning room where they'd been sitting. Missy was about to sit down in her chair when she suddenly sucked in her breath. Her face wore a startled look.

"Go get Delia," she said.

Kitty stared in amazement as a puddle of water slowly spread in a circle around Missy's feet.

❖

Grady felt as though he'd swallowed a stone as he faced Walter Browning. He knew very little about the overseer except that he was the son of the man who had raped Delia, years ago, and fathered her child. This Browning was middle-aged with thinning black hair, but he was as strongly built as his slave laborers. Grady doubted that he could beat him in a fight, even though Browning was at least twenty years older. Besides, the overseer carried a pistol strapped to his belt, and was rumored to be lightning quick with it. Grady saw no way to avoid a second scourging with the lash.

"Missus Fuller wants Grady whipped," Lewis told Browning. Grady heard the sorrow in the butler's voice. "Forty lashes. She says he's supposed to work in the fields from now on."

"Did he steal something?"

"No, not that I know of, sir."

"Okay. There are some slave shackles hanging up in that second shed over there," Browning told Lewis. "Go get a pair for me." He studied Grady while they waited. "What did you do?" he finally asked.

Grady was much too angry to explain to this white man that he'd refused to father a child for Missus Fuller's convenience. His rage was certain to boil over, making his punishment even worse. "You better ask her," he mumbled.

232

"You can bet I'll do just that," Browning said. "But right now I'm asking you."

"I . . . um . . . I ain't exactly sure, sir." If he knew nothing else, Grady knew it was always better to play dumb than to lose his temper or show disrespect for white people.

Lewis returned with the chains, and Browning led Grady to an iron hitching post used to tether animals. Grady had fastened countless pairs of manacles to other slaves' wrists and ankles when he'd worked for Coop, but he'd been too small to wear them himself when he'd been taken from his family in Richmond. The heavy irons fit him now. For the first time in his life, he felt what it was like to have the cold metal clamped tightly around his own wrists, securing him to the post. Browning left him standing alone in the icy mist while he walked up to the Big House to talk with Missus Fuller.

Waiting, knowing the pain that was to come, added to Grady's torture. In a few minutes he was going to be whipped. Again. For no reason. Grady wanted to roar in outrage, but no one in heaven or on earth would even hear or care.

He was more certain than ever that there was no God. Or if there was, that He had no love or mercy to spare on him. In less than one hour, Grady had lost his job, his horses, and his home with Delia and Kitty. Being born a slave was certainly a curse, but at least his favored position as a driver and his home with the two women had made his life tolerable for the past few years. Now, at the whim of a white woman, he not only faced a brutal punishment but was also being reduced to an animal—a beast of burden, laboring from dawn to dusk. He sank to the ground, leaned his head against the iron hitching post and waited as despair overwhelmed him.

It seemed like a very long time passed before Browning returned. When he did, he was carrying a whip coiled in a tight circle. He stood staring down at Grady for a long time, as if deciding how to begin.

Grady rose to his feet. "Just get it over with," he said. He gripped the rail with both hands, bracing himself.

Browning didn't move. "I've never given a slave forty lashes in my life," he said quietly.

Grady said nothing. He wouldn't beg. The foggy morning was damp and cold, but he felt a bead of sweat run down his back as he waited, his muscles tensed. His mouth felt as dry as cotton. He wondered if he dared ask for a drink of water.

"You've been Mr. Fuller's coachman since Old Jesse died, haven't you?" Browning asked.

"Yes, sir."

"Shame about them taking all of Mr. Fuller's horses away," Browning said. "Missus Fuller told me all about it." He paced in place.

Grady wondered what Browning was waiting for. Was someone else coming to do the dirty work? Was he going to make all the other slaves gather around to watch? As much as Grady dreaded the pain, he longed to get the ordeal over with.

"You know, if Mr. Fuller were here he would never allow this," Browning said as he unwound the long whip. "Slaves are valuable property, and he doesn't like his property damaged. There have been a few times when a slave stole from him. And a slave tried to run off, once. But even then, Mr. Fuller took them to the auction block. He never had any of them whipped."

Grady closed his eyes, not daring to hope that he'd be spared.

"Mr. Fuller liked the way you kept his stables. Said you were a hard worker, that you knew a lot about horses . . ." He took a step back. "Tell you the truth, I don't think he'd like me doing this. Especially for no reason that I can see."

Grady was certain that his heart would beat right out of his chest as he waited. Browning paced in circles for another long, agonizing minute, then reached into his pocket.

"I can't do this," he said, pulling out a key. He unfastened one of Grady's hands and slid the chain free from around the post. "I don't suppose you'll tell Mrs. Fuller that I disobeyed her, will you?"

Grady exhaled. "No, sir."

"A lash or two out in the field is one thing . . . but I never did give out forty. Mr. Fuller won't allow it."

"Thank you, sir." Grady was so weak with relief that he could barely walk. Browning led him into a storage shed, then refastened his shackles, anchoring him to a metal ring in the floor. He locked a second pair around Grady's ankles.

"I'm going to leave you in here for a few days until everybody cools off—and to make sure you don't get it in your mind to run away. After that, there's plenty of work around here for you to do. You'll put in a full day like all my other field hands, come springtime."

Browning went out, the door creaking shut behind him. Grady heard the bolt slide closed on the outside. The shed was dark and damp and cold. It smelled of moldy wood and tobacco. But by some miracle, he'd just been spared forty lashes. Tears came to his eyes, and he wondered if Delia had been praying.

❧

Kitty couldn't stop worrying about Grady as she sat with Missy Claire through her long, hard hours of labor. Delia had sent for the slave midwife who delivered all the slaves' babies, and together they helped Missy through her ordeal. The older women made Kitty leave the room during the final two hours, but she heard Missy's screams, nonetheless. Kitty didn't feel one bit sorry for her. Nor did she care if Missy lived or died. At times, Kitty couldn't hold back her tears as she recalled the ugly welts on Grady's back from being whipped the first time and as she imagined him suffering that agony and humiliation a second time.

Kitty managed to whisper the story to Delia in one of their free moments, and the little woman nearly collapsed to the floor before Kitty steered her to a chair. "O Lord," she moaned. "O Lord, not my Grady. Not again." She'd been tearful ever since, as if the news had broken Delia's heart.

Nearly twenty-four hours after her water broke, Missy Claire had a baby boy. She named him Richard. The midwife brought a young

Negro woman named Patsy up to the Big House from Slave Row to be his wet nurse.

Kitty dreaded returning to the little cabin now that Grady was gone, but in the end she didn't have to. Missy was afraid to stay in the Big House with a strange field slave, and she made Kitty and Delia both sleep in the house with her and the baby.

On the night after the baby was born, Kitty awakened to see Delia tiptoeing from the room. "Where you going?" she whispered.

When Delia turned around, Kitty saw her tear-swollen eyes and knew the answer even before she spoke. "If you're going down to see Grady, I want to come, too," Kitty said. She threw her blanket aside and started to rise, but Delia hurried over to her, whispering so they wouldn't awaken Patsy.

"No, I think you better stay here, honey. If Missy calls for one of us and we ain't here, there'll be even more trouble. Besides, Grady may not want you to see him all tore up."

Kitty lay down again, but she didn't go back to sleep.

❧

The sound of the shed door creaking open awakened Grady. He sat up, his heart hammering, but he was unable to see anything in the darkness.

"Grady? You in here?"

He sagged with relief at the sound of Delia's familiar voice. "Yeah, over here."

He saw her tiny form outlined in the open doorway before she pushed the door closed again. He longed to stand up and sweep her into his arms but his chains were too short to allow him to stand. Delia bent over him and kissed his forehead, gently holding his face in her hands. "You okay, honey?" she asked, her voice choked with tears.

"Browning didn't whip me, Delia. He said Massa Fuller would never allow it, so he didn't do it. I'm okay."

"Thank the Good Lord," Delia breathed. She dropped to her knees beside Grady and hugged him tightly. Grady felt such a rush of renewed gratitude and wonder at being spared that he nearly whispered "Amen."

"I brought you a few things," Delia said when she could speak. "Praise God you won't be needing any doctoring, but I wrapped up some of your clothes and things in this bundle. Thought you might need your blanket, too."

"Thanks, Delia."

"You're shivering, honey. Want me to put it around your shoulders?"

"Yeah." He'd been afraid that he would take sick if he had to sleep on the dirt floor one more night in the bone-chilling February cold.

"I brought you some food and water, too, but you best eat it all now so Walt Browning don't find out about it."

Grady had to bend his head nearly to the floor in order to feed himself, the short chains hindering his movements. He hated for Delia to see him this way, but the food was welcome, just the same. He hadn't eaten in nearly two days.

"Kitty tells me you're gonna have to live down on Slave Row from now on," Delia said.

"Looks that way," he said, swallowing a chunk of corn bread. "Massa don't need a driver if he ain't got any horses."

"Well, I put a couple of Kitty's pictures in with your things. I know how much you like them. Thought maybe you could hang them up in your new place. Be a little like home, anyway."

"Is Anna okay?" he asked quietly. "Missus Fuller didn't punish her, too, did she?"

"No, she's fine—worried sick about you. She wanted to come with me, but I told her she better not be giving Missus Fuller any more reasons to be mad."

"I hate that woman." Grady felt a shiver travel through him that had nothing to do with the cold.

"If it makes you feel any better, Kitty ain't making excuses for her this time."

"Good." He felt Delia's eyes studying him in the darkness.

"Grady, honey, please don't waste your life hating people. You're the one who's gonna suffer for it, not them. Don't you know you're poisoning yourself?"

He didn't answer. He had finished eating, and he didn't think he could bear to hear one of Delia's sermons about Jesus when he was chained to the floor like an animal. Grady had nothing more to say. He gulped down all of the water, then leaned over as far as he could and kissed her cheek. "Thanks for coming, Delia. And thanks for the food and things. You better head back now, before you get into trouble."

She slowly rose to her feet, then caressed his hair for a moment. "I'll be praying for you, honey," she said.

He smiled at her in the darkness. "Yeah. I know you will."

❦

FULLER PLANTATION
APRIL 1862

On a warm day in springtime, Kitty looked out one of the front windows and saw Massa Fuller walking up the long driveway to the Big House. She thought she must be dreaming.

"Missy Claire!" she called. "Missy Claire, come quick! Massa's home!" Kitty didn't wait for the butler but ran out into the foyer and opened the door wide for him.

"Welcome home, Massa Fuller! I know Missy's sure gonna be pleased to see you. And wait till you see your beautiful new baby boy."

"Thank you. It's good to be home." He smiled wearily as he leaned his rifle against the hall table. He slid a canvas pack from his shoulders, and Kitty could tell by the way that it thumped to the floor that it was very heavy. Massa Fuller looked exhausted. His boots were falling apart, and the handsome uniform that he'd worn at his wedding was muddy and ragged.

"Kindly fetch your mistress," he said. But Missy Claire was already hurrying into the hallway from the morning room. She flew into his arms.

Kitty looked away as they embraced, remembering how wonder

ful it felt to be held in Grady's arms that way. She hadn't seen him since he'd been sent down, two months ago, and she missed him.

"Kitty, run upstairs and fetch the baby," Missy said. "And be careful with him. We'll be in the morning room."

Baby Richard was asleep in his cradle, his hands curled into tiny fists. He had no hair and his skin was as pale as Missy's was, but Kitty had grown to love him as she'd helped take care of him these past two months. Sometimes she would close her eyes as she cuddled him in her arms and imagine that he had beautiful coffee-brown skin and wooly black hair—and that he belonged to her and Grady. She lifted Richard from his cradle, careful not to wake him, and carried him downstairs to meet his papa.

Massa Fuller rose from the sofa as Kitty carried Richard into the room, but he didn't ask to hold him. Instead, he stood gazing down at his new son for a long moment, and the lines of fatigue that were etched in his face grew soft.

"I can't tell you how wonderful it is to see new life again, after so much—" His voice faltered slightly, then faded into silence.

"He looks like you, Roger," Missy Claire said. She remained seated on the sofa. Massa Fuller touched his sleeping son's hand, then sank down beside his wife again.

"You think so?" he asked.

"Of course. He's been surrounded by so many Fullers," she said, gesturing to the portraits on the walls, "what other choice did he have?" They laughed together, and Kitty felt another stab of loneliness. Maybe if she talked to Massa Fuller alone and begged him to let Grady come home—maybe he would allow it. Massa Fuller had always been good to Grady.

The baby stirred in her arms and yawned. "Shall I take him back upstairs now, Missy Claire?" she asked. She knew better than to offer him to Missy to hold. She seldom wanted to.

"Not yet," she replied. "He seems content for now."

Kitty remained standing, rocking the sleeping baby in her arms. She was a little surprised that Missy and her husband didn't want their privacy after being apart from each other for so long. She decided to daydream about Grady as she waited, but when she realized that Massa was talking about the war, she suddenly became alert. This was the first real news she or any of her fellow house slaves had heard in months.

"Mother sent me a Charleston newspaper," Missy said, "and I read about the naval battles last month. I was so proud that our little Confederate navy was victorious."

"Yes, the battle of the ironclads must have been a sight. We've enjoyed several land victories as well, I'm happy to say. But it always comes down to numbers. I heard about a battle up in Shiloh, Tennessee, earlier this month, where we had the Yanks all but licked until they sent for reinforcements. Our men always fight better than theirs do, but there are always more of them than there are of us."

"Have you heard from Ellis?" Missy asked.

"I recently received letters from both my sons. Ellis is in Yorktown, Virginia, bracing for a huge assault that may be coming soon. The Union commander is expected to launch an attack against the Peninsula this spring with the goal of taking Richmond. Rumors are that he has amassed an enormous arsenal and a hundred thousand men. But Ellis says they're dug in behind earthworks and they're ready for him. The news from John," Massa said with a sigh, "was worrisome, I'm afraid. He left the Citadel and enlisted in a new South Carolina regiment as soon as he became of age. He isn't sure where he'll be sent yet."

"What about you, Roger? Will you be sent up to Virginia, too?"

"No, too much is happening down here at the moment. I don't know if you've heard, but Fort Pulaski fell into Union hands. It guarded the harbor of Savannah."

"No, I hadn't heard. Thank God Charleston is well protected."

"Yes, the Yanks will have a tougher time there. But what's worrisome about the fall of Fort Pulaski is that more and more slaves are escaping to Union-held territory, and the Yankees are refusing to return them."

"I thought the Fugitive Slave Law said that they had to return them."

"It does. But Major General Hunter isn't honoring it. He's calling the fugitives 'contrabands of war,' like any other property that's been confiscated during wartime. Of course, word of this has spread to the slaves somehow, and more and more of them are trying to escape to Union-held territory—all along the coastal area between Charleston and Savannah."

Kitty didn't realized how tense she had become as she'd listened to this news until she felt the baby squirm in her arms. She looked down and saw that his eyes were open. If he began to cry she would have to take him upstairs—and then she would miss the rest of the conversation. She shifted Richard to her shoulder and rubbed his back, humming softly to soothe him.

"For now, I'm stationed close by," she heard Massa Fuller say, "but our lines shift constantly to protect the railroad. We're more like bush-fighters than regular combatants. Our lookouts watch all of the Union's movements along the coast, and we're able to move quickly if an attack on the railroad seems imminent. We know all the inlets and rivers and waterways in this area much better than the Yanks do. So if we spot Union vessels heading up one of them, we know where they'll end up and we can be ready for them. We've placed mines and other obstructions in the main waterways, and we have batteries placed in all the strategic places. So far, we've been able to keep the enemy confined to the Sea Islands and off the mainland."

Later that evening, Kitty walked down to Slave Row for the first time, looking for Grady. She was afraid that he would hear the rumors about slaves not being returned to their owners, and he would try to run away. She needed to warn him that the Confederates had lookouts everywhere and were guarding all the waterways. It would be nearly impossible for him to get off the mainland to safety.

The stench of Slave Row, the atmosphere of squalor and hopelessness, nearly made Kitty turn back. But Grady suddenly stepped out of one of the huts, spotting her before she had a chance to change her mind.

"Anna? What are you doing here?" he asked in surprise.

Kitty wondered if she would have recognized him if he hadn't spoken first. He looked older and rougher, his wooly hair longer and poorly trimmed. His body was leaner yet more muscular, if that was possible. But the biggest shock was seeing him dressed in rags when he'd always worn his coachman's livery with such pride.

"Is there someplace we can talk?" she asked. "I can't be gone from the house too long." He led her inside the hut he'd just come out of, and she had to battle not to show her shock at how he was forced to live. The room had a fireplace but little else—most of the space on the dirt floor was taken up with rough, narrow wooden beds with cornshuck mattresses. Three other men Grady's age lay on three of the beds, but Kitty knew which bed was Grady's even before he gestured to it and invited her to sit. He had decorated the walls above it with her drawings.

Kitty sat down and quickly told him what she had heard that morning. The other three slaves also listened intently. As Kitty expected, Grady reacted to the news with anger. "I ain't giving up! There has to be a way to get free from here!" he said in a low, harsh voice.

"Grady, listen, I'm going to talk to Massa Fuller about you. Just as soon as I can get him alone, I'll ask him if you can come home and—"

"No, don't do that," he said quickly. "It'll only make trouble for me. And maybe for you, too. Supposing Missus Fuller finds out I wasn't whipped?"

Kitty's eyes filled with tears. "I miss you," she said softly.

He reached out to stroke her cheek. His hand was rough and callused, his forearm scarred with insect bites. "You drawing any new pictures since I been away?" he asked.

Kitty hesitated. "I can't . . . I ran out of paper again."

"And you won't ask your missy for more." He made it a statement, not a question.

"Missy don't have any paper, either," she said, shaking her head.

"She can hardly get enough to write letters on now that there's a blockade."

The anger faded from his eyes. Sorrow took its place. "You better be going," he said. Kitty knew he was right. If it was painful for her to see him again, how much harder must it be for him to see her, and to be reminded of all that he'd lost? She stood. Grady rose from where he'd been sitting on the bed across from her. Kitty leaned toward him and held him in her arms for a long moment, just to remember what it felt like.

He hugged her in return, but nothing was the way it had been. His embrace was brief and passionless, his homespun shirt rough beneath her cheek. He no longer smelled of soap and leather and horses the way she remembered. She stepped away again.

"Bye," she whispered.

"Good-bye, Anna."

CHAPTER

16

FULLER PLANTATION, SOUTH CAROLINA
APRIL-NOVEMBER 1862

The horn blew before the roosters crowed or the sun rose, and Grady's long, exhausting day began. Instead of meals in the kitchen with Delia and Kitty, he had to cook his own rations as best he could and pack his dinner can to carry with him into the field. The foremen doled out rations of smoked pork and cornmeal each week, but it seemed to Grady that he never had enough to eat, that hunger gnawed around the edges of his stomach all the time.

He walked the long road to the fields with the other slaves each day, carrying a hoe or a shovel or tugging one of the mules along by its bridle. He would leave his dinner can at the top of the row, waiting as long as he could before eating it, knowing that it would be after sundown before he ate again. And even then, he would have to cook the food himself.

Each morning he'd be given a task to do, and he'd work until it was complete, sometimes until after dark—every day but Sunday. The work changed with the seasons but the fatigue and monotony were always the same. And it would be this way until the day that he died and they buried him by torchlight after the day's work was finished.

When winter was nearly over, Mr. Browning assigned Grady to one of the mule-drawn plows and gave him a quarter-acre of ground to till each day, in preparation for planting. They weren't planting cotton this year, the overseer said, because the harbor in Beaufort was still occupied and there was no way to ship the cotton past the enemy blockade of the coast. Instead, they would plant wheat, rice, and other food crops. The Confederacy always needed food.

As soon as the seeds sprouted, the task of hoeing began, and the fight against weeds continued endlessly through spring and summer. Browning couldn't be everywhere at once, but he rode up and down the rows on his mule, his lash flying every time he saw a slave chop a plant by mistake or overlook a weed or labor too slowly.

Browning knew about Grady's experience with horses, and he often made him work with the mules. The animals were strong but proverbially stubborn, and Grady's horse tricks seldom worked with them. He had to resort to brute force to get them to do what he wanted, and his arms ached at night from wrestling with them. When the spring rains came, the mules' hooves had to be fitted with wooden boots to keep them from sinking into the mud. Since Grady knew how to shoe a horse, it was his job to help fit these boots into place—and a miserable job it was. Massa's horses had never kicked him, but he often found himself knocked to the ground by one of the mules. And in Grady's half-starved condition, the ugly bruises were slow to heal.

When the ground began to dry out, Grady shoveled muck out of the ditches that would be used to flood the rice fields when it was time. They sowed rice twice—in early April and again in June to avoid the migrating birds that swooped down to feast on the newly planted seeds. Grady watched the bobolinks fly overhead, listening to their distinctive call, and he thought of Amos' words long ago in Richmond. *"That's freedom, boy . . . flying away anytime you want, going wherever you want—just like that bird. . . . You gotta plan for it, boy. Know where you gonna go and how you're getting there. Otherwise they catch you right away and whip you 'til you wish you was dead."* Ever since they'd fled Beaufort and Grady had missed his opportunity to escape as they'd waited for the Port Royal Ferry, freedom was all that he thought about. He would plan for it this time. He would be ready. He would not let another chance pass him by.

In time, Grady learned ways to help take his mind off his aching hunger and boredom. Sometimes as he drove the mule-drawn plow up and down the rows, he imagined that he was driving Massa through the streets of Charleston or Beaufort again, and he would try to recall each building and landmark. Other times he would rehearse the fiddle in his mind while he hoed, dreaming that he was still in New Orleans with Beau, before Massa Coop had forced him to play for the slaves. Grady would concentrate on all the fingerings and how to move the bow, humming the melodies in his mind and trying to see how many songs he could still recall after all this time.

But the most painful days were the ones when he couldn't stop thinking about Anna. He would re-create the details of her face in his mind, or envision her delicate hands as they sketched a tree or a flower. He would remember what it felt like to hold her in his arms, until the pain would overwhelm all his other sorrows—the ache of his muscles, the blistering heat, his never-ending hunger.

The other slaves often sang to help drown their troubles, and when Grady first heard them, it made him angry. They sang as they traveled to the fields, and as they worked throughout the day, and as they journeyed home at night, weary in body and spirit. He wanted to shout for them to stop. Why were they singing? Music was an expression of joy they couldn't possibly know. The fact that most of the songs had something to do with God added to his bitterness.

But as time passed, Grady gradually began to see that these work songs created a sense of community and shared hardship among his fellow slaves. Like Grady's own mental exercises, singing helped pass the time, relieved the boredom of their monotonous tasks, and distracted them from their pain. When they had to labor together as a group, the Negro foreman set the pace and rhythm of their work with song. But most of the time the songs sprang spontaneously and unplanned. Someone would sing a line, and the others would quickly join in, echoing the words, adding verses of their own. Some of the tunes were lively, but many were mournful and hauntingly beautiful.

And one day, without making a conscious decision, Grady joined them. The release he felt as he sang along with the other slaves—his brothers and sisters—was even greater than what he'd felt when he'd learned to play the fiddle. This time it was his music, slave music, not a white man's song. No one compelled him to sing. And he was very surprised to find that the music offered hope for a changed life, a better life:

> My army cross over; O, Pharaoh's army drowned!
> My army cross over, we cross the river Jordan....

Even the songs that talked about Jesus had an undercurrent of rebellion and a yearning for freedom that Grady grew to love:

> Ride in, kind Savior! No man can hinder me.
> O, Jesus is a mighty man! No man can hinder me....

He rehearsed his plans to escape as he sang, "Brother, keep your lamp trimming and a-burning . . . for this world almost done" or "Way down in the valley, who will rise and go with me? We'll run and never tire, Jesus sets poor sinners free." They could sing about freedom and the overseer couldn't stop them as long as freedom from slavery was disguised behind words of dying and going to heaven:

> We'll soon be free, when the Lord will call us home.
> My brother, how long before we done suffering here?
> We'll walk the golden streets when Jesus sets me free.
> We'll fight for liberty, when the Lord will call us home.

Grady labored all that long, hot summer beneath a broiling sun, the humid air as thick as wet cotton against his skin. He dreamed of sailing down one of the waterways to freedom as he and the others opened the reservoir gates and watched the water pour through the channels to flood the rice fields. He thought of Anna's love of color when he saw the rows and rows of ripening rice, the stalks a vivid yellow-green against the muddy water. When the heads of rice began to bend down, he helped drain the water again so the fields would dry before harvest—and he wondered if he would live this way until the day he died.

On a sweltering Sunday in August, Grady's only day off, he sat outside his hut watching all the other families on Slave Row. He saw children playing, husbands and wives enjoying an hour or two together, and his longing for his own family was so great that he suddenly decided to sneak home and visit Delia and Anna. He knew that he stank of sweat and dirt, so he carefully rinsed out his shirt first, and laid it in the sun to dry while he shaved and washed himself as best he could. But when he arrived at the little cabin he'd once shared with the two women, he found it empty. He stared up at the rear façade of the Big House, bitterly disappointed, and remembered that house slaves didn't get a day off.

Grady returned to his own hut on Slave Row, his loneliness multiplied. As he sat staring at the dirt, trying to ignore the smells of cooking food and the sounds of activity all around him, he heard a woman's voice. "Hey, there. You look awful sad sitting all by yourself."

Grady looked up. One of the young slave women who had worked beside him in the rice fields all week, smiled down at him. She was pretty and shapely but not as lovely as Anna.

"I just been cooking some greens," she said. "You want to come on down to my place and have some?"

Grady's stomach rumbled at the thought. Many of the other slaves managed to grow a little extra food in gardens of their own after the workday was finished. This girl was making a huge sacrifice in offering to share what little she had with him. He couldn't take her food.

"Thanks. But I ain't hungry," he lied. He expected her to leave, but she surprised him by sitting down on the step beside him.

"Every time I see you, you're all alone," she said. "What I can't figure out, is why a good-looking fella like you don't have a dozen gals cooking for him. Don't you know we all need each other to help make this sorry life of ours a little easier?"

Grady thought of his life with Coop—a lonely existence without companionship. He'd worked with William every day, but the servant had remained cold and distant, as if unwilling to get close to Grady and risk seeing Coop kill him as he'd killed the first "Joe." Grady's life with Delia and Anna had been very different. He had still been a slave, but the love they'd shared made it bearable.

"I know. You're right," he said. "But I have a wife. I'm already married."

"You are? Where is she?"

"She works up at the Big House. Lives up there, too."

"And you don't ever get to see her?"

He shook his head.

"What's she like?"

Beautiful, he wanted to say. *Trusting and naïve.* She noticed colors and saw beauty everywhere, in things he never even noticed. But she had no more self-respect than a dog. "She draws pictures," he said, instead.

The girl looked at him as if she'd never heard of such a thing. "What do you mean?"

"Come inside, I'll show you." He rose to his feet and led her into the deserted shack, pointing proudly to the drawings pinned to the wall over his bed. The girl crawled onto the bed and knelt there, studying them for a long moment, straightening the heat-curled edges with her fingers.

"Mmm. These are really something," she said. She turned around to face Grady again but remained seated on his bed. "I heard you used to be Massa's coachman. Why'd he send you down?"

"He didn't, Missus Fuller did. Besides, Massa ain't got any more

249

horses for me to take care of. The Confederates came and took them all away for the war."

She didn't seem to be listening. Instead, she was looking him over from head to toe and smiling at him in a way that stirred his blood.

"Why don't you come on over here and sit down?" she asked, patting the mattress beside her. Grady's heart speeded up. He was so tempted, so lonely. Why not forget his miserable life for a little while, and take whatever love was being offered to him? Why not close the cabin door and take this girl in his arms and drown out his pain any way he could?

But Grady knew from experience that loving someone only led to more sorrow, in the end. He and this girl might grow to like each other—and then they might be separated in the blink of an eye, the same way he and Anna had been. He remembered how Anna had sat in the same place this girl was sitting. How she had stood to say good-bye and held him in her arms before she left.

"Thanks," he mumbled. "But I . . . I love Anna. My wife." Grady was astonished to discover that it was true. And that he was unwilling to risk loving one more person in this life—and losing them.

"Oh." The girl looked disappointed and a little angry. She slowly climbed off the bed and stood close to Grady, resting her hands on his chest, looking up into his eyes. "Well, if you ever change your mind, let me know."

Grady's longing was almost more than he could bear. He gently lifted the girl's hands from his chest and ducked out of the shack before he changed his mind.

⁂

Once a week Mr. Browning drove into town to pick up supplies and the mail, and he often took Grady along to wrangle the mules and help load the wagon. It was the only chance that Grady and the other slaves had to hear the latest news about the war and all the battles that were being fought. There might not have been many trade goods to buy in the general store these days, but the white men who gathered there loved to talk about the War for Southern Independence.

Grady quietly rejoiced when he learned that the city of New Orleans had fallen into Yankee hands. He imagined Massa Coop's capture and arrest and pictured the slave trader rotting in a filthy jail cell like the ones where Grady and Coop's other slaves had lived. Grady paid especially close attention when he heard that several battles were being waged near his old home in Richmond, Virginia. His hopes for freedom for his mama and Eli soared as a huge Yankee army marched all the way up the Virginia Peninsula that spring and summer, determined to conquer the city. But as the summer months passed and the last Yankee soldier was chased back to Washington City in defeat, Grady's hopes were crushed. In August, the entire town celebrated the second Rebel victory at a place called Manassas. And September brought news that the Rebels were on the move, marching into Yankee-held territory in Maryland. While the plantation owners rejoiced at these victories, Grady despaired.

By the time the long days of harvesting and threshing began, Grady had become a trusted member of the slave community. Each time he made a trip to town and back, the men would gather in his hut at night to make whispered plans for escaping.

"There's nearly a hundred of us and only the overseer to stop us," one of them said. "Why wait any longer? Let's escape now."

But Grady remembered Anna's warning and passed it along. "It's too risky. We can never tell for sure where the Confederates are. They move all up and down this stretch of low country, guarding the railroad. They know this area. And they have lookouts watching. The only way we can safely get past the Confederate lines is if the Yankees attack and the Confederates all head off to stop them."

"Even then, we'd need boats to get to the Sea Islands where the Yanks are," someone added.

"Unless the Yankees come to the mainland," Grady said. "I hear that the Yanks sometimes come ashore to help slaves escape—and they're not returning us to our owners."

Plotting with the others buoyed Grady's hopes. They pooled all of their knowledge, gathering information about the land routes and waterways. Before the harvest was over, they had formulated a plan. All they needed was the right opportunity, when the Rebel soldiers were distracted, to put their plan into action. Grady was certain he would know when that golden moment had arrived.

One cold fall afternoon, while Grady was checking one of the mules for a sprain, he heard an unfamiliar sound. He paused to listen, gradually recognizing it as the sound of marching feet. He jogged to the edge of the pasture to peer through the trees and saw thousands of Confederate soldiers hurrying down the road past the Fuller Plantation. Grady had watched Massa Fuller drilling new recruits in Beaufort, and he knew that these men were marching on the double-quick. He'd never seen so many soldiers this close to the plantation before—probably two or three thousand of them—and he wondered what it meant. Before the dust cloud had a chance to settle again, Lewis came hurrying down to the barn from the Big House.

"Missy's needing a wagon and team of mules, right away," he said.

"What's going on?" Grady asked. "Did them soldiers say anything when they came by?"

"They said the Yankees are coming. Whole bunch of them landed at McKay's Point. The soldiers told Missus Fuller she better get out. They're all in an uproar up at the Big House and fixing to run."

"Where's she going? With the soldiers?"

"No, the soldiers are heading toward Pocotaligo and she's going to her daddy's plantation on the Edisto River. Wants a wagon right away."

Grady felt the sudden panic as if it was contagious. But his concern was for Delia and Anna, not Missus Fuller. "She's leaving now? Today? What about Delia and Anna? Are they going with her?"

"Missus Fuller never said who's going. She only told all of us to help load the wagon so she can leave first thing in the morning.

Don't know nothing else. She says to leave the wagon up by the house so she can pack everything, and bring the mules back first thing in the morning."

It was only after Lewis left that Grady suddenly realized what all this meant. He glanced around the barn to make certain Mr. Browning wasn't around, then whispered to his fellow slaves, "This is it! This is the chance we've been waiting for! We can all be free!"

"What's going on?"

"The Yankees have landed here on the mainland at McKay's Point. All the Rebels are heading to Pocotaligo to stop them. We'll be able to circle to the south and get past the Rebel lines. Browning can't chase all of us, especially if we split up into groups and go in different directions, the way we planned. Once we get to McKay's Point we'll be free. The Yankees won't return us to our owners."

"We gonna have to act soon, I reckon."

"Yes. Tonight when the moon sets," Grady said. "Start spreading the word to all the others."

"What about bringing Missus Fuller her wagon?"

"Let me do it," Grady said. "I need to talk to my wife and Delia."

Grady parked the wagon in the yard outside the rear door and waited, delaying as long as he dared, hoping that one of the women would come out to talk to him. At last the door opened and Anna and Delia came out of the house together. As much as he longed for Anna's embrace, he stayed away from her, unwilling to risk Missy Claire's anger if she happened to look out the window and see them together. But there was no harm if Delia hugged him, and her embrace was as welcome as a warm fire on a cold day.

"Lord, Lord, honey! I hardly recognized you," she said. "You driving Missy Claire's wagon for her tomorrow?"

He shook his head. "I'm all through with being a slave," he said quietly. "Me and the others gonna steal away to the woods tonight. Once we get to where the Yankees are, we'll all be free."

"You can't run away, Grady!" Anna cried. "They'll send the dogs out after you if you run!"

Her fear made him angry. "Who will? Ain't nobody left to chase us but the overseer. He can't catch all of us, can he?" He folded his arms across his chest and raised his chin in defiance to show her he was unafraid, that they had nothing to fear. "You don't have to go with Missy Claire, you know. She can't make you go with her."

"What do you mean? She's our missy. We have to do what Missy says."

"No you don't," he said in a low, harsh voice. "We don't have to do nothing she says no more, now that the Yankees are here. Y'all can come hide in the woods with us tonight . . . unless you think house slaves is too good to run off with field hands."

"Nobody's thinking that," Delia said.

"Then come with us," he urged.

Anna gazed into the distance as if trying to make up her mind. "Missy says the Yankees ain't our friends," she said after a moment. "She says they gonna have their way with all the women and—"

"Don't you know them white folks is lying?" Grady felt desperate to convince her, but he didn't know how.

"Missy Claire don't lie! I been with her just as long as I can re-member, and she—"

"Go on with your fancy white missy, then, if you want to be her slave so bad." He spat on the ground near his feet, frustrated by her blindness, and sick with anger and fear. What if she wouldn't come with him?

Delia stood beside the wagon, not saying a word. But they all looked up a moment later when one of the upstairs windows slid open with a loud scrape. Missy Claire leaned out of it.

"Kitty! Get back up here this instant!" Anna turned and ran straight into the house. Grady felt as though he'd been punched in the stomach.

"How can I convince her to come with me, Delia?" he asked.

"I don't know, honey."

"But you're coming with me, right?" He gripped Delia's slender shoulders, desperate to convince at least one of the women he loved to join him.

"Let me think on it awhile," she said. "I'll meet you later, when Missus Fuller ain't looking out the window. I'll be in the cemetery by my daughter's grave after dark. Can you meet me?"

"I'll be there."

CHAPTER
17

FULLER PLANTATION, SOUTH CAROLINA
NOVEMBER 1862

As soon as it was dark, Grady crept out of his cabin and hurried through the trees to the slave cemetery to talk to Delia. Mr. Browning often patrolled the plantation grounds at night, armed with his rifle, and Grady hoped that the overseer wasn't patrolling tonight. As word of the planned escape had spread, everyone on Slave Row had been trying to act normal, trying to pretend that tomorrow was just another workday. But Grady noticed the extra tension and excitement in the air as everyone waited for the moon to set, waited to be free. He wondered if Mr. Browning had noticed. The overseer had several sets of shackles in his toolshed. He could easily chain up all the leading men for the night, to prevent them from running.

The cemetery was very dark, shaded by a grove of oak trees. Grady saw Delia standing in the fenced-in yard beside the little grave. He hoped that she had come to her daughter's grave to say good-bye before she escaped with him. Grady had spent all afternoon trying to figure out a way to convince Delia and Anna to leave with him tonight. If there was ever a time when he wished he could pray, this was it. He went to Delia and stood beside her, waiting for her to speak first.

"You got yourself a good plan?" she asked. "Did you take your time and think everything through? I know you heard plenty of stories about all the other slaves who've tried running. You know all the things that can go wrong and what will happen if they catch you?"

"I know the risks," Grady replied. "Me and the others have been talking about this and planning it ever since we came here from Beaufort. Tonight's our chance, Delia. We can do it. We're gonna be free."

"Inside your heart is where you're free," she said softly. "And that only happens when you know the Lord. If your sins are forgiven and you're His child, then you're free. If not, then even if you make it over to the Yankee side, you still ain't gonna be free."

Grady struggled to control his impatience, unwilling to argue with Delia. "We're waiting until the moon sets," he said. "Are you and Anna coming with us?"

Delia gazed down at the grave without answering. In the long silence that followed, Grady was aware of the sighing wind, the rustle of Spanish moss in the branches overhead, the murmur of insects.

"I don't come here to this grave to be sad," Delia finally said. "I come here to find hope. I know that my baby has gone on to a better life."

Grady stifled a groan. She was going to start talking about the Lord and how they'd all have a better life in heaven someday. He didn't want to hear it. He wanted a better life now. "Can we talk about heaven some other time, Delia?" he asked as gently as he could.

"I don't mean heaven, honey. If you was to dig up this grave, know what you'd find in that pine box?" She smiled up at him and her eyes filled with tears. "Rocks—ain't nothing inside it but rocks."

"Rocks?" he repeated.

"That's what I said, ain't it? My baby girl ain't buried in this here ground."

"Well, where's she buried, then?"

"She ain't dead, Grady. She's gone free."

"You ain't making sense, Delia."

"Remember how I told you that her daddy was a white man? How she's just as light-skinned as you are? Well, one day when my baby was five years old, I met some real kind Quaker folks who were visiting down here from the state of Pennsylvania. They offered to take my little girl up north with them, so she wouldn't have to be a slave no more. Said they'd adopt her as their very own daughter and everything. So I let her go."

Tears spilled down Delia's face, and for a long moment she couldn't speak. Grady wrapped his arm around her and pulled her close. They stood side by side, looking at the grave in silence.

"They dressed my baby all up in pretty little white girls' clothes," Delia said when she could continue, "and they drove away with her one night. I told everybody that my baby took sick, and then I let on like she died. Had a funeral for her and everything. But she's gone north, honey. She's free."

Grady remembered how he'd been torn from his mother against her will, and he marveled at the strength of Delia's love to let her child go. "You set her free," he said softly.

"Hardest thing I ever done, because I loved that girl like my own life. This here is the second hardest—saying good-bye to you. I guess you know how much I love you, too."

Grady looked down at her and nodded, barely able to speak. "Come with me, Delia. Please."

"No," she said simply. "No, honey, I can't do that."

"Why not? We'll both be free, just like your daughter. Maybe we can go up north and find her. All we have to do is cross the Rebel lines. You know I'll take good care of you. I'll carry you on my back if I have to. Please, Delia. I can't leave you behind."

"Well, you're just gonna have to, because I ain't going. I prayed about it, and the Lord told me I still got work to do for Him right here." She freed herself from his embrace and abruptly walked away.

"Wait . . . Where are you going?"

"I have something to give you before you go," she called over her shoulder. "Come down to the cabin with me and I'll show you." She walked so briskly that Grady had to hurry to keep up with her.

He drew a deep breath as he stepped into the cabin they'd shared for so many years, as if he could inhale all the memories they'd shared, as well, and store them inside. He'd only been back once since Missus Fuller sent him to Slave Row. Now he gazed around at the familiar rooms, remembering his first day on this plantation—how Delia had pulled him into her arms and allowed him to cry.

"I can't leave you, Delia," he said, swallowing the lump in his throat.

"Yes, you can, honey. Here . . . these are for you." She handed him a pile of folded clothing with a hat lying on top. "I borrowed some of Massa Fuller's clothes from his bureau up in the Big House." Grady recognized the tailored suit and starched white shirt that Massa sometimes wore to church on Sundays.

"What's this for?"

"Massa ain't needing them, right now," she said. "I know you're taller and bigger through the shoulders than he is, but they'll do. When my daughter put on white girls' clothes she fooled everybody. You put these on, and I know you can pass for a white man if nobody's looking too close. Keep Massa's hat on your head so they don't see your hair. Them Rebels ain't never gonna know you're a runaway slave. You'll be free, honey."

Grady couldn't imagine it. He was certain that for the rest of his life he would always be looking over his shoulder, always expecting to be caught and dragged back and whipped. He longed to know what it would be like to walk down the street, a free man. But he was not at all certain that he wanted to pose as a white man—the very race he hated—in order to do it.

"There's just one favor I want to ask when you go," she said.

"Anything, Delia."

"Take Kitty with you."

"Anna? But she said this afternoon that she was afraid to run."

"I know. That poor child can't make up her mind what to do. I know it ain't none of my business, but she loves you, Grady. Whether you love her or not, take her with you."

"I do love her," he said softly. He was surprised to admit it. He couldn't bear the thought of leaving her behind, maybe never seeing her again. He longed for both of them to be free so they finally could be husband and wife. "I'll gladly take her—but how do I convince her to come?"

Delia sighed. "I'm going up to the Big House now, to take care of Massa's baby. I'm gonna send your wife back down here. Show her you love her, Grady. Give yourself to her tonight. I know you always been afraid to love her, afraid you'll lose her like you lost everybody else, but the white folks can never keep you apart once the two of you are free. And it don't matter if she has your baby now, because he'll be free, too. If you give Kitty your love tonight, I know she'll make up her mind to go with you when the moon sets."

Grady pulled Delia into his arms and held her tightly, bracing himself for another loss. He wondered if he would ever see this beloved little woman again, or hold her in his arms. When he pulled back to look at her face one last time, they both were crying. "I wish you'd come with us, Delia."

"I'll never stop praying for you, honey. Not for a single day. Not as long as I have breath in this old body."

Delia wept as she walked away from Grady and hurried across the yard to the Big House. O Lord, this was hard! Just as hard as that day, more than thirty years ago, when she had let her baby go. Now Delia was saying good-bye to two more of her children, because that's just what Grady and Kitty were to her—beloved children. But they weren't hers to hang on to, any more than her first daughter had been. They belonged to the Lord, and she had to leave them in His hands.

She hoped she had done the right thing in telling Grady to sleep with Kitty tonight. She hoped it would change Kitty's mind. Surely she would go with him once she saw how much Grady loved her, wouldn't she? Kitty did love him—Delia was certain of that. And he loved her—as much as that poor boy would allow himself to love anybody.

Delia longed to keep Grady here, keep both of them here. But Grady's anger was growing more dangerous every day. If he didn't get his freedom soon, if one more tragedy happened to him, his rage was going to explode, destroying him and anyone who got in his way. As much as Delia hated losing him, she knew that his wounds would never heal until he was free. And there was more hope for that healing to take place if he had Kitty in his life. In time, she could help soften all of his hatred with love and tenderness. Otherwise, letting Grady escape alone would be like turning a caged animal loose, bent on revenge.

"Lord, take care of them," she prayed. "They're in your hands."

Delia thought of her real daughter, still remembering her as the five-year-old child she had said good-bye to, so long ago. But her baby would be all grown up by now. She was probably a mother herself. It was hard to imagine, but she would be as old as Massa Roger was. They'd been born only a month apart. The hardest thing was not knowing, never hearing from her baby or knowing for certain that she was all right. Delia would probably never know what became of Grady and Kitty, either, after she let them go.

O Lord, this was so hard.

Delia dried her tears before she went inside the Big House so that Kitty wouldn't see them. She slowly climbed the stairs to the nursery where Kitty was holding baby Richard in her arms, humming softly as she rocked him to sleep.

"You make up your mind about going with the others tonight?" Delia asked her.

Kitty nodded. "I thought it all over like you said, Delia—all the way back to the beginning. But no matter how much I want to be with Grady in the end, the story just ain't gonna end up like that. I ran off once before with my mama and papa, and . . . and it ended . . ." She couldn't finish. "I'm scared, Delia. I'm just so scared."

"I know, honey. I know you are." She lifted the baby from Kitty's arms and laid him in his cradle.

"Are you going with Grady?" Kitty asked.

Delia didn't answer. She patted the baby's back until he settled down to sleep again, then she put her arm around Kitty's waist. "Honey, I think you should go with him. You know Grady's gonna take real good care of you. It ain't gonna be like when your folks ran off. The Yankee soldiers are real close, this time. Soon as you reach them, you'll be safe."

"But what if we get caught?"

Delia didn't say *trust Jesus*. She didn't want to make a promise that wasn't hers to keep. She knew that Kitty's father had been a man of faith, trusting the Lord. Kitty would never believe her. Instead Delia said, "But what if you *don't* get caught? Then you and Grady will be free. It's what he wants more than anything else, what he needs."

Kitty swallowed. "I didn't tell him good-bye."

"He's waiting down at our cabin right now," Delia said. "You go on down there and talk to him. I'll stay here with the baby."

"But what if Missy—"

"I'll tell her you went down to pack your own things. Heaven knows, you spent all day packing hers."

Kitty hesitated.

"Go on, honey. I'll be here when you get back. I ain't going no-where."

❧

Kitty had thought about escaping with Grady all afternoon, and she just couldn't face the fear and the darkness that were her earliest memories. She'd made up her mind to return to Great Oak Plantation with Missy, where it was safe. Now she needed to convince Grady to stay where he would be safe, too.

There was no light burning in the cabin, no smoke rising from the chimney. She wondered if Delia was mistaken, if Grady had left already. But when she opened the door, she saw him sitting at the little table.

"I thought you'd be gone by now," she said, relieved that he wasn't.

"Not until the moon sets. Come with me, Anna."

She slowly shook her head. "I can't."

Grady stood and moved toward her in the darkness. "May I hold you?" He didn't wait for her reply but drew her into his arms, clinging to her as if he planned never to let go. And she didn't want him to.

The tears she had held back all day began to flow. She wanted so badly to be with him this way forever. But her parents had wanted to be together, too. And her story would surely end the same way that theirs had. Kitty had seen the armed Rebel soldiers today. There were thousands of them. The slaves would surely be recaptured. She wept, overwhelmed with fear for Grady.

"Shh . . . it's okay . . . it's okay," Grady murmured. His strong arms tightened around her as if he sensed her fear. She felt safe in his arms. But she had felt safe in her papa's strong arms, too. The men who had chased Papa had been stronger. They'd carried guns. Papa hadn't been strong enough to save her.

Then Grady started kissing her, his lips brushing her neck, her cheeks, her forehead. His lips found hers, and she forgot everything else but this moment and the overpowering love that she felt for him. Nothing, no one, could ever separate them.

"I love you, Anna," he whispered. "I want to sleep with you tonight. Not because Missy wants us to, but because we want to."

Kitty allowed him to lead her to the bed. Then he stopped, gazing down at her in the moonlight, waiting for her answer. His hands felt warm as they caressed her back, her shoulders, her face.

"We're married, Anna. I belong to you. But only if this is what you want . . ."

She could scarcely breathe. "I do want it," she whispered. She pulled him close, returning his kisses with her own. She trembled and didn't know why.

"Don't be scared," he said. "I would never do anything to hurt you."

Time and space seemed to vanish as Kitty lost herself in Grady's love. Delia had told her that married love was a gift from God, and tonight Kitty wept with the sheer joy of it. She reveled in the safety and warmth of his arms, awestruck by the wonder of belonging to each other alone. Grady had allowed himself to be vulnerable with her, and she with him. The scars on his bare back were hers alone to soothe and caress.

All her life she'd been Missy Claire's possession, but on this glorious night she belonged to Grady, the man she loved, and he belonged to her. She lay content in the warmth of his arms as the moon slowly crawled across the sky and sank below the horizon.

"I want to be with you this way forever," Grady whispered. "Every night . . . the way we are right now."

She wept and kissed him again, certain that he would stay with her now, to take care of her, protect her. It stunned her when he said, "Run away with me tonight. Please, Anna."

Her heart pounded with terror at his words. She clung to him tightly, unable to voice her fears. In the midnight stillness, she heard an owl calling.

"That's the signal," Grady said. "The moon has set. Come on, the others are ready to go." He climbed out of bed and began to dress. She watched him but she was unable to move, her limbs paralyzed with fear. She couldn't seem to breathe.

Anna remembered her parents and the nightmare returned—not as a worn and faded dream this time, but as a living memory, vivid with color and sound. She felt her family's fear as they slogged through the eerie swamps, heard the sound of horses and dogs splashing through the water behind them, gaining on them. Her papa's breath had come in ragged gulps as he ran and ran with Anna in his arms. She saw the terror on her parents' faces when they were captured.

Anna had always forgotten the end of the dream—until now. Now she saw each blow of the whip across her parents' backs and heard their tortured screams. She relived all of it, all the way to the end, and heard her mama screaming her name as the men dragged her away. She saw Papa's body dangling from the Great Oak Tree, his face a deep, violent purple.

"No . . ." she whispered. "Grady, no!"

He returned to the bedside and took her face in his hands, covering it with kisses. "Come on, Anna. Please, we have to hurry."

She gripped his arms in desperation, clinging so tightly she saw him wince. "Stay here with me! If you love me, stay here! Where it's safe!"

"I do love you. But we can be free." He gently pried her hands loose and began picking up her clothes, handing them to her one by one. "Trust me, Anna. Everything will be all right."

"How do you know that? How do you know we won't be caught and whipped and tortured?" She couldn't catch her breath. She felt as if she'd been running and running, just as her parents had.

"Anna, I *have* to go. I've waited all my life for this chance. Please come with me."

He began to dress her as if she was a child, slipping her frock over her head and patiently buttoning each button. The voice was Grady's, but he was a stranger to her, dressed in a starched white shirt and a dark vest and suit coat. Why was he wearing white men's clothes? He looked every inch an elegant gentleman, not a slave. She loved him, longed for him. But her fear was greater.

"Don't go, Grady! Please don't go! I don't want to lose you! I don't want you to die!"

"I won't die. We'll be free. Come with me Anna, *please*!" His dark eyes filled with tears. "Here's your shoes. Hurry, put them on."

She shook her head, clutching the shoes to her chest.

"Anna, I'm begging you! Come on!"

He bent to lift her into his arms and carry her, but the thought of being taken against her will made her hysterical. "No, no, no!"

He quickly put her down and backed away, covering her mouth with his hand. "Okay, okay . . . shh . . . shh . . ." Her mama had urged her to be quiet the same way as they'd crept through the swamp.

Outside, the owl hooted again, signaling to Grady. Anna sensed his urgency, his despair. He went to the door and gazed out, then turned back, his eyes pleading with her, his face wet with tears.

"Anna, *please!*"

She shook her head.

Grady wiped his eyes with his fist and drew a deep breath. "Good-bye, then," he said.

And he ran out into the night.

Kitty couldn't stop trembling, couldn't breathe normally for a very long time. The night was quiet except for the soft rustling of tree branches in the wind. There were no baying dogs, no pounding hooves, no gunshots echoing through the swamps. But Kitty couldn't move from the bed.

She gazed down at the cornshuck mattress where Grady had lain beside her. She saw the dented imprint of his body.

But Grady was gone.

Part Two

❧

Has God forgotten to be merciful? Has he in anger withheld his compassion? Then I thought, "To this I will appeal . . . I will remember the deeds of the Lord; yes, I will remember your miracles of long ago."

Psalm 77:9–11 NIV

FULLER PLANTATION, SOUTH CAROLINA
NOVEMBER 1862

Kitty lay awake in the empty cabin for the rest of the night, too distraught to sleep. Any moment now, she would hear the tramp of marching feet, the sounds of gunfire. The Rebel soldiers would capture Grady and the others and haul them into the plantation yard in shackles. She would have to watch the overseer flog her husband to punish him for escaping.

As the room grew light, Kitty could no longer bear waiting. She put on her shoes and walked across the backyard to the Big House, passing the loaded wagon still parked outside the door. She had forgotten that she and Missy were fleeing today, too.

Upstairs in the nursery, Delia walked the floor with the baby. She halted midstep when she saw Kitty and gaped at her in surprise. "What are you doing here?"

"I came to help you with the baby. Missy said we have to leave real early, and I thought—" She stopped when Delia lowered her head and began to weep. The little woman sank down on the bedroom chair as if she was very old, still cradling the baby. Tears leaked from behind her closed eyes.

"What's wrong?" Kitty asked.

Delia finally looked up. "Is Grady gone?"

"Yes. He ran off with all the others last night."

"And you didn't go with him?"

Kitty shook her head. "No, I—"

"O Lord, honey . . . why not?"

Delia's grief confused Kitty. She struggled for a way to explain her fear to Delia, but before she could utter a word, Missy burst into the room.

"Kitty! Get in here and help me get dressed. Delia, get the baby ready to go. Where's the wet nurse? Tell her to hurry up and feed Richard so we can leave."

Kitty and Delia looked at each other. The mat where the nurse slept was empty. She must have escaped with all the others. "S-she ain't here, Missy. Want me to go look for her?" Kitty asked.

"No, I want you to help me get dressed. Delia, put the baby down and you go look for her. And send someone up to the house to harness the mules to the wagon."

Kitty knew that there was no one to do it. Grady and all the others were gone. But before either Delia or Kitty could move, someone pounded on the front door downstairs. Kitty's heart hammered with fear at the sound. They waited for Lewis to answer it, but he must have run off as well.

"Where's Lewis?" Missy asked. "Go and see who's at the door, Kitty."

She ran downstairs and opened it to find Mr. Browning, the white overseer. He studied Kitty in silence for a long moment, then looked up and saw Missy standing at the top of the stairs.

"They're gone, ma'am," he said. His voice shook with anger. "The slaves have all run off."

"What . . . what do you mean?" she asked as she slowly descended the stairs. Delia followed her down.

Lynn Austin

"I blew the horn to start the workday, just like always, but nobody came. When I checked the cabins, there wasn't anybody left except a few old-timers. The rest of your field slaves have all run off."

"What about my house servants? Where's the baby's nurse? And my butler? And . . . and my coachman? Who's going to drive me to Great Oak Plantation?"

"I'm afraid they're all gone, ma'am. Your driver ran off with all the others."

Missy whirled to face Kitty. "But he's your husband! Did you know he was going to run away? Why didn't you warn me?"

Kitty didn't know what to say. She was afraid to speak for fear she would make Missy even angrier—or worse, betray Grady. And she didn't want to make a mistake and say something that would help Missy and Mr. Browning find the runaways and bring them back. But before she could figure out what to say, Delia spoke.

"Don't blame her, ma'am. Kitty and her husband ain't been living together since you sent him down to Slave Row. How's she supposed to know where he's at or what he's up to? I never heard Lewis or Patsy say a single word about running off, and I been working with them every day."

"What are we going to do?" Missy asked Mr. Browning.

"If it's okay with you, ma'am, I'm going to load my rifle and start tracking them. I'll see if I can round up some help from a couple of neighboring plantations and borrow their dogs. Our soldiers aren't far from here. They're expecting a battle near Pocotaligo, but they can be on the lookout for the runaways, too. We'll catch them all, ma'am. Don't worry."

Kitty felt faint with fear at his words.

"I'm going to my father's plantation today," Missy said. "Would you kindly hitch the mules to my wagon for me before you start the search? And find someone to drive it. I want to leave immediately."

"Of course, ma'am."

By the time Kitty fixed Missy's hair and helped her get dressed, she barely had enough time to run down to her own cabin and grab

271

a few belongings. They had filled the wagon to overflowing with Missy Claire's things, and there wasn't much room to spare, but Kitty made sure that she packed a picture of Grady. It was the one she'd drawn a long time ago, on the first day they met.

On her way out of the cabin, she saw the bed that they'd slept in, the covers still rumpled from their one night together. Kitty could no longer stop her tears from falling, nor did she care if Missy Claire saw them. She was leaving. Grady wouldn't know where to find her again, nor she him. Once she reached Great Oak Plantation, she might not hear news of the runaways for a very long time—if ever.

Back at the Big House, Missy was frantic, barking so many commands that Kitty couldn't keep track of them all. She helped Delia climb onto the wagon, then ran upstairs and brought the baby down for her to hold. The overseer had harnessed the mule team and ordered an elderly slave who had been too old to flee, to drive. He stood beside the wagon with his wife, clutching a bundle of their belongings and waiting for someone to help them climb aboard.

"That old woman stays here," Missy Claire said, pointing to the old man's wife. "There isn't enough room on the wagon for both of you."

"Please, I can make room," Kitty begged. "I'll leave my bag—"

"I said no!"

Kitty hated Missy at that moment. Grady had been right about her—and about all white people. They never cared how many families they tore apart this way, how many times slaves had to say good-bye to the people they loved. If only Kitty could have convinced Grady to stay with her last night, instead of running headlong into danger. If only they could be together forever. Now it was too late.

She saw the old couple's love for each other as they embraced and kissed each other good-bye. Then Mr. Browning helped the husband climb up on the driver's seat. Kitty looked back as they drove away and saw the man's wife standing where he had left her on the side of the road. She was still there when the wagon finally rounded a curve and Kitty lost sight of her.

⚜

By the time the sky grew light, Grady figured he and the other slaves had walked a good long distance from the plantation. The harvested wheat and rice fields had given way to marshy woods, then swamps. Cold water had seeped into his tattered shoes until his toes were so icy he could barely feel them. Massa Fuller's suit coat was warmer than Grady's homespun shirt would have been, but the other slaves weren't dressed as warmly as he was. Grady worried about the women and children.

As planned, the slaves had divided into several groups, each heading in a different direction to confuse any dogs that might be tracking them. Grady traveled with twenty-two others—nine men, six women and seven children. He had helped carry a little girl on his back, for much of the night, thinking of Anna and the story of her parents' failed attempt to escape.

Dawn made it easier to find a path through the maze of inlets and swamps, easier to avoid snakes and alligators and other hazards. But Grady worried constantly that someone would spot them, especially when they skirted around the edges of a plantation or came within sight of a road or the railroad tracks. Back on Slave Row, he and the others had debated a long time about whether or not to travel during the daytime. Some had argued that they needed to cover as many miles as they possibly could, and therefore they should keep walking day and night so their pursuers wouldn't catch up with them. Others had insisted that they hide and rest during the day so that roaming Confederate soldiers wouldn't discover them. A group of twenty-two slaves tramping through the woods would immediately raise suspicion. And Grady knew that Mr. Browning would quickly spread the alarm, asking all the surrounding plantation owners—and soldiers—to be on the lookout for the runaways. Grady had sided with those who wanted to keep running day and night until they reached safety.

But by noon of the first day, after walking for nearly twelve hours, many of his fellow slaves were too weary to walk another step. It had started to rain shortly after dawn, soaking all of them and adding to their misery. They finally stopped in a dense grove of cypress trees to rest. "Any idea where we are?" one of the men whispered to Grady.

"Not exactly," he replied. "But the little bit I can see of the sun tells me we're heading in the right direction. And I tasted this water. It's brackish, so that means we're getting closer to the ocean."

Another slave joined their huddle. "Think it's safe enough to follow the road for a while if we find one? Everybody's feet are so wet and cold they can't hardly walk."

"I know—mine are, too," Grady said. "But them Confederate soldiers is probably sticking to the roads for that very reason. We need to be staying in the woods."

"The Yankees came to the mainland by boat, right?" the first slave asked. "Well, this coast is a mess of rivers and salt marshes. How we ever gonna find the place where they landed without running into the Rebels?"

It was a question that Grady had been asking himself all night. He didn't know the answer. They might have to wander through the swamps for quite a while before they met up with the Yanks—unless the Yanks won the battle. They were expecting a fight near the town of Pocotaligo. If the Yankees won, all of this territory would fall into their hands as the Rebels retreated toward Charleston. He and the others might be safe right now and not even know it.

Before he could think of a reply, Grady suddenly smelled smoke. He looked around in alarm and saw that a group of women had kindled a fire.

"Hey! Put that fire out!" he said, rushing over to them. "You want to get us all caught? Someone's bound to see the smoke." He tried to kick dirt onto the flames to put them out, but someone shoved him aside.

"Stop it!" the man said. "Our feet's half frozen. Let the women and little ones warm up a bit, then we'll douse the fire."

274

"Don't be a fool!" Grady said. "The soldiers have lookouts. They'll spot the smoke and send armed men to check it out."

"Ain't no Rebels around here. They're all off fighting the Yankees."

"We don't know that. Hey, come on!" Grady grew more and more alarmed as the fire continued to burn, but there was nothing he could do about it. Two of the fathers with small children held Grady back while their wives helped the little ones get warm near the flames. The wood and fallen leaves they were using for fuel were damp from the rain, creating even more smoke.

"Let go of me," Grady said as he struggled to break free. "If you won't listen to reason, then I'm gone. I ain't gonna stay here and get caught. Who's coming with me?"

Every one of the men shook his head as the slaves crowded around the fire, desperate to warm themselves. Several of the children were crying, their teeth chattering with cold. If only the rain would let up and the sun would come out, then they could dry out and get warm without a fire. Of all the rotten times to have unusually cold weather and rain! Grady wanted to rage at God for refusing to help them in even the simplest way.

"I'm leaving y'all, then," he said quietly. "I ain't staying by a fire that the Rebs are sure to spot." No one protested. They had talked last night about having Grady pose as their white master if they were discovered, since he was dressed so differently from all of them. He could make up a story about getting lost in the woods or something. But now it was almost as if his clothing and lighter skin set him apart as someone who was different from them. They chose to stick with each other rather than join him.

"Good luck to you," he said and strode off into the woods alone.

⁂

By sundown Grady was exhausted. Several times during the day he had wandered close enough to a road or a house to see people and signs of activity. He had briefly considered taking the road, trusting his disguise as a white man to help bluff his way past any danger, but he had finally discarded the idea. How would he explain why he wasn't serving in the Confederate army? They might shoot him for a deserter. And if they asked him to read something or write his name, he'd be unmasked for sure.

Grady ate very little of his meager food supply as he walked, determined to make it last as long as possible. On the second night, the sky was just as cloudy as on the first, slowing his progress through the gloomy swamps. It was next to impossible to see where he was going as he picked his way through the dense brush. Without the moon or stars to guide him, he might be traveling in circles or back toward the plantation, for all he knew. Weary and discouraged, Grady finally decided to lie down beneath a clump of scrub oaks and sleep until daylight. He was just too tired, too lost, to go on.

As he lay on the cold ground, waiting for sleep to come, a verse of scripture that Eli had once taught him drifted through his mind: *I will both lay me down in peace, and sleep: for thou, Lord, makes me dwell in safety.*

Immediately, Grady was angry with himself for remembering it. It seemed a mockery. Why was he thinking about God? During all these years, God had never once offered help to Grady when he needed it. He hadn't helped Kitty's parents, either, and they had called on Him, believed in Him. Exhausted and furious, Grady finally fell into a restless sleep.

※

The drive to Great Oak Plantation seemed like a very long one to Kitty. It didn't help that the damp, foggy day was gray and cheerless, and that she was cold and miserable most of the way as she rode in the back of the farm wagon. They drove through scented pine forests, past salt marshes and swamps, following the route of the Charleston and Savannah railroad tracks much of the way. She saw several plantations along the road, and a few other wagonloads of fleeing refugees, like themselves. But over and over, her thoughts returned to Grady, worrying about him and the others, wondering where he was and if he was safe.

Late in the morning, the old driver stopped to rest and water the mules. Kitty helped Delia climb down so they could stretch their legs while they waited. "You seem so sad today," Kitty said to the older woman. "Are you okay?"

Delia sighed and gazed into the distant woods. "I guess I'm already missing my boy. Grady's been just like a son to me these past few years, and it sure was hard to say good-bye and let him go. But I know you're feeling the same thing as me, ain't you?"

"Yes," she whispered. "I'm so worried about him, Delia. Aren't you?"

"No, honey, I don't waste time worrying. I pray. That's what I been doing all morning. Every time I think of the danger he's in, or I start imagining all sorts of bad things happening to him, I know it's time to get praying, instead."

Kitty wished that her own fears would go away that easily. She wished that prayer really worked. She knew better. "My papa prayed when we tried to escape, and it didn't do us any good at all," she said.

"You don't know that," Delia said a little sharply. "You don't know how God answered those prayers. Praying ain't about getting your own way. It's about asking God to have His way."

"But if God's mind is already made up, why bother praying at all?"

"I suppose different folks have different reasons," she said with a sigh. "But for me, praying helps me remember that the Lord is in charge. I been picturing Grady in His hands all morning and asking the Lord to watch out for him—no matter what He sees fit to have happen."

Her words shocked Kitty. "Delia, no! What if God wants him to get caught?"

"Then that's what's best for Grady." She spoke the words so softly that Kitty barely heard her.

"You don't really mean that!"

"Yes, I do. God let His own Son die because He had a better

idea in mind. Now, I don't know why He let your folks get caught or what's gonna happen to Grady. But I do know that we can trust the Lord, even when we don't understand why things happen the way they do."

"I'm scared, Delia. I'm scared for Grady and so scared that . . . that I'll never see him again."

"I know," she said, wrapping her arm around Kitty's waist. "But you're trying to face your fears all alone."

"I am alone—except for you."

"No, you're not. The Lord's been beside you all your life, watching over you just like a father. I put Grady into His hands when I said good-bye to him last night, and I'll bet your mama and papa put you in His hands, too. Jesus knows how we're suffering. Did you know they whipped Him, too, and hung Him from a tree?"

Kitty pictured the Great Oak Tree and shuddered. "Was he a Negro like us?"

"He was God's Son, and God ain't no color at all."

Kitty was still thinking about Delia's words when they finally arrived at the plantation late that evening. Two years had passed since Kitty and Missy Claire had lived here, but everything looked unchanged, the Great Oak Tree still standing sentry on the hill above the Edisto River. She felt exhausted and a little dazed as Mammy Bertha and Daisy and the other servants hurried out of the house to greet them and help unload the wagon. Bertha lifted baby Richard from Delia's arms.

"My, oh my! Ain't he a little darling?" Bertha said. "We ain't been having a baby boy in this house in a long, long time. Only girl babies. My, my what a treat."

As soon as Missy Claire explained the reason for their flight, Missus Goodman took charge. "You must stay here where it's safe, Claire, until those Yankees are driven away for good. As soon as I heard that they'd landed in Beaufort, I told your father that Roger's plantation was much too close to all the danger. I'm glad you've come home."

The word jolted Kitty. She had been born on this plantation, had lived here most of her life—but it didn't feel like home anymore. Home had been the little cabin she'd shared for such a short time with Delia and Grady. Tears sprang unexpectedly to her eyes when she remembered their only night together.

"Kitty! You haven't heard a word I've said!"

She came out of her reverie to hear Missus Goodman yelling at her. "I'm sorry, ma'am. I'm listening now, ma'am."

"It's about time! I ordered you to take the baby's things upstairs to the nursery. Mammy Bertha will show you where to put them. I assume you're his nurse?"

"Um . . . n-no, ma'am. I . . ."

"She couldn't produce a child," Claire told her mother. Kitty knew by Missy's tone that she was still angry about it. "I had to use one of the field slaves. But she apparently ran off this morning with all the others."

Missus Goodman glared at Kitty for a long moment as if that had been her fault, too. "I'll send Daisy down to the Row to fetch a new nurse. In the meantime, you'd better start obeying me, girl, if you know what's good for you. Now get upstairs!"

"Yes, ma'am." Kitty grabbed a bundle of the baby's clothes and gestured to Delia to follow her.

"Just a minute," Missus Goodman said, stopping Delia. "Where do you think you're going? Who are you?"

Delia lowered her eyes. Her voice was calm. "My name's Delia, ma'am. And I been the mammy over at Massa Fuller's house these many years."

"Well, Claire won't be needing you anymore. Mammy Bertha will take care of the baby from now on. My overseer will find you a place down on Slave Row."

Her words stunned Kitty. She nearly cried out in protest but caught herself just in time.

"You can help Kitty carry Richard's things upstairs," Missus

Goodman told Delia, "then someone will take you down to speak to the overseer."

"Yes, ma'am." Delia suddenly looked very old to Kitty. She remembered the cold, drafty cabins and meager food portions on Slave Row and feared that life down there would be the death of the little woman she loved.

"She can't do this to you," Kitty whispered as she led Delia up the servants' stairs. "You raised Massa Fuller and his sons since they was tiny babies. What would Massa say if he knew?"

Delia laid down her armload of satchels on the nursery table. "It don't matter what he'd say, because he ain't here. Missus Goodman runs this house, and it's up to her to decide."

Kitty could no longer stop her tears. She lay down her own bundles and took Delia into her arms, clinging to her. "I don't want to lose you," she wept. "I already lost Grady, and I don't want to lose you, too."

"I know, honey. I know. . . ."

"Why do things just keep getting worse and worse? Why does every bit of happiness we find always get snatched away from us again? I should have gone with Grady last night. We both should have."

"No, I believe this is where the Lord wants me," Delia said quietly.

Kitty pulled back to look into her eyes. "How can you say that? After what just happened?"

Delia didn't answer. "I surely will miss you, honey," she said instead. "You come on down and visit me whenever you can, okay?" She gave Kitty one last hug before she left.

Kitty struggled to absorb the fact that she would no longer be with Delia. She was back to where she started, living at Great Oak Plantation, working for Missus Goodman and Missy Claire, all alone in the world. For a horrible moment it seemed as though the past few years with Delia and Grady had been only a dream. Kitty quickly dug in her satchel for the picture she'd drawn of Grady, gazing at it through her tears to assure herself that he had been real, that he had loved her.

Kitty had been a slave since the day she was born, but for the first time in her life she felt like one—a captive, forced to labor for other people against her will. She closed her eyes and prayed to Delia's God—her papa's God—that wherever Grady was tonight, he was safe. And that he was free.

19

SOUTH CAROLINA
NOVEMBER 1862

Grady awakened when something sharp prodded his shoulder. He opened his eyes and saw the barrel of a gun. The bayonet that was attached to it poked his shoulder again. For a long moment his heart seemed to stop beating.

"Get up!" a voice said.

Grady's heart started up again, pounding as if it would burst. They'd caught him. Rebel soldiers had caught him.

"Stand up. Nice and slow," the man with the gun said. "Hands above your head."

Grady obeyed, his limbs stiff and numb from sleeping on the cold ground. Massa's suit was wrinkled and coated with dirt and leaves. When Grady could take his eyes off the bayonet, he saw that the gun was loaded and ready to fire.

"Hey, Johnson," the man holding it called. "Come over here and check this fellow for weapons."

A second soldier stepped forward and carefully rifled through Grady's clothing. The only weapon Grady had was the tool he used to trim horses' hooves. He'd taken it from the stable and sharpened it on a whetstone before leaving home. The man named Johnson found it and slid it into his own pocket.

Grady squinted in the scant daylight, trying to focus on his captors' faces. The sun hadn't quite risen on another overcast day, and he wondered how the Rebels had ever found him. They didn't seem to have dogs. As he shook off his sleep and battled to rein in his panic, he realized that the men wore dark blue uniforms. They didn't look at all like the outfits that Massa Fuller and his Confederate soldiers wore.

"Y'all are Yankees?" he breathed.

"You bet we are."

Grady's knees went weak with relief. He was wide-awake now. He looked past the loaded rifle and into the clearing where more than a dozen men searched through the bushes, alert for enemy soldiers. It startled Grady to see that some of them were Negroes. They carried rifles with bayonets attached and wore Yankee uniform jackets, just like the white soldiers. A Negro soldier carrying a gun was such an unbelievable sight that Grady wondered if he was dreaming.

"Hey, Captain, come here!" Johnson called. "We caught a fancy Rebel gentleman trying to sneak off. Should we just go ahead and shoot him?"

Grady panicked. "Wait! I ain't a Rebel! I'm a slave. I ran away from Massa Fuller's plantation two nights ago. I'm trying to escape to y'all. Let me show you." He knew that his dark wooly hair would prove it, but when he started to remove his hat, the soldier jabbed the bayonet against his ribs.

"Hold it! Get your hands up! You move again, and I just might have to kill you."

"Listen," Grady pleaded. "I stole my master's clothes so I could fool the Rebels. But I'm a Negro, just like him." He tilted his head toward a black soldier who had wandered over with the captain to stare at him.

"You sure look white to me," Johnson said. "What do you think?" he asked the Negro soldier.

"He's all dressed up just like my massa," the Negro replied. "I say shoot him." He turned and walked away.

"Wait! Please!" Grady begged. "I'm light-skinned because I'm half white."

"Now, that's a good one, isn't it?" Johnson said. "What these Rebs won't think of to save their scrawny necks."

"Yeah, who would ever sleep with a Negro?" The three men laughed at the idea.

Grady felt a rivulet of sweat roll down his neck. "It's true," he said. "My white massa used my mother for . . . for his pleasure. She was his slave. I'm half white." He hated admitting that his father was white, that his mother had been abused that way. And he hated that these men thought he was white, like they were. He wasn't anything like them.

"What do you think, Captain?" the gunman asked. "His story sounds made-up to me."

"He talks just like a Southern boy. He's probably a spy."

"Shoot him. Who cares about one more dead Rebel?" Johnson said.

"Wait! I know how I can prove it," Grady said. He had a desperate idea, but his hands were still raised in the air and he didn't dare lower them. "Lift up my shirt and look at the scars on my back," he said. "Nobody ever done something like that to a white man."

The soldier kept the gun trained on him while Johnson walked around behind Grady. He felt his jacket being jerked up and his shirt pulled out of his trousers, then the damp morning air bathed his bare back.

"Oh my gosh! Come here and look at this, Captain."

The officer peered behind Grady to look. "He's telling the truth. I saw a slave at an abolition meeting back home who had been whipped for trying to escape. His back looked just like that." He called to the Negro soldier again, and he came over to look, too.

"Yes, sir, that's just what some massas like to do to us."

The soldier who had captured Grady finally lowered his gun. "Sorry, friend. No hard feelings?" He extended his hand for Grady to shake. Grady stared at it, his own hands still raised in the air. No white man had ever offered to shake hands with him as an equal before. But the gun was lowered. They weren't going to kill him. He gripped the soldier's hand in his own clammy palm.

The captain thumped Grady's shoulder. "You're free, son."

Grady heard the words, understood what they meant, but he couldn't comprehend them. He took off his hat and wiped his sweating brow with his sleeve.

"Are there any others with you?" the Captain asked.

Grady struggled to think clearly as a floodtide of emotions washed over him. "Um . . . yeah. About a hundred of us escaped from Massa Fuller's plantation. B-but we went our separate ways yesterday."

Anna. He had left Anna behind. She would be free right now if only she had come with him. They would both be free.

"Come on over here and join your brothers," the Negro soldier said. The other Negroes beckoned to him, welcoming him. One of them held out a canteen of water to him.

"I-I can't believe I made it," Grady murmured. He accepted the canteen and tilted his head back to take a long drink, hoping to hide the tears that had sprung to his eyes. But when he lowered the canteen again, the man who had given it to him had tears in his eyes, too.

"You don't have to be ashamed," he said. "We all know exactly how you feel. My name's Joseph. What's yours?"

"Grady."

"Well, Grady, you can start praising the Lord right now, because you ain't never gonna be a slave again."

Grady closed his eyes and allowed his silent tears to fall. He had nothing in the world except his freedom, and that was enough.

❧

All that glorious day, his first day of freedom, Grady had to remind himself over and over again, *I'm free! I'm a free man! I'm not a slave anymore!* He could scarcely believe it was true. If only Anna had come with him. And Delia. If only they could feel the way he felt right now.

Grady followed the band of Union soldiers as they scoured the woods for more runaways, and by some miracle they found thirty-seven other slaves from Massa Fuller's plantation and led them all through the woods to the landing site. Another squadron of soldiers arrived a few hours later with twenty-three more rescued slaves. Then to Grady's astonishment, he suddenly recognized one of the Negro soldiers in the second squadron. The big man was several years older than when Grady had seen him last, but the tension and anger on his dark face looked exactly as they had years ago.

"Amos!" Grady called out to him.

The big man looked up, puzzled, then slowly walked toward Grady. He carried his rifle with both hands, his finger on the trigger. "Do I know you?"

Grady quickly removed his hat, suddenly remembering that he still wore white men's clothes. No wonder Amos looked him over with distrust and suspicion. "Yeah, Amos. It's been nine years and I guess I've grown some since you saw me last. But we was in the slave pen together in Richmond. You looked out for me. We both got sold on the auction block to that slave trader."

Amos' face relaxed, coming as close to a smile as Grady had ever seen. "Right, I remember now. You was just a boy. . . . Now look at you! I thought you was some rich white man."

"I stole these clothes from my massa when I run off," Grady said with a grin. "But here you are with a gun and everything. How'd you get to be a soldier?"

"The Yankees come to our plantation near Savannah and set us all free," Amos replied. "They talked me into joining Hunter's regiment and gave me a gun. I finally got a chance to kill some white men, just like I said I would. Why don't you join us?"

"And take orders from them?" Grady asked, gesturing to the white soldiers. "No, sir! I ain't ever doing what any white man says again."

"Not even for the chance to kill a few of them? Help set our people free?"

"Oh, I still plan on killing plenty of white men," Grady said. "But I ain't taking orders anymore or being a servant to nobody. Besides, I don't need their permission if I want to kill somebody."

"Suit yourself," Amos said with a shrug. "They always willing to sign you up if you're changing your mind."

An officer shouted for the soldiers to begin lining up. They were about to board the boats. They told the rescued slaves to crowd in wherever they could.

"Where you headed?" Amos asked as he prepared to leave. Grady considered the question for the first time.

"Um ... I don't know. Where's this boat going?"

"Beaufort. We're camped near there," Amos replied.

"Then I guess that's where I'm going, too."

Amos nodded. "Maybe I'll see you around."

The ship with Grady on board arrived in Beaufort late that afternoon. He walked around town in a daze, barely recognizing the place. Supply boats and warships bristling with cannons filled the harbor. White men in uniforms swarmed everywhere, and the Stars and Stripes flew from every flagpole and church steeple. Soldiers tramped in and out of the finest houses along Bay and Craven Streets as if they owned them, using them as their headquarters or to house officers or store army supplies. Even the pretty white church that Massa Fuller used to attend had been turned into an army hospital. Vandals had pillaged and ransacked many of the homes, tearing down fences and outbuildings, chopping down trees. In one short year, the quiet beauty of pre-war Beaufort had vanished.

But Grady was free. He could stroll down the sidewalk heading anywhere he wanted, anytime he wanted, and nobody could stop him or shove him into the gutter. Dressed in Massa's clothes, Grady was treated just like a white man in downtown Beaufort, although he saw many former slaves on the docks and in the streets who were being mistreated by the Yankees. Even so, he made up his mind not to pretend he was white. He was a Negro and proud of it.

As night fell and the sky began growing dark, Grady's stomach rumbled with hunger. He had eaten the last of his food onboard the ship that afternoon, and now he was starved. He had no money, no friends, nowhere to sleep that night. Unsure what to do or where else to go, he walked the familiar route to Massa Fuller's town house, circling around, by habit, to the rear carriage gate in the backyard. The washhouse and slaves' quarters appeared deserted. He crossed the yard to the abandoned stables and ran up the stairs two at a time to the room he'd shared with Anna. He found it just as they had left it when they'd been forced to flee.

Grady hurried downstairs again, and was heading over to the kitchen to scrounge for food when he noticed smoke rising from the town-house chimney. He halted. As he stood staring at the back door, wondering what to do, it suddenly opened and Jim walked through it. Grady was astonished to see that the former slave wore one of Massa Fuller's jackets and was smoking one of his cigars. Jim glared at him with suspicion for a long moment before Grady thought to remove his hat.

"Hey, Jim. It's me—Grady," he called.

"Grady? I almost didn't recognize you. What're you doing here?"

"I run off from Massa's plantation a few days ago. Didn't know where else to go, so I came here."

Jim grinned, the cigar clamped between his teeth. "So you're a free man now, eh? Just like us. Ain't it great? Come on inside. Minnie will be tickled to see you."

"Come in . . . into the house?" Grady stammered. He had never been allowed inside before, but Jim held the door open wide for him.

"Sure. Who's gonna stop you? Massa Fuller ain't coming back with all these Yankees hanging around town, that's for sure. Me and Minnie got the whole place all to ourselves."

Grady followed Jim inside the Big House for the first time in his life, astounded by what he saw. Beautiful furniture and carpets and household goods filled room after room, making the town house even more lavish than the fancy hotels where Massa Coop used to stay. Minnie was nearly unrecognizable in a white lady's dress made of shiny, rose-colored material and lots of lace. She even wore one of those things beneath her skirt that made it stick out like a bell. Like Jim, she was wearing her former owners' clothing—but then, so was Grady.

Minnie had set the dining room table with bowls and tableware for the two of them. A delicious-smelling pot of stew and dumplings waited in the middle of it. "Want some dinner?" she asked. "We was just sitting down to eat when Jim thought he saw somebody snooping around out back."

"Yeah, thanks—if you got enough, that is."

"We can make do." She pulled another shiny white bowl and some silverware from a dining room cabinet and set a place for Grady at the table. He hesitated, then finally sat down at his master's polished dining room table, certain that he was dreaming. He had to keep telling himself that there was no reason to be nervous, nobody was going to burst through the door and punish him for sitting at a white man's table. These were his friends, Minnie and Jim. Massa Fuller was gone, and Grady was free.

"Where's your pretty little wife?" Minnie asked.

Grady had to draw a deep breath before he could answer. It pained him to recall that Anna truly was his wife in every way. He loved her. But at the moment, he had no idea where she was. "She . . . um . . . she couldn't come with me." He was relieved when Minnie let it go at that.

"What're your plans now that you're free?" Jim asked.

"I ain't really made any, yet," Grady said with a sigh. "I been planning how to escape for so long that I ain't thought about what comes afterwards."

"Well, you're welcome to stay here with us," Minnie said, "even though we ain't got a lot. We been eating from Massa's cupboards, but the food won't be lasting forever."

"It's different being free," Jim added. "Ain't no massa giving us things no more. Folks like us gonna have to make a living now, if we want to eat."

"How you been doing that?" Grady asked.

"Well, Minnie's washing clothes for the white soldiers, and I been earning money at the docks, unloading freight. We was amongst the lucky ones who got jobs right away because we was living here when the Yankees first come. But it's getting harder and harder to find work these days. I hear that more than ten thousand slaves was set free—just on the Sea Island plantations alone. Yes, sir, there's plenty more folks looking for work than there's work to do."

"You could try one of the plantations," Minnie said. "I hear the army's letting slaves take over their masters' cotton crops and promising to pay them wages when it's sold."

"I ain't picking cotton," Grady said, "and I ain't working for white men no more."

"It's gonna be awful hard to make a living, then," Jim said gravely. "If I was as young as you, I'd join the army. They got Negro soldiers now."

"Yeah, I know. Some of them was the ones that found me." They ate in silence for a while before Grady asked, "How'd you end up back in Beaufort? Last I heard you and Martin had escaped after heading out to the fort with Massa Fuller."

Jim lifted his bowl to slurp the last of his stew, then handed it to Minnie for a refill. "There was too many Yankees for Massa and the others to fight off. We helped ferry them all out of there when they had to give up the fort—and I saw a lot of dead and wounded men that day, I can tell you. But as soon as I got the chance, me and a few others just took off and hid in the woods during all the ruckus. The town was deserted by the time I come back here for Minnie. Yankees moved in a few days later."

"What happened to Martin?"

"I don't know," Jim said with a shrug. "Last I saw him, he was help-ing Massa and the others at the fort. Ain't seen him or Massa since."

"You look all tuckered out, Grady," Minnie said when the meal was finished. "You should have yourself a good night's sleep before you go deciding anything. Why don't you let Jim show you upstairs where we been sleeping?"

It took Grady a moment to realize that she was inviting him to sleep upstairs in the town house, not up above the stable where he used to sleep. He didn't move, unable to picture himself doing it. Sitting inside the house at Massa's dinner table had been a huge step for him; sleeping in Massa's bedrooms would be even bigger. "I think I'm tired enough to sleep just about anywhere," he finally said. "Even standing up."

They talked a little while longer before Jim finally convinced Grady to follow him upstairs. He led him to an enormous room with a four-poster bed draped with curtains. The mattress, which was made of feathers and piled high with pillows and blankets, looked so soft and deep that Grady wondered if he'd sink down and suffocate in all that luxury. He suddenly thought of Anna, remembering their only night together and the way she had felt in his arms. How wonderful it would be to sleep beside his wife in this big, soft bed. He longed to see her wearing Missus Fuller's fancy clothes, like Minnie did, and living here in the town house.

"Ain't that bed something?" Jim asked, interrupting his thoughts. "White folks have it pretty good, don't they?"

"Yeah. They sure do." Grady was so angry he couldn't think of anything else to say. While he'd been sleeping on cornshucks all these years, in smelly stables and drafty cabins, the white folks had slept in rooms like this one. He'd never been inside Massa Coop's house in New Orleans or Massa Fletcher's house in Richmond, but they probably looked much the same as this.

"Build yourself a little fire in the fireplace, if you want," Jim said. "There's plenty of wood. I'll see you in the morning."

Grady stood for a long moment, surveying his new room. If only

Anna had come with him. They could sleep here together tonight—in freedom. But she had chosen to go with Missy Claire instead of him. It angered him to realize that she hadn't been torn away from him against her will, the way all the other people in his life had been. The choice had been hers to make. Grady made up his mind in that moment to forget her. She wasn't his wife, Anna, anymore. She was Kitty—a white woman's slave.

As he finally undressed for the night, Grady suddenly knew what he wanted to do with his newfound freedom. He would make his way back home to Richmond. He could do that now, couldn't he? As a free man, dressed in white men's clothes, he could board a passenger ship and sail up the coast, just like Massa Coop used to do. Once he reached Richmond, Grady would help his mama and the others escape.

But first he would need to earn boat fare. Grady had no idea how much it would cost or how he would earn it. The only money he'd ever held in his hands was the loose change Massa had given him to buy drawing paper for Anna. Those coins had seemed like a lot of money as they'd jangled heavily in Grady's pocket. He'd been very surprised when the store clerk made him hand them all over just to buy a pile of paper.

Grady climbed into the feather bed, too tired to make any more plans. For the first time in his life, softness and warmth enveloped him as he drifted off to sleep. But anger battled his exhaustion throughout the long, restless night.

❧

"Do you know where that regiment of slave soldiers might be camping out?" Grady asked Jim the next day at breakfast.

"I hear they're a little ways outside Beaufort, on the grounds of Old Fort Plantation. Know where that is?"

"Yeah, I drove Massa Fuller there a couple times."

"You planning on joining up?" Minnie asked as she handed Grady a plate of biscuits.

"No. Just going to see an old friend."

The warm sun shone brightly as he set off to find Amos. Why couldn't the weather have been this fine on the day Grady and the others had escaped? Seemed like God was always on the white men's side.

It took Grady an hour to walk the three miles to Old Fort Plantation, perched on a small spit of land along the Beaufort River. The Big House stood at the end of a long, tree-shaded avenue, looking tattered and war-torn since the last time he'd visited with Massa Fuller. Off in the woods, the neat encampment of white canvas tents appeared deserted, but Grady quickly spotted the men marching up and down an empty field in neat columns and rows. With their crisp, orderly movements, the Negroes looked just as fine as Massa Fuller's white soldiers had looked when they'd drilled on the Green out at the Point last year.

Grady sat down to watch them, still amazed to see slaves in uniforms, carrying guns. The field slaves he'd worked with on the plantation used to shuffle to work on slow, dragging feet, their shoulders slumped, their spirits beaten down. He'd never seen Negroes like these men—their chins raised in pride, their shoulders squared, their feet lifted high as they marched in step with shouldered rifles. But the man shouting all the orders was a white man, and that spoiled everything for Grady.

The soldiers finally paused for a break around noon, and he found Amos. He was the biggest man in the troop and easy to spot. Grady accompanied him to the mess tent and waited beside him while Amos stood in line with the other soldiers. An atmosphere of contentment seemed to fill the camp, and the men laughed and joked with each other as they lined up for their food.

"Seems like you have it pretty good around here," Grady said.

"Yeah, most of us was field slaves before. We're getting plenty of food now, and warm blankets and clothes, too." He gestured to his new uniform.

"I need to ask you something," Grady said. "You're from Richmond, ain't you?"

"Yeah, I was born there," Amos replied. "Left my wife and five kids behind when I was sold."

"I want to go back and find my own family," Grady told him, "but I ain't sure how to do it. You know how much it costs for a ticket on a boat? Or how to get a job on one that's heading there?"

Amos gave him an odd look. "I guess you ain't following the news. There's a war going on right now."

Grady gestured impatiently. "I know that."

"Well, passenger ships can't be sailing into Confederate ports any time they feel like it. They can only go to cities like Beaufort that the Yankees already took. Them Rebels have forts and armed batteries guarding all their rivers and ports. And Union warships are patrolling up and down the coast, stopping ships."

Amos reached the head of the line and paused to fill his tin mess plate, then he led Grady to a makeshift bench outside his tent. "Want some food?" he asked.

Grady shook his head. "How can I get to Richmond, Amos?"

"You can't, boy. The Rebels made Richmond their capitol, like Washington City. The Yankees been trying all last spring and summer to get in there. Didn't you hear about that?"

"I thought the white folks was making it all up, about keeping the Yankees out. It was hard to find out exactly what's been going on in the war, since they had me working as a field hand."

Amos grunted in sympathy. "Yeah, well, them Rebels have Richmond all closed up behind earthworks and such. Even General Mc-Clellan and thousands of Yankee soldiers weren't able to get in there last summer. Word is that a new general is gonna try again soon, and that they're marching down that way right now. But if you're thinking of going after your family, it ain't gonna work. They's still slaves. If you go anywhere near Richmond, them white folks gonna catch you and make you their slave again, too."

Grady stood and paced a few steps, his fists clenched in frustration. "How can I help my family get free, Amos?"

He chewed his food, thinking. "Only way I know is to march into Richmond with the Yankees. That's why I put on this uniform. When we finish drilling and learning how to fight, I'm hoping to get up there myself and save my own family. And you can bet I'll be killing every last Rebel I find along the way."

This discouraging news wasn't what Grady had wanted to hear. "Thanks anyway," he mumbled. He said good-bye to Amos and set off across the camp toward the road, hoping that another plan would come to mind on the long walk back to town. He was crossing the parade grounds when one of the white officers intercepted him.

"Hello there," the man said with a friendly smile. "Are you interested in joining the First South Carolina Volunteers?" It astounded Grady to be addressed as an equal by a white man—even more so when Grady recognized him as the officer who had shouted all the orders to Amos and the others as they'd drilled. Grady hesitated for a long moment, his lifetime habits of submission and fear still deeply ingrained. Then he summoned the courage to answer as a free man—an equal.

"No, thanks. I ain't taking no more orders from any white men."

The soldier looked surprised but not angry. "You misunderstand. The men don't obey us because we're white but because we're officers. We have black officers, too."

"You mean Negroes like me giving the orders?"

"That's right. Colonel Higginson is in charge of this regiment and he's white, but he's been fighting all his life for equality and freedom for the slaves. He even went out to Kansas during the troubles a few years back and fought like a wildcat to keep it from becoming a slave state. He gave money to support John Brown and the slave rebellion at Harper's Ferry, too."

Grady nodded as if he understood, but he had no idea what the man was talking about.

"Colonel Higginson agreed to lead this regiment as a kind of experiment," the white man continued. "If we can succeed—and we're certain that we can—we'll show the nation that there's no difference at all between our two races. We believe that you Negroes will fight just as good or even better than whites do because you're fighting for your freedom. Everyone up north is watching, you know. This is your chance to prove that your race is just as good as ours. Besides," he added with a grin, "you'll get paid every month and get plenty to eat. And Colonel Higginson plans to start school lessons in the evenings to teach everyone how to read and write. Think about it."

It sounded much too good to be true to Grady. He wondered if it was a trick to get all the Negroes to enlist so that the whites could enslave them again. "No thanks," he mumbled and began the long walk back to Beaufort.

Later, as he passed the harbor where Jim worked, Grady saw his fellow Negroes laboring with their backs bent, their faces downcast— still wearing rags and working for meager pay. Watching them, it seemed to Grady that freedom had never come. He couldn't help comparing them with the Negro soldiers he'd seen that morning, carrying themselves and their weapons with pride.

Back at Massa's town house, smoke curled from the chimney of the washhouse. Grady peeked inside to see Minnie scrubbing the white men's laundry, and it made him angry. He didn't want to labor on one of the plantations or do menial work like Jim and Minnie. Grady wanted to walk into Richmond as a free Negro. He wanted Massa Fletcher to meet the son he'd sold—a free man now, carrying a gun. It was what the white folks had long feared—Negroes with guns, coming back to get even, searching for the justice they'd long been denied. Grady wanted to aim a gun at Massa Fletcher's head and make him cry and beg the way Grady and his mama had begged on that last day. After he'd seen his white father's fear and listened to his pleas for mercy, Grady would pull the trigger and blow his brains out.

But in the meantime, how would he get there?

Three days later Grady had made up his mind. He walked back to the army camp and found the white officer he'd spoken to.

"I've decided to join your Negro regiment," he said.

"That's great. I'm Captain Metcalf. What's your name?"

Grady didn't hesitate. He knew exactly who he was. "My name's Grady," he said. "Grady Fletcher."

BEAUFORT, SOUTH CAROLINA
NOVEMBER 1862—JANUARY 1863

It didn't take Grady long to adjust to the routine of army life with the First South Carolina Volunteers. After a lifetime of slavery, it felt natural to him to sleep on the ground, rise early every morning, and eat simple army rations from a tin plate—more natural than sleeping in a feather bed and dining at Massa's polished table had. And he certainly felt more comfortable in his new woolen uniform than in Massa Fuller's Sunday clothes.

Grady had spent hours watching the white troops drill on the Point last year, and he already knew many of the commands and maneuvers. But the happiest moment came when the ordnance department issued him a new Springfield rifle. Holding a weapon in his hands, responding to the command "Battalion! Shoulder arms!" gave him a feeling of power and control that he'd never known before. He honed his marksmanship skills as diligently and lovingly as he'd once practiced the violin. And every time he aimed at a target, every face he imagined on it was white.

More than eight hundred other Negroes had enlisted in Grady's regiment, undergoing the transformation with him from degraded slaves to proud soldiers. Some days he felt like an item for sale in one of Beaufort's storefront windows as he drilled, his every movement watched by military experts and newspaper reporters and countless visitors from the North, all curious to see a battalion that was made up entirely of black soldiers.

"It won't always be easy to live under such scrutiny," Colonel Higginson had warned the men in one of his speeches. "Your successes will be reported and applauded, of course. But if even one of you makes a mistake, it will reflect badly on the entire regiment. And a disaster like Bull Run . . . well, our little experiment with colored troops would quickly come to an end in that event."

"What happened at Bull Run?" Grady asked Captain Metcalf later that day.

"Our soldiers turned tail and ran when the Rebels attacked them," he said, wincing.

"White soldiers?" Grady asked.

The captain nodded. "For many of those men, it was their first time in battle. That's why the colonel is afraid for all of you. None of you has seen combat before."

"We won't run," Grady said. "We faced a death sentence every day of our lives when we was slaves, while you white folks was scared of getting your feet wet. Just give us a chance to fight. You'll see."

Grady lived and worked with his fellow Negroes day and night, just as he had when he'd been a slave. But because of the freedom each man felt and cherished, the atmosphere in camp was vastly different from what it had been on Slave Row. In the daytime the camp rang with the sound of drums and drill commands and laughter. At night the men gathered around their campfires until taps was played, telling stories and roasting peanuts and sweet potatoes as the moon shone through the silvery moss above their heads.

Grady's only disappointment was that all of the ranks in Amos' company had been filled, and he wasn't able to join his friend. Instead, the army assigned him to a new company under Captain Metcalf.

Grady shared a tent with a former slave named Joseph Whitney, the man who had let him drink from his canteen the day the Union soldiers had found him. He was about the same age and height as Grady, but so thin and angular that he might have been made from matchsticks. His coal-black skin was every bit as dark as Grady's was light. Everything about Joseph irritated Grady, including his name, which was a painful reminder of his years with Massa Coop. But most grating of all was Joseph's religious fervor. He'd even earned the nickname "Preacher" from the other men because of it.

"Do you know the Lord Jesus?" Joseph had asked Grady on their first day together as tentmates. Grady had mumbled a reply and tried to ignore him, but by evening he had already heard enough preaching.

"Listen, Joe," he said. "No offense, but I don't want to hear all your God-talk. I've had that stuff shoved at me all my life, and never once has God done me any favors."

"He sent His Son to die for you—"

"Enough!" Grady said, holding up his hands. "That's exactly the kind of talk I mean. I don't want to hear it. There's plenty of other fellas around here who're happy to listen to your preaching, but not me. Understand?"

"I'll be praying that you—"

"No!" he said, interrupting. "I don't want you praying for me, either. Just leave me alone, okay? If you can't talk to me about regular things, then don't be talking to me at all."

Joseph wore the hurt expression of a long-suffering saint. It made Grady angrier still. But when Joe invited a friend with a fiddle over to their campfire that night, and they sat around singing and playing hymns, it was the last straw. Grady went up to the plantation house to see Captain Metcalf first thing the next morning.

The five-minute walk from the campground to the war-ravaged house was a picturesque one, passing down the long avenue beneath moss-draped oaks. But even the pleasant, mist-shrouded scenery couldn't soften Grady's resolve. *"You belong to God,"* Delia had once told him. *"And He's gonna chase you down and hound your steps until He gets you back.*" Well, if God was planning to use Joseph to torment him, then Grady intended to halt those plans right now.

"I want a different tentmate," he told the surprised captain. "I can't be having him preach at me all day and fiddling hymns at me all night."

"I'm sorry," Metcalf said, frowning. "But an army camp isn't a hotel room that you can check in and out of every time you're inconvenienced. We can't have men changing tents every day or two."

"Talk to him, then. Tell him to shut up about God."

The captain looked taken aback by Grady's irreverence. It was a moment before he replied. "You'll have to work out a compromise between the two of you," he said slowly. "Joseph has a right to freedom of speech and freedom of religion."

Grady returned to camp determined to avoid Joseph as much as possible. It wasn't hard to do. The men spent all day drilling and learning maneuvers, but during their free time every evening, they naturally gravitated to whichever activities interested them. Joe went to prayer meetings or sang hymns with some of the others. Grady often went to hear a Negro woman from up north teach the alphabet and read lessons from a schoolbook.

But every now and then, nearly all of the men would spontaneously gather together to hold a "shout," sitting around a campfire singing chorus after chorus of the old slave songs they'd once sung on the plantation, accompanied by an assortment of instruments. The men would clap and dance and drum their feet in rhythm as they celebrated their newfound freedom. The songs both drew Grady and repulsed him because of the memories they stirred. He remained on the sidelines at those events, feeling the music deep in his soul, but unwilling to join his gangly tentmate and the others as they sang about the Lord Jesus and going to the Promised Land.

December brought wind and rain and swarms of sand flies. It also brought the disappointing news that General Burnside and the Union army had suffered a defeat up in Fredericksburg, Virginia. Captain Metcalf and the other officers seemed depressed by the news, and they shook their heads as they talked about the 12,600 Union casualties. But those numbers meant nothing to Grady, who had never learned to count that high. To him, the defeat meant that Richmond remained in Rebel hands, and that his mother and the others were still slaves.

He hoped that he would finally get a chance to fight in the new year. He was ready. But the fact that his regiment was working hard to build a permanent camp here worried him. The tents all had wooden floors now, and each company had its own wooden cookhouse. The men had pitched in to dig a well and build a fireplace in the guardhouse to warm the soldiers on duty. An outbuilding that had once housed a cotton gin now housed a hospital. And nightly school lessons with teachers from up north would soon be offered in a big circular tent made from discarded canvas. The camp had become quite comfortable—and much too permanent for Grady's liking. He wanted to march north and fight.

Two months after Grady enlisted, Colonel Higginson announced plans for a New Year's celebration. On January 1, 1863, President Lincoln's Emancipation Proclamation would go into effect, officially setting all of the slaves in the Confederate states free. Grady had looked forward to the day ever since he heard the news. Maybe now he could stop looking over his shoulder, worrying that his freedom would come to an end, expecting at any moment to be chained and beaten and returned to slavery.

He volunteered to help dig pits in the sandy soil and cut down trees for spits to cook the oxen for the feast. The smell of roasting meat filled the camp that night as Grady and the other men took turns rotating the spits by hand and tending the smoldering fires while the meat cooked for the celebration.

"Looks like there's gonna be plenty of meat tomorrow," Joseph said as he sat alongside Grady near one of the pits. "Ten oxen! I ain't ever seen that much beef before, have you?"

"No," Grady replied. He grudgingly recalled being well fed by Massa Coop, but even Coop hadn't offered him roast beef.

"Did your massa let his slaves have parties and such?" Joseph asked.

The slave gathering in Charleston came to Grady's mind, celebrating Massa Fuller's marriage. But then the more painful memory of the celebration that had followed his own wedding left him unable to reply.

"My massa always treated us on Christmas Day," Joseph said, breaking the strained silence. "But it wasn't nothing like this. The cook told me they was fixing a real fancy concoction for us to drink tomorrow, made with molasses and ginger and cider. Should be a real fine celebration, don't you think?"

Grady raked the coals with a stick to stir the embers. "Yeah," he mumbled. "Real fine." He wondered why he still felt bitter about anything the white folks gave him, even a celebration.

"Do you recollect where you was this time last year?" Joseph asked. "What you was doing?"

"I could've been free this time last year," Grady said. "We had to leave Beaufort earlier that fall, and I could've run off then and been free. Instead, I was fool enough to stay and drive Massa's wife to the plantation."

"She must have been grateful to you, though, for helping her."

Grady looked up from the coals to glare at Joseph. "Not her. She rewarded me by sending me down to Slave Row."

"That's where I was a year ago, too," Joseph said. "Me and my sisters and brothers all living in a cabin with our folks. Sure is hard to believe we're all free now, ain't it? When we get married and have children, they'll all be born free. Never have to know what slavery's all about. You got a wife or a girlfriend, Grady?"

He slowly rose to his feet, weary of this painful conversation, depressed by Joseph's unending cheerfulness. "No," he lied. "No, I ain't never been married."

❧

Guests began arriving about ten o'clock the next day for the celebration, most coming by land, some on steamers sent by General

Saxton. Hundreds of women came, the wives and mothers of the other Negro soldiers, including Joseph's mother and sisters. Grady thought of Anna and Delia, of how proud they would be to see him marching in his new uniform—then he quickly pushed them from his mind.

There were older men in the gathering, as well, former slaves who were too old for military duty, dressed in their Sunday best. One of them reminded him of Eli, renewing Grady's resolve to fight for his family's freedom. Many white visitors had come, too, the wives and families of the white officers, as well as white schoolteachers and missionaries who had come down from the North to teach the freed Sea Island slaves to read and write.

Grady and the other soldiers assembled by companies in their camps, then marched across the plantation grounds to the grove of live oaks near the river where a platform had been built for the dignitaries. White soldiers from the Eighth Maine Regimental Band played such a stirring march for them that Grady felt as if he could lick an entire regiment of Rebels all by himself.

The ceremony began at eleven-thirty with the chaplain's prayer. Then President Lincoln's Proclamation was read. What Grady had scarcely dared to believe would ever happen, was now officially true: on this, the first day of January, in the year of our Lord 1863, all persons once held as slaves in the Confederate states were declared "thenceforth and forever free."

He gazed up into the sky to stop his tears from falling and saw a flock of birds swooping overhead. He was free—as free as they were. This time last year, he'd been a slave. Now, and for the rest of his life, he was a free man.

"Praise the Lord," Joseph murmured beside him. "Praise the name of the Lord!"

Grady knew that Delia would have echoed Joseph's words if she had been here. He wished he could say them, for her sake, but he couldn't.

He looked over at the platform again as a chaplain from New York presented Colonel Higginson's colored regiment with a brand-new United States flag. It had come all the way from New York, where it had been hand-sewn by donors. It unnerved Grady to realize that there were white folks up north who were on his side, folks like the Quaker couple who had helped Delia's daughter escape to freedom. These people didn't see Negroes as inferior, deserving of slavery, but as men and women of dignity. Some of them had worked all their lives, as Colonel Higginson had, to help set the slaves free. Grady thought that maybe he'd like to live up north after the war. He would take his mother and Eli and the others up there with him. He wouldn't bother asking Anna. She would refuse, preferring to stay here with Missy Claire.

Colonel Higginson lifted the flag high in the air and waved it—Grady's flag, his country's flag. Grady added his voice to those of the other men in his regiment as they roared their approval, loud and long.

When the cheers died away into silence again, a single male voice, shaky with age, suddenly broke into spontaneous song:

> My country, 'tis of thee,
> Sweet land of liberty,
> Of thee I sing!

A moment later, two women's voices joined his. Grady saw white people glancing at their programs, then at each other, and he knew that the song hadn't been planned; it had simply sprung forth.

> Land where our fathers died,
> Land of the pilgrims' pride
> From every mountainside
> Let freedom ring!

The choked voices sang on and on, verse after verse. Other slaves who knew the words joined in. Grady could no longer stop his tears from falling. He looked around and saw tears on every face. And when the song finally ended, the silence that followed it felt holy.

Later, there were speeches; Grady's regiment sang; the band played. There was good food and laughter and joy on every face. But for Grady, that simple unplanned song, performed by unknown persons, remained the most powerful memory of that day.

His people's souls had been unloosed—their hearts set free in song.

❦

GREAT OAK PLANTATION
FEBRUARY 1863

Delia sat on the front step of the slave cabin, rocking little Rosa to sleep in her arms while three older children played near her feet. Delia had raised a lot of babies in her life, and except for her own daughter, they had all been white. But oh, how she'd grown to love these little slave babies with their dark brown eyes and smooth brown skin. It was hard work feeding and changing and chasing nearly a dozen children every day, with only Old Lucy to help her out. But sometimes in the evenings, when things quieted down, Delia had time to do what she loved best of all: tell stories to the older boys and girls. Her favorites all came from the Bible, of course, stories like Jonah and the whale or Daniel and the lions. These kids didn't hardly know what lions were, and she was scared, at first, that she'd give them all nightmares by telling them.

"But there ain't no lions around here," she'd assured them. "Those lions are all living far away, in the land where us colored folk come from a long time ago." Someday when the children were older, she would tell them about the land of the Mountain of Lions, where their ancestors came from. They needed to know.

This was a different life for Delia down here, much different from living in the Big House where it was warm and dry, with plenty to eat. Down here, she was cold and hungry much of the time, especially since she gave most of her own food away to the little ones. It broke her heart to see their little stomachs empty

306

all the time. Yes, she knew that the Lord had sent her down here for a reason.

Little Rosa finally fell asleep in her arms. Delia slowly rose to her feet to carry her into the cabin, but when she looked up, there was Kitty walking up the path. Kitty smiled when she saw Delia and quickened her pace. How many months had it been since they'd seen each other?

"Oh, honey, I'm so glad to see you!" Delia said as she hugged Kitty with her free arm. "Let me put this baby in the house, and then you and me can talk." She hurried through the open door and laid Rosa on the mattress beside the other sleeping babies. Old Lucy, who helped Delia with the children, sat dozing in a chair beside them.

"So what brings you way down here on this fine day?" Delia asked as she sat on the front step beside Kitty.

"Missy Claire and Missus Goodman went off visiting without me today, so I asked Bertha if I could come see how you was doing. Bertha said I should stay home and rest because I been feeling sick and kinda dragged down lately, but I said, 'I want to go see Delia. She'll make me feel better.'"

"I'm so glad you did, honey."

"I been hoping all this time that they're letting you watch the babies with Old Nellie instead of making you chop cotton and such. Nellie took care of me when I was small. Is she still here?"

"No, she went to be with Jesus before I come. I'm working with a woman named Lucy, and she's loving these babies as much as I do." Delia spied one of her toddlers wandering off and shouted to him. "Henry! You get on back here. Don't you make me chase you, now."

"I was always running off like that," Kitty said with a smile, "making poor Nellie chase me. Here, I brought you some food. I never had enough to eat when I was living down here, and I been worrying about you getting enough."

Delia untied the cloth bundle that Kitty handed her, and the aroma of smoked pork and hot corn bread drifted out. "Thank you, honey. I'll save this for later. But don't you be worrying yourself on my account. The Good Lord's been taking care of me."

One of the babies started fussing inside the cabin and Delia jumped up to fetch him before he woke Lucy or one of the other children. When she returned with the baby in her arms, Kitty was holding a pencil and an odd-looking piece of paper. "What you got there, honey?"

"This? It's an old envelope I found in Missy's trash. The outside is used, but I unfolded it so I could use the inside, see?"

"You gonna draw yourself a picture?" she asked.

"I was hoping you'd let me draw one of you."

"Of me?" she said with a laugh. "You should be drawing something nice to look at, not my homely old wrinkled-up face."

"I thought maybe if I had a picture of you, I wouldn't be missing you so much. I have one of Grady, and it helps me remember . . ." Her voice choked and she couldn't finish.

Delia squeezed Kitty's hand with her free one. "You hearing anything about him and the other runaways?"

"Not a word. Missy Claire gets letters from Massa Fuller, but she never lets on what he says. Sometimes it makes me crazy not knowing what happened." She paused again to brush away a tear. "I'm sorry, Delia. I didn't come down here to be all sad. I brought you something else. I copied my picture of Grady for you on another old envelope."

Delia moved the baby to her other knee and reached to take the paper from Kitty, holding it well out of the squirming boy's reach. The drawing was such an excellent likeness of Grady that Delia caught her breath. He looked defiant, his proud chin thrust forward, his arms folded across his chest the way he always used to do, as if he were mad at the whole world. She whispered a silent prayer that wherever he was right now, that he had found peace in his heart.

"Thank you, honey," Delia murmured. "You're right, it surely is a comfort to see his face again, even if it's just a picture." She laid the drawing aside, out of the baby's reach, and turned to Kitty, who sat with paper and pencil in hand. "What do you want me to do, honey? Do I need to sit still and pose or something?"

"No, just sit there and talk to me, Delia. I'll draw."

"Okay. But the first thing I'm needing to do is change this boy's diaper. I reckon that's why he's kicking up a fuss. Can you fetch me a clean one from inside? And get that old quilt to lay him on. I'll change him out here."

Kitty found what Delia needed inside, then helped her spread the folded blanket on the ground. She picked up her pencil again and began to sketch as Delia lay the baby on his back and knelt beside him. "You say you ain't been feeling too well, honey?" she asked as she untied the diaper. "What's wrong?"

"It ain't nothing serious. I'm just feeling so tired all the time, like I could just sleep and sleep. I don't hardly feel like eating, either. Of course, Missy don't care. She keeps me working all day long, no matter how tired I am. But sometimes I think I could just lie down in the middle of the floor and—"

She stopped so abruptly that Delia glanced up at her. Kitty was holding her hand over her mouth, trying not to retch after getting a whiff of the dirty diaper. Suddenly Delia knew what was wrong. She swayed, barely stopping herself from falling sideways. "Oh no. Oh no," she murmured.

Kitty leaned forward to help her. "Delia? Are you okay? I'm sorry, but the smell—"

Delia gripped Kitty's arm. "Did you sleep with Grady the night he left?" But she knew from Kitty's expression what the answer was before the girl had a chance to reply. Her face showed a mixture of deep joy and an even deeper sorrow.

"Oh, Lord, honey! You're gonna have his baby!"

Kitty's eyes went wide. "H-how do you know?"

"I know. Oh, honey, I know."

Kitty covered her face with both hands and wept.

The poor girl was pregnant. And Delia knew just as surely as the sun rose every morning that it was all her fault. She had meddled in matters that were none of her business, encouraging Grady to sleep with Kitty on that last night, promising him that she would escape with him if he did. Delia had tried to take control of things instead of trusting God, and now she'd created an awful mess. It was her fault that Kitty was gonna have a baby all alone, with no husband to help raise it. Her fault that Grady's child would be born a slave. Delia could never forgive herself, much less ask Kitty or Grady or the Lord to forgive her. But what to do now? What to do?

Delia left the bare-bottomed baby kicking and squalling on the blanket and pulled Kitty into her arms. "It's gonna be okay, honey," she soothed. "Everything's gonna be okay."

"I'm having a baby? Grady's baby?"

"You poor thing. You don't know whether to be happy or sad, do you? Well, it's okay to feel a little of each. Being a mother's the most wonderful thing in the whole world—and also the most painful. There's no joy like a mother's joy. And there's no pain greater than a mother's pain. It's like being in love—there's nothing more wonderful than being with the man you love. And nothing more painful than losing him."

"But . . . I thought you didn't love the father of your little girl. I thought that he, you know . . ."

"I didn't love her father. But I loved my husband."

Kitty pulled back to stare at her. "You were *married*? Delia, you never told me! Where is he? What happened to him? I know that your daughter died, but—"

"She didn't die." Delia saw Kitty's confusion and sighed. "I guess I better tell you the whole story, from the beginning." She patted Kitty's shoulder, then knelt beside the baby again, sifting through her memories for a place to start while she soothed and diapered him.

"My mama was the Fullers' cook before Faye was," she began. "Mama's gone now, living in heaven with Jesus. Papa is, too, God rest his soul. He worked as a carpenter for the Fullers, making wagon wheels and barrel staves—anything, you name it. I had two brothers and three sisters, all older than me. I was the youngest. They's all gone and buried now. I been with the Fullers for so many years that I saw lots of folks come and go—Massa Roger's grandparents, then his parents, then his first wife. I saw Massa and his sisters born into this world and those boys of his, too. So many folks come and gone . . . gone just like you and me someday.

"The Fullers had lots of visitors, back in the old days, and old Missus Fuller had a sister called Miss Carrie who lived down Savannah way. Miss Carrie didn't get on too well with her husband, so she spent a lot of time visiting the Fullers. And she always came with her coachman—a fine, handsome young fella named Shep. His daddy was a Negro preacher-man so he named his son Shepherd, after the Good Shepherd. Young Shep turned out to be a mighty fine preacher himself, and he taught me that psalm by heart: 'The Lord is my Shepherd; I shall not want. He maketh me to lie down in green pastures . . .'"

Delia finished diapering the baby, and she sat him on the blanket beside her. He chewed on his fist, cooing happily while Delia continued.

"Shep had a Bible, and he knew how to read it. He used to hold meetings at night when the white folks were partying and couldn't hear us. He taught us all about Moses, and how the Lord heard the slaves' cries and delivered them from bondage. Shep said the Lord Jesus was gonna be our deliverer, too, and He'd hear us and help us, if we cried out to Him.

"I wish you could've heard the singing and praying and rejoicing at those meetings. I reckon the white folks thought we was having a party, too, but we was praising God and storming heaven with our prayers." She paused to look up at Kitty. "I believe He's answering them right now. I believe that's what this war is all about."

Kitty looked puzzled, but she didn't interrupt.

"Well, Shep and I fell in love and decided to jump the broom. We knew it was gonna be a hard life, because we never knew when we was gonna see each other or how long Shep would be staying when he did come. But we was happy for those hours we had. Oh yes. Shep's faith in the Lord was as big and as wide as the whole state of South Carolina. And even though things was hard for us, we was happy.

"It was right around that time that the overseer, the first Mr. Browning, took a liking to me. He was a married man with a family of his own, but the doctor says his wife ain't supposed to have any more babies. So he put me in a little cabin of my own, so he could come and go anytime he wants. Nothing I can do about it, either."

"Did Shep know?" Kitty asked.

"He knew. It just about broke his heart. He cried along with me, because we knew I belonged to him, not Mr. Browning. But Shep told me not to hate him. He said I had to forgive him. And I been trying to do that. All these years, I been trying.

"Then one day Shep drove Miss Carrie home to Savannah, and they never came back. She died of a fever all of a sudden. The Fullers went to her funeral, but they left me home. And Shep couldn't come driving all the way to Beaufort to see me no more, now that his missus was gone."

"So you never saw him again?" Kitty asked softly. "You don't know what happened to him?"

Delia shook her head. "I heard Old Missus Fuller saying one day, that Shep's massa was a gambler and he was running up so many big debts that he had to sell his slaves to pay them off. But I never did learn whether or not he sold Shep. It's been some forty years now, and I ain't never seen my husband again."

Delia closed her eyes for a moment, trying to picture Shep in her mind. She wished she had a drawing to remember him by. She looked up to tell Kitty how blessed she was to have a drawing of Grady and saw the poor girl's tears. Delia never should have told Kitty her story. She never should have dashed all her hopes of ever seeing Grady again—even if it turned out to be true.

"Believe me, honey," Delia said softly, "I know how you're feeling. My biggest sorrow was that I never had Shep's child. At least you'll have that. Your baby is a gift from God, a little part of Grady to remember him by."

"I'm so sorry for you, Delia." Kitty reached for her hand.

"No . . . my husband gave me something even better than a child—he taught me about the Lord. Shep's the one who told me all about Jesus and how much He loves us. He taught me to be thankful each day—for what the Lord has given, thankful for the good and the bad. We learn a lot more from the bad than from the good, you know."

Kitty's hand slid from hers as she leaned back, gazing at Delia in surprise. "How can you be thankful, Delia? How can you still be praying and believing in God after everything that happened to you? Everything you lost?"

"I'm not sure I can explain it, honey. I just keep looking to the Lord, my Heavenly Massa, no matter what. His love is always there, through it all."

Kitty was quiet for a long moment, then said, "Tell me about your daughter."

Delia drew a deep breath. "Shep had been gone for more than a year when I found out I was gonna have a baby. I knew right away who the daddy was, but that overseer never so much as looked at his little girl. She was just another slave to him, not his baby."

"And did she die or didn't she?" Kitty asked.

"No, she didn't die. I had a funeral and made a grave and everything, so that it'd look like she had. But she's gone free. I used to go to a colored folks' church in Pocotaligo, and that's where I met up with a Quaker family from up north. My baby had very light skin, you know, just like Grady's, and these white folks offered to take her up north with them where she would be free. So I let her go."

"That must have been hard," Kitty said in a whisper. "What was her name?"

"I named her Love. My little Love. I wanted to remind myself that it ain't her fault what her daddy done. She would always help me remember to love my enemies." Delia paused, biting her lip. "I know things is hard for you right now, honey, but if you let God shine His love on you, He can make something beautiful out of even the darkest hours of your life. That's what He'll do with your child—Grady's child. . . . But Lord, Lord, how I wish you'd gone with him."

"Me too, Delia. Me too."

CHAPTER

21

BEAUFORT, SOUTH CAROLINA
FEBRUARY 1863

Excitement spread to every corner of the First South Carolina Volunteers' camp. Grady could feel it—the expectancy of change in the air. Their training was nearly complete, and the real business of fighting was about to begin. Every man was busy polishing his rifle, shining his boots, and brushing his uniform to look his very best. Grady took extra care shaving and combing his hair, primping the way he used to do before going courting. The memory brought Delia to mind, and with it the ache of loneliness.

He quickly drew a breath and exhaled, pushing the pain aside. Today was going to be an important day, not a sad one. Grady's regiment of colored troops was marching into Beaufort in dress parade to be reviewed by General Saxton himself for the first time. A week ago Colonel Higginson had put them through their paces in preparation. At the end of the drill, he'd ordered them to hold up their right hands and pledge themselves to be faithful to those slaves who were still held in bondage. Grady had sworn by all that was in him to keep fighting until every last slave was free—or die trying.

Yes, change was coming . . . he could tell. Today the men would prove to General Saxton that they were ready. Then the army would finally let them march and fight.

Grady glanced around at the other dark, proud faces as they lined up, nearly a thousand soldiers in straight, even ranks. The color-sergeant, Prince Rivers, came forward to address the men before they marched. The former slave had been a coachman in Beaufort, like Grady, and they had met before the war. Now Sergeant Rivers stood before them, more than six feet tall, as noble and dignified as any white officer.

"Listen, boys—" he began.

"Call us men!" Grady shouted. Sergeant Rivers paused, glancing around to see who had spoken. "Excuse me, sir," Grady said. "But call us men. And keep calling us that until we believe it." He heard shouts of agreement all through the ranks. The sergeant smiled slightly and began again.

"Listen, *men* . . . don't be gawking all over the place when you march through town. Keep your eyes looking straight ahead of you. You're gonna be marching past white soldiers and officers who ain't never seen the likes of us before. They been drilling a whole month for every week that we have. Let's show them what we can do . . . *men*."

There was a roar of approval and the drums began to pound. Grady's heart thumped with the beat as they set off on the three-mile march to Beaufort. The Eighth Maine Regimental Band stood waiting for them at the edge of town and led them down Bay Street with a brisk march. The blood-stirring music coursed through Grady's veins like a rush of fire. He knew they looked extraordinary, every chin lifted with pride, every foot in perfect step. He risked a glimpse without turning his head and saw the white soldiers staring in amazement as the First South Carolina Volunteers marched through Beaufort in disciplined ranks. These were slaves—ignorant slaves—looking as fine as any white regiment ever looked.

The troops reached the eastern edge of town, turned, and marched back through Beaufort once again. Grady knew they had done well, but it still wasn't enough. He wanted a chance to prove he could fight, to earn the respect he deserved. They halted at the parade ground and drilled for an hour for the officers' review. Then they marched back to camp singing John Brown's song and dozens of others. Grady felt dizzy with exhilaration.

"I'm proud of you, men," Colonel Higginson announced before dismissing them. "I'm going to speak with General Hunter and tell him we're ready to fight."

An enormous cheer followed his words. Grady lifted his fist high in the air and shouted until his throat ached. At last! The time had finally come for him to avenge his life of bondage. He would fight for his dignity, fight to reclaim what had long been denied him as a slave.

❦

Four days later Grady stood onboard the *John Adams,* steaming down the Beaufort River on his regiment's first mission. General Hunter had authorized an expedition along the Georgia coast into Confederate-held territory. Their orders were to confiscate cotton crops, to acquire much-needed lumber for the Union army, and best of all, to liberate slaves. Any able-bodied men they freed would be welcomed into their ranks as recruits.

Grady stood near the rail as the ship reached the mouth of the Beaufort River and headed out into the open sea. It was the first time he'd been on a ship since his years of traveling up and down the Atlantic coast with Coop. The air was brisk up on deck, the salt spray cold on his face, the winter seas rough and choppy. But Grady didn't want to go down below where Coop had always confined him. It was well worth the chill to experience this exhilarating sense of freedom.

After an hour or so at sea, Corporal Robert Sutton came up on deck to stand alongside him. "How come you ain't getting seasick like a lot of the other men?" he asked Grady. "You must have a strong stomach for the sea."

Grady liked the powerfully built corporal. The former slave loved to talk and could entertain the soldiers with his stories for hours.

"I spent four years on the sea," Grady replied. "Guess I got used to it."

"Was you working on a steamer or something?"

"No . . . my massa was a slave trader." Grady decided to bring the bad memories out into the open in hopes it would finally drive them away. He knew that Sutton wouldn't insult him with misplaced pity. "Massa Coop had me sailing with him from Richmond to New Orleans and back again, trading slaves. Never got to stand out here, though. Most of the time I was down in the hold with all the other cargo."

"I'll bet you seen more of the world than I ever did," Sutton said.

"Yeah, I reckon so. How come you ain't sick?"

"Who says I ain't?" Sutton chuckled and Grady laughed along with him. It felt good to laugh.

"Where you from, Corporal?" Grady asked.

"All the way down in Florida—right where we're headed. Colonel Higginson asked me to pilot the boat up the St. Mary's River for him, seeing as I know them waters so well. That's the river dividing Florida from Georgia, you know. My old massa run a lumbering operation, so I told the colonel I know where there's plenty of lumber. Told him it's about time we went to work. I don't believe in lying around camp eating rations."

"I know. Me neither," Grady said with a smile. "How'd you manage to escape from your massa?"

"I went down the river one night in a stolen dugout. I liked being free so much that I went back for my wife and child. Yes sir, I been up and down that river plenty of times. Gonna be a real pleasure steaming up there with all these guns, though." Sutton gestured to one of the cannons mounted behind them.

"You know a lot about ships?" Grady asked.

"No, but I know that the one we're on used to be a ferryboat up in Boston, until the army turned it into a gunboat. Now she's armed with a thirty-pound Parrott gun, two ten-pounders, and an eight-inch howitzer. She's ready for a fight, I'll tell you. And so are the other two ships we're sailing with—the colonel's flagship, the *Ben DeFord*, and the *Planter*. You ever hear the story of the *Planter*?"

"No, I don't think so."

"Oh, it's a good one!" Sutton leaned against the rail, his face animated as he told Grady the story. "A slave from Beaufort named Robert Smalls captured that steamer right out from under the Rebels' noses! He was a first-class pilot, you see. Knew all these waters like the back of his hand. So he ended up aboard the *Planter*, working for a Confederate captain named Relyea who was known for always wearing a beat-up straw hat. Well, last spring while they was stopping in Charleston, Smalls and six other slaves hid themselves on board, waited until three o'clock in the morning, then fired up the engines and cast off.

"First they sailed upriver where their wives and children was waiting. Then they turned around and headed out to sea. It was real dangerous sailing past Fort Sumter, don't you know. If they went too fast, the Rebels would figure something's up—and sink her straight to the bottom. So Smalls put on Captain Relyea's straw hat and stood on deck so the watchman up at the fort could see him. Smalls even knew which signal to give with the ship's whistle.

"Now, usually the *Planter* would be turning and heading for Morris Island once she was past the fort. Instead, Smalls opened her up and headed for the Union blockade fleet a few miles out. On the way, he took down the Rebel flag and raised a white one. Not only did Smalls and his men and their families all escape, but the Union got herself a fine ship, perfect for navigating these shallow coastal rivers."

Grady smiled when Sutton finished. He imagined Delia telling that story over and over to crowds of eager listeners. "You're right, Corporal," he said. "That's a great story."

The journey to St. Simons Island off the coast of Georgia proved uneventful. The *John Adams* soon lay anchored with several other naval vessels in the calm waters of St. Simons Sound, waiting for the slower-moving *Planter* to catch up. Grady felt restless and ready for action as he stood gazing at the distant beach and abandoned plantation houses. When Colonel Higginson began assembling a team to go ashore, he quickly volunteered.

"The Rebels have abandoned all their forts on St. Simons Island," the colonel explained, to Grady's great disappointment. "But some of the men from our regiment were forced to help build those batteries while they were still slaves. They said that the Rebels used brand-new railroad iron to reinforce their magazines and bomb-proofs. Those iron bars would be worth their weight in gold to the Union if we could dig them out of the sand."

It wasn't what Grady had imagined himself doing when he'd enlisted, but he figured anything was better than standing around on a ship all day. He boarded a large flatboat with the other men, and once ashore, the Georgia slaves easily guided them to the buried treasure. The sun beat down on the exposed beach, forcing Grady to shed his uniform jacket as he and the others shoveled through nearly twelve feet of sand. His fellow soldiers seemed to thoroughly enjoy this demolition work, and Grady couldn't understand their laughter and high spirits. Weren't they tired of such backbreaking tasks after all these years? Didn't the fire of revenge burn as hotly in their souls as it did in his? What good was a gun if he couldn't kill anyone with it?

After unearthing nearly one hundred iron rails, the men set off across the island to forage for farm animals and to rescue any remaining slaves. Grady enjoyed rifling through the white folks' plantations. He and his fellow slaves deserved a portion of the food and livestock they had labored to produce. And he loved seeing the expressions of joy on the former slaves' faces when he offered them their freedom.

The ships set sail the next morning, dropping off the freed slaves in the town of Fernandina, and reaching Fort Clinch at the mouth of the St. Mary's River by late afternoon. "I'm assembling a corps of troops for another mission," Colonel Higginson announced after dinner.

Most of the men quickly volunteered, eager to join him. But Grady held back this time, waiting to hear what the mission entailed. He was willing to fight, but he would no longer break his back for the white men. When the colonel said, "We'll be conducting a night-time raid on a Rebel camp," Grady caught his breath. This was it: the chance he'd waited for all his life.

"Corporal Sutton is going to guide us up the St. Mary's as far as Township Landing, fifteen miles upriver," the colonel continued. "We'll go ashore there and pay a surprise visit to Captain Clark's Rebel cavalry, camped nearby. We'll likely come under fire, so your courage will be tested for the first time. But it's a chance to apply what we've learned in training camp."

So many men volunteered that there wasn't room for them all on the two ships making the run. Grady was grateful for his good health when Colonel Higginson decided to winnow out all of the men who were coughing and might spoil a surprise attack. Grady's tentmate, Joseph, was just recovering from a cold and was devastated at the thought of being left behind. Grady overheard him begging at the colonel's feet.

"Please let me come, sir! I'll throw myself on the ground and scrape a little hole to cough into before I'll ever make a sound! Please, sir!"

Higginson smiled, evidently amused by Joseph's zeal. He allowed him to come.

They waited until after dark to begin the trip upriver so that the plume from the ship's smokestack wouldn't give them away. The colonel addressed the volunteers one last time before they cast off, offering anyone who wanted it a chance to change his mind.

"The Rebels have heard all about our regiment," he told them. "They've heard that we have freed slaves fighting against them now, and they're all in an uproar about it. Before you volunteer for this mission, you need to know that the Rebels will show you no mercy. They won't be taking any prisoners of war. If you're captured, they'll either shoot you outright or return you to slavery."

The news didn't deter Grady in the least—or anyone else. He stood beside Joseph at the bow of the ship as the journey began, his rifle loaded, his body tensed and ready to kill. "I ain't showing them no mercy, either," he murmured. "The more white men I kill, the better I'll feel."

Joseph turned to face him, studying him in the darkness. "Killing in battle is one thing. After all, we're trying to win a war. But hating people . . . Hating ain't good, Grady."

He remembered Delia trying to preach him the same sermon and it made him angry. "Why don't you go talk to the white men, then? Seems like they're hating us as much as I'm hating them."

"Not all of them hate us, and not all white men are bad. There's good ones and bad ones, just like us colored folks."

"Yeah, well I've seen more than my fair share of bad ones," Grady said. "I ain't no worse than any of them."

"If you're comparing yourself to other men, then you're using the wrong measure. You need to be comparing yourself to God's standard—"

"Don't preach to me," Grady warned.

Joseph paused for a long moment, then asked, "What about Colonel Higginson? And Captain Metcalf and Captain Trowbridge and all the other white officers?"

"What about them?"

"Are you hating them, too, just because their skin's white?"

Grady didn't answer. The truth was that he avoided them as much as possible, wishing his race knew enough about warfare to go into battle without any white men. It was only because of the white man's prejudice that Negroes had never studied to be army officers. And there was no doubt in his mind that with the proper training, a black man could be a four-star general.

"Colonel Higginson and the others could be with a white regiment right now instead of with us," Joseph continued. "But they're volunteering to lead us—even though they're all knowing that they won't be sent to a prisoner-of-war camp, either, if they're captured. The truth is, the Rebels plan on killing the white officers right along with us."

Grady looked at Joseph for the first time. "Why would they do that? They're white men."

"That's their punishment for working with us. The Rebels are saying that any white officer they catch leading a troop of Negroes is gonna be treated just the same as a Negro and killed on the spot."

"Is that true?" Grady glanced up at the darkened pilothouse where Colonel Higginson stood in the shadows beside Corporal Sutton.

"Yes, sir, I swear it's true," Joseph replied. "Not all white men are like our massas, you know. A good many of them are wanting to see us set free—and that includes Colonel Higginson and all the men who're volunteering to lead us."

Grady still didn't understand why they would do that. But he had a new respect for these white officers who willingly shared his race's scorn and the Rebels' hatred.

"You know, Jesus done the same thing," Joseph said softly. And for some reason Grady didn't interrupt him or walk away. "Jesus was God's Son. He never had to live on earth or suffer and die. But He became a man, just like us. He took on our shame and sin and was willing to die for us."

His words sent a shiver of unease through Grady. "Why?" he asked.

"Same reason," Joseph said with a shrug. "He wanted to set us free."

Grady did walk away then, unwilling to allow any disquieting thoughts to disturb his plans for revenge. The moon shone dully off the swiftly flowing water as he stared into the darkness ahead. They rounded each bend in the river never knowing what lay ahead, heightening his sense of danger. He gazed up at the hills and meadows on shore and knew that he was heading deep into Rebel territory for the first time since his escape. He imagined thousands of Confederates waiting in ambush around the next bend in the river, and he felt alert, tense, and fully alive. Every light on the ship had been darkened, every voice whispered like the lapping of waves against the hull. He walked over to a group of soldiers standing beside one of the heavy guns.

"They say the Rebels will let ships go upriver," he heard one of them say, "but it's a trap. They'll build snags so they can attack us from their batteries on the way back."

"Yeah? Let them try it!" Grady said, his rage building again, along with his tension. "I've got plenty of ammunition."

The ships finally halted just below their destination of Township Landing, and Corporal Sutton went ashore with a small advance force. By the time Grady's ship rounded the point and docked at the landing, Sutton's men had silently surrounded the sleeping inhabitants' homes.

"Ain't nobody running off to tell the Rebels we're here, Colonel," Sutton reported to Higginson with a proud grin. "We can take them by surprise. They're camping about five miles from here, down a logging road through them woods."

It was after midnight by the time Grady and the others started down the path behind a small advance guard. The sense of wariness and danger he'd felt on board ship was heightened tenfold as he crept through the silent forest. His rifle was loaded and ready, his bayonet fixed. They would catch these white boys by surprise and kill them while they slept.

The pine woods were damp and fragrant, the bed of needles soft beneath his feet. The only sounds were the quiet tramp of feet, the *glug* of frogs in a nearby marsh, the distant yelp of a dog on some small farm hidden deep in the woods. The moon barely penetrated the thick forest, and Grady squinted into the darkness as his eyes tried to adjust to the scant light. They marched for more than two miles, hearing nothing, seeing nothing.

Suddenly the advance guard halted. They motioned for Grady and the others not to make a sound as they came to a halt behind them. Grady strained to see into the blackness, every nerve stretched tightly. Then he heard it—the distant sound of galloping horses. He remembered hearing those thudding hooves on the darkened road the night the white paddyrollers had caught him. He'd been defenseless against them back then. They'd captured him and tied him up and flogged all the flesh off his back, simply because they could. But tonight Grady had a gun. Tonight he would have his revenge.

Before he and the others could react, a rider on a white horse appeared out of the gloom on the shadowy path, leading a pack of cavalry. The two forces saw each other at the same moment, and the surprised Rebel in the lead reined his horse to a halt. He drew his pistol and fired just as the advance guard raised their rifles and fired. A volley of shots echoed through the silent woods like thunder as Grady and the others quickly took cover in the bushes. His heart pounded wildly, but he knew exactly what to do. Kneeling behind a bush, Grady calmly lifted his rifle and aimed at a target he couldn't see. He heard the whiz of bullets overhead, the deafening roar of hundreds of rifles all around him, but he waited until he spotted a burst of fire in the darkness from a Rebel rifle. Then he carefully took aim where he'd seen the flash—and fired. His ears rang from the discharge.

Grady ducked his head and quickly reloaded, cursing his fumbling fingers, wishing he could reload and fire faster. Voices cried out as bullets struck their mark on both sides, but Grady aimed, fired, reloaded—over and over again, his hearing deadened by the noise.

How long had they been fighting? He lost all track of time. In a way it seemed as if he'd been marching through the silent woods only a moment ago, yet it also seemed as if he'd been firing into the night for an eternity. Gradually, the enemy fire slackened, then stopped. He heard Colonel Higginson call, "Cease fire!"

Grady lowered his rifle and glanced around. Every man was in an offensive position, bravely standing up to the enemy. Not a single one of them cowered in the bushes. But the Confederates were gone. They were the ones who'd turned tail and run. Grady's company had experienced their first fight and they'd been victorious. He wanted to cheer.

"Let's keep going and finish this," Corporal Sutton said. Grady and the others agreed. But Colonel Higginson shook his head.

"All hope of surprise is lost. We won this round. The Rebels are the ones who fled in defeat. Let's fix some stretchers and attend to the wounded."

One of Grady's fellow soldiers had been killed. Seven others lay wounded and bleeding—some of them dying. The first sight of these casualties left Grady shaken. He had come to kill white men, not to be wounded or killed by them. Grady had taken an oath to help free his fellow slaves or die trying, but until this moment he hadn't truly faced what that meant. He didn't want to die. Death wasn't in his plans. But as he looked at his dead and wounded comrades, he realized that it hadn't been in their plans, either.

"It's okay, Colonel," he heard one of the wounded men say, when Higginson knelt to console him. "Freedom is sweeter than life."

Grady felt a moment of stomach-churning fear as he glanced around for Joseph and couldn't find him. Then his gangly tentmate stood from where he'd been kneeling in prayer beside the dead man. Grady exhaled in relief. As skinny as Joseph was, those Rebels probably couldn't hit him on a clear day with the sun shining.

Grady helped load the wounded onto stretchers and carry them back through the woods to the landing. They marched with their weapons loaded, their eyes and ears alert, fully expecting a counterattack at any moment. When it didn't happen, Colonel Higginson assured them that it meant complete victory. "We must have hit them pretty hard," he said. "No decent cavalry would let a small infantry force like ours march through their territory without a fight."

Grady volunteered to stay onshore with the colonel and a small squadron to guard the settlement until morning. He remained alert all night, waiting for another fight, eager for it, but the attack never came. Filled with unspent fury, he watched his fellow soldiers load a piano from the plantation house onto the ship the next morning to deliver to the Negro children's school in Fernandina. Then at the colonel's signal, Grady helped set the house on fire to prevent the Rebels from using it again.

On the return journey down river, Grady's ship docked at another small town to retrieve a much-needed load of lumber. Three white-haired Southern ladies waited to greet them, waving white handkerchiefs.

"They gonna tell you they's on our side," Corporal Sutton warned the colonel, "but they's really Rebel spies. You wait and see—as soon as we're on our way again, their menfolk will be waiting round the first bend to ambush us."

Colonel Higginson greeted the women politely—too politely, Grady thought. He knew the women were lying when they insisted that they weren't Rebel sympathizers or spies. He gritted his teeth when he saw how they addressed only the colonel and the other white officers, casting cold, disdainful glances at any Negroes who ventured near them. Grady easily recognized their racism for what it was, having experienced it all his life. He worried that the colonel had fallen for their flattery until he overheard him say, "If our ships are ambushed as we're leaving, I can promise you ladies that we will return and torch your town."

Higginson ordered some of the soldiers to spread out and guard the town from a surprise attack while the rest of the men quickly loaded the lumber onboard. Grady and two others climbed up the cupola of one of the houses to stand watch. It was still early morning, and the feathery mist rising from the river and the distant fields looked like fairy smoke. He thought of Anna and wished he could share the view with her. Then, as he scanned the woods for signs of Rebels, he wondered how long it would take to forget her.

When the colonel finally signaled to reboard the ship, Grady felt bitterly disappointed that there hadn't been a fight. He was ready for one after his first taste of combat last night. But shortly after the vessels got underway, a sudden volley of explosions rocked the ship. Everyone dove for cover, dodging a rain of shrapnel and splintering wood and bullets. The gunners ran to their weapons to return fire, but the attack ended as quickly as it began.

Grady's heart thudded with excitement and readiness as the colonel made good on his threat and returned to shore to set the town on fire. Something deep inside him found immense satisfaction as he listened to those white ladies begging for mercy . . . and he watched their pleas go unheeded.

The ships returned safely to Fernandina with no further Rebel attacks. But rather than soothing Grady's need for action, the night's work left him feeling very unsatisfied. He'd savored only one tantalizing taste of combat, and he hungered for more. Enemy troops still roamed the woods along that river, and he longed to hunt them down and kill them all. Even after staying up all night, he felt much too edgy to sleep. So when the colonel announced a second nightlong mission, Grady quickly volunteered again. They would venture further upriver this time, to the town of Woodstock, deep in Rebel-held territory, to acquire a supply of new bricks to repair Fort Clinch.

The expedition sailed up the St. Mary's River after dark, just as they had the night before, with Corporal Sutton piloting the ship by moonlight. The river was calm as Grady stood watching from the bow, the tide flowing with them. Conversation onboard was subdued as everyone prepared for action, wondering if they'd be attacked from the shore batteries again. They sailed past the old ladies' town that they had burned the previous night, then past Township Landing, where they'd fought the Rebel cavalry. But there was no sign of the enemy.

The riverbanks loomed steeply on either side of them as they steamed farther upstream, and the current grew swifter and more treacherous. Branches and snags littered their path, and the ship grounded eight times as the captain tried to navigate the river's sharp bends. When they lay stranded on one sandbar for half an hour, the colonel put everyone on alert, fearing a Rebel attack. Grady knew that one well-placed cannonball would sink the ship and doom them all. But the enemy seemed not to be expecting a second foray into their territory so soon after the first, and Grady's ship finally reached the sleeping town of Woodstock just before daybreak.

The soldiers scrambled ashore with orders to surround the town and make certain that no one crept away to alert the Rebels of their arrival. Once all the roads were secured, Grady and the others went house-to-house, rounding up all the white men to hold as temporary prisoners and urging all the slaves to board the ships to freedom. He took great pleasure in rousing these white folks from their homes and beds, savoring their fear at being held at gunpoint by former slaves. Dogs barked and babies cried and roosters crowed in the pandemonium of rushing feet and shouted orders. But the loudest protests came from the white women who were outraged at being held captive by armed Negroes as they watched all their slaves go free.

The regiment's orders had been to show restraint, using force only when absolutely necessary, and not a shot was fired throughout the entire operation. But Grady saw the loathing and disgust for his race in every white person's eyes, and he longed for an excuse to shoot one of them. When his work was finished, he went to Colonel Higginson with a request.

"The slaves we're setting free ain't got a thing in the world, Colonel," he said. "Can't we rummage through town and maybe take some bedding and stuff that they might be needing? Ain't it all their hard work that earned everything their massas have?"

Colonel Higginson shook his head. "I'm sorry, Private. We have permission to forage only for things we need ourselves."

"What about that piano we took last night?" Grady asked.

Higginson looked embarrassed. "Well . . . that was against regulations. I'm afraid I got a little carried away. We're not allowed to loot from civilians or burn a town unless there's proof of collaboration with the Rebels."

He must have seen Grady's anger and frustration, because a moment later he added, "Come with me, son. Corporal Sutton and I are about to pay a visit on one of the town's leading citizens—the proprietress of the sawmills and lumber wharves. Corporal Sutton was once her slave."

Grady followed Sutton and Colonel Higginson to the town's largest home, upset to realize that his natural inclination was to circle around to the servants' entrance. Instead, he followed the colonel up the steps to the front door. Higginson introduced himself to the lady of the house adding, "And I'm sure you remember Corporal Robert Sutton, ma'am?"

She gave her former slave a look of utter contempt and said, "We called him Bob."

Grady imagined himself facing his former mistress, Missus Fuller, and spitting in her face. His admiration for the corporal grew when he saw how the man maintained his poise and dignity.

When the colonel finished informing her that the Union was confiscating her lumber, Sutton turned to Higginson and said, "I'll show you her slave jail now, sir."

They walked around back to a small building that was no larger than a corncrib. Grady saw the bolt and chain in the middle of the floor, and his fury mounted as he recalled being shackled to the floor of the slave hut for three days at Missus Fuller's orders. This slave jail also contained three pairs of stocks, including one that was small enough to confine women and children.

"Do they . . . do they use this on *children*?" Higginson asked in a hushed voice.

Corporal Sutton nodded. Grady knew that when he'd been a boy, Coop would have shackled him along with all the other slaves if the bonds had fit his wrists.

"What is this?" Higginson asked as he examined an odd metal contraption with chains and spikes.

"Massa use that to torture us slaves," Sutton said quietly. "Once he's putting us in that thing, we can't sit, stand or lay down without suffering. We just have to balance ourselves as best we can till it's over, sir."

Grady saw the colonel's horror. For several long moments Higginson was unable to speak as powerful emotions rocked through him. He took the set of keys that hung on a nail on the wall and handed them to Sutton. "You keep these, Corporal," he said quietly. "You've earned them."

When the lumber, bricks, and newly freed slaves were all loaded onboard, Higginson ordered his soldiers to take all of the town's white men along as hostages. They would be transported to the mouth of the river before being released, he told them, in order to discourage the usual Rebel attacks on the voyage downstream.

The ship's gun crews stood ready near their weapons as they left

the wharf. Grady chafed when he and the other soldiers were ordered to remain belowdecks where it was safe. The hot, crowded
hold brought back memories of all the years he'd spent traveling
with load after load of slaves, bound for the auction block, and his
stomach clenched like a fist. He had to remind himself that he was
free now; that these slaves were heading toward freedom, too; and
that the white men huddling in the corner were his prisoners.

Suddenly a volley of explosions shook the boat. Grady ducked
instinctively. A soldier near one of the portholes shouted, "The Rebels
are attacking from the bluffs!"

The cannons on the deck above them roared as the ship returned fire.
The boom of rifles seemed deafening in the hold as the soldiers who
crowded near the portholes fired their weapons. Grady felt trapped,
imprisoned in the bowels of the ship with no way to fight back.

"Let me out!" he begged the soldier guarding the hatch. "Let me
fight!" But the man shook his head, and the ship steamed downriver
until the noise finally died away.

Grady exhaled in frustration. He rechecked his weapon to make
sure it was still ready, then inspected his ammunition pouch. He had
just convinced himself that it was safe to sit down and relax when he
heard a cannon explode on the top on a nearby bluff. The ominous
scream of a falling artillery shell followed, growing louder, coming
closer, until it crashed into the river alongside the ship with a roar.
He knew by the way the vessel rocked, and by the burst of water that
sprayed the deck above him, that the shell had fallen very close to
them. It would only take one to sink them. And if the ship grounded
again or got entangled in a snag, it would make an easy target.

A hail of bullets hammered the deck above him, and he heard
the sounds of splintering wood and shattering glass. Belowdecks,
chaos reigned as the women and children wept and screamed, and
his fellow soldiers begged for a chance to fight. Grady ran to the
hatch again with his rifle. "Let us up on deck!" he shouted. "Give us
a chance to fight back!" He could barely hear the reply above the din.

"The colonel says to stay below! Your rifles ain't any good at this distance!" Bitterly disappointed, Grady could only hunker down with the others until the ship steamed out of range.

An hour passed, and the Rebels made no more attacks. Exhausted, Grady finally managed to doze for a few minutes. The hushed murmur of excited voices awakened him. He scrambled to his feet. "What is it? What's going on?" he asked Joseph.

"The colonel's just sending us the news," he said somberly. "Mr. Clifton, the ship's captain, was hit by a Rebel bullet in the first attack."

"Is he okay?"

Joseph shook his head. "They killed him, Grady. He died standing right there at the helm." He paused, then added, "He's a white man, you know. And he gave his life to help free a boatload of slaves."

Grady returned to where he'd been dozing and sank down. Joseph had tried to tell him that not all white men hated him, that the officers in his regiment were risking their lives for the slaves' sakes. He remembered Colonel Higginson's emotional reaction when he saw the slave jail, but Grady still couldn't comprehend it. He'd never experienced anything but hatred between the two races, yet on this mission, white and black had fought together against a common enemy, facing death for the same cause. Before the war he would have called any man a liar if he had tried to tell him such an alliance was possible.

Later that afternoon, when all danger was past and the men were allowed up on deck again, Grady saw Joseph and a small group of soldiers kneeling in prayer by their dead captain. The man's body was shrouded, the color of his skin hidden from view—and Grady was able to look past it for first time in his life and see the man beneath. Captain Clifton had earned Grady's deep respect and admiration. This white man had taken upon himself the wrath of all those who hated the Negro race—and had died for their sakes.

Grady recalled what else Joseph had told him on their voyage upriver. It was the same thing Eli had taught him long ago in Richmond, and what Delia had tried to tell him back at Massa Fuller's plantation: God's Son took the scorn and sin of the human race upon himself and had died for their sakes.

But the old question quickly rose to taunt Grady: <u>Why had Jesus deserted him,</u> then? Why had He allowed him to suffer all these years? Delia had compared Grady's life of slavery to that of Joseph's in the Bible; she said Joseph's suffering had made him strong so that God could use him to save his family. *"Ever think that maybe the Lord's preparing you to save your black brothers and sisters?"* she had asked.

It had seemed inconceivable, back then. But that was exactly what Grady was doing right now.

He quickly turned and stumbled belowdecks to escape his disturbing thoughts. Over in one corner huddled a group of white men who would gladly kill him or enslave him again, if given the chance. Grady was still not sure he was willing to trust a white man as his friend. And he was certain that he wasn't ready to trust Jesus again, either.

22

GREAT OAK PLANTATION, SOUTH CAROLINA
SPRING 1863

Missy Claire stood before her open wardrobe and pouted. "I'm so tired of these same old dresses. I haven't had anything new to wear in ages."

Kitty ran her fingers over the fine, brightly colored gowns hanging in Missy's wardrobe, savoring the smooth rustle of silk and taffeta. Missy owned dozens of beautiful dresses. Why on earth would she need a new one? But Kitty knew better than to ask.

"I can fetch one of your mama's seamstresses from down on the Row," Kitty said as she reached to straighten the hatboxes on the top shelf. "She'll be glad to sew you a new one."

Missy turned to glare at her. "And what, may I ask, is she supposed to use for fabric? Ugly old homespun like your dress?"

Kitty quickly lowered her arms to hide the frayed side seams of her homemade dress. She'd worn it since before the war began and the rough fabric was threadbare. Now, as her figure changed with pregnancy, she'd had to alter the dress to fit, raising the waistline and re-stitching the bursting side seams. She'd sewn it at night by candlelight, after all her other work was done, and the shoddy workmanship embarrassed her.

"Can't you send to Charleston for some new cloth, Missy? I remember all the fancy stores they have there, filled with bolts and bolts of beautiful cloth—so many that you could scarcely make up your mind which ones to buy, remember?"

"Don't be stupid. There's nothing in Charleston, either."

Kitty stared at her mistress in surprise. "There ain't?"

"Of course not. The stores have been nearly empty ever since the Yankees started this tiresome war."

Kitty thought she remembered everyone saying that the Southern states started the war by firing on Fort Sumter—but she didn't argue with her mistress. "You mean . . . *all* them stores in Charleston? How can they all be empty, Missy Claire?"

"Because the best fabric comes from abroad and the ships that run the Yankee blockade usually bring goods that are needed for the war. The few nice things that are available are outrageously priced." She sank down in her chair with an angry sigh, as if it was all Kitty's fault. "I haven't worn a ball gown in ages. And I hate being cooped up here all winter and missing the social season. Father promised we'd go to Charleston for Easter—and I *always* had a new outfit for Easter. I'll be so embarrassed with nothing new to wear."

Kitty knew that it was her job to cheer up her mistress and help her see the brighter side of things. She thought for a long moment before saying, "Seems like if all them stores is empty then ain't nobody else gonna be wearing a new gown for Easter, Missy Claire."

"Well, yes . . . I suppose that's true," she said. "Mother says that a lot of women are having their dresses turned."

"What does that mean, Missy Claire? They wearing them inside-out or something?"

Missy managed a thin smile. "No, silly. You know how the bottom hemline gets frayed and the collars and cuffs get worn? Well, their seamstresses take the dresses apart, turn the fabric around, somehow, and re-cut them so the worn parts don't show."

"Oh, I get it. They make a brand-new dress out of the old ones." Kitty turned to Missy's wardrobe again and sorted through the gowns. "You know, some of these colors go real nice together. You could cut up this skirt and use it to trim the hem of this dress where it's frayed and it would look real pretty, see? And this dress is a little worn out but the lace is still nice. You could sew it on this bodice and make it look brand new."

Missy sat forward, looking excited for the first time. "What about that plaid gown? Could we fix that one, too?"

"Sure thing, Missy. See how nice this green dress matches it? We could cut up the green one and make a new ruffle around the hem of the plaid one . . . maybe put parts of the green on the bodice, too."

"You always did have a good eye for things like this," Missy said grudgingly.

"Want me to go fetch the seamstress? She'll help us figure out how to do it."

"All right," Missy said with a sigh. She waited until Kitty got as far as the door to add, "And don't dawdle!"

Kitty made a face as soon as she was out of sight, chafing at Missy's command. What difference would it make if she did dawdle? Missy had no place to go and nothing to do. It wasn't like the wardrobe was on fire and she had to fetch water to put it out.

Kitty took her time descending the stairs, wrapping a shawl around her shoulders before heading outside. She stood in the doorway for a moment listening to the call of birds down by the river, enjoying the few moments of peace away from Missy's whining voice. Halfway across the yard she felt her baby's fluttering movements and halted. She'd felt this quickening for the first time only a week ago and the sensation was still wonderfully new. Life! A living child—Grady's child—moved and grew inside her.

Tears filled her eyes as she thought of Grady. Was he alive or dead? Slave or free? What if they never found each other again and were separated forever, just like Delia and her husband, Shep? But as Kitty felt the baby move again she took comfort in the fact that a part of Grady would always remain alive in his child. At least she had that.

"I could have taken a nap in all the time you've been gone," Missy complained when Kitty returned with the Negro seamstress.

"I'm sorry, Missy Claire. I was hurrying just as fast as I could."

"Oh, I'm sure you were. Did you explain to her what I want her to do?"

"Yes, Missy Claire. I thought I'd just lay the dresses all out on the bed like this so she could see them." Kitty began removing the gowns from the wardrobe, piling the ones they would combine on top of each other as she explained her ideas to the seamstress. Missy supervised from her chair as if all of the ideas had been hers, warning them from time to time, to be extra careful with her delicate silks.

"Such beautiful colors . . ." Kitty said as she ran her hand over the plaid taffeta.

"Yes, thank goodness Roger hasn't died," Missy said. "Where would I ever find black fabric? Besides, I hate black. I couldn't bear it if I had to wear black for an entire year!"

Kitty hid her shock at Missy's heartlessness. If Grady died, Kitty would mourn his loss for the rest of her life. But Missy had never been in love with Massa Roger. At least she and Grady had loved each other—and that was one thing Missy could never take away from her.

"What about a new bonnet?" Missy said suddenly. "I can't wear my old ones. I always bought a new bonnet for Easter."

Kitty saw the seamstress roll her eyes, but the woman had her back to Missy. Kitty would have made a face, too, but she didn't dare. "Maybe we can fix a new hat from all the old ones," she said. "We'll find one that ain't looking too bad and make a little ruffle from leftover dress fabric. If we use a bit of matching ribbon . . . pick the best flowers . . ."

Kitty reached to the top of the wardrobe to pull down Missy's hatboxes and heard a ripping sound as the side seam of her dress gave way. "Oh!" she cried and quickly lowered her arms.

"What was that tearing sound?" Missy asked. "What did you do?"

"Nothing, Missy Claire. Just my own dress ripping a little bit."

"Come here and let me see. Lift up your arms."

Kitty did as she was told.

"What a mess!" Missy said when she showed her. "And you expect me to trust you with my gowns? Look at this! And why is the waistline way up above your waist? Who sewed this?"

"I did, Missy Claire. The side seam was about to split and—"

"Look at you! You're putting on weight. Turn around."

Kitty cringed as Missy eyed her changing figure.

"You never used to be so . . . so full on top." Missy's eyebrows raised as the truth suddenly dawned on her. "Wait a minute! Are you pregnant?"

"Yes, ma'am," she said softly. "I believe so."

"Why, you little hussy!" Missy looked as though she might slap her. "You're a married woman! You're not supposed to be carrying on with other men."

"But I ain't been carrying on. This is my husband's baby, ma'am. Honest!"

"How dare you lie to me! I waited for months on end for you to have a baby, and your worthless husband wasn't able to sire one."

"But this is his baby—"

"I don't believe it. You told me you haven't seen him since they took the horses away and I sent him down to Slave Row. Were you lying to me then or are you lying now?"

Kitty didn't know what to say. If she told Missy that she had seen Grady one last time then Missy would be angry with her for disobeying—and she would know that Kitty had been aware of his escape plans. What if Grady had already been caught? Would telling the truth get him into even more trouble? When Kitty didn't answer or try to defend herself, Missy gave a triumphant smile.

"I knew it! That couldn't possibly be your husband's baby. I can count off the months since I sent him down, you know. Mother was right when she said marriage means nothing to you people."

Kitty's entire body trembled with fury. She wanted to rage at Missy and tell her that she was wrong! Slave women loved their husbands. It was their white owners who were always breaking up marriages and separating husbands and wives. White people had separated Kitty's parents—and Delia and Shep. Missy herself had separated the old man from his wife when he drove Missy here. And Missy had sent Grady down to Slave Row and forbidden them to live together. Kitty longed to scream at her, to make her see the truth. There was no other man in Kitty's life except Grady. She loved him, missed him desperately. Missy was the one who had married for selfish reasons. She didn't even care if her husband died—only that she would have to wear black.

But Kitty didn't say any of those things. She turned away from her mistress, blinking back her tears as she lifted one of Missy's dresses from the bed. "Guess I better be ripping out some of these seams, Missy Claire, so we can start sewing you some new dresses." She sat down near the window with a pair of scissors and carefully picked away at the tiny stitches of a side seam. She kept her head lowered, struggling not to cry.

"What's wrong with you?" Missy asked a few minutes later. "Are you pouting?"

Kitty forced a smile, her eyes bright with unshed tears. "Oh, no, Missy. There ain't nothing wrong with me. I'm just concentrating, that's all. Your seamstress sewed such tiny little stitches that I can barely see to pull them out."

"Well, my gowns are very important to me, you know. It isn't my fault that this stupid war has forced me to trust them to the two of you. Just make sure you don't make a mess of them. If you do, I'll have your hide."

❧

St. John's River, Florida
March 1863

Grady heard an ominous rasping sound as the ship's hull scraped against a sandbar. The vessel slowed, then stopped with a sickening

339

jolt as it ran aground. His heart speeded up as he scanned the wooded shoreline in the darkness, watching for the telltale flash of enemy artillery fire, aware that his stranded ship made an easy target for a Rebel attack. But only the waning moon and millions of shimmering stars lit the night sky.

The steam engines reversed, grinding loudly as they labored to free the ship. After a tense twenty minutes, the ship was underway again, steaming up the winding St. John's River toward Jacksonville, Florida. Grady's regiment had begun the journey upriver at two o'clock in the morning after waiting at the river's mouth all evening for their escort of navy gunboats. He had thought of Anna as he'd watched a flock of pelicans swooping for fish above the mirror-like water, filling the enormous pouches that hung from their bills. She would have loved to sketch that beautiful scene.

Colonel Higginson had planned to arrive before dawn and take the sleeping city of Jacksonville by surprise, but the St. John's River had proved difficult to navigate. The expedition lost valuable time as the ships took turns getting stranded, and they finally had to leave one grounded gunboat behind as the tide changed and the river began to ebb.

Grady recognized the outskirts of Jacksonville as the sky grew light, remembering the city from his travels there with Massa Coop. The wooded shoreline gave way to cultivated meadows and distant houses, then the ship rounded the last bend and the city came into view. Coop had done a fair amount of business here, selling slaves to white folks for the lumbering trade. It was a pleasant city, with neatly laid streets, serene houses, and rustling shade trees. Except for the city's mills—charred husks of bricks and twisted metal, burned by the fleeing Rebels the last time the Union army had invaded— Jacksonville appeared peaceful and untouched by the war.

But Grady knew that the calm appearance might disguise a Rebel ambush. He held his breath, gripping his rifle as his ship's gunners readied their weapons, bracing himself for the first volley of shots or boom of enemy artillery. But the city remained quiet as his ship reached the dock. He could hear his heart pounding in his ears as he prepared to disembark with the rest of the invasion force, fanning out and taking defensive positions as they'd been trained to do. An artillery unit set up their howitzers on the wharf behind him, preparing for an attack—but the attack never came. Moments after they landed, the First South Carolina Volunteers had made Jacksonville, Florida a United States military outpost without firing a single shot.

Grady's regiment had accomplished the first stage of its objective, the capture of Jacksonville, but he was deeply disappointed that it had fallen so easily. He had been ready for a fight—jubilant, in fact—when orders had come to strike their camp outside Beaufort and prepare for permanent deployment in Florida. He and the others had worked steadily for twenty-four hours, packing up all their tents and equipment and hauling everything out to the waiting ships on flatboats. Their mission was to invade and occupy as much of Florida as they could, driving out the Rebels, freeing the slaves, and recruiting all the able-bodied men into their ranks. The regiment's courage had been proven on the expedition up the St. Mary's River, Colonel Higginson had told them. No one could deny the slaves' valor in combat. Now their behavior as victors would be tested. The Northern press was watching, waiting to report how a Negro occupation force would treat their former oppressors.

Jacksonville lay spread out over a large area, with dense woods beyond the city limits. The regiment would be spread very thinly as they guarded the town. If the Rebels attacked with a force larger than their own, Grady's regiment might be overrun. Grady and the other men spent much of the first day making their presence known, checking for ambushes, and planning the fortifications and entrenchments they would need to build in order to secure the town. Oddly, they found only a small number of slaves for a city this size.

"Our owners heard how the Yankees been freeing all the slaves," an elderly Negro told Grady, "so the Rebels took all the strongest men away already. Moved them all inland, out of reach." His words made Grady more determined than ever to fight his enemy.

341

"Don't worry," Captain Metcalf promised, "once we're established here, we'll make some forays upriver to find those slaves and free them."

Grady's troops spent the long day in suspense, expecting a Rebel counterattack, preparing for it. As night fell, the regiment's scattered companies bedded down in various parts of town, with guards on the alert for a nighttime assault. Grady felt exhausted from the tense day and lost night of sleep. He slept restlessly, with his shoes on and his gun close beside him.

The hard work of fortifying Jacksonville began at dawn. Redoubts needed to be built, trees cleared to create a buffer zone, houses razed and trenches dug. The men took turns performing the heavy labor and doing picket duty to guard against enemy raids. Grady's own encampment was in a grove of linden trees on the outer edge of town, and he spent the morning chopping down trees to barricade the main road out of Jacksonville.

As he labored to build defensive works around the camp that was to be his new home, Grady noticed a lone white man standing on the front porch of a house across the street, watching the laborers. He was one of the few whites left in this part of town, living in one of the few occupied houses on the street—in the last row of homes at the edge of Jacksonville. Something about the man reminded Grady of Massa Coop, and he felt the same prickle of fear he'd felt as a boy when Coop had scrutinized his every move, waiting for him to make a mistake, hoping for an excuse to beat him. The "watcher" haunted Grady, and even as he lay in his tent at night with Joseph snoring beside him, he imagined the man on his porch, staring at him in the darkness.

Grady soon learned that the Rebels were camped nearby. They began creeping forward at odd hours to skirmish with Union pickets on the outskirts of town or to harass the squads that were sent out to forage in the region around Jacksonville. Life in Grady's regiment became a continuous round of hard labor, daily skirmishes, and nightlong vigils. And whenever Grady glanced at the last row of houses, he glimpsed the man watching from his porch or standing like a shadow in his front window.

Grady wondered if the man was a spy—if he was sneaking past the pickets somehow, to carry information to the Rebels. It was clear that someone was providing them with information. The Rebels had a locomotive-mounted cannon, and they traveled down the rail line to bring the weapon within range of the city, bombarding the Union camps each night before disappearing again. One night, the bombs fell much too close to the colonel's headquarters for it to be a coincidence. Grady had been on guard duty and he'd watched in horrified fascination as the shells streaked through the night sky like falling stars and exploded in a shower of deadly fragments.

The man on the porch even stood the same way that Massa Coop used to stand, with his arms cocked stiffly on his hips and his feet widespread. He dressed as neatly as Coop, too, in a white shirt and a dark, well-tailored suit and vest. But Coop was from New Orleans, and the Yankees had captured that city a year ago. Grady had heard all about it last spring when he'd gone into Pocotaligo with the overseer for supplies. Coop wouldn't be able to trade slaves anymore, now that Union warships were blocking all the southern ports. Grady tried to put the resemblance out of his mind.

But one day he noticed that the men on guard duty had a pair of field glasses. They were using them to watch for Rebels hiding in the woods. Grady decided to satisfy his curiosity about the "watcher" once and for all.

"Can I borrow them glasses for a little while?" he asked. He found a place where he could view the porch and still be hidden behind one of the tents. But for once the man wasn't there, and Grady was forced to wait—an eternity, it seemed. He was about to give up and return the field glasses, when he finally spotted the "watcher" hurrying up the street toward his house, coming from the direction of town. The man kept his face lowered until he was opposite Grady's encampment, then he quickly glanced over at it before hurrying up the porch steps.

343

Grady caught his breath. If that wasn't Coop it was someone who looked exactly like him. He had the same stern, narrow face and shrewd eyes, even if his drooping mustache and fringe of receding brown hair had turned iron gray during the past six years. It had to be Coop. But it couldn't be. Was it him—or wasn't it?

The question haunted Grady for days. He borrowed the field glasses a second time, then a third, and each tantalizing glimpse made him more and more certain that it was his old enemy. Then, on a foraging raid upriver to bring back provisions and to free the area's slaves, Grady learned that the squadron's guide, Peter, was a former slave from Jacksonville.

"Can I ask you a question?" Grady said as he took Peter aside. "Are you knowing a lot of white folks in this town?"

"A fair amount. I'm living here all my life. Why?"

"If I take and show you a white man living near our camp, think you could tell me who he is?"

Peter pulled on his bottom lip and shrugged. "Maybe I can and maybe I can't. Take me there and we'll see."

Grady's heart speeded up as they neared the house. The "watcher" stood outside on his porch. Grady still felt a jolt of childlike panic each time he saw the man, and he remembered his four years of unrelenting fear.

"That's him. That's the man," Grady said. But as he and Peter approached, the man quickly disappeared into the house. "You know him?" Grady asked.

"Nope. That fella ain't from Jacksonville. If he's who I think he is, he just come here about a year ago with a big pile of money. Paid cash for that house. I heard someone say that the Yankees chased him out of his other home. Keeps to himself, mostly."

"Did he come here all alone?" Grady asked.

"I believe he brought his wife and a couple of slaves."

William. If one of those slaves was William, then Grady would be certain. But nearly all of Jacksonville's slaves had left the city on

Union ships shortly after being set free. "Are any of his slaves still staying here in Jacksonville?" he asked hopefully.

Peter shrugged again. "I can ask around. What's your interest in the man?"

"I'm trying to figure out if he's my old massa. Looks a lot like him."

"And if he is . . . ?" Peter asked.

"Then he's a slave trader."

Peter's reaction was instantaneous. Grady saw his revulsion in his tightly clenched fists and angry grimace. Edward Coop was Peter's enemy—every slave's enemy.

"My massa made his fortune sending young gals to brothels and tearing families apart," Grady continued. "He used to torture and beat us slaves just for the fun of it."

"I'll ask around," Peter said in a husky voice. "I'll be sure and let you know."

Peter returned a few days later. "I found a gal who says she worked for the man's wife until y'all got here. She says they move here from New Orleans—and her massa's name is Coop."

A shudder rocked through Grady. His stomach clenched with hatred—and fear.

"I take it that's the fella," Peter said.

Grady could barely speak. "Yeah. That's him."

Grady wanted to yank Coop from his porch and beat him to within an inch of his life before hanging him from the gallows in the city square. He resisted the urge to dash across the street and grab him right now, knowing he couldn't accomplish anything alone. He spent the next few hours trying to think of a way to prove to the authorities that Coop had once been a slave trader and deserved to hang—and he finally remembered Amos. The big man was part of Grady's regiment, but his company had been assigned to guard a different part of Jacksonville. Weeks seemed to pass in between skirmishes, nightly guard duty, and fatigue duty, until Grady finally had enough time off one Sunday afternoon to hunt for Amos.

"I found Massa Coop, the soul trader," Grady told him without preamble. "He's living here in town. You remember what he looks like? Think you can back me up when I turn him in to the authorities?"

"Turn him in? For what?"

"He should hang for being a slave trader. And he killed at least one slave that I know of."

Amos gave a bitter grunt. "They won't arrest Coop just for killing one of us. And there still ain't no law against trading slaves. Besides, the whites would never believe our word against another white man's. Coop probably has all them white officers fooled into thinking he's a kindly old Southern gentleman. And if he's got money, he'll just buy his way out of trouble."

Grady exhaled in frustration. "What can we do? I don't want to see him go free."

"Oh, he ain't going free, boy. You and me are gonna kill him ourselves."

A tremor of unease shivered through Grady, but he quickly brushed it aside. It would be justice to kill Coop. What about all the slaves Coop had tortured and killed, all the suffering and abuse he'd caused—separating families, sending young girls to brothels? Didn't God demand justice for all of that? If Grady felt uneasy, it was probably just fear that he might be caught. He certainly wouldn't feel any guilt for killing Coop.

"I know plenty of fellas who'll be willing to help us kill a white slave trader," Amos continued. "We just have to come up with a plan to make sure we ain't caught."

Grady's mind was already scheming. "What if we waited until a night when I'm on guard duty? There's a guard post close to Coop's street. It should be easy to sneak on over there and break into his house, if I'm the one on watch. And if Coop is found dead in the morning, ain't nobody gonna care."

Another long week passed until Grady was scheduled for guard duty, the second watch of the night. He requested a pass and hurried across town to Amos' camp to let him know.

"I'll be there," Amos said. And Grady saw a hint of a smile cross the big man's face.

The night they'd chosen turned out to be perfect, with cloudy, moonless skies and a blanket of damp, gray fog. But Grady waited, interminably it seemed, for Amos to arrive. His watch was nearly over when four shadowy figures finally drifted out of the fog, startling Grady, at first. Amos and the other three men wore slaves' rags, but Grady knew by the army-issue rifles they carried that they were soldiers just like him.

"I was afraid you weren't coming," Grady breathed.

Amos shook his head as if to dismiss his doubts and whispered, "Which house?"

Grady glanced around before leaving his post, then signaled for the others to follow him across the street and around to the backyard. The door was barred from the inside, but one of Amos' men quickly broke a rear window, muffling the sound with his army blanket. They all climbed through it. The modest house was as dark as a cave inside. Grady stood in the inky stair hall, waiting to move until his eyes adjusted, but Amos and the others quickly spread out to search all the downstairs rooms, as silent and stealthy as cats. They found no sign of Coop.

Amos had just started to lead the way upstairs when a dark figure appeared at the top of the steps. Even in the dark, Grady knew it was Coop. He saw a glint of metal in Coop's right hand—a pistol—and was about to shout a warning to Amos, when the huge man moved as fast as a panther, tackling Coop around his knees. Coop tumbled down the stairs, and his gun bounced to the floor before he could fire it. The knot of men quickly converged around him, raising their rifle butts to beat him, but Grady pushed them away.

"Wait a minute. I need to be sure." He jabbed the barrel of his rifle against Coop's chest and bent over him. Grady saw the man he hated and spit in his face.

"Remember me?" Grady asked, removing his hat. "The slave you lost in a poker game? You called me Joe, but my name is *Grady*."

He kicked Coop in the ribs as he said his name. "Got that? *Grady!*" Even now, he felt the anguish of being a helpless boy, of suffering a brutal beating simply because he'd clung to his name. Now Coop was helpless. Grady kicked him again.

"I don't know what you're talking about," Coop growled. He was breathing rapidly but his expression showed anger, not fear.

"Don't you remember beating me, like this?" He gripped his gun by the barrel and smashed the butt of it against Coop's head until he cried out in pain. "Go ahead and yell," Grady breathed. "Cry for mercy, just like all those slaves you bought and sold. Nobody cares, Coop. Nobody's gonna listen to you—just like you refused to listen to all their cries."

Grady stepped back and let the others take their turns, kicking Coop and clubbing him with their rifle butts. Grady allowed them to vent their rage for a minute, then he held up his hands to stop them. He wanted to drag out the torture, make Coop suffer in agony as he waited for the end. He wanted to hear Coop beg.

"Hold it," Grady said. "We'll give him a minute to pray for God's mercy because we ain't gonna show him any. You deserve to die, Coop. We're gonna kill you now, in cold blood, just like you killed your first slave named Joe. Remember him? Except your death will be a lot quicker than his."

"Go ahead and kill me now," Coop gasped. "I don't believe in God."

Grady froze, shocked by his confession. "You . . . you *what*?"

"That's right. Religion is just a bunch of myths and lies to appease simple fools like you."

Cold dread slithered through Grady at Coop's words. "You . . . you ain't sorry for all the harm you done, all the slaves you tortured and killed?"

"I don't have to apologize to any paltry god for my life, and I don't intend to. Just kill me—unless you lack the guts, *boy!*"

Grady lifted his rifle butt and brought it down on Coop's head. He tried to strike him a second time but Amos and the others pushed him aside to swarm all over Coop, beating him and kicking him for what seemed like hours until Coop finally lay still.

"Hold it a minute," Amos said. The men backed away. Amos knelt to feel the vein in Coop's neck and said, "He's dead."

Coop's cold gray eyes gazed sightlessly at the ceiling but the rest of his face was unrecognizable. Grady couldn't take his eyes off him. This was what he'd wanted, what he'd dreamed of doing for years. He should feel triumphant, victorious. Instead, he felt as if his limbs had turned to stone.

"Let's get out of here," Amos said. He gripped Grady's arm and pulled him down the hall and through the house. The men climbed out through the window again, leaving the door barred, and disappeared into the shadows as silently as they'd come.

Grady stood in Coop's yard for a long moment, disoriented. Then he remembered his abandoned post and broke into a run. He shivered as the damp fog enveloped him, and he realized that he was wringing wet with sweat—that he stank of it. He'd been gone less than ten minutes, and his turn at watch surely wasn't over yet, but as he dashed across the street he saw a man standing in his place.

"Halt! Who goes there?" the figure called. Grady recognized Joseph's voice. He remembered that his tentmate was scheduled to relieve him. Grady gave the password and Joseph lowered his rifle.

"Ain't you coming on duty a little early?" Grady asked. He tried to act casual but his voice shook. His entire body shook.

"Where were you?" Joseph asked. He stared at Grady as if he'd never seen him before.

"I . . . um . . . I went to check something out over there." He tilted his head in the general direction of Coop's house. "Heard a noise. Turned out to be nothing."

He followed Joseph's gaze as he looked down at Grady's hands—and he saw that he still gripped his rifle by the barrel, like a club, the way he'd gripped it as he'd smashed it against Coop's head. Even in the dark, smears of Coop's blood glistened on the gunstock.

His hands were sticky with blood, his light skin stained dark with it. He slowly lowered the rifle, resting the butt on the ground, out of sight.

"What's going on, Grady?" Joseph asked.

"Nothing. See you in the morning." He walked away as casually as his trembling limbs would allow and sank down inside their tent. Joseph couldn't leave his post to follow him.

Grady sat for a long time, waiting to regain control over his shaking hands. When he thought he could use his fingers again, he fumbled in his knapsack for a bandana and a canteen of water, using them to scrub the blood off his rifle and his hands. But now the telltale blood stained the bandana. Grady crawled out of the tent on his hands and knees and burned the evidence in one of the smoldering campfires.

Back in his tent, he still couldn't sleep. He didn't know why. It couldn't be guilt—he had no reason to feel guilty. Coop deserved to die. As his racing mind replayed the night's events, Grady decided that what he felt wasn't guilt, but fear. Joseph had seen the blood on his hands.

Grady pretended to be asleep when Joseph came in from his watch. He waited until he heard his tentmate snoring, then got up and went outside long before reveille, feeding wood into the campfire until it blazed. At roll call, Captain Metcalf asked for volunteers to carry supplies to one of the distant picket lines, and Grady quickly offered to go. He returned to camp late in the afternoon and was dismayed to see Joseph watching for him outside their tent, waiting to speak with him.

"You missed all the ruckus across the street this morning," Joseph said somberly.

Grady feigned surprise. "Oh, yeah? What's going on?"

"Some white man who lived in that house over there was found dead. His wife's claiming that a band of Negroes broke in last night and beat her husband to death. She's hiding in the closet until morning, too scared to move."

"White folks lie all the time," Grady said with a shrug. "They're blaming us for everything."

"She says one of them had on a Yankee uniform—just like ours."

Grady could tell by the way that Joseph's eyes bored into his, that he knew the truth.

"The provost marshal is wanting to talk to you and me," he continued.

Grady's stomach made a slow, sickening turn. "What for?"

"He wants to know if we saw or heard anything last night when we was on watch."

Grady forced himself to hold Joseph's gaze, challenging him. "Did you see anything on your watch?"

Joe shrugged his bony shoulders.

"Me neither," Grady said.

"Well, we're still supposed to go see the marshal. Captain Metcalf said for us to hurry on over there as soon as you got back. Come on."

Grady tried to act unconcerned as he walked toward headquarters, but inside he was trembling uncontrollably. If the provost marshal asked for details, Grady knew that Preacher Joe was much too religious to ever tell a lie. Grady wished he knew exactly what his tentmate had seen, but he couldn't think of a way to ask him without admitting his guilt. Maybe he should threaten Joseph, drop a few hints that he also might die mysteriously in the night if he said too much. But before Grady could finish weighing the idea, Joseph spoke.

"Can I ask you a question, Grady?"

He nodded, his heart racing.

"Why'd you join up? Was it so you could kill a few Rebels, get revenge?"

Grady considered a moment before answering. Joseph knew how much Grady hated white men. He would see right through him if he lied. "Sure. Killing Rebels was part of the reason. But mostly it was to help set our people free."

"Well, you got your freedom," he said dryly. "And thanks to us, every slave in Jacksonville is free. So—has that been enough to satisfy you?"

Grady knew that the answer was no. So did Joseph. Grady hadn't been able to hide his restless, pent-up anger from anyone, least of all his tentmate. Grady was not a happy man, and Joe knew it.

"How can I be satisfied?" Grady said angrily. "You know this is more than just a fight to win our freedom. We're still fighting for respect and dignity."

"And you think being mad all the time, shooting off your anger and rage at white folks, is the best way to be winning respect and dignity?"

"If we don't fight for what we deserve, our people are never getting it."

Joe shook his head. "I don't agree. Dignity ain't something we need to be fighting for or trying to earn. It's something we had all along. We're God's children, made in His image."

"Why are you preaching this stuff to me?" Grady said bitterly. "Go tell it to all the white men who hate our guts. They think we're animals, not people. Try telling them we're all God's children. They'll laugh in your skinny black face."

"Some people were hating Jesus so much that they crucified Him. But that didn't change who He was. I don't need a white man's opinion to know that I'm worthy in God's eyes. I'm His child, and I don't care what any man thinks about me, white or black." He slowed to a halt and turned to Grady. "Ready?" he asked.

Grady looked around, as if emerging from a fog, and realized that they had reached the provost marshal's house. His stomach lurched. "Sure. After you," he said coolly, but his knees felt rubbery as he followed Joe up the steps. They told the officer's aide why they had come, and he offered them seats while they waited.

More than fifteen minutes passed but neither of them spoke. The longer he waited, the more ill Grady felt. He was afraid he might vomit. Joe would surely tell the truth. Maybe he already had. Maybe that's why Captain Metcalf had sent them here together.

Grady would be arrested and tried and hanged for killing a man who deserved to die. Coop was white. The provost marshal was white. The men Grady would face at his court-martial would all be white. Grady was black, and that was the end of the matter. A white man like Coop could kill a black man like Grady, but not the other way around. Grady had seen the gallows in Jacksonville where a Negro had been lynched for "insulting" a white woman. Grady's crime had been much worse. He had *killed* a white man. He didn't stand a chance of escaping the gallows.

At last the provost marshal called for them. Grady and Joseph went into the man's office together and stood before his desk. The officer looked up briefly as he continued to shuffle papers around on his desk.

"Thank you for coming," he said gruffly. "I assume you've both heard about the civilian, Edward Coop, who was found beaten to death last night?"

"Yes, sir," they said together.

"Did either of you hear or see anything unusual while you were on watch last night?"

Grady cleared his throat and hurried to speak first. "I might have heard something, sir," he began, but the marshal interrupted him.

"Which watch were you on?"

"The second one, sir. I even crossed the street and went over to check it out, but things was pretty quiet when I got there. I didn't think I should be straying too far from my post, in case it was the Rebels. I was just coming back when my friend Joe came on duty." Grady turned to face him, forcing himself to meet Joseph's gaze. He tasted bile as he asked, "Ain't that right, Joe?"

"Yes, sir. I saw Grady coming back."

Grady held his breath. Joe must have seen the blood on his hands and on the butt of his rifle. Surely he'd noticed the odd way Grady had carried it.

"Then what happened?" the marshal asked Joe. "Did you see or hear anything after that? During your own watch?"

Joseph paused for a long moment. "No, sir. Everything was quiet on my watch."

The officer exhaled. "Very well. Give my aide your names and the name of your company. And if anything else comes to mind, please let me know right away. I'd like to get this matter cleared up as quickly as possible."

Grady walked from the room like a blind man. He staggered from the house feeling worse than when he'd gone inside, his nausea so severe that he had to stop and lean against a lamppost until it passed. Joseph stopped and waited beside him, but Grady couldn't look at him. He couldn't comprehend why Joe had protected him, why he hadn't told the provost marshal everything he had seen.

Eventually Grady's dizziness passed. The two men walked nearly all the way back to camp before Joseph finally spoke. "God knows what happened to that poor fella," he murmured. Grady heard the irony in his voice and was more certain than ever that Joe knew the truth.

"Don't waste your pity or your prayers on him," Grady said quietly. "The man was a slave trader. He caused our people untold suffering and got rich destroying lives. Besides, I know for a fact that he murdered at least one of his slaves—whipped the man to death. Feel sorry for him if you want to pity someone. Edward Coop got exactly what he deserved."

"It's up to God to be dealing out vengeance, not us," Joseph said.

"Yeah? Well, Coop told me that he didn't believe in God."

"Then he's in hell."

There was something about Joseph's matter-of-fact certainty that sent a shiver through Grady. It was the same feeling of icy horror he'd felt last night when Coop had confessed that he didn't fear God's judgment.

"If you had any part in his death," Joe continued, "then you'll be living with it on your conscience for the rest of your life. But just so you know, God will forgive you if you ask Him to."

"I don't want to hear—" Grady began. But Joseph halted and spun to face him.

"Well, for once in your life you're gonna hear it, Grady. If you don't want me telling everybody that I saw you coming from that direction with blood all over your hands and on your rifle, then you're gonna have to shut up and listen to my preaching."

"Okay, okay . . . I'll listen," he said, holding up his hands.

"Maybe this Coop fella was a murderer, like you say. But if you're taking justice in your own hands, then you're a murderer, too. That guilt is gonna start eating away at you in time to come, and when it does, I want you to remember something. I want you to remember that God will forgive you for everything you done if you ask Him to."

His speech made Grady uneasy, but he resisted the urge to interrupt, afraid of what Joe could do with the knowledge he had.

"Three of the greatest men in the Bible were all murderers," he continued. "Before Moses led all the slaves out of Egypt, he once killed an overseer when he thought nobody was looking. And King David—the man after God's own heart—was sleeping with another man's wife, so he fixed things up for her husband to be killed. David ain't pulling the trigger, but he may as well have—the man's blood was on his hands."

Grady saw Joseph's gaze stray to his hands, and he had to resist the urge to hide them behind his back.

"The third man was the Apostle Paul," Joe said. "He's standing by and cheering the murderers on when they're stoning an innocent man named Stephen to death."

"Why are you telling me this?" Grady asked quietly.

"Because later on, God forgave them all when they repented. Not only that, He used all three of those men to do great things for Him." Joe started walking again, his voice thick with zeal. "There ain't no doubt that our race has suffered. Ain't no question that the white folks deserve to pay for all they done to us. But I believe that God can use our suffering to teach us to have faith in Him. And who knows? Maybe someday we can be showing the white people how to obey Jesus' command to love our enemies—even when they don't deserve it."

Delia had preached a similar sermon to Grady. So had Eli. Grady wondered why God didn't just give up on him and leave him alone. Then he recalled Delia's warning that the Lord would hunt him down and hound his steps like a master chasing his escaped slave until He finally got him back. Grady already felt hounded. The seething anxiety that twisted through his gut felt nearly as painful as the lash. He steeled himself to ask Joe the question he dreaded to ask.

"So are you ever gonna tell anybody about what you saw last night?"

"No. Not this time. But I will if there's a next time."

Grady exhaled but he felt no relief. "I don't get it," he said. "You believe in all that Bible stuff—good and evil, the Ten Command- ments, 'Thou shalt not kill'—right? So why didn't you turn me in?"

"Because I'm a sinner, too, Grady. Jesus says anyone who sins is a slave to sin, and that's just what I was. But now, the Bible says, we have been purchased by God. It's just like someone put me on the auction block and sold me to a new owner. Everything in my life changed. My new massa set me free, and if the Son sets you free, you are free indeed. I don't have to be serving that old massa no more, and neither do you. It's time for you to get free from your sin, Grady. Jesus bought and paid for you, and He wants to set you free."

Grady couldn't help remembering how his life had changed when Massa Fletcher put him on the auction block and sold him to Coop. Nor could he forget the glorious sense of freedom he felt under his new owner, Massa Fuller. When Old Jesse had driven him down the shell road from Beaufort to the plantation, leaving his life with Coop behind forever, Grady had felt . . . born again.

"Jesus forgave me the same day I asked Him to," Joseph said. "He gave me a second chance, and now I'm serving Him. That's God's grace. He keeps offering us His love, even when the only thing we deserve is death." He gripped Grady's shoulders, forcing him to face him. "You could hang for killing that man, Grady. But God's giving you a second chance. Use it."

23

JACKSONVILLE, FLORIDA
SPRING 1863

Grady stood onboard the *John Adams* and watched the houses of Jacksonville burn, the bright flames dancing through their windows and licking their rooftops. Bitter smoke filled his nostrils and permeated his uniform. He felt ash on his tongue and in his throat. Then the ship rounded a bend in the river and the city disappeared from sight. His regiment had strict orders *not* to burn the city they were abandoning—and they hadn't. It had been white soldiers who had ignited the blaze, not the colored troops. Grady watched the plume of smoke billowing into the sky above the trees and imagined all the fortifications he'd worked so hard to build being reduced to ashes. But at least the Rebels wouldn't be able to make use of them.

In a way, Grady felt relieved to be leaving Jacksonville. He'd heard nothing more about the investigation into Edward Coop's death, but every time he glimpsed Coop's house across the street, his stomach had churned. Was it fear or guilt? Grady couldn't decide. At least now he would no longer have to see the house, a daily reminder of what he had done.

But they shouldn't be abandoning Jacksonville after occupying it for barely a month. Why were they all leaving? Even the two regiments of white soldiers that had arrived to serve as reinforcements had been ordered to leave. There was no reason for it that Grady could see. The city had been secure in Union hands. In fact, Colonel Higginson had announced plans to move his men upriver seventy-five miles to Palatka and establish a second foothold farther inland. But suddenly the order had come, recalling the entire expedition, evacuating Jacksonville. Everyone Grady talked to about it felt as bitterly disappointed as he did.

As he stood at the ship's rail, he saw Captain Metcalf come up from belowdecks to stand alone in the stern. Grady usually avoided white men, but his need to understand why they'd left Jacksonville outweighed his natural aversion. He crossed the rolling deck to where the captain stood and saluted.

"Excuse me, Captain. I'm sorry to be bothering you, but . . . but I don't understand why we're leaving. Seems like the wrong thing to be doing." Grady was aware that his anger was showing—in the way that he stood, in the tone of voice he used, and in his scowling features. He wished he could disguise his resentment, but he didn't know how. Anger had ruled his life for a very long time.

"I understand your frustration," Metcalf replied. "A lot of us are leaving Jacksonville with heavy hearts."

"But why give up a place that we worked so hard to secure?"

"That's the way war is," the officer replied, spreading his hands. "Men in the lower ranks like you and me are seldom told what the orders from above are all about. We just have to trust that the people in command know what they're doing. They can see the bigger picture. We're part of a much larger plan than what we can see."

Grady had the eerie feeling that the captain was delivering one of Joe's sermons or Delia's lectures, telling him to trust God no matter what, even when things didn't make sense. But Grady needed to know that his life, his hard work, did somehow make sense.

"But what did it accomplish?" he persisted. "All that time we spent reinforcing the city. Was it just a waste?"

"Well, no. I can see a couple of things." Metcalf leaned against the rail and faced Grady. He was talking to him as an equal—as if Grady were a white man. Grady still wasn't used to that, but he shoved his astonishment aside for a moment to concentrate on what the captain was saying.

"For one thing, you may not realize it, but everything our regiment does is groundbreaking. Folks thought slaves were simple, fearful creatures who would run off in a panic when the first bomb exploded. You proved them wrong. Other people said slaves would never be able to handle military discipline—that they were flighty and lazy, quick to give up and slow to learn. But there have been fewer disciplinary actions and desertions in our regiment than in any white regiment in the Union army. People have been watching us. Our every move is reported in the Northern presses. And thanks to our success, several other all-Negro regiments have formed. There's one up in Massachusetts that's made up of free Negroes, not slaves. You should read some of the articles that they're writing about us in the newspapers."

Grady nodded, but he still couldn't read. His lessons had ended when the regiment left for Jacksonville. He determined to return to his studies when he got back to Beaufort and learn to read those newspapers for himself.

"We broke new ground in Jacksonville, too," Metcalf continued. "When those two white regiments arrived, it was the first time in history that white and black soldiers served together on regular duty. I witnessed a lot of mutual respect between the races back there. You proved that skin color doesn't matter on the battlefield."

While Captain Metcalf was speaking, Colonel Higginson himself—the regiment's commanding officer—walked over to join them. Grady was stunned when Higginson entered the stream of conversation as if all three of them were white.

"I'll tell you what else it accomplished," the colonel said. "After John Brown's slave rebellion, many Northerners believed that if we gave a slave a gun he'd exact vengeance, indiscriminately killing men, women, and children all over the South. That hasn't happened. Except for that one civilian fatality, no whites were ever harmed in Jacksonville. And we only have the word of the man's wife that it was Negro soldiers who killed him. Frankly, I don't believe that it could have been anyone from my regiment. I've found my soldiers to be honest, honorable men."

Grady stood very still, holding his breath. He didn't dare speak, afraid he would betray his guilt. But when the colonel turned to him, Grady couldn't help averting his gaze, pretending to look at the passing scenery.

"The former slaves' exemplary behavior under arms has shamed the nation," Higginson continued. "A lot of people up north are feeling guilty for not coming forward sooner to help free the slaves."

"What's your understanding of why we're leaving?" Captain Metcalf asked the colonel. "Were the troops needed elsewhere? Were there too few to hold the post alone?"

"Maybe one of those was the case," Higginson said with a shrug, "and maybe not. I'll tell you what I think—but I have no proof. Our slave regiment has made history and changed a lot of prejudices. But there are still people in Congress who aren't so eager to see slavery abolished. They're willing to compromise with the South in order to bring this war to an end. Our regiment has freed a great many slaves . . . I wonder if maybe the pro-slavery people wanted the recruiting to halt."

Anger boiled up inside Grady before he could stop it. "Anyone who's thinking slavery is okay ought to come down here and try being a slave himself for a while! He ought to see how he likes being *owned* by someone. How it feels to be so powerless that even your own wife can't be yours."

The colonel nodded faintly and rested his hand on Grady's shoulder. "I hope you realize, son, that the end of the war won't bring an end to the battles your race will face. No, I'm afraid your fight is only beginning."

GREAT OAK PLANTATION

Missy Claire's face flushed with anger as she confronted her father at the dinner table. "You promised you'd take me back to Charleston for Easter! You can't go back on your promise now!" Kitty had never heard Missy speak to Massa Goodman in that tone of voice before, and she shrank back into the doorway, fearing that both of their tempers would erupt. But Massa Goodman's response was surprisingly patient.

"We can't sail down the Edisto River anymore, Claire. Our soldiers have barricaded it near Wiltown Bluff to keep the Yankees out. Besides, we'd never get past the Union fleet that's anchored outside Charleston harbor. It's a dangerous trip, even for the blockade-runners—and they do it at night in ships that are much smaller and swifter than ours."

"Can't we go by carriage?"

He exhaled. "It's a long, rough journey by carriage. The spring rains turn the roads into mud pits this time of year. We'd need a team of Negroes just to push us out of all the bogs. That's why I go back and forth on horseback. Can't you wait until summer?"

"No! I'm so bored out here! I want to visit with my friends in town and see our cousins. It's been two years since I've been to Charleston. Please, Daddy. You promised."

He kept his eyes on his plate as he cut off a piece of meat and chewed it slowly. "Don't you think your baby is a bit young to travel so far?"

Missy frowned. "The baby isn't going. He's staying here with Mammy Bertha."

Kitty looked at her mistress in surprise. She couldn't imagine leaving her own child behind for months at a time. Babies grew so fast, changed so quickly. Kitty would miss little Richard while she was in Charleston, and he wasn't even hers.

Richard had just celebrated his first birthday in February and was learning to toddle around the nursery on his sturdy white legs. It hardly seemed possible that a year had passed since Richard was born. That was the day Kitty's life had changed so horribly, the day the Confederates had come for the horses and Missy had ordered Grady whipped and sent down to Slave Row.

"I wish you would change your mind about going to Charleston," Massa Goodman said. But Kitty could have told her massa that the more he tried to discourage Missy Claire, the more determined she would be to go. Missy never gave up on anything until she got her own way.

A week later, the seamstress finished altering Missy Claire's gowns, and Kitty packed them into steamer trunks for the trip to the city. Massa Goodman had been right—the carriage trip was a long and grueling one, through mud that was axle deep in places. And when they arrived, the Charleston that greeted them was a very different place from what it once had been.

The city had deteriorated during the war, and the bustling streets looked nearly deserted now, the stores boarded up and emptied of goods. A devastating fire had raced through the downtown area during the winter of 1861, destroying a large part of it. Massa Goodman said there was very little money or manpower to rebuild it. And with Union warships anchored off the bar, bristling with cannons, much of Charleston's population had fled the city in fear.

The town house also seemed deserted without the large retinue of slaves that usually traveled from the plantation for the social season. Massa Goodman had ordered much of the family's furniture and other valuables to be stored in the basement for safekeeping after the fire, and the huge rooms seemed bare. Missy insisted on having a big dinner party for all of her friends who were left, but it wasn't the grand affair that the Goodmans' parties used to be. Kitty not only had to help Missy get ready, but she was also needed in the kitchen to help Cook, since the town house was so understaffed. As she also helped serve the dinner that evening, Kitty heard Missy's friends exclaiming over her clothes.

"How on earth could you afford a new gown, Claire? Roger must be filthy rich."

"Oh, it isn't new," Missy replied proudly. "I had to remake my old ones, just like everyone else, in order to be fashionable."

"Well, you've done a beautiful job! Look at those colors. What an eye you have! You're ingenious."

Missy glowed in the warmth of their compliments. "Thank you," she purred.

Kitty knew that she deserved the praise, not Missy. But it would never cross Missy's mind to give her slaves any credit, much less thank them. Grady would be furious if Kitty told him the story. In the past, she had never understood why he'd hated Missy Claire so much. But as she listened to her mistress accepting applause for her ideas and hard work, she felt robbed.

Kitty's back ached from being forced to stand throughout the long meal in her pregnant condition. When Missy had been pregnant, she would complain if she had to walk more than ten feet, much less serve a meal or stand in one place for hours. Kitty tried to think of other things to take her mind off her discomfort and began paying attention to the dinner conversation.

"I heard that the Yankees now have an entire regiment made up of former slaves," she heard one of the guests say. "They wear Yankee uniforms and carry guns and everything, just like real soldiers." There were cries of outrage all around the table.

"That can't be true!"

"How can anyone even think of giving weapons to such an ignorant race?"

"Not only that," the guest continued, "but every place that regiment goes, they're stealing our slaves and promising them freedom."

Kitty wanted to hear more, but Missus Goodman sent her down to the warming kitchen to refill the gravy dish. By the time she returned, the guests were no longer discussing Negro troops.

"Rumors are flying all over town that the Yankees are massing a fleet of ironclad ships over in Port Royal Sound. They're going to attack Charleston."

"That's not news," Massa Goodman said. "Charleston has been a Yankee target since the very beginning of this war. They're calling us the 'Cradle of the Confederacy' because we were the first state to secede from the Union."

"And don't forget, the first shots were fired here at Fort Sumter," someone added.

"The Yankees know how much the rest of the South looks up to Charleston," another guest said. "As long as we're one of the few ports open to blockade runners, we serve as a symbol of the South's resistance to tyranny."

"Yes, well, I'm afraid that the threat of a Union naval attack is real this time," Massa Goodman said somberly. "In the past the Yankees have made the mistake of attacking Charleston's batteries and forts. Now that the Yankees have a fleet of ironclads, General Beauregard is afraid they will make a mad dash past Fort Sumter to fire directly on the city and force it to surrender."

"But we live right on the waterfront," Missus Goodman said in alarm. "Perhaps we should go back to Great Oak and—"

Missy Claire struck the table with her fist, making the teacups rattle. "No!" she said stubbornly. "I'm tired of running away. First the Yankees chased me out of Beaufort, then they drove me from Roger's plantation and practically made me a prisoner at Great Oak. I won't run any more. I hate those Yankees for ruining my life this way."

Kitty remembered her mistress' fear on all of those occasions, and saw her bravado for what it was—an act to impress her Charleston friends. She wished she didn't have to listen to Missy's whining anymore. She wished she could sit down and ease her aching back and burning feet. But even when the meal finally ended, Kitty's work wasn't finished. As she washed dishes out in the kitchen with the other slaves, she shared what she'd heard at the dinner table.

"They're saying the Yankees got slave soldiers in uniforms now, fighting for the Union," she told them.

"I don't believe it," Alfred said. "White folks won't never let us join their army. They think we're no better than animals."

Kitty knew that Missy Claire and her mother certainly believed that—and Kitty herself once believed it, too. That's why Grady used to get so mad at her. Did she still believe that her race was inferior? She remembered standing in this very kitchen a long time ago and hearing Delia say that white people and black people were no different in Jesus' eyes, except for the color of their skin.

"It's true about the Negro soldiers," Massa Goodman's footman added. "I heard the same thing, through the grapevine. Every place those black soldiers is going, they're setting folks free. President Lincoln made a big proclamation saying they could do it, too."

Again Kitty thought of Grady, wondering if he was free. It was what he'd longed for more than anything else—even more than he'd longed to be with her. She wondered what he would do with his freedom once he got it.

"The Yankees might be coming here," Kitty added. "They're all worried over in the Big House, saying that the Yankees are getting a big fleet of ships together and coming here to bomb Charleston. Missus Fuller's wanting to go back home."

"Do you suppose we'll be free if the Yankees come here?" Bessie asked.

"Yes," Kitty replied, remembering what had happened in Beaufort. "If the Yankees come, get on over to their side just as fast as you can. Don't believe a word the white folks is saying about the Yankees, either. They're our friends."

On Easter Sunday, Kitty rose early to help her mistress get ready for church. Missy Claire wanted to look extra special in front of all her friends in her "new" Easter bonnet and dress. But Kitty was curious about the church service itself. Delia had talked about Jesus as if He was her best friend, and she was always encouraging Kitty to pray and to trust in the Lord. If only Missy Claire would let her come inside the church with her, so she could see for herself what it was all about.

The April morning was warm, the sun shining brightly. When they reached the church, Kitty climbed down from the wagon instead of staying on the seat with the driver, and followed her mistress up the stone steps. Missy stood talking with a group of her friends for a while and didn't notice Kitty at first. But when the church bells began to toll and it was time to go inside, Missy nearly stumbled over her.

"Kitty! What are you doing underfoot?"

"May I please come inside, too, Missy Claire?"

"What for? You never go to church. Why would you want to come inside? You won't understand a thing."

Kitty knew that Missy would never believe the truth, so she said the first thing that came into her head. "It's hot out here, Missy Claire. I want to get out of the sun."

Missy laughed. "I might have known there would be a stupid reason. Okay, but you'll have to sit up in the balcony with all the other darkies. And for goodness' sake, mind your manners. You can't talk or make noise during the service."

"I won't, Missy Claire. I promise."

Kitty climbed the steep, winding stairs with the other slaves to the balcony where they would be out of sight. She found a place to sit on a hard wooden bench and looked down where all the white people were. She gasped at the sight. The center of the long narrow church was filled with pews of white people, but along both outer walls were the most magnificent windows Kitty had ever seen. They were made up of thousands of tiny pieces of colored glass, and as the sun shone through them into the church, they lit up in a dazzling explosion of color and light. Wherever the light fell, it speckled the floor and the walls and even the people with prisms of brilliant, jewel-like color.

Kitty stared and stared, afraid to blink, afraid she was dreaming. At first she saw only the glowing rainbow of blues and reds and purples and greens. But when she had finally drunk her fill, she noticed that the windows were more than a random array of hues. They formed pictures. And the pictures told stories. She studied them as the huge pipe organ resounded and the church service started, and she quickly decided that the bearded man who appeared in many of the windows must be Jesus.

One window showed Him hanging in agony on a wooden post, and she remembered Delia telling her how they had whipped Jesus and hung him on a tree to die. On another window, several white children surrounded Him, crawling onto His lap. His hand rested tenderly on one child's head. But the window that was closest to Kitty captivated her the longest. A woman lay slumped at Jesus' feet. Kitty saw suffering and despair in the droop of her shoulders and in her lifeless limbs. But Jesus stretched out His strong hand to her—even though her hand looked limp and helpless as she reached for His.

Kitty finally drew her eyes away from the compelling picture, back to the dazzling church sanctuary, and realized something else: the windows didn't look at all like this from the outside. She had waited for Missy outside of this church countless times, and the windows had always appeared gray and somber against the beige stone building. She'd had no idea what magnificent colors were hidden on the inside.

She felt a shiver of awe when she remembered what else Delia had told her: *"If you let God shine His love on you, He can make something beautiful out of even the darkest hours of your life."* Is this what Delia meant? Could God shine into her life the way the sunlight came through those windows, making it alive with color and beauty?

The singing and chanting ended after a while, and Kitty began to listen as the minister spoke about the darkness they were all suffering through in this time of war. He spoke about Jesus' suffering and His death on the cross. But then the minister's expression turned to one of joy as he told the congregation, "Jesus Christ is alive! He is no longer in the grave, but He has risen! And Jesus is here with us today—even in Charleston, South Carolina, even in our darkest hours. He will help us, if we turn to Him. Jesus said, 'Ask and it will be given to you. . . .'"

He urged the people to bow their heads in prayer, trusting Jesus to answer them—just as Delia had urged Kitty to do. She bowed her head like everyone around her and closed her eyes.

"Ask," the minister had said. Maybe it was like making a wish. Of all the many things Kitty needed right now, there was one thing that she wished for above all the others.

"Jesus," she prayed in her heart, "I don't know how you can ever answer this prayer, but the one thing I want most of all is to find out about Grady. I just want to know if he's dead or alive, if he's still a slave, or if he's finally free. Please, that's all I ask. I ain't expecting to ever see him again. I just need to know if he's okay . . . and if he's free."

Kitty lifted her head as the minister said, "Amen." And she looked again at the vibrant glass picture of Jesus and the begging woman. He was bending forward, moving toward her. The woman lay helpless at His feet, but Kitty knew that Jesus was going to help her. He was going to lift her up.

❧

The Coosaw River, South Carolina

A rush of excitement pumped through Grady's veins as he huddled with his fellow soldiers and listened to Captain Metcalf explain the mission.

"We'll be crossing the river, heading deep into Rebel-held territory, so it will be dangerous. If we manage to make it to the railroad, our orders are to sabotage the rails and retreat. But even if we don't get that far, it's okay." He paused to wave away a swarm of mosquitoes that buzzed around his face. "The Navy is planning something big. The fleet is leaving Beaufort and heading to Charleston soon. And so our secondary mission is to let the Rebels know we're still here. We can't let them make a bid to win back Beaufort while the fleet is away. The Coosaw River is the Union's front line, and it's up to our regiment to hold it."

It was after midnight when Grady and the others paddled silently across the glassy river to the mainland. Joseph was among those who volunteered to stay behind to guard the boats and ensure a safe retreat. The rest of the men headed down a small footpath into the forest. The woods were cool and damp, the earth spongy-soft beneath Grady's feet. He inhaled the scent of pine, heard the whine of mosquitoes, his senses humming with readiness. He had never felt more alive in his life. He hoped that they would meet up with Rebels tonight. Grady was ready for them.

They halted several times, the men crouching behind rocks or lying down beside fallen logs while scouts crept ahead to investigate any unusual noises or unfamiliar movements. When the all clear was given, the men would rise from their hiding places like specters, and once again the woods would come alive with soldiers. No one spoke, the men stepping as lightly as cats.

After nearly an hour of hiking, one of the scouts returned with news. "There's a Rebel encampment just over yonder in a cluster of empty farm buildings. Ain't nothing left of the farmhouse but a burnt pile of timber and stones. I seen two men keeping watch, and I don't know how many's asleep, but judging by the tents, I'd say we're about evenly matched."

Captain Metcalf thought for a long moment. "If we skirt around them and head for the railroad, they could ambush us on our way back. And if they discover our boats we'll be stranded . . ."

Grady's heart pounded as he waited for the captain to decide. He wanted to fight these Rebels. Cutting the railroad could wait.

"On the other hand," Metcalf continued, "the element of surprise is in our favor, and—"

"And we can still cut the railroad after we've finished them off," Grady interrupted.

"Yes," Metcalf said with a wry smile. "That's what I was about to say."

"Let's go after them!" Corporal Rivers said.

Captain Metcalf agreed. He divided his men, sending some of them with the corporal on an indirect route through the woods to flank the enemy. Grady went with the larger force to make a frontal attack. After checking their rifles and bayonets, they started forward through the dense woods behind the scout. The closer they got to the Rebel camp, the faster they marched, until Grady was jogging as quickly as the uneven terrain would allow. But before they were within rifle range, an alert Rebel sentry spotted their advance and sounded the alarm. Within moments, the quiet night erupted in a volley of gunfire.

Bullets struck four of the men marching in front of Grady, and they fell to the ground at his feet. He and the others continued forward, taking their places in the front ranks. As the hostile fire intensified, the captain signaled for them to take cover and fire from behind rocks and trees to give the flanking force a chance to sneak up from the side. Grady crouched behind a tree stump, well protected from the three Rebels who fired back at him from behind a tent. He loaded and fired and reloaded as rapidly as he could, unable to see their faces in the dark, but imagining them to be the same white boys who had bullied and whipped him. When his bullets hit their marks and his three enemies no longer returned fire, he longed to stand up and cheer with his fist raised in victory.

The skirmish continued at a dead heat until Corporal Rivers' men swooped down on the surprised enemy's flank, overwhelming them. Grady foresaw total victory—until two Rebels suddenly charged out of one of the farm buildings on horseback and raced out of the clearing, escaping into the woods. Grady swore beneath his breath. The riders would bring reinforcements—possibly a cavalry troop. Captain Metcalf would have to forget about cutting the railroad and retreat to the boats before the cavalry arrived.

But in the meantime, the Rebel fire slackened as their casualties mounted. Grady and the others began moving forward again at the captain's signal, killing off the last pockets of resistance, forcing the surrender of those who remained. Grady didn't want to take prisoners. If it was the other way around and the Rebels had won this clash, every last Negro prisoner would either be killed or returned to slavery. He and the other men fanned out through the encampment, rustling through the bushes and checking each building as they hunted for Rebels. Grady was determined to kill them all without mercy.

As he rounded the corner of a corncrib, he heard a low moan. He froze, his rifle raised, his finger on the trigger. Four Rebel soldiers lay in a tangled heap in the bushes. Three of them were obviously dead, and the one who was moaning was badly wounded. Grady inched forward cautiously. The injured man slowly turned his head and looked at Grady.

It was Massa Fuller.

For a long moment Grady stopped breathing. Fuller still gripped his rifle in one hand, but his other arm had been hit. Grady saw the torn sleeve and gaping wound, still oozing blood. Fuller slowly laid his rifle on the ground at Grady's feet, unable to reload it with one hand. He had blood all over him, soaking his clothes and the grass beneath him. But there wasn't nearly as much blood on him as there had been on Massa Coop, by the time Grady had finished with him.

Massa Fuller didn't say a word, didn't surrender or plead for his life. Without knowing why, Grady turned to the soldier who had jogged up alongside him and said, "Go on, I'll deal with him." The soldier nodded and hurried away, leaving them alone.

Now Massa Fuller would beg and plead for his life the way Grady's mama had pleaded with Massa Fletcher. White men didn't show mercy, and neither would he. He thought of all the slaves who had begged not to be sold, not to be separated from their families or sent to brothels. White men had been deaf to their pleas, and now it was Grady's turn to be deaf.

A lifetime of hatred flooded through him, spilling over until he trembled with rage as he stood over his former master. He wondered if Fuller even recognized him. Grady was a man now, in a Union

371

army uniform, not a docile slave in livery. He kicked Fuller's rifle away from him and asked, "You remember me?"

Fuller nodded. Grady saw pain in his eyes from the wound to his arm, but not fear. "Shoot me if you must, Grady," he said.

Grady lifted his rifle and took aim. Why didn't Fuller beg?

Out of nowhere, the memory came to Grady of how he had fallen on his knees at Fuller's feet after the poker game in Beaufort, begging him not to sell him back to Coop. *"Your old massa offer him a lot of money,"* Jesse had told Grady the next day. *"Massa Fuller refuse to sell you."*

Then another memory came to him—of how angry Massa Fuller had been at the paddyrollers for whipping him. Fuller's clothes had been stained with Grady's blood as he'd helped him to Delia's cabin. Massa had given Delia medicine to doctor his wounds and had come to check on him every day. Grady recalled the handful of silver that Fuller had given him to buy drawing paper for Anna. He remembered Anna's tears of surprise and delight. And for one brief moment in time, Grady looked beyond Fuller's white skin and saw the man beneath it—a man who had been good to Grady.

Sweat poured down Fuller's face, plastering his sandy hair to his forehead. "I believe in God's grace," he said quietly. His voice was strong and steady. "I'm not afraid to die."

If it was the other way around and the Rebels were about to kill Grady, could he say the same thing? Did he believe in the God of grace whom Joseph had preached about? Grady knew that he had been angry with God ever since he'd been snatched from his home in Richmond. Why hadn't God helped him? But as angry as he was, Grady never stopped believing that God existed. Unlike Massa Coop, Grady did believe in Him. And Grady also knew right from wrong. Joe had spoken the truth when he'd said that Grady's guilt would eat away at his soul. If he had died in tonight's battle, Coop's murder would still be on his conscience. Grady had never repented or asked God to forgive Him. The moment that his heart stopped, he would be in hell—with Coop.

Grady shook his head as if to clear these disturbing thoughts from his mind. His race had been wronged, his people oppressed. They deserved a chance to fight back and avenge the crimes against them. But in the call of a nightingale singing in the branches above his head, Grady thought that he heard Delia's voice, warning him that he was poisoning himself with his hatred. He had escaped to freedom. He had celebrated President Lincoln's Emancipation Proclamation along with all the others. But Grady knew that he wasn't free. He was still a slave to his hatred and his sin.

The soldier that Grady had sent away returned, stopping at his side. "Captain says we're getting ready to leave. We got wounded men that are needing a doctor. You want help with this prisoner?"

Grady shook his head. "He's dying. He asked me to shoot him and finish him off. Go on, I'll be right there."

Grady would add another murder to his sins. Two crimes would now eat away at his conscience—because Coop's bloodied corpse still haunted Grady, even though he'd left Jacksonville, even though the daily reminder of his sin no longer stared at him from across the street. And as he thought about killing Fuller—thought about being killed himself—Grady realized that he wanted to be free of his guilt almost as much as he'd once longed for freedom from slavery. He wanted God's forgiveness.

"I'm sorry," he prayed aloud as he stared down at Fuller. "I'm so sorry. . . ."

Massa Fuller winced and held up his uninjured hand as if trying to ward off Grady's bullet.

"Forgive me," Grady whispered. "Please."

He swung his rifle to the right, aiming into the bushes, three feet from Fuller's head. He pulled the trigger and fired. The shot sounded deafening in the quiet night, echoing off the buildings as if he had fired several shots.

Then Grady turned away without a word and ran back with the others to the waiting boats.

❦

CHARLESTON, SOUTH CAROLINA

Two days after Easter, Kitty stood outside with Missy Claire on the piazza of the town house and watched as a fleet of nine ironclad Union warships steamed into the bay toward Charleston. Massa Goodman looked very worried as he gazed through his telescope at the unfolding drama. Missy tried to act brave in front of her sisters and cousins, but Kitty could tell by the way she twisted her handkerchief in her hands that she was terrified. She begged her father so often to tell them what was happening that he finally stopped answering her altogether.

Downstairs in the slaves' quarters, Bessie and Alfred and the others were quietly gathering their belongings, hoping for freedom when the Yankees landed. But Kitty didn't entertain dreams of freedom herself. If she'd been too frightened to flee with Grady, who had vowed to take care of her, she knew she would never be able to find the courage to flee on her own or with a group of slaves she barely knew. Kitty was all alone in the world except for Missy Claire. Who would take care of her if she left? How would she live? And what about her baby?

In the end, none of those questions mattered. The battle that began at two-thirty in the afternoon was all over with by five-thirty. Instead of steaming past the forts and shelling the city, as everyone feared, the ironclads attacked Fort Sumter once again. And in spite of the frightening noise and smoke and fury of battle, the fort withstood the onslaught once again. None of the ironclads made it past Charleston's defenses. "In fact," Massa Goodman told them as he stared out to sea, "one of the ships appears to be badly damaged. It's being abandoned."

It sank the following morning after the Rebels brazenly stole all of her guns.

The wild rejoicing in Charleston's city streets lasted throughout the night and continued into the next day—longer than the actual battle had. In the slaves' quarters, everyone mourned. To their eyes, the Rebels seemed to be winning the war. Alfred summed up everyone's feelings when he said, "Guess we better be getting back to work. Looks like we're gonna be slaves forever."

❦

Kitty was the one who answered the door the day the telegram came. She brought it into the drawing room and gave it to Missy Claire, then watched as she opened it and read it. When Missy Claire screamed, Kitty turned and raced upstairs, calling for Missy's mother.

"Roger is wounded! He's been wounded!" Missy repeated over and over. Missus Goodman gave her some laudanum to prevent the hysterics, but Missy couldn't stop weeping.

Massa Goodman met every locomotive that arrived on the Savannah & Charleston rail line until he finally found Massa Roger on one of the hospital trains. The servants drove him back to the town house in Massa's carriage and set up a bed for him in the first-floor drawing room.

For the first few weeks, Kitty wasn't allowed into the room with Massa Roger at all. But she could tell by the worried look on everyone's face that her massa was gravely ill. When the weather turned unseasonably hot, Missy Claire finally allowed Kitty into the room, ordering her to stand beside Massa's bed and fan him to help cool his fever.

The first glimpse of him shocked Kitty. He was ghostly thin, his skin whiter than paper. The doctor came every day to change his bandages and to check to see if the wound on Massa's arm was healing, but he made no comment in front of Kitty. Massa seemed to drift in and out of consciousness, moaning in pain, and Kitty waved the fan until she thought her arms would break off.

Then one afternoon while Kitty was fanning him, Massa's eyes suddenly fluttered open. He gazed around, blinking, and his eyes no longer had the feverish glaze she had seen in them for so many weeks.

"Missy Claire!" she cried. "Missy Claire, I think he's waking up!"

Claire dropped the book she was reading and hurried over to sit on the bed beside him. "Roger? Roger are you okay? Are you in pain?"

He licked his parched lips. "Claire . . . ?"

"Yes, darling. I'm right here."

"Where . . . where's our son? I want to see Richard."

Missy looked uneasy. "He's with his mammy at Great Oak, where it's safe. We'll go there when you're well enough to travel. You'll see how big he's grown."

Massa Fuller gazed up at the ceiling, not at Missy, and Kitty was surprised to see tears shining in his eyes. "Did you know that my son Ellis was killed?" he asked.

"Yes, Roger, I'm so sorry." She lifted his pale hand from the sheet and held it between hers. "I got the letter you wrote to me, but I guess you never received my reply."

"They buried him where he died, up in Fredericksburg."

Missy swallowed. "What about John? Have you heard from him?"

"The last time he wrote, he was still in one piece," Massa said, sighing. "That's more than I can say for myself."

"But you're getting better, Roger. You're going to be okay."

Kitty didn't realize that she had stopped fanning until Claire made a face at her and motioned for her to continue. As the breeze from her fan ruffled Massa's sandy hair, he turned to stare at her, his gaze intense. It was as if he was studying her, and his inspection lasted for such a long time that Kitty grew uncomfortable. Was it because she was pregnant? Kitty didn't dare meet his gaze but even with her eyes averted, she was sure that he was studying her face, not her stomach.

"Can I get you some water, Massa Fuller?" she asked softly.

"No." He glanced at Claire, then back at Kitty. "They're using Negro soldiers now," he said.

"Well, that's what we all heard," Missy said with a huff, "but I didn't want to believe it. What a disgraceful thing to do—trying to turn our slaves against us. And I can't imagine giving guns to such ignorant creatures, can you? Are you certain that it's true?"

"I was wounded in a firefight against a band of them," Massa said. "They were all in uniform. They had white officers, but the soldiers were Negroes. We think they came to the mainland to try to cut the railroad."

"They'll probably try to cut our throats if we're not careful. Listen, darling, can I get you anything? Do you want Kitty to fetch you some broth to sip?"

Kitty looked at him and his eyes held hers for a moment before she remembered to look away.

"I recognized one of the colored soldiers," Massa said quietly. "He was my former coachman, Grady."

The fan slipped from Kitty's hand as she stumbled backward. She had to lean against the wall to keep from falling over.

"You mean Kitty's husband?" Claire asked. "Why, the ungrateful wretch! After all we've done for him, imagine him turning against us that way."

Massa shook his head. "That wasn't what happened, Claire. Grady spared my life."

Missy stared at him as if she didn't believe him. *"What?"*

"It's true. I was lying there, wounded and defenseless. The three men alongside me were all dead. Grady could have taken me prisoner—and I probably would be dying in some squalid prison camp right now. He also could have killed me on the spot. But he didn't. He pretended to shoot me—for the others' sakes, I suppose. Then he simply walked away."

Kitty felt faint. She needed to sit down. Missy didn't seem to notice her distress, but Massa Fuller did. "Are you okay?" he asked her.

Missy Claire turned on Kitty before she could reply. "Did you know about this? Did you know that your husband is fighting against us, now?"

"N-no, ma'am."

"You're a liar! I don't believe you!"

"How would she know, Claire?" Massa Fuller's voice was gentle.

"Well, what if he's in contact with her?"

"How?" he asked. "None of them can read or write."

"He *shot* you, Roger! That ungrateful boy *shot* you!"

"I was wounded in battle, Claire. There's no way to know whose bullet it was that hit me."

"But they were Negroes! I don't want to look at another one of them! Get out of my sight!" she screamed at Kitty.

Massa Fuller reached for Missy's hand. "Claire . . . don't take it out on her."

But Kitty knew by the look of pure hatred on her mistress' face that she needed to get out. Quickly. Kitty hurried from the room and ran blindly down the back stairs to the warming kitchen. She staggered into the room, barely making it to a chair before her legs gave way. A fire smoldered in the fireplace and the room was very hot. Kitty couldn't breathe.

"You okay?" Bessie asked. "What's wrong? You look like you seen a ghost."

"Grady's alive! My husband . . . H-he escaped, and he's safe, and he's a soldier in the Yankee army!"

"You dreaming, girl?"

"No. Massa Fuller just told me. He saw him. He saw Grady!"

Kitty wished that Delia were here. She needed to talk to her, needed to make sense of what she'd just heard. Grady hated white men. He longed for revenge, wanting to kill every white man that breathed. But when he'd had a chance to kill Massa Fuller, he hadn't done it. Kitty couldn't imagine why.

Then another thought struck her: if Grady was a soldier, then he was in terrible danger. Massa Fuller's son had died in the war, and Massa had been badly wounded. What if something happened to Grady, too?

"Can I get you anything?" Bessie asked.

"No . . . I-I need air."

She got up and stumbled outside. The sun was so bright that it hurt her eyes. As she lifted her hand to shade them, she suddenly remembered how brightly the sun had shone through the dazzling church windows on Easter Sunday.

Then Kitty remembered her prayer.

God had answered her prayer! She had asked to find out about Grady, and now, by this miracle, she had learned that Grady was alive. That he was free.

She felt the sun's rays, warm and comforting on her bare arms. And for the first time in her life Kitty felt the warmth of God's love. It overwhelmed her! He had answered her prayer. He had listened to her, a mere slave.

"Thank you," she sobbed as she sank to her knees on the warm paving stones. "Thank you."

CHAPTER
24

PORT ROYAL FERRY, SOUTH CAROLINA
JULY 1863

Grady sat outside his tent near the picket line, bending close to the newspaper as he struggled to read it by candlelight. Across from him, Joseph also leaned close to the light, the pages of his Bible rustling softly as he turned them. The summer night was muggy and warm, the midges and mosquitoes relentless. But Grady was barely aware of them, or of the gentle night sounds all around him—the chirp of crickets, the hoot of an owl, the sweet whine of fiddle music nearby—as he read news of the war. The Rebel general, Robert E. Lee, had led his army north to invade the Union states.

"I sure wish I was up there where all the fighting is," Grady said with a sigh.

Joe nodded but didn't look up. "The Lord knows which battles He's wanting us to fight."

Grady folded the newspaper to the next page and scanned the headlines, his finger moving along the typewritten words as he carefully sounded out each one. The more he practiced, the better he could read. He'd had to swallow his pride, at first, and learn like a child, starting with his ABC's, making baby noises as he'd memorized the sound each letter made. But once he'd caught on, Grady couldn't learn fast enough. Joseph had gone with him to the school tent every evening, and now they shared the same candle. But while Grady read the newspapers to learn how the war progressed, Joseph practiced his new skill by reading his Bible. A group of missionaries from up north had offered New Testaments to any former slave who wanted one. Joe had chided Grady when he had politely refused.

"God's word is 'a lamp unto my feet, and a light unto my path,'" Joe had quoted. The verse sounded familiar to Grady, and he wondered if Eli had taught it to him. "With your whole life ahead of you," Joe persisted, "don't you think you might be needing to see which way to go?"

Grady shrugged but didn't reply. He was trying to be patient with Joe, figuring he owed him something in return for not turning him over to the authorities. Whenever Joe's preaching got to be too much, Grady would quietly excuse himself. And Joe seemed to be learning his limits. Now he only preached to Grady a little at a time.

"Hmm, I like that tune," Joe said suddenly. Grady looked up, his finger still holding his place on the page.

"What did you say?"

"That tune that Willie's playing on the fiddle . . . Hear it?"

Grady cocked his head, listening, and recognized the slow, haunting melody of the slave trader's song. A long time ago at Massa Fuller's wedding, another fiddler had called it that when he'd played it for Grady. He frowned at this unwelcome reminder of Massa Coop and Massa Fuller and pointed to his newspaper to change the subject.

"It says here that another regiment of colored troops under a white colonel named Shaw just arrived down here from Massachusetts, to fight with us. They ain't former slaves though, they're free men. Colonel Higginson says that our regiment paved the way for them."

Joe grinned and his thin face glowed in the dim light. "Want to hear what I just read?" He didn't wait for Grady to reply but began to read in a slow, halting voice. "'When I cry unto thee, then shall mine enemies turn back. . . . In God I have put my trust: I will not be afraid what man can do unto me.'"

"You better be afraid," Grady said. "They can kill you, Joe. That's what man can 'do unto you.'"

"They can kill my body, but not my soul. That belongs to God."

Grady made a show of indifference, turning the newspaper to the next page, folding it in half, scanning the headlines. But who did his soul belong to? He'd asked God to forgive him for killing Coop, but Grady didn't feel any different. As he listened to Joe humming the slave trader's song along with the fiddle, he wondered if God had even heard his prayer.

GREAT OAK PLANTATION

Kitty moaned as the carriage bounced over a rut, jarring her. For most of the way home on this long ride from Charleston, her abdomen had been tightening as hard as a stone with each jolt and bump in the road. Now the squeezing was becoming very painful as the spasms gripped her back and spread all through her middle.

"You okay?" the driver asked. "Want me to slow down?"

"No, please don't," Kitty breathed. "How much farther?"

"Just another mile or two. We're almost there."

She sat high on the seat beside the driver, with Cook and Daisy crammed in beside them. The sun beat down relentlessly, and the damp air wrapped around Kitty's skin like a wet wool blanket. Clouds of dust from the road filled her mouth and lungs, and she longed for a drink of water. If only Missy would let her ride in the coach with her and Missus Goodman. The journey would have been just as long and tiring, but at least she would be out of the sun and dust—and the coach had springs to cushion the long, bumpy ride.

The decision to return to Great Oak had been made in a hurry. Thousands of Union troops had landed on Morris Island to attack Fort Wagner. "If they win control of that strip of beach," Massa

Goodman had warned, "they could easily shell the city from there." He had elected to remain in Charleston as part of the home guard. Massa Fuller had returned to fight with his regiment, in spite of Missy's tears and pleas, his bandaged arm in a sling. The women had decided to return to the plantation.

By the time the carriage pulled into the yard at Great Oak, Kitty was in so much pain that Daisy and Cook had to help her climb down from the seat.

"Kitty, make sure you hang my gowns in the wardrobe right away, so they don't wrinkle," Missy ordered as she stepped out of the carriage. "And don't forget . . . Kitty! Are you listening to me?"

She was struggling to make sense of the orders Missy was issuing, but she felt so light-headed that she was afraid she might faint.

"I'm sorry, Missy. I been having pains—" She inhaled sharply as another one gripped her. She doubled over, clutching her middle.

"Are you having your baby?" Missy demanded.

"I-I think so," Kitty gasped.

"Well, for heaven's sake, go someplace else and have it, not in my house." She hurried up the front steps and into the house as if Kitty's condition was contagious.

"Here, now, let me help you," the driver offered after all the trunks had been unloaded from the carriage.

"Take me to Delia's cabin," Kitty breathed. "It's down on the Row."

"O Lord, you poor child," Delia moaned when she saw her. "You come right on in and lay down. How long have you been suffering?"

"I don't know . . . it was taking forever to get home. . . ." She gasped as another pain twisted through her. Delia shooed two toddlers off her bed and helped Kitty lie down, then mopped her sweating face with a cloth.

"I'm going for the midwife, honey," she told her. "Don't you be having that baby till I get back, you hear?"

Kitty smiled faintly despite her pain. Then tears of relief and joy filled her eyes. Delia was here with her. She had come home to Delia, and now everything would be okay. Thank God for the Yankees. If they hadn't attacked when they did, Kitty would still be in Charleston having her baby in the slave dormitory, all alone. As grueling as the carriage ride had been, at least it had brought her home to Delia.

The next few hours in the stifling cabin all blended together in a haze of pain and sweat. Kitty was barely aware of Delia smoothing the hair off her brow, or of the midwife helping her onto the birthing stool, as pain gripped her like a fist and tried to rip her in half. Then her baby was born. Kitty heard his helpless cry, and her painful struggle was forgotten in a rush of love.

"It's a little boy, honey," Delia told her. "You have a son."

The midwife wiped him clean and wrapped him in a cloth. Kitty stretched out trembling arms to take him. He was so beautiful, so warm and weightless as he rested in her arms, his smooth brown skin so perfect. And he was hers! Her child. She couldn't recall ever holding something so beautiful that was hers alone.

As she gazed down at him, the baby's face puckered into a scowl, as if he was angry at the whole world. "Look, Delia," she whispered in awe. "I see his daddy . . . don't you?"

"Oh yes. He surely does have Grady's proud chin. You gonna name him after his daddy, honey?"

Kitty drew a shaky breath. "I can't—it's too hard. Just seeing his face this way is hard enough. I can't be saying his name, too. . . . I miss him so much."

"I understand. You can name that little boy whatever you want to. You're his mama."

A tear rolled down Kitty's cheek. "Grady was always talking about how much a person's name means. He once took a beating for wanting to be called by the name his mama gave him. And he always called me Anna, the name my mama gave me. Missy Claire is the one who called me Kitty." And as she gazed at her baby, she finally understood what Grady meant. It was an act of love and ownership for a mother to name her child. It was her right and no one else's. She vowed to think of herself as Anna from now on.

"Do you want me to call you Anna, too?" Delia asked.

"Would you?"

"Sure, honey." Delia stroked the baby's head, her brown hand dark against his bronze skin. "Is there someone else you'd like to name him after? Your own daddy, maybe?"

Anna thought for a moment. "I can't hardly remember my daddy, but I don't ever want him to be forgotten. He died trying to help me be free."

"What was his name, honey?"

"George." She looked down at the tiny boy in her arms and kissed his soft brow. "I'll name you George," she told him. "After your granddaddy."

Delia helped Anna get settled in bed, and the midwife showed her how to nurse her baby. The warmth and closeness brought tears to her eyes each time he suckled.

The next three days were among the happiest ones that Anna had ever lived. The only memory that came close to it was the night she had spent with Grady. But at the close of the third day, Mammy Bertha walked down from the Big House to see her.

"How you doing, girl?" she asked. "My, what a beautiful baby boy. He sure is looking strong and healthy, ain't he? You should be right proud of yourself."

"He's a hungry fella, too," Anna said with a smile. "Seems like he's wanting to eat every time I turn around."

"I suppose you know that Missy Claire sent me to fetch you," Mammy Bertha said, her smile fading. "You better be coming back up to the Big House, first thing tomorrow morning. She can't get along without you, and she's putting us through all kinds of misery. We can't do nothing to please her."

"I'll be there," Anna promised. But her mind raced in a hundred directions as Bertha said good-bye, trying to picture how she would work things out. "What am I going to do?" she asked Delia.

"Well, when slave babies are this little and still needing their mamas to feed them, the field slaves make a sling and carry their little ones all around with them. I'll show you how to do it. They're carrying them right along to the fields while they're working or laying them down at the end of the row to sleep in the shade."

The next morning, Delia helped Anna wrap baby George in her shawl so she could carry him up to the Big House with her. Anna arrived well before dawn so she could be in Missy's room the moment she awoke and called for her. Since George slept for so many hours every day, Anna planned to ask Mammy Bertha to find him a place to sleep in a corner of the nursery, somewhere. But Anna was still carrying little George in his sling when Missy woke up and called for her. She hurried to her mistress' bedside.

"I would like my breakfast now, and—what is that *thing* around you?" Missy asked.

"This here is my little baby, George—"

"How dare you bring that child in here!"

"You said you needed me to work and . . ."

"I do need you, but not with a baby hanging on to you like an opossum."

"But I have to feed him every little while, Missy Claire. How else will he eat if I—?"

Missy threw the covers aside and climbed from the bed so swiftly that Anna jumped back a step. Claire's face flushed pink as her temper flared. "I don't care how or what he eats—that's not my problem. You didn't care how my poor Richard would be fed after he was born, and I was forced to get a nurse from Slave Row. You'll just have to do the same thing."

The summer morning was very warm but Anna suddenly felt cold with dread. "Oh no, Missy Claire. Please don't make me do that. H-he won't be any bother. I promise—"

"You're my chambermaid, not a wet nurse. Now get him out of here immediately, and don't bring him into this house again!"

Anna hugged him tightly to herself, her panic rising at the thought of being separated from her baby. "No!" she cried. "No, please, Missy Claire!"

Missy's eyes widened. "How dare you tell me no!"

386

"I need to be with him.... He's my baby!" She fell to her knees, gripping Missy's nightgown as she wept and begged. "Please, Missy ... please."

"Stop it! Get up!" Missy said, slapping Anna's hands.

"Please don't take my baby away from me. He—"

"The child will be reared on Slave Row, and that's the end of it."

"Then send me down to Slave Row with him. I'll work in the fields from now on, I don't care, but I don't want to leave my son!"

"You'll do what I tell you or I'll have you whipped."

"Go ahead and whip me. Make me chop cotton—"

"If you don't stop fussing this instant, I'll sell your son to the slave auction."

"No!" Anna screamed. Her fear and despair were so great that she could scarcely breathe. "No, you can't sell him! He's mine!"

Missy Claire slapped her across the face, but Anna barely felt it, her agony at the thought of losing George so much greater.

"Don't you *dare* tell me what to do!" Missy said. "He's my property, not yours, and I can do whatever I want with him. I'll throw him into the river, if I please."

"Never!" Anna cried, hugging him fiercely. "I'll drown myself with him, and you won't have either one of us as your slaves!" She no longer cared if she made Missy angry. In fact, she hoped Missy would be so furious that she would banish her to Slave Row forever. Anna would defy her, insult her—whatever it took to be sent down with her son. "My son is a human being, not your property!" she cried. "You can't take him away from me! You can't!"

"Oh no? Watch me!" Missy yelled for Mammy Bertha and Daisy, and ordered them to pry George loose from Anna's arms. Anna tried to shield him with her body, the same way her papa had shielded her from the paddyrollers' dogs. She understood her parents' desperation—and she also understood Grady's rage. George was being ripped away from his mama, just as Grady had been ripped away from his. But Anna would not give up her son without a fight. She would not.

She screamed and fought with all her strength, but Massa Goodman's butler came running upstairs to help them, and they finally tore George loose from her arms. She heard his frantic, helpless cries as Bertha hurried away with him, and she remembered her own mother screaming, calling her name as the men dragged her away. Anna knew a fury powerful enough to kill, for her baby's sake. She rose from where she lay huddled on the floor and flew at Missy Claire.

"I hate you! I hate you!" she cried as she beat her mistress with her fists. "I wish you were dead!"

It took the butler and two footmen to restrain Anna. They carried her, kicking and screaming, out of the Big House and down to the slave jail, shackling her to the post inside the hut. She lay on the filthy floor, weeping in rage and despair.

By the end of the day, Anna's breasts were so full and sore that she wept in pain. She felt bruised all over from the beating she'd taken as the men had pulled her away from Missy. She only hoped that she had hurt Missy just as badly.

She'd had nothing to eat or drink all day. But sometime after midnight, while the plantation slept, she heard a key rattling in the lock. The door swung open and Delia slipped inside, bringing Anna's baby to her. Sobbing, she put George to her aching breast and fed him.

"I know, honey . . . I know," Delia soothed. She cradled Anna in her arms the same way Anna cradled George. She felt the little woman's love comforting her, quieting her aching heart. Anna knew the risk that Delia was taking. Missy would surely punish Delia severely if she got caught.

"How . . . how did you know . . . ? Where did you get the key?"

"That don't matter, honey," she said. "At least we know, now, why the Good Lord sent me down here to take care of the slave babies—why I ain't working up at the Big House like I used to do at the Fuller Plantation."

"Yes," Anna said. And she also understood why her parents had taken the risk they had when they'd attempted to escape. They loved her. They wanted her to be free. She kissed George's tiny fingers and

388

asked, "What am I going to do, Delia? He's Missy Claire's property. She owns him, and she can do whatever she wants with him. She threatened to sell him or throw him into the river."

"Even Missy Claire ain't that mean."

"But someone else will nurse him. He'll never know his mama or his—" She couldn't finish.

"You know I'll take good care of him, honey. You know I will."

"But why does it have to be this way? Why does my child have to suffer, just because he has black skin? He's no different from Missy's son. What matters is what kind of a man he grows up to be, not the color of his skin."

"God knows how you're suffering, honey. Look what they did to His Son."

"Why is Missy doing this to me?"

Delia sighed. "Because everything in her life is flying out of control, with the war and all. I guess you're the one thing she's always been sure of, and she's wanting you all to herself."

"Don't defend her, Delia! I hate her! I hate her so much!" She remembered how Grady used to say the same thing, and now she knew why. "I wish Missy was dead!"

"Anna . . . Anna. Don't start hating. You saw what it did to poor Grady. He poisoned his heart with bitterness, until there was no room left for love."

"Now I understand why, Delia! I know how he feels."

"And are you wanting your little baby boy to grow up hating, too? Because he will, you know. He'll learn whatever his mama teaches him. Jesus can't be listening to our prayers if we don't forgive."

Anna felt despair pulling her down, immobilizing her with its massive weight. "What am I going to do?" she sobbed.

"Pray, honey. Ask Jesus to light the way for you."

Anna suddenly remembered her Easter prayer, and how God had miraculously answered it. "Oh, Delia!" she cried. "In all the excitement of George's birth, I forgot to tell you. Grady's free! He's free, and he's a soldier fighting with the Yankees."

Delia went very still. "Where are you hearing about all this?"

"Massa Fuller told me. He saw Grady! I went to a church in Charleston, and I prayed and asked Jesus to please tell me, somehow, if Grady was alive. And Jesus answered my prayer."

"And you're saying that Grady's free? For sure?"

"Yes! He's alive and he's free. He's with the Yankees."

"Oh thank you, Lord," Delia whispered. "Thank you." Her voice trembled with tears.

Anna remembered the beautiful church window and the woman who lay slumped at Jesus' feet. She was as helpless as Anna was right now. But Jesus had stretched out His strong hand to help her, to lift her up.

"Delia, I want to ask Jesus for something else," she said. "He helped your daughter go free, and I want to ask Him to help George. I want my baby far, far away from here, away from Missy—even if it means never seeing him again. Will you help me pray?"

"Of course, honey."

"I want my baby to be free."

25

BEAUFORT, SOUTH CAROLINA
JULY 1863

Grady stood outside Colonel Higginson's tent with a select group of men, listening intently as the officer outlined his plans. "Excuse me, sir," Grady interrupted. "What'd you say the name of that river was?"

"The Edisto. It's about halfway between Beaufort and Charleston."

The name sounded familiar to Grady, for some reason, but he couldn't figure out why. He pulled his mind back to the mission Colonel Higginson was describing, eager for another chance to fight the Rebels.

"Our goal is to destroy a bridge on the Charleston & Savannah Railway," Higginson said. "But in order to do that, we'll need to sail some thirty miles up the river, deep into Rebel-held territory. And as always, we want to rescue as many slaves as we possibly can. There are several large rice plantations on the Edisto."

Grady realized, suddenly, why the name sounded so familiar to him. Great Oak Plantation—Missus Fuller's family's plantation—was on that river. It was where Anna and Delia had gone. He sat forward, his heart racing.

"When do we leave?" someone asked.

"Tonight. We'll have a full moon and a flood tide," Higginson said. "We want to take the Rebels by surprise, arriving at their doorstep at daybreak, before they even have a clue that we're coming. That means sailing at night so the smoke from our stacks can't be seen. But the Edisto is shallow and winding. We'll need the full moon to navigate.

"Ten miles below the railroad bridge is Wiltown Bluff," Higginson continued. "The Rebels have an armed battery there, and they've placed obstructions in the river. We'll need to silence the battery and clear a passage through the barricade before we can continue upstream and burn the bridge."

When the briefing ended, Grady returned to his tent. He had promised himself that he would forget about Anna, but he couldn't stop thinking about her as he and Joseph packed their gear for the mission. He wondered if they would pass her plantation, if he would have an opportunity to rescue her and Delia. And if he did find her, he wondered if she would come with him this time. It still hurt him to recall how he'd pleaded with her to escape with him—and how she hadn't trusted him enough to overcome her fear.

"What're you so heated up about?" Joseph asked.

Grady realized that he had been shoving and slamming things all around in their tent as he packed, his face creased in anger. "Rebels," he mumbled, hoping that would satisfy Joe. But he was remembering Anna's cringing submission to Missy Claire, her refusal to think of herself as anything but a slave. He shouldered his knapsack with a grunt. Let her stay a slave, then, if that's what she wanted.

Their three ships sailed from Beaufort late that afternoon, reaching the mouth of the Edisto close to midnight. They had no guide as they ascended the shallow, muddy river, and Grady felt a breathless anticipation as they approached each turn, listening for the enemy, waiting to be fired upon. He had read in the newspapers about all the great battles being fought in other parts of the country, with thousands of troops locked in combat. But Grady thought he preferred the more adventurous life of a bush fighter, ascending dangerous rivers in the darkness, fighting hand-to-hand, freeing his fellow slaves. Tonight the riverbanks remained dark, the unnerving silence broken only by the startled cries and flapping wings of herons nesting in the reeds. The full moon revealed the outlines of graceful plantation houses along both sides of the river, but Grady had no way of knowing if one of them was Anna's.

They reached Wiltown Bluff shortly after four in the morning. Captain Metcalf ordered Grady and the others to take cover as the ship opened fire on the Rebel battery that guarded the river. The Rebels quickly returned fire, and Grady had to cover his ears to deaden the sound as the thundering roar of artillery rocked the predawn stillness. It seemed to last forever. He wondered if his or any of the other ships would be sunk in the brawl. But all three ships still were afloat when the Rebel guns gradually fell silent. The smoke of battle cleared, and Grady gazed in amazement at the shoreline. The dawning sun revealed hundreds of slaves, running down the dikes through the lush green rice fields, cheering as they headed toward the boats.

Grady joined the first boatload of troops that went ashore, his heart racing as he scanned the faces of the slaves waiting there, searching for Anna's. The ragged collection of men who tugged Grady's boat through the marshy reeds and onto the riverbank stared at him and the other soldiers in astonishment. "You're Yankee soldiers?" they asked again and again. "And you're black, like us?"

Captain Metcalf tried to get information from them about the size of the Rebel force that was stationed on the bluff. But the slaves' excitement was so frenzied, as men, women, and children raced to the river to greet their saviors, that none of the slaves seemed to understand what the captain was asking. Hundreds of jubilant souls surrounded Grady—the men reaching to grasp his hands in thanks; the women weeping for joy, their bundled belongings balanced on their heads; the children hopping from foot to foot with delight as they carried their younger siblings on their backs. One old woman reminded Grady of Delia as she knelt in the grass repeating, "Bless the Lord . . . Oh, bless the Lord."

But she wasn't Delia. And Grady grew desperate as he asked the men who swarmed around him, "Who's your massa? What's your massa's name? Is it Goodman?" No one seemed to hear him. Most were too incoherent with joy to reply.

When an elderly man finally told him, "It's Elliot. We was working for Massa Elliot," Grady felt his disappointment like a blow to the gut. But he forced himself to put Anna out of his mind as Captain Metcalf rallied the troops and gave the order to assault the hilltop battery.

Grady knew that they might be walking into a trap. They made easy targets as they ascended the barren slope. And he wondered briefly if he was prepared to die—if God had really forgiven him for killing Coop. But no shots greeted them as they jogged up the hill. They found the Rebel battery abandoned.

The captain sent a band of skirmishers into the woods to hunt for the Rebels. Another band went to search the plantation house and other buildings. Grady returned to the riverbank to help transport the waiting refugees to the ships. Each time he lifted a child in his arms or helped a woman onboard, he thought of Delia's words to him on that long-ago night, after the white boys had whipped him: *"Ever think that maybe the Lord's preparing you to save your black brothers and sisters?"*

Meanwhile, the obstructions that the Rebels had planted in the river proved difficult to remove. Progress was so slow that lunchtime came and went, the tide began to ebb, and all hope of a surprise attack on the bridge was lost. Grady paced impatiently beneath the blistering sun. He felt the heat from the wooden deck through the soles of his shoes, as warm as a bed of coals beneath his feet.

At last the barricade was cleared. Colonel Higginson left the *John Adams* behind for a rear guard and told Grady and the others to crowd aboard the two smaller boats for the ten-mile journey to the railroad bridge. They sailed with torches lit, ready to set it ablaze. But by now the tide was so low that both ships continually ran aground, frustrating everyone. Slowly, mile by mile, they made their way north, passing acres of emerald rice fields on both shores. Grady knew that those fields should be filled with laborers on this sultry July day. Instead, they were strangely deserted. There were no joyous mobs of slaves rushing out to meet them, like the mob that had greeted them early this morning.

The route grew more and more treacherous. At one point, when the other ship lay aground, two excited slaves paddled out to Grady's ship in a dugout canoe. "Are there any more of you onshore that need to be rescued?" Colonel Higginson asked.

"No, sir. We been hiding in one of the rice canals all day, waiting for y'all. The overseer move everybody else away from the river when they heard y'all was coming."

"What's the name of your plantation?" Grady asked them. "Who's your massa?"

Again, the reply was disappointing. "His name's Massa Ferguson, sir."

The ship was finally freed to continue upstream. But a scant two miles below the railroad bridge, Grady's boat ran aground on a mudbank. Unwilling to waste any more time, Colonel Higginson waved the other boat on, ordering them to steam ahead and burn the bridge without them. The ship soon disappeared from sight around a bend.

Grady pounded the rail with his fist in frustration. Grounded! Now he wouldn't even have the satisfaction of watching the bridge go up in flames. When Joseph came to stand beside him at the rail, Grady's anger boiled over. "Why is God always on the Rebels' side?" he asked. "Why can't He help us, for once, instead of working everything in their favor?"

"What makes you think He's helping them?" No sooner had the question left Joseph's lips when the boom of artillery fire sounded close by, coming from upstream.

"Hear that?" Grady said. "The Rebels have been waiting for us all day, and now they're firing on our other ship. We're sitting here with no way to help them. Why would God do this to us?"

"If we was smart enough to figure out what God was doing, then that would make Him pretty small, wouldn't it?" Joe said. "You really want a God like that? A God you can figure out?"

"All I know is, every time I ask Him for help, He's turning His back. We came here to set some slaves free, and look at that—there ain't even a single slave left over there to save." He gestured angrily to the empty rice fields on the shore across from them. "We been getting stuck so many times that the Rebels had all the time in the world to be moving their slaves away from here. Now, what reason would God have for doing that?"

"I don't know, Grady," he said quietly, "but I'm trusting that He has a good one."

Grady shook his head, staring at the distant plantation house, its roof shimmering in the wavy heat. Then an egret caught his attention, wading near shore. Something unseen startled it, and the bird stretched its broad white wings to soar above the boat landing. Grady followed the path of its flight to the top of the hill above the landing—and that's when he saw it: an enormous oak tree. The pale silver moss that was entwined with its leaves swayed gently in the breeze.

Grady drew in his breath so sharply that Joe asked, "What's wrong? You seeing Rebels?"

Grady didn't reply as he quickly scanned the crowded deck. "Where's those slaves we rescued from the dugout?"

"Over there," Joseph said, pointing. "What's wrong, Grady?"

He jogged across the deck, not caring that he interrupted the slave's conversation with Captain Metcalf. "Do you know this plantation?" he asked, pointing to it. "What's the name of it?"

The slave seemed to take forever to reply. "Why, I believe that's Great Oak. Owned by the Goodmans."

Grady turned to Joseph, grabbing his lapels. "That's where my wife is!"

"Your . . . your *wife?*" Joe stared at him as if Grady had lost his mind. "You never told me you had a wife."

"Her name is Anna," he said frantically. "She works in the Big House."

Joseph gently pried Grady's hands loose. "Then maybe she's still up there. Maybe they're just hiding the field slaves, not the house slaves."

"Let's take one of the skiffs ashore and find out," Captain Metcalf said. "I'll come with you."

"Me too," Joseph said.

Grady didn't know what to do. Suppose Anna refused to escape with him after these men risked their lives to go ashore with him? Grady was afraid to be hurt a second time, afraid to have the others see that his wife didn't love him enough to trust him.

Joseph tugged on his arm. "Come on, Grady. You have to try, even if she ain't there. Maybe we can help somebody else."

Captain Metcalf quickly gathered a squad of volunteers, and Grady found himself climbing into the skiff with them, rowing toward shore. He felt dazed and breathless—and more afraid than he'd ever been in his life.

"I hope I'm not leading y'all into an ambush," he murmured as they approached the quiet landing dock.

"That ain't likely," Joseph said. "Don't you think the Rebels would have attacked our ship by now, seeing as we're stuck?"

"Which way should we go when we land?" Captain Metcalf asked.

"I-I don't know. I ain't never been here before." The men looked at him as if he was crazy. "My wife worked for Massa Fuller's wife, and this is her daddy's place," he explained. "She packed up and came here the night I escaped."

Joseph bowed his head and closed his eyes, praying out loud. "O Lord, please lead us to her. Please help Grady find his wife and bring her home, safe and sound."

His prayer made Grady's entire body tremble—with anger and with something else that he couldn't quite place. He wanted to yell at Joseph to shut up. God had stayed a long way off, all these years, unheeding when Grady had needed Him the most. But there was something else in Joe's simple, heartfelt prayer that made Grady feel like a little boy, seated on Eli's knee. He longed to have that little boy's faith again—to believe that Massa Jesus heard and answered his prayers.

He stepped from the boat on rubbery knees and hurried up the driveway, glimpsing beautiful gardens to the right, the carriage house and other outbuildings to the left.

"Slave Row must be that way," Joe said, gesturing to the left.

The captain nodded. "We'll start there."

Grady knew that Anna was most likely up at the Big House, but he felt relieved that they were going down to the Row first. This risky trip ashore would be worth it if they managed to save a few other slaves, even if Anna refused to come with them.

Joseph and Captain Metcalf ran to search inside the stable and carriage house. Grady and the other men hurried toward the slave huts. The first few cabins they searched were empty. But as he ran to kick open the door of the next cabin, he heard a baby crying inside. He halted, unwilling to scare the occupants, and slowly opened the door.

Delia! Delia was inside. Grady couldn't believe it.

She sat on the bed, surrounded by children, staring up at him in surprise. Then recognition lit her face. "Grady? O Lord, Lord!" she cried as she sprang to her feet and into his arms. She seemed even smaller than Grady remembered. "The Good Lord brought you here—He brought you!" she wept.

Grady could scarcely comprehend that he had found Delia. And if she was still here at Great Oak, then that meant that Anna must be here, too. He released his grip.

"Get your stuff together, Delia, you're coming with me. I'm going up to the Big House to find Anna, and then we're leaving." He turned to go.

"No, Grady, wait!"

"I ain't arguing with you, Delia. This time you're coming." He ran out the door and was halfway across the yard when he heard her calling to him.

"Grady, stop! Come back! She ain't up there! Anna ain't up at the Big House."

He halted. His racing heart felt as if it might burst inside his chest. They had taken Anna away with all the others. He wouldn't be able to save her. He slowly walked back toward Delia. "Where is she?" he asked.

Delia motioned for him to follow her as she led him to a window-less, stone building behind the outhouse. "Kick the door in, Grady," she said. "I ain't got time to be stealing the key again."

He stared at Delia, unable to comprehend what she was saying. What were they doing here? He needed to find Anna. They were wasting time. Why had Delia brought him here?

"Go on, kick it in," she repeated. "Anna's inside."

He backed up a step and did as Delia said, aiming his foot as close to the lock as he could. He had to kick it three times before the metal locking pin bent far enough for the door to fly open. Anna sat slumped on the floor, her wrists in shackles, the shackles chained to a post. Grady couldn't imagine what she was doing there. Why was his beautiful Anna caged like an animal? She was covered with sweat and filth, and her dazed eyes were filled with despair.

But then she recognized him, and her expression changed to one of joy and disbelief. "Grady . . . ? Grady, is it really you? You're really here?"

He dropped to his knees beside her and wrapped her tightly in his arms. Tethered to the post, she couldn't hug him in return. He wanted to ask her what they'd done to her, why she was here, but tears choked off his words. Instead, he took her face in his hands and covered it with kisses.

"Is it really you?" she repeated. "You came for us?"

"Yes," he whispered. "Yes." She felt so small and broken and fragile. What had they done to her? It made him half crazy to imagine. But then a sense of urgency suddenly gripped him. "We have to get out of here," he said. "Where's the key to these shackles?"

"I don't know," Delia said. "The overseer must have it."

Grady stood up to examine the shackles. They were too strong to break. The only way to free Anna was to pry the ring they were fastened to, out of the post. He glanced around the shed, searching for something to use as a pry bar and decided to try his steel bayonet. It seemed to take forever to wedge the weapon into the ring and force it open. And it required every ounce of strength he had. But the chain on Anna's shackles finally came free. He lifted her to her feet and looked around. For some reason, Delia had disappeared. Grady hoped she had returned to her cabin for her belongings.

"Come on!" he told Anna. "You're coming with me this time."

"Yes, Grady! Yes!"

He half-supported, half-carried her as they raced back across the lawn. Anna was crying uncontrollably, babbling as if trying to tell him something. He wasn't listening. Whatever she'd been through, he would deal with it later. He would help her heal.

When they reached Delia's cabin, Anna ran inside ahead of him and scooped up one of the babies in her arms. She had to hold it awkwardly with her hands still bound.

"Come on, Delia," Grady said. "We have to hurry."

Delia shook her head. "I ain't coming."

"No! Not this again!" he shouted. "Don't try and tell me God's wanting you here! I'll tie you up and carry you to the boat if I have to!"

She rested her hand on his arm to calm him. "It ain't that, honey. I can't leave all these little ones here alone." She gestured to the cabin full of children, and Grady saw them as if for the first time. There were at least a dozen children of various sizes and ages. Most of them were crying.

"Where's Lucy?" Anna asked. "Can't she watch them?"

"She passed on, honey. I'm here all alone, now. Go on, Grady. You got your wife and baby to look after."

"My . . . my *what*?"

"That's your baby, Grady. Your son." Delia gestured to the child in Anna's arms.

Anna nodded, hugging the child as tightly as her bound wrists would allow. Grady stared at them, speechless, and slowly realized what Anna had been trying to tell him. He couldn't grasp it. He had a son?

"The overseer loaded all the field hands into wagons this morning when they heard that the Yankee gunboats was coming," Delia explained. "They took the house slaves, too. Left just me and the babies. Who knows when they'll be bringing all their mothers back home. Go on. Get going, now. I'll be praying for you."

Grady knew that Delia wouldn't change her mind. He pulled her into his arms and hugged her fiercely, devastated that he would have to leave her behind a second time.

"Go on, honey," she said, freeing herself from his grip. "Take your wife and son—and may the Good Lord watch over all three of you."

Grady wiped his eyes on his sleeve and reached for Anna. He wrapped his arm around her shoulder, gripping his rifle in his other hand, and hurried out of the cabin. They raced toward the landing together.

Captain Metcalf and the others had found only one or two old-timers in the cabins, and they were leading them toward the waiting rowboat. Joseph saw Grady coming and his narrow face lit with joy. "Bless the Lord, is that her, Grady? You found your wife?"

Grady could only nod. Anna was coming with him. Anna and his son.

His son.

Grady felt dazed as the soldiers pulled him and Anna onboard the gunboat. As he led her downstairs belowdecks, he slowly became aware once again of the sounds of battle in the distance upstream and of his ship's engines laboring as the crew tried to free them from the mudbank. And his son was crying. Grady realized that he had been crying pitifully ever since Anna had snatched him from his bed in Delia's cabin. Grady found a quiet corner where they could sit down, and the distraught cries finally stopped as Anna put him to her breast and fed him. Grady watched, and the love he felt for both of them overwhelmed him.

"I'll be right back," he whispered. He went into the engine room and asked to borrow some tools. Then he sat by Anna's side again as she fed their son and began sawing her shackles off.

"Are you okay, Anna?" he asked. "What happened? Why'd they chain you up like that?"

"I hit Missy Claire."

"You . . . you *what?*"

"She wouldn't let me be with our baby, and she said she was gonna sell him to the slave auction or throw him into the river—"

"Oh, God!" Grady reacted instinctively, dropping the tools as he enveloped Anna and his son in his arms. As his horror slowly subsided, he released his grip and gazed down at the baby. He was asleep. His tiny brown face was as wrinkled as Delia's, his arms and legs curled tightly against his body. He had Anna's long eyelashes and beautiful, full lips. Grady saw a drop of milk in the corner of his mouth and wiped it with his finger.

"I just started hitting Missy—hitting her over and over," Anna said. "I couldn't stop. I wanted to kill her."

Grady couldn't believe what she was telling him. Anna, who had taken so much abuse from Claire all these years, who had never stood up for herself, had endangered her own life to defend their child. He shuddered at the risk she had taken, aware of what might have happened to her. Striking a white person was a crime punishable by death. He heard the tremor in his own voice as he said, "I'm surprised that all she did was lock you up."

"No, Missy told them to give me forty lashes. They were going to do it this morning but the overseer found out that the Yankee warships was coming, so he didn't have time." She looked up at Grady and her eyes filled with tears. "And then you came."

He held her tightly again, overwhelmed at the timing that had brought him there at the right moment.

"Delia and I prayed and asked Jesus for help," she said. "I prayed that He would help set our baby free—and now he is free."

The ship lurched suddenly as it broke free from the mudbank. The baby awoke, startled, his frail arms and legs jerking in fright. Grady reached instinctively to stroke his head, to soothe him. The ship began to move. He remembered questioning God a few hours ago, asking why He had grounded them here when they were supposed to burn a bridge. Now he knew why. But he heard the thunder of Rebel guns in the distance and knew that they still weren't safe. He felt an overpowering urge to protect his family, to get them safely back to Beaufort or die trying.

"Anna, we're moving again. These shackles will have to wait until later. I need to go back up on deck with the other soldiers. We have a job to finish. Stay down here where it's safe, okay."

"Please be careful, Grady," she whispered.

He took the stairs two at a time as he raced up on deck. The ship had stopped again, and Grady quickly saw why. The second boat was floating back downstream, coming toward them. "Our engine is disabled," he heard the captain shout to Colonel Higginson. "Our engineer was struck by a shell and killed."

Colonel Higginson lowered his head and closed his eyes. Grady wondered if he was praying. When he raised it again he nodded solemnly. "It's getting late. We need to turn back. We'll have to forget about the bridge."

The tide was turning, as well. The colonel ordered the crippled ship to float downstream ahead of Grady's vessel, carried along by the current. In spite of the fact that their mission had been aborted, that they had failed to burn the railroad bridge, Grady was surprised to discover that he didn't feel his usual anger and frustration. God had a reason for this trip that Grady never could have foreseen.

They continued downstream, mile after mile. Grady was about to return belowdecks to sit with his wife when he heard the deadly boom of a cannon. The shell whistled sickeningly as it arced through the air toward him, and he watched in horror as it struck their sister ship a few dozen yards ahead. A long, straight stretch of water loomed in front of them before the river curved around a spit of land. The Rebels had planted a battery at that point, and their cannons were aimed squarely at the approaching vessels. Grady's ship was heading into their trap with no way to escape.

"Take cover!" the colonel shouted.

Grady dove for the stairs with all the others, but even belowdecks there was no escape from the deadly bombardment. The vessel shook as her cannons returned fire, but it made a much-too-easy target for the waiting Rebels. Shell after shell struck the ship, exploding in a deadly rain of shrapnel and wood splinters and glass. Grady raced toward the corner where he'd left Anna, nearly tripping over a soldier's lifeless body, and sloshing through a puddle of river water that was seeping inside. He pulled Anna away from the hull, into the center of the ship where it was safer, then crouched over her and their baby, shielding them with his body.

The deafening sounds of battle heightened the chaos around him—bombs exploding, glass and wood shattering, men screaming. But above it all, Grady could hear his son's helpless, terrified cries. He had been sleeping so peacefully in Delia's cabin, until Grady had come along and yanked him awake. Now the baby found himself in this terrible, frightening place and he couldn't possibly know why. If only Grady could make his son understand that he loved him, that he would rather die himself than watch him suffering such terror. If only he could explain that this incomprehensible horror was, in reality, for his son's own good. At the end of this perilous journey was something so much better than a safe cabin on Slave Row—there was freedom. But the gulf between Grady and his son was too great. There was no way to help him understand.

"I'm right here," he murmured. "Please trust me . . . it'll be okay . . ."

After what seemed like hours, the deadly explosions gradually faded into the distance as the ship finished running the gauntlet and steamed out of range. She was badly damaged, but miraculously still afloat. Grady rose slowly to his feet and stretched his cramped body. He felt a burning sensation in his neck and reached to remove a wood splinter. "Are you okay?" he asked Anna. "Is the baby okay?"

"Yes," she replied. But the baby was still screaming, and she focused all her attention on him as she tried to soothe him.

Grady looked around. Injured men lay everywhere, moaning softly. He could see daylight through a gash in the ship's hull. And crumpled beneath that hole, lay three bloodied bodies. One of them was Joseph's.

"No . . . oh, no . . ." Grady breathed. He wove his way through the tangle of wreckage to kneel by his friend's side. "Joe! Joe, can you hear me? Are you okay?"

Joseph turned to Grady, staring at him with dazed eyes. He smiled faintly. "I guess I'm still this side of glory, if you're here," he murmured. "But I think I've been hit."

"Where?" Grady saw blood all over the front of Joseph's jacket, oozing from a jagged tear above his belt. He gently loosened the buttons, then tried to hide his horror when he saw the gaping wound in the middle of Joe's stomach. "You're gonna be okay," he said, willing it to be true. "I'm gonna find you a doctor."

Joe grabbed his arm to stop him before he could rise. "Are your wife and baby okay?"

Grady bit his lip. "Yeah. Just shook up."

Joe's grin broadened. "She's real pretty, Grady. How come you never told me you was married?"

Grady wondered how Joe could be talking about this now, with a hole blown through his gut. Then he realized that he probably needed a distraction from his pain. Grady took a deep breath. "I don't know why I never told you . . . I'm sorry. I guess I just don't like talking about myself, much."

"God answered our prayer, Grady. You found your wife."

Grady didn't realize that he had reacted until Joe's smile faded. "What's wrong?" Joe asked. "Why're you frowning like that? Don't you believe that it was God who helped you?"

"Yes, I believe it," Grady replied. "But you said God answered *our* prayer. And I didn't pray, Joe. I was too afraid to pray. He answered *you*."

Joe's grip on his arm tightened. "Don't you be listening to that old devil when he tells you God can't forgive you. It's a lie, Grady. Okay?"

He nodded, unable to speak.

A moment later, Captain Metcalf knelt beside them. "How are you doing, Joe?"

"He needs a doctor," Grady said before Joe could reply. "Where is he?"

The captain hesitated. "He's taking care of Colonel Higginson at the moment. The colonel was hit, too."

Grady felt a surge of nausea. "Is he gonna be okay?"

"Let's hope so. Listen, I'll make sure the doctor sees Joe, next."

Grady returned to Anna's side when the doctor finally arrived, unable to watch as he probed Joseph's wound, afraid to ask him if he thought Joe might die.

An hour later, the battered ship finally reached Wiltown Bluff. Grady helped transfer his friend and all of the other wounded men onto the *John Adams*, since it could make the trip to Beaufort much faster than the other two vessels. Anna and the other refugees moved with them, joining the noisy throng of slaves who had been rescued earlier that morning. Anna looked exhausted as she sat huddled in the hold with their baby, sitting between piles of bedding and other belongings.

"Why don't you try and rest for a while?" Grady said. But no sooner had he spoken, than he heard the unmistakable sound of artillery exploding. The Rebels were attacking the ship from their shore batteries again, as it continued the journey downriver.

"Is this ever going to end?" Anna wept as missiles whistled through the air above them.

"Yes," Grady promised, cradling her in his arms. "This ship is stronger and faster than the other one was. We'll get through this, soon—and you'll be free."

She flinched as cannons roared and thundered all around them. "What's it like, Grady? Being free?"

He leaned his head against hers, kissing her hair. "Imagine you and me together like this . . . and nobody telling us we can't be. Imagine working and doing things for each other and for our son, all day long, instead of for somebody else. You can go wherever you want to go, and do whatever you please without nobody ever stopping you. I can buy you the biggest pile of paper you've ever seen, and you can draw pictures all day long if you want to—and you won't even have to squeeze them all together on one page." He held her tighter as a bomb exploded nearby. "And freedom means that this little boy of ours can grow up into a man without ever knowing what it's like to be somebody's slave."

"I'm so glad you came back for me!" She was silent for a long moment, then said, "Grady . . . I'm sorry I didn't go with you, before. I'm so sorry for being scared."

"That's all behind us now," he said, kissing her again. "Let's not be talking about it no more."

Once again, the ship steamed past the Rebel battery and moved safely out of range. Grady finished filing off Anna's shackles, then fixed a bed for her on his army blanket. He stayed with her until she fell asleep with their son beside her. But Grady was too uneasy to sleep. He went out onto the quarterdeck, where all the injured soldiers were, and searched for Joseph.

"How you doing?" he asked when he found him.

"Better," Joe said weakly. "The morphine helps."

Grady cleared his throat. "Listen, I never thanked you for helping me rescue my wife today. And I'm real sorry that I made fun, the other day, when you read me that Bible verse about being afraid of what man can do—"

"Hey, forget it, Grady. I meant what I said. I ain't afraid of dying. I'll be going home to see my heavenly Father. We're all free up there, you know."

Once again, Grady shuddered when he recalled Joseph's certainty that Coop was in hell. "Just don't be getting in a hurry to go to heaven, okay?" Grady said. "You're gonna make it. They're gonna fix you up good as new when we get to Beaufort."

Grady looked around at all the other injured men and swallowed. He might easily have been one of them. "You needing anything, Joe? A drink of water or something?"

Joe shook his head.

Grady remembered the day he'd met Joe—his first day of free-dom—and how Joe had offered him a drink from his canteen. "Mind if I sit here with you for a while?" Grady asked.

"You might have to listen to me preach, you know."

"That's okay. I'm getting used to it."

Joe closed his eyes for a long moment. When he opened them again he met Grady's gaze. "Are you gonna stay mad at God forever?" he asked softly. "I know you been through a lot in your lifetime, but God never stopped loving you, Grady. He heard your cries all that time. And He had His own reasons for not answering the way you wanted Him to. He just couldn't explain it in a way you'd understand."

Grady remembered the baby's frightened cries this afternoon, and how he'd pleaded with his son to trust him. Maybe God really hadn't abandoned Grady years ago in Richmond. Maybe it was just like Delia had said—God wanted to use all the hardships Grady had endured to lead him and so many others to freedom. The generals who were overseeing the war could see the picture so much clearer than the men on the front lines.

"You're gonna do great things for God, Grady. I know it," Joseph said. "That's why the devil's making you suffer so much—just like Job."

Grady shook his head, still not ready to believe that he would ever have as much faith as Joseph did. "No, you're the preacher, Joe. Not me," he said. "That's why you have to get better."

❧

Grady was relieved to learn that his friend was still in stable condition when they docked in Beaufort the next day. Ambulances met the ship at the wharf, and Grady helped carry the wounded men off first. He was dismayed to see Colonel Higginson lying pale and wounded on one of the stretchers. Captain Metcalf crouched down to speak with him, and Grady overheard Higginson say, "When I think of the slaves we rescued, I know that the day was worth all it cost, and more."

Grady gazed out at the gray-blue water to stop his tears. Higginson—a white man—thought Grady's wife and son worth dying for.

When he'd pulled himself together again, Grady hurried down belowdecks to fetch Anna. He had been dreading this moment, knowing that he would have to abandon the two of them on the wharf and return to camp with the other soldiers. How could he bear to leave Anna? She had never been on her own before, without Missy Claire telling her what to do.

He was still weighing what to say to her when Captain Metcalf came alongside him and clapped his hand on Grady's shoulder. "Take two days' leave, son. Get your family settled."

Grady closed his eyes. The relief he felt staggered him. But more than that, a white man had shown sympathy for him and his family. "Thank you, sir," he said. "Thank you so much."

Part Three

Let this be written for a future generation, that a people not yet created may praise the Lord: "The Lord looked down from his sanctuary on high, from heaven he viewed the earth, to hear the groans of prisoners and release those condemned to death."

Psalm 102:18–20 NIV

Beaufort, South Carolina
July 1863

It felt funny to Anna to be off the ship and standing on dry land again—and so strange to be back in Beaufort without Missy Claire. The sun was very warm as it shone down from the cloudless sky and glared off the water, but she couldn't seem to stop trembling. "Where are we gonna go?" she asked Grady. He didn't reply.

All the other soldiers lined up to march back to their camp, but she'd heard the white officer telling Grady that he could spend two days with her. She wondered what would happen after that. Anna wished Grady could stay with her and their baby from now on, but she knew that he couldn't. He was still a soldier. They would still have to live apart.

A group of white ladies from a church up north had gathered all of the other rescued slaves together, promising them food and a place to stay if they came to the mission on St. Helena Island. They said that they could learn to read and write there, too. Anna wondered if it was true. But Grady took her arm and led her away, toward Bay Street, before she had a chance to hear more.

"Where are we going?" she asked again.

"To Massa Fuller's house."

Anna froze, clutching little George to her chest.

"It's okay," Grady said gently. "There ain't nobody there but Minnie and Jim. Missy Claire ain't coming back here as long as the Yankees are in town."

Anna knew that she had no other choice. The baby needed diapers and blankets and things, and she had escaped with nothing but the clothes on her back. She had already torn up her apron and petticoat to swaddle him on the ship. Maybe it would feel like home to be living in their room above the stable again, with the sweet smell of hay and horses. But when they reached the town house, Grady led her toward the back door, not the stable. She halted again.

"Why are we going in there?"

Grady's arm tightened around her shoulder. "Because that's where you and our son are going to live." He knocked on the door, and when no one answered, he opened it himself and led her inside. He shrugged off his knapsack and propped his rifle beside it near the door.

There were plenty of signs that the house was occupied—the curtains were open, Minnie's shawl lay draped over a chair, the aroma of bacon filled the air—but at the moment, no one was home. It was strangely quiet. Anna felt as though, any moment now, Missy Claire would yell at her to come upstairs, or would emerge from one of the rooms barking orders.

"I don't think I can stay here," she said.

"Anna, listen—"

"No, Missy Claire is everywhere, Grady. Everything reminds me of her."

"But you don't have to be afraid of her no more. You ain't her slave. You're free."

"I know. I ain't scared of her," Anna said, struggling to put her feelings into words. "I'm scared of the way I feel about her. I hate her, Grady. When she said she would sell our son or throw him into the river, I wanted to kill her. And now that I'm here in her house, all those feelings are coming back again."

Grady closed his eyes. "I know. It ain't easy changing the way you feel. But Delia used to say that hating people was like drinking poison and expecting them to die." He smiled faintly and said, "Come upstairs with me." He rested his hand on her back and gently urged her forward, moving up the steps and into one of the guest bedrooms. He gestured to the four-poster bed. "I slept here after escaping last fall," he said. "Did you ever sleep in a bed like this? It's as soft as a cloud, Anna, not all scratchy like cornshucks. Which bed do you want our boy to be sleeping in? Go look at our room above the stable, then tell me if you think he deserves that one—or this one."

"This one," she said fiercely. "He's every bit as good as Missy Claire's son."

"I know. And you're just as good as Missy Claire—better, in fact." He stroked his fingers down her cheek. "You would never be throwing her baby into the river. You deserve to sleep here, too." He gestured to the bed and said, "Lay him down on there for a while. Your arms must be tired of holding him." She hesitated, afraid to relive the terrible experience of losing him, of having her arms emptied.

"It's okay," Grady said. "I promise you that nobody will ever be taking him away from you again. Trust me." Anna did trust him. He had returned for her and their son. He had brought them here to safety. She bent and laid the baby on the bed. He squirmed for a moment, then fell asleep again.

"He's a fine-looking boy," Grady said hoarsely. "What's his name?"

"I'm calling him George."

"No!" Grady shouted so loudly that the baby startled awake. But Anna moved to soothe her husband first, resting her hands on his chest. She could feel his heart pounding against his ribs.

"Grady, what's wrong?"

"Why did you name him *that*?"

"I-it was my daddy's name. What's wrong? Please tell me . . . what's wrong?"

She watched as he struggled for control. "George Fletcher was my first massa's name—my father's name."

"Oh, Grady . . . I can change it—"

"No," he said, exhaling. "No. I don't want you to do that. Your daddy died trying to help you escape. He was a good man who loved you. You're the baby's mama, and you should name him whatever you want."

Anna wrapped her arms around Grady's waist and rested her head against his chest. "Are you sure?"

"Yes."

All the tension had gone out of him, and she knew that he meant what he said. He seemed so different to her. Broken, somehow—as if the anger and resentment he'd stored up over the years had shattered into dust. Even his hands seemed gentler as he caressed her back.

"Where did Missus Fuller keep her clothes?" he asked suddenly. "You could use a new dress."

Anna leaned back to look up at him, to see if he was joking. His face was serious. It was hard enough to imagine living in Missy's house. But wearing her clothes? "It ain't right to be taking her things and—"

"Anna. How much has she been paying you for all the work you done all these years? Don't you think she's owing you at least one dress?" He bent and kissed her before she could reply, and the love she felt from him, for him, brought tears of joy to her eyes. "Listen," he said as he pulled away again, "it ain't enough to be a free woman. You got to start thinking like one, too. I don't want you teaching our—teaching George—to think like a slave. Free people get paid for the work they're doing. And free people are sleeping in houses, not stables."

Anna looked down at her son, asleep like a tiny prince on one of Missy Claire's softest feather beds. A fierce protectiveness rose up inside her. "I'll do it, Grady," she said. "I'll start thinking like a free woman from now on, I promise—for George's sake."

She slept in Grady's arms that night, in the big four-poster bed, with their son clutched tightly to her side.

❧

Grady's two-day leave ended much too soon. He wished he had more time to help Anna get settled and to teach her all the things she needed to know, like how to shop for food and things. He had given her all of the money he'd saved from his army pay, and he'd promised Minnie and Jim that he'd keep on paying every month, if they would take care of Anna for him.

It had been hard saying good-bye to Anna. But he'd decided to leave a little early, giving himself time to walk to the Pinckney Street mansion near the Green that had been converted into a Union hospital. He needed to see Joseph before returning to camp.

"I'm looking for my friend, Private Joseph Whitney," he told the hospital clerk. "He's in my regiment—Colonel Higginson's regiment—the First South Carolina Volunteers. He was wounded two days ago on the *John Adams*."

The clerk looked away for a moment, and there was something in his expression that made Grady feel queasy. The man sorted through his papers as if searching for Joe's records, but Grady had the sick, certain feeling that the clerk already knew the answer. His heart thudded painfully as he waited.

"I'm sorry, son," the clerk finally said. "Private Whitney is dead."

"No," Grady breathed. "Are you sure?" The clerk simply nodded.

Grady wrestled with his grief on the long, hot walk back to camp, wondering how he could ever face their empty tent. And even though he knew that Joe was gone, even though several of his fellow soldiers met him along the row of tents to talk about Joe and to share his grief, Grady still expected to find his lanky friend sitting outside their tent reading his Bible or to hear his familiar voice saying, "Bless the Lord, Grady!"

They buried Private Joseph Whitney in the soldier's cemetery beneath a grove of huge oak trees above the river. Silvery moss drooped from the tree branches like tears. Captain Metcalf had postponed the funeral until Grady returned from his leave so that he could be part of the military escort. Grady and two other soldiers fired the rifle volley over Joseph's grave.

Joe had been so well loved and respected that nearly every man in the regiment attended his funeral. His simple coffin, draped with the United States flag, looked much too small to contain him. The other men sang hymns as the coffin was lowered into the grave, but Grady's throat was so tight with grief that he could scarcely breathe, much less sing. He didn't hear much of the chaplain's eulogy, only his final words, so hauntingly like Joe's: "His body is in this grave. But we know that our friend Joe is home now, with his Lord."

Grief hung heavily over the entire camp that night. The crickets and cicadas sounded deafening without the laughter and good-natured banter that usually enlivened the summer evenings. "Ain't nobody to preach to us no more," Grady heard one man sigh.

An aching restlessness filled Grady's heart. He longed to do something for Joseph, but he didn't know what. Joe's friend Willie sat beside his tent with his fiddle in his hand, but he seemed too distraught to play it. Grady walked slowly over to him.

"Can I borrow that for a minute?" he asked. Willie looked surprised, but he handed the fiddle and bow to him. Grady hesitated a long moment, then put it beneath his chin, adjusting the strings, trying a few tentative notes. The feel of the smooth wood in his hands, the vibrations that shivered through him, stirred painful memories. But Grady had to play.

He closed his eyes and began with a slow, sad tune—the one that Joe had always liked, the slave trader's song. Then, one after another, Grady played all the songs that the slaves had once sung as they'd marched to the fields—mournful, haunting tunes that sounded painfully sweet on the violin, like a child's voice. He wasn't aware that all of the murmuring voices had fallen silent, that everyone was listening. Nor was he aware of the tears that streamed down his face as he played.

He lost all track of time, stopping only when he ran out of songs.

Then he wiped his face on his sleeve and handed back the fiddle. "Why don't you play some more?" Willie asked, his voice hoarse.

"I-I can't," Grady said. But when he looked around and saw the grief on all the men's faces, he realized what he had done. The music had stirred up a lifetime of pain and sorrowful memories, forcing them to relive it all.

"Play something happy," Willie said with a tearful smile. "Joe wouldn't want us to be sad."

Grady knew that he owed the other men that much. There had been happy times, too, in the slave quarters as they had gathered with their wives and families. And there had been happy times with Joseph, sitting around the campfire every night and singing about Jesus. Grady owed it to them to bring those memories back, as well. He wasn't being forced by Coop to play for the slaves this time. The men wanted him to play.

He lifted the fiddle to his chin and played one of the happy, faith-filled songs that Joe had sung every night. He played as many as he could remember—songs about freedom and the Promised Land and crossing to heaven's shore. Before long, all of the men were singing and clapping and stomping their feet in rhythm. Grady heard laughter again, and he played until his own sorrow lifted and his fingertips grew too sore to play another note.

Exhausted, he gave the fiddle back to Willie and headed toward his tent for the night. Grady braced himself to endure the loneliness of his first night without Joe, without Anna. But Captain Metcalf intercepted him before he could duck inside.

"I didn't realize you could play like that, Grady. How come we never heard you play before?"

The question made him uneasy. "I . . . um . . . I don't own a fiddle."

"Listen, the officers are having a get-together in Beaufort next week. Colonel Higginson promised to come, if he's feeling better. If I find you a fiddle, will you play for us?"

Grady's reaction was instantaneous. Anger and rage boiled up inside him until his entire body trembled with it. If he had still held the fiddle in his hands, he might have smashed it over the captain's head. He wanted to yell at Metcalf, *"I don't play for white men!"* but he stopped himself in time.

"We'll be happy to pay you," the captain added.

All the heat of Grady's fury died away in a wash of shame. He had urged Anna not to hate, but he still overflowed with it himself. And as hard as Grady had tried, he hadn't been able to get rid of it. Seeking revenge against Coop hadn't cleared it out. Grady had been a free man for eight months, but that hadn't changed his heart either, nor had helping to free his fellow slaves. He knew that God alone could change him—and only if Grady admitted that the hatred and bitterness were there and asked for help.

And Grady wanted to change. He didn't want to hate someone just because he was white. Good men like Colonel Higginson and Captain Metcalf had shown him that it wasn't the color of a man's skin that counted, but the heart of the man beneath it.

Grady drew a deep breath and stretched out his hand to his captain. "Find me a fiddle to play, and we've got a deal."

⁂

Every morning Anna awoke with the same heart-racing feelings of panic. Missy Claire was calling her! She needed to run and fetch a basin of warm water so Missy could wash. She had to empty the chamber pot and open the curtains to let in the light. Missy needed her breakfast brought to her, needed her hair fixed, her corset laces fastened, her hoops tied in place. For more than ten years Anna had jumped to obey Missy's every command, and now those commands—and their commander—were absent from her life. She couldn't get used to it. Daydreaming was no longer forbidden, dawdling no longer a crime. She could sit down to rest if she was tired, a luxury she had never known. She had promised Grady that she would think like a free woman, but that promise was proving much more difficult to keep than she'd imagined.

Of course, caring for little George occupied a great deal of Anna's time. He wanted to be fed every few hours and his diapers needed to be washed every day in order to keep a fresh supply. She helped Minnie with the cooking and housekeeping. But even though the remainder of Anna's day was hers to do with as she chose, she still couldn't shake off the guilty feeling that Missy was hovering nearby, waiting to chastise her for her laziness.

"Why don't you get out and go for a walk?" Minnie urged her one sunny afternoon. "That little baby must be needing some fresh air."

That was what free people did, Anna told herself. They went for walks anytime they wanted to with no one to stop them. But where would she go? She considered several possibilities as she tied the baby in his sling and put on one of Missy's old bonnets to keep the summer sun out of her eyes. A stroll along Bay Street would be nice, but there were always a lot of soldiers there—white soldiers. And she didn't want to go near the shopping areas without Minnie, afraid to endure all the flirtatious attention she always received. She finally decided to walk the few short blocks to the pretty white church that Missy Claire used to attend. She wanted to see if the windows were as beautiful as the church windows in Charleston had been. She would show George the magnificent colors, let him bask in the rainbow of light.

Anna left the town house through the back door, her belief that the front door was for white people still too deeply ingrained to disregard. George seemed to enjoy the rolling motion of their leisurely stroll and quickly fell asleep, cuddled close to her heart. She found the church easily, pleased that she remembered the way—and was surprised to see a flurry of activity in the peaceful little churchyard. She stood across the street, watching as Negro soldiers dressed just like Grady came and went through the open doors. She had planned to view the windows from inside if the church was open, but she quickly changed her mind when she saw how busy it was. Besides, a quick glimpse of the side of the building told her what she had come here to learn—all of the windows in this church, to Anna's great disappointment, were made of clear glass.

Still, she was reluctant to return home. She stood watching the soldiers from the shade of an oak tree across the street, rocking from foot to foot so that George would remain asleep, and wishing that one of the soldiers would miraculously turn out to be Grady.

"Can I help you find someone, ma'am?" a voice beside her asked.

Anna turned, startled, and the Negro soldier tipped his hat to her. "Sorry if I frightened you. You looked as though you might need some help. Are you here to see someone at the hospital?" He didn't talk like any slave she had ever met, and he wore a pair of wire-rim spectacles on his nose like the ones Massa Goodman wore when he read the newspaper. Anna had never seen a Negro with spectacles before. Then she noticed that his arm was in a sling.

"Is that church a hospital?" she asked. The man nodded. "I-I was just out for a little walk with my baby when I saw all the soldiers. My husband is with a colored troop."

"Is that right?" he asked, adjusting his glasses. "Which one?"

"The First South Carolina Volunteers—here in Beaufort."

"That's a slave regiment, isn't it? I'm with the Fifty-fourth Massachusetts. At least I was until I crossed paths with a bullet a few weeks ago. I'm hoping the surgeon will let me rejoin my unit, now that my arm is healing. We're stationed on Cole Island."

"How come you're talking like a white man?" Anna asked, surprised at her own boldness. She hoped she hadn't offended him. His quick smile reassured her.

"Probably because I've lived among white men all of my life. I was born a free man in Boston, Massachusetts—to free parents. I've read about slavery in books, but it's even more appalling than I'd imagined, now that I'm seeing it in person."

Anna hugged her sleeping son and felt a little thrill of hope. George could be just like this man someday, reading books and talking so fine, and wearing white men's spectacles. George would be raised a free man, too, with free parents.

"How'd you get hurt?" she asked the stranger.

His smile faded to deep sadness. "Our regiment led the assault on movie "Glory"

Fort Wagner a few weeks ago. Nearly half of us didn't make it back in one piece, including our colonel, Robert Gould Shaw. He was killed." He paused, and Anna saw him struggle with his emotions. "The Fifty-fourth Massachusetts demonstrated our race's bravery to the entire nation—but what a terrible price to pay."

"We're grateful to you," Anna said softly. "To all of you Yankees for coming down here and fighting for us—you helped set my baby and me free. I would gladly pay you back, if I knew how."

His friendly smile returned. "I can think of a way. It would really cheer up all the men if a lovely lady such as yourself were to pay them a visit while they're in the hospital. They'd enjoy seeing your baby, too. You would help them remember what their sacrifices were for."

"Me?" she asked. He nodded. "Okay. I-I'd be happy to do that."

The soldier offered Anna his arm, the way white gentlemen always offered their arms to the ladies they escorted. It took her a moment to respond to his surprising gesture, then she graciously accepted, allowing him to lead her across the street and through the graveyard into the church.

Anna's first reaction to the hospital was one of horror. She had seen casualties onboard the ship with Grady, but there were so many, many more here—men with gruesome wounds and without arms or legs. Her new friend seemed to understand her shock, and he introduced his fellow soldiers to her one at a time, slowly easing her into the converted sanctuary. Instead of seeing mangled bodies, Anna saw lonely, wounded men, far from their wives and families. She could offer them a drink of water, help them eat a few bites of food, let them stroke George's plump cheek as they talked about their own children. By the time Anna said good-bye, she already knew that she would come back tomorrow and the next day, helping in any way that she could.

It was only after she returned home that afternoon, that her towering fear began to build. Any one of those suffering men could be Grady. His regiment might be ordered to attack a Rebel fortress just like Fort Wagner. Grady could easily be wounded—or killed. She lay alone in bed that night, his place empty beside her, and she saw his face on every wounded body she'd seen today. The baby seemed to sense her distress, and he fussed and cried nearly all night long. As Anna walked the floor with him in the dark, wishing Delia were there to console her, she slowly realized what Delia would tell her if she were there: *"Pray, honey. Ask Jesus to help you."*

Anna had no idea how long a war like this one might last, how long Grady would be in such terrible danger. It seemed to her that the fighting had already been going on forever. But she knew that twice before Jesus had answered her prayers—and she needed to keep on praying until the war ended and Grady was safe.

"Do you know which church Delia used to go to here in Beaufort?" she asked Minnie the next morning.

Minnie pursed her lips in thought. "Don't know the name of it, but it wasn't the same one Massa belonged to. Delia's church was a couple blocks north of here, I think—on Charles Street."

Anna found it a few days later, after her daily visit to the hospital. She asked the old man who was sweeping the church steps what time they held Sunday services. She made up her mind to go there.

The following Sunday, when she and George crowded into the sanctuary with hundreds of other people, she was surprised to discover that it wasn't at all like Missy's church. This service seemed more like a celebration than a somber ceremony, with so much shouting and clapping and singing it was a wonder that George remained asleep through it all. And all the people sat mixed together, no matter what color skin they had.

But the most surprising moment came when the Mueller sisters, white missionaries from a church up north, stood up and sang a duet. Anna listened in amazement, slowly realizing why the beautiful tune brought tears to her eyes. It was the song that her papa used to sing to her. After all these years, she still recognized it. One of the verses spoke about a path through fiery trials, and she remembered how Papa had hummed the melody to calm her fears as he'd carried her in his arms through the swamp.

When the service ended, a knot of people gathered to talk with the two sisters. Anna waited to one side, determined to speak to them, as well. Finally, the older woman noticed Anna and separated herself from the group.

"Did you want to speak with one of us, dear?" she asked. "My name is Ada Mueller." Anna's heart raced in fear. What had ever possessed her to come forward to see a white woman? She was about to apologize for interrupting her, to turn and run from the building, when the woman rested her hand on Anna's shoulder. "It's okay. You don't have to be afraid," she said.

Anna glanced up. Ada's eyes were gray, like her dress, and very gentle. Anna quickly looked away again. "I'm sorry for bothering you, ma'am," she murmured. "I was just wondering if you could tell me the words to that song you sang—the ones about the path."

"Of course. The words are beautiful, aren't they? The hymn is called 'How Firm a Foundation.' I'll be glad to write them down for you, if you'd like."

Anna quickly shook her head. "That won't help, ma'am. I can't read."

"Would you like to learn how? My sister and I hold classes here every evening."

Anna was afraid to believe it. Slaves were forbidden to read or write. But free people could learn. "What about my baby? I-I can't leave George—"

"You don't have to leave him. You're very welcome to bring him with you. Several of the other women bring their children, too."

Miss Mueller reached out her hand and gently lifted Anna's chin until she was forced to face her. "Look at me, dear," she said softly. "We're all brothers and sisters in Christ in this place. And there isn't any hatred or discrimination when He's our Lord and Master. In His kingdom, we all have the same color skin."

27

BEAUFORT, SOUTH CAROLINA
JUNE 1864

"Catch him, Grady! Don't let him crawl away."

Grady swiveled around and reached for his son, grabbing George before he crawled off the edge of the blanket and into the dirt. "Hey, come back here!" he said, laughing. George giggled as Grady lifted him high in the air, then set him on the blanket again. The three of them sat together in front of Grady's tent on this warm spring day. Grady had been watching his wife, not their son, unable to take his eyes off her as she sewed the new corporal's insignia onto his uniform.

This would be the last time Grady saw her for a while. Tomorrow morning his regiment was leaving for Folly Island and the start of a new campaign to conquer Charleston and the remaining Rebel forts that guarded the city. He knew that the fight he was about to face would be fierce and dangerous. He hadn't told Anna just how dangerous.

"I'm sure gonna hate it when you're gone," Anna sighed. "It's been so nice having you close by all this time and being able to come and visit you."

"I know," Grady said. "Let's hope the war ends soon, so I can come home for good."

They had been able to see each other quite frequently over the winter months, especially after Grady's regiment had moved to a new winter camp further north on Port Royal Island, closer to Beaufort. The men had named it Camp Shaw, in honor of the white colonel who had died along with so many of his Negro troops at Fort Wagner. In late December Grady's regiment had been assigned to share provost duty in Beaufort with a white regiment. Anna had strolled over from the town house whenever he was on duty and watched him and his fellow soldiers as they proudly policed the streets and kept the peace.

The new camp was built on a rise overlooking the river. Grady and his family had often sat together during his free time, inhaling the scent of pine from the trees that fringed the camp and watching ships glide past on the silvery river. On Sundays, Anna sometimes came to the new "praise house" the men had built for school and prayer meetings, made of poles and brush and the delicate gray moss that hung from all the live-oak trees. The regiment had held regular inspection and drills in camp that winter, and little George loved to come and watch with Anna, reveling in the excitement of rolling drums and shouted commands. Grady would glimpse him on the sidelines, holding Anna's hands as he stood on his wobbly legs, his dark eyes dancing with delight. Grady swallowed, realizing just how much he would miss both of them.

"Don't forget," he reminded her, "if you're wanting news about us, we're not called the First South Carolina Volunteers anymore. They changed it to the Thirty-third U.S. Colored Troops—even though we really were the first colored troops."

"The thirty-third," she repeated.

"Right. And our commander is Lieutenant Colonel Trowbridge from now on."

She stopped sewing. "How is Colonel Higginson? I thought he was only going to be on sick leave for a month?"

"He was. But now Captain Metcalf tells me that the colonel is still too weak to come back." Grady felt a new wave of sorrow for the white man who had been injured on their mission up the Edisto River—the mission that had saved Anna's life. But as dangerous as that expedition had been, Grady knew that the campaign he would begin tomorrow would be real warfare, with thousands of troops engaging in battle and bloody assaults against heavily fortified batteries and fortresses. He hoped that Anna would never learn the truth of what his regiment was about to face.

"I'll keep on praying for Colonel Higginson," Anna promised.

"Good. I heard that they're naming one of the slave settlements near here Higginsonville, in his honor," Grady said. "A lot of people are owing their freedom to him."

He reached to grab his son a second time, prying a rock from his chubby fingers moments before he would have thrust it into his mouth. The boy howled.

"You almost done with that sewing?" Grady asked above the noise. "I have something for you, but I don't dare let go of this rascal."

"Yes. I'm done." She bit off the thread and held up the uniform jacket for him to see. "I'm so proud of you, Grady. A corporal!"

"I hope to be making sergeant before I'm through," he said. "Here, let's trade." He took the jacket from her and tipped George into her arms. She was so much better at controlling their squirming son than he was. He shoved his arms into the coat sleeves as he ducked inside the tent to retrieve her present. "Close your eyes," he called before emerging again. He peered out to see if she had obeyed him, then laid the package of drawing paper he'd bought for her on the blanket, out of the baby's reach.

"Oh, Grady!" she breathed when she opened her eyes. "Where did you get this? How . . . ?"

"I had to send away for it, since none of the stores in Beaufort had any. And here's a gum eraser and some new drawing pencils, too." He had used the money he'd earned playing fiddle for the officers, but it was worth every penny to see Anna's surprise and delight. "I'm expecting to see lots of pictures when I come back," he added.

She let go of George for a moment and wrapped her arms around Grady's neck, hugging him tightly. "Thank you, thank you!" she said. "I wish I'd had this paper a week ago. I have a present for you, too, but it would of been nicer on this paper."

She reached into her bag and pulled out an old book. Carefully tucked inside was her present to him—a drawing of George. Anna had captured perfectly the sweet curve of his plump mouth, his dimpled cheek. Grady felt a shiver of awe at his wife's talent. But what on earth had she drawn it on? He turned it over to look at the back and saw an old receipt for a sack of horse feed.

"Hey! You ain't supposed to be looking at the back," she said, gently slapping his hand.

"What is this?" He smiled, amused by her resourcefulness.

"I found an old pile of papers in Massa's desk for things he was buying long before the war started. I picked two or three that I didn't think he'd be needing anymore."

Anna could read nearly as well as Grady could now, and he was proud of her. Then he realized what she'd said and grinned wider. "There's more than one?"

"Yes. This is your other present." She pulled another receipt from the book and Grady saw her neat, careful printing on the other side instead of a drawing. "Those are the words to my papa's song," she told him. "I copied them from Miss Helen's hymnbook. I want you to keep them and read them while you're away."

Grady felt his throat constrict as he silently read the words:

> When through fiery trials thy pathway shall lie,
> My grace, all sufficient, shall be thy supply;
> The flame shall not hurt thee; I only design
> Thy dross to consume and thy gold to refine.

He couldn't speak. He pulled Joe's well-worn Bible out of his pocket and carefully tucked her two gifts inside it.

"I'll be praying for you every day," she told him, biting her lip. She was trying to be brave, but he knew that she was thinking about all the wounded men she'd helped at the hospital. He knew how afraid she was for him.

"They're wonderful presents, Anna," he said when he could speak. "I couldn't ask for a better gift . . . unless it was a picture of you."

She smiled shyly. "I thought you might say that." She pulled out a third yellowing receipt. "This one's for a bolt of cloth for Missy's dress," she said. "Turn it over."

She had drawn a sketch of herself on the other side. "I had to go in Missy's room and use the mirror on her dresser in order to draw it." When he remained silent, she asked, "Is it okay?"

"You're so beautiful, Anna," he murmured, looking at her, not the portrait.

She reached to embrace him again. "Come back to us, Grady," she whispered. "George needs his daddy and I . . . well, I wouldn't want to keep on living without you."

⁂

BEAUFORT, SOUTH CAROLINA
FEBRUARY 1865

Anna closed the newspaper. Sometimes she wished she hadn't learned to read when the words described such terrible suffering. This news was old—the newspapers she was using to practice her skills were always months old by the time the Mueller sisters got them from their church up north. The horrible events the papers described were already over and done with, but they were no less shocking.

The Union general William T. Sherman had marched through the state of Georgia with some sixty thousand men—a number too big for Anna to comprehend. They had pillaged the land like a plague of locusts, from Atlanta all the way to Savannah, Georgia, devouring every scrap of food and leaving a trail of destruction some sixty miles wide in their wake. General Sherman's goal had been to make life so difficult for Georgia's women and children and old people that the Rebels would have to surrender. Thousands of white families were now homeless and starving. The tens of thousands of slaves who had trailed behind the army were free—but they had no place to live and nothing to eat, either. Not a scrap of food remained in the devastated countryside.

General Sherman had reached Savannah by Christmas, a few months ago. Now he and his men had invaded South Carolina, hell-bent on vengeance in the state that had given birth to the rebellion. Anna shuddered at their ruthlessness. On their way to burn the capitol of Columbia, Sherman's soldiers had destroyed every one of South Carolina's farms and plantations that lay in their path, slaughtering more farm animals than they could possibly eat, simply to keep the citizens from using them. How would all those starving women and children live?

Anna glanced down at George playing beside her on the school-room floor, and she whispered a prayer for little Richard Fuller. That poor baby. The war he was suffering through wasn't his fault. He had done nothing to deserve going hungry or being homeless. She wondered about Delia, as well. There never had been food to spare down on Slave Row, but with Sherman's army plundering the land, Delia would starve for certain. Anna said a prayer for her, then another one for Massa Fuller. He'd lost his oldest son and had been badly wounded himself. She wondered if he would survive this war—and if he would have a home to return to, if he did.

Finally, after much wrestling, Anna was able to say a prayer for Missy Claire. The Mueller sisters had taught her that if she wanted the Lord to hear her prayers for Grady, she had to forgive other people the way Jesus had forgiven her. And Anna was desperate for the Lord to spare Grady, terrified that he would be killed. She dreaded the day that she would look down at one of the stretchers at the army hospital and see him. She had watched so many soldiers die already.

"Lord, please be with Missy Claire today," she prayed. "She always

430

needed a lot of help, and . . . well . . . I know you can give her what she's needing most."

Anna looked up when she finished her prayer and saw that Ada Mueller had finished talking to the two women who had just joined her class. Anna had been waiting to give her present to the two sisters until all of the other students had gone.

"Miss Ada?" she said. "I have something for you. I drew a picture to say thank you for all that you and Miss Helen have been teaching me." She carefully removed the drawing from the large book that she carried it in to protect it, and handed it to Miss Ada. The sketch showed the classroom where the sisters taught every evening, and two freed slaves in homespun with kerchiefs on their heads, watching Miss Helen expectantly. Miss Ada was bending over a little Negro girl, helping her learn to write.

Miss Ada's face went very still. She didn't seem able to speak. She looked as though she might cry, and Anna wondered what she had done wrong.

"This is magnificent," Ada finally said. "You—you drew this?"

"Yes, ma'am."

"My goodness," she breathed. "My goodness! Have you drawn many more pictures like this one?"

"Well, yes. My husband bought me some paper last spring, and I been drawing just about everything I see ever since. I have some more of the school, and all the ladies and children in your class, if you're wanting to trade that picture for a different one."

"Oh no, dear. No, I wouldn't trade this for a million dollars. It's so . . . so poignant, so moving. . . ." She gazed from the picture to Anna and back again. "My brother publishes a newspaper in Philadelphia. Would you ever consider selling some of these to him, to print in his paper?"

Now it was Anna's turn to be speechless. She couldn't possibly believe what Miss Ada was saying—someone would pay money for her pictures? And print them in a newspaper? But she also knew that Miss Ada would never tell a lie.

"W-why would he pay me to draw?" Anna asked shaking her head.

"If your other work is anything like this, you've offered a truer picture of what life is like down here for a freed slave than any photograph ever could. You've shown their poverty, the difficulties they face as they struggle for an education. Yet you've captured hope in these people's faces—and beauty and joy. Anna, dear, this is a work of art."

Anna wasn't sure what that meant, but tears filled her eyes at the thought of earning money, of being able to help Grady and George get along. For the first time since Grady had snatched her out of the slave jail at Great Oak, Anna felt truly free. People who were free received payment for the work they did.

"Yes, Miss Ada," she said. "I'll be happy to sell your brother all the pictures he wants."

❋

CHARLESTON, SOUTH CAROLINA
FEBRUARY 1865

"The rumors are true," Captain Metcalf told Grady and the others. "The Confederates have abandoned Fort Sumter. The mayor of Charleston has surrendered the city." The cheers that followed his announcement were so deafening that Grady was certain they could be heard all the way across the harbor in the city that they'd besieged all these months.

A few hours later, boats arrived to ferry the regiment ashore. Grady saw smoke billowing into the sky from fires set by the Rebels as they'd hurried north to engage Sherman's army. It seemed unbelievable to Grady to be setting foot in Charleston after occupying the sandy, coastal islands across the harbor since last June. He had taken part in the Battle of Honey Hill and in the capture of Fort Gregg. Wounded men from his regiment had been sent back to the hospitals in Beaufort, and Grady had worried that Anna would see them, would recognize that they were his comrades, and would be overwhelmed with fear for him. He'd had a few close calls from enemy artillery shells, but thankfully, he'd remained safe.

Now Grady just wanted it all to end. He was tired of seeking revenge, tired of fighting. He wanted the war to be over so he could live out his life with Anna.

It was an odd feeling to walk the once-familiar streets of Charleston as a victor, to see white people scurry into their homes in fear and draw their curtains closed as he marched past. The last time he'd walked through Charleston, he'd been another man's property, fit only to drive a carriage. Now he wielded the power of a conqueror over these people. But somehow the victory felt hollow as he viewed the ravaged city.

Hundreds of buildings had been destroyed, some by fire, others by Union artillery shells. Still others crumbled dangerously, about to topple. Nothing remained of the church where Massa Fuller had been married except a burned husk. Starving people—black and white— begged for food. But it was the sight of so many homeless, drifting slaves that moved Grady the most—sheep without a shepherd.

His first task was to help fight the fires that had raged for a day and a half. The blistering heat and choking smoke made that battle nearly as dangerous as warfare. When the inferno was finally under control, Grady's regiment was assigned to picket duty around the city's undamaged buildings to halt the looting. It seemed ironic to him that he and other former slaves now worked to save the property of a people who hated them. And his Negro troops were clearly hated. They faced jeers and brickbats and spitting wherever they went. Snipers took potshots at them from among the ruins. Grady confided his resentment and simmering hatred to Captain Metcalf one evening.

"It's only a few misguided individuals," the captain assured him. "Remember, Grady, not every person in Charleston hates Negroes. Don't let the actions of a few speak for all Charlestonians."

Grady recalled Colonel Higginson's warning that the end of the war might not bring an end to the battles that Negroes would face. "But how do I fight those few?" he asked. "How can I be helping my people get the respect we deserve as human beings?"

Metcalf sighed. "It's not up to you to fight every battle for your people. You weren't at Gettysburg or Fort Wagner, were you? You didn't fight at Petersburg or Shiloh—only where you were sent. Your war will be won over time, Grady, by every soldier doing his part, right where he is. We can only do what we're asked to do today."

The following morning thousands of Charleston's slaves poured into the streets as Grady's regiment marched past. Throngs of ragged, cheering children skipped alongside them. Women lifted small babies, like George, high in the air so they could see their deliverers. Grown men stretched out their hands to them, wanting to touch them, thank them. Grady saw tears on every face, arms raised to heaven in praise, and it was hard for him and the other soldiers not to be overwhelmed with emotion, hard to keep marching.

Then someone in Grady's regiment began to sing. Grady recognized the song from his years as a slave. It was one that he and the others had sung as they'd trudged to work in the fields every day:

> My army cross over; O, Pharaoh's army drowned!
> My army cross over, we cross the river Jordan . . .

Grady immediately joined in, and soon everyone was singing—men and women, soldiers and slaves, their voices raised in a joyful song of victory for all that they had won, for how far they had finally come:

> We'll cross the danger water, my army cross over
> We'll cross the mighty river; O, Pharaoh's army drowned!

❧

BEAUFORT, SOUTH CAROLINA
APRIL 1865

It seemed to Anna that she had waited breathlessly, for days, for the latest news. First Richmond had fallen to the Yankees. Then Gen-

434

eral Grant had Lee and his men on the run outside of Petersburg. Rumors said that the Confederates were badly outnumbered, weary, starving. Thousands of Lee's men had already deserted. At Anna's school, at the hospital, on the town's street corners, everyone waited for the good news of a final surrender.

And then one sunny spring morning, the church bells in Beaufort began to ring. Shouts of joy filled the streets. Jim rushed into the warming kitchen to tell Anna and Minnie that General Lee had truly surrendered. The war was over. Soon they would all live in peace. Anna hugged her two friends and wept for joy.

"Mama?" little George whimpered. He was watching her, clinging fearfully to her skirts as if unable to understand her tears or the noisy celebration in Beaufort's streets. She lifted him into her arms and kissed him.

"It's okay, honey. Mama's happy, not sad. Pretty soon your daddy's coming home."

For Anna, her own long, dark night was finally over. Grady had survived the war. Her little family was free. A dreadful thought had long resided in the back of her mind, that if the South somehow won, or if the North grew tired of all the fighting and bloodshed and called a truce, that she and Grady and George would be returned to slavery again. But the Union was clearly victorious. No one could ever take away her freedom.

"Let's go celebrate with Miss Ada and Miss Helen," she told her son. The sisters had taught her that free people—even white people—served the Lord Jesus as their Massa. Anna knew that the little church would soon be ringing with songs of praise for Jesus, their true Deliverer. And she wanted to join them.

GREAT OAK PLANTATION, SOUTH CAROLINA
JUNE 1865

The war was over. Delia was free. She had watched her fellow slaves walk away from Slave Row with their belongings bundled inside their tattered quilts—and nobody stopped them. Some of the slaves lugged the plantation's dugout canoes to the river and paddled off downstream. Others followed the long, sweeping driveway past the Big House and disappeared down the road. Delia wondered what they would do with their freedom. They'd been so overjoyed when they'd heard the news, dancing and celebrating for an entire day and night. But how would they live tomorrow and the next day?

Delia had watched them pack up and say good-bye, and she'd felt a mixture of sorrow and joy. "You're welcome to come along with us," several people had offered. "You know we'll be taking good care of you." But Delia was much too worn out to go anywhere. She spent the rest of that spring in the same shabby cabin where she'd lived for the past year and a half, scratching around for food in the meager gardens that the other slaves had left behind.

She knew that the war was really over when Massa Fuller arrived at Great Oak Plantation one warm June afternoon. Delia watched him trudge up the driveway, slump-shouldered and weary, the uniform he'd worn at his wedding five years ago a tattered pile of rags. She beamed with happiness when she saw him, this white man she had suckled along with her own daughter and reared into manhood. Massa Roger was safe.

"Thank you, Lord," she murmured. "Thank you for watching over him."

Yes, the war was over and Delia was tired—bone-weary tired. Life here in South Carolina had been very hard this past year, the white folks suffering just as much as the colored folks. There hadn't been much food for any of them to eat, with the soldiers from both sides taking all of their chickens and pigs, and plucking the crops right out of the garden as fast as they could grow them. She'd heard stories about all the plantations that had burned, and she thanked the Good Lord that Great Oak didn't lie in the Yankees' path. She wondered how her home—Massa Roger's place—had fared. Whenever she thought of "home," Delia always pictured the Fuller Plantation.

That evening, Delia walked up to the Big House and asked to speak with Massa Roger. He came to the door in his shirtsleeves, his face gaunt and sallow, his injured arm shriveled and crippled-looking. But he smiled with surprise and pleasure when he saw her.

"Delia—you're still here? You're free now, you know. You don't have to stay around here any more."

"I know. But I want to ask you something, Massa Roger. I want to know if you'll take me back home to your plantation, when you go. It's where I was born and raised, and I been living there most of my life."

"Is your family still there?"

Delia shook her head. "I don't have no family, Massa Roger. They all dead and gone. But I'd sure like to live out my days there, if that's okay with you. I'm willing to work for my keep."

"Of course." He smiled sadly and Delia wondered if the sorrow he felt was for her or for himself—or for both of them. He had once loved her freely and unashamedly as a child. She remembered the warmth of his little arms around her neck as he'd hugged her and called her Mammy Delia.

"I'm taking Claire and Richard back home at the end of the week," he told her. "You may certainly come with us."

By the time Delia reached home at last, the suffering and senseless destruction she'd witnessed along the way had left her deeply depressed. All those plantation houses—beautiful, graceful homes—burned to the ground. All those ruined fields and barns. Such a waste. Every tired breath she'd drawn had reeked of smoke. But what brought her the most sorrow were the people—not only the hundreds of slaves wandering hungry and homeless, but the white refugees, as well. Women and children like Missy Claire and little Richard. Confederate soldiers like Massa Roger, making their weary way back to homes that no longer existed. So much sorrow. So much hatred in this world.

But Delia thanked the Good Lord when she saw that the little cabin she'd shared with Grady and Anna was still standing. Tears filled her eyes as she walked through the empty rooms, wondering how Grady and Anna were, and what had become of them now that the war was over. She longed to see her Grady again, but she doubted that she ever would. The same was true of her daughter up north. Delia often wondered if she even remembered her real mother anymore, or if she lived such a happy life of freedom that her five years of slavery had been long forgotten.

Delia tidied up and made her bed and swept away some of the dust. Then she sat outside on the doorstep, so tuckered out that she felt winded. A verse of scripture that Shep had once taught her floated through her mind: *"Come unto me, all ye that labor and are heavy laden, and I will give you rest."* Yes, Delia was ready for a good, long rest.

She stared down the deserted road, remembering a time when she had been young and pretty and full of strength, a time when the road brought a steady stream of visitors to the Fuller Plantation. But whenever she'd heard the merry jingle of carriage bells, her heart had leaped and danced. It meant that Shep was here! Delia smiled, remembering how his owner, Miss Carrie, had demanded bells on her carriage so that everyone would know when she arrived from Savannah. Those bells had made such a happy, joyful sound. Delia would race to the window whenever she heard them—and there Shep would be, sitting tall and proud on the driver's seat, his face stretched wide in a handsome grin.

Shep would have to finish all his work before he could see Delia, wiping the dust off the carriage and greasing the wheels, feeding and tending the horses. And she would have to finish her work in the Big House, as well, polishing the furniture and serving the meals. But when evening fell, Delia's husband would come to her in their tiny cabin, and he would hold her in his arms and kiss away her tears. And all the long months that they had spent apart would seem like a fading dream.

"How long can you stay?" Delia would always ask.

Shep would smile his wide, loose grin and say, "I can stay until the Good Lord needs me someplace else."

Now, as Delia sat on the weathered step, she realized that Shep was the real reason she had returned home to this cabin. Not only was it filled with warm memories of him and the love they'd shared, but it was also the only place in the whole world where Shep knew where to find her. If he was still alive after all these years and the upheaval of war, if he could somehow find a way to return to her, then this is where he would come.

The summer night was sultry, the midges annoying. Delia had eaten very little all day, but she was too tired to get up and fix dinner. She sat on the steps and watched the fireflies winking in the bushes, the stars pricking through the covering of night, one by one. She felt an ache in her shoulder, a weight on her chest and knew that grief and longing and sadness had caused them. She leaned against the doorframe and closed her eyes, waiting for the pain to subside.

Then Delia heard them—the jingling carriage bells—faintly at first, then growing louder, clearer.

She opened her eyes and it was morning. She was surprised at how light it was. Sunshine filled the yard, and she wondered how she could have slept on the cabin doorstep all night. The sound of jingling bells grew closer, a happy sound that lifted Delia's heart to the skies. The approaching carriage rolled down the long driveway and drew to a halt.

Shep stepped down.

But for once he didn't take care of Miss Carrie's horses first. Instead, he hurried toward Delia's cabin, smiling broadly. Delia thought it must be the tears that blurred her vision, but he didn't look a day older to her than when he'd driven away so many years ago. She slowly rose to her feet, afraid to wipe her eyes, afraid to blink for fear he would disappear.

"Shep!" she whispered. "Oh, Shep!"

He stretched out his strong hand to her and she felt the calluses on his palm from holding the reins.

"Delia, honey, we're free," he said. "I've come to take you home."

<hr />

BEAUFORT, SOUTH CAROLINA
SEPTEMBER 1865

"Kitty!"

Anna dropped the book she was reading and looked up. Missy Claire glared at her from the drawing room doorway, holding her son, Richard, by the hand. "What are you doing in my house?" Missy demanded.

Anna's heart leaped to her throat. She had heard the back door open and close, heard footsteps approaching down the hall, but she had assumed it was Grady. Her first instinct was to scramble to her feet and apologize to Missy for sitting on her sofa, for reading her book, for living in her house. But George was asleep with his head on her lap. Besides, Anna was a free woman now. She remained seated, calmly stroking George's wooly hair, fighting the impulse to stand.

"We been living here for a while now, Missy Claire. And we've been taking real good care of your house for you."

"You have some nerve," she said, "sitting there as if you owned the place. And that's my dress you're wearing!"

"Yes, ma'am. I made it over to fit me, seeing as my dress was all worn out."

"Get out!" she yelled, pointing toward the back door.

Anna had long been afraid that this day would come. Ever since the war had ended last April, she'd wondered how much longer she and George would be allowed to live here. Grady had only returned home from the war two days ago. They'd been so overjoyed just to be together again, and so in love with each other, that they hadn't had time to talk about what they would do next or where they would live if Massa Fuller wanted his house back.

Anna set the book on the table beside her and slowly rose to her feet. George felt heavy and warm and cuddly as she lifted him in her arms. The surprise and panic she felt had passed, and Anna faced her mistress with her chin held high. "I think you'll see how nice Minnie and Jim and me have been keeping your house for you, Missy Claire. There ain't nothing ruined or missing either, except some food that was in the pantry . . . and this dress."

"Get out this minute!" Missy said, stepping into the room. Anna looked down at three-and-a-half year-old Richard. She had cared for him like her own child, walking the floor with him, bathing him, loving him. But he glared up at her with the same resentful stare that his mother wore. Anna rubbed George's sweaty back, promising herself that she would never teach him to hate.

"I learned how to read and write," Anna said without knowing why. "I'm a teacher myself, now."

Missy gave a short, humorless laugh. "The blind leading the blind. No doubt you're teaching people who are just as stupid and ignorant as you are."

Anna smiled sadly. "I don't know why you hate me, Missy Claire, but I don't hate you. I'm not your slave anymore, but if you need any help getting settled, I'll do what I can for you."

"Are you going to get out of my house, Kitty, or should I call my husband and have him throw you out?"

"It's gonna take me a few minutes to gather all our things together, but I'll go. And my name ain't Kitty, ma'am. It's Anna."

❦

When Grady returned from his errand downtown, there was a wagon parked near the carriage house. He hurried up the driveway, wondering who it could be, and found himself face to face with Roger Fuller. His old massa gave a start of surprise, but the worried look quickly left Massa's face.

"Oh, Grady! It's you. I saw the uniform, and for a moment I . . . What are you doing here?"

Grady suddenly felt like the trespasser that he was. "My wife has been staying here with Minnie and Jim," he said slowly, "taking care of the place for you. I was mustered out of the army last week. I just got here myself a few days ago."

"I see."

Grady could tell that Fuller was just as uncomfortable as he was. Neither of them seemed to know what to say. He gave his former master a quick appraisal and saw how much the war had aged him. His skin looked brittle and yellowed, like the old receipts Anna had used to draw her portraits. Fuller's arm, which had been severely wounded the last time Grady had seen him, hung from his shoulder, gaunt and awkward, as if it hadn't healed properly.

"Yes, my arm is still a bit troublesome," Fuller said, following Grady's gaze. "I have difficulty holding on to things with this hand. Makes it hard to drive a team of horses."

"I see you got yourself some new ones," Grady said. He walked over to survey the team, running his hand along the first one's flank.

"Nothing like the horses I used to have, are they?" Fuller said a little sadly.

"You ever get them back again?" Grady asked, remembering Blaze.

"No, I'm afraid not."

Grady tried to act casual, but his unease was slowly turning into panic. Massa Roger had returned home to Beaufort, and now Grady would have to find someplace else for his family to live. He had no idea where that might be.

"You planning on living here in Beaufort for a while?" he asked.

Fuller sighed. "The government claims that I owe four years' worth of taxes on this house. Since I can't pay them, the place will have to be sold at auction."

"But you're a rich man, Massa Fuller."

"Not anymore. I invested everything in Confederate bonds to support the war effort. They're worthless now, of course. Claire and I came to pack up some of my family's things, then we're moving back to the plantation. If I sell some of my land and a few other valuables, I should be able to keep the plantation in the family for my sons."

Grady had no idea why Fuller was confiding in him, but he found himself pitying his master. Grady had never had anything, and so he had nothing to lose. How much worse it would be to have had everything in the world—and to have lost it.

"If you need help loading your wagon, I can help you," Grady said. The look Fuller gave him was so stripped of pride, so naked and vulnerable, that Grady was immediately sorry he had made the offer.

"Thank you, Grady. But I can't pay you."

Grady swallowed his own pride in return. "I have no place to live, Massa Fuller. If you let me and my family stay in the room above your stable, we'll call it even."

Fuller nodded, staring at the ground. Then Grady remembered Delia, and his pulse raced. "Massa Fuller? Do you know where I can find Delia? Last time I saw her she was at Great Oak with Missus Fuller. She's always been like a mother to me, and I'd like to find her and take care of her if I can."

"She was at Great Oak," Fuller said, "but she asked to come home with me to live on my plantation again. She said she wanted to live out her days here."

Joy and relief flooded through Grady. "I'll be glad to drive your wagon for you when you're ready to go back. Anna and I want Delia to live with us."

Fuller looked away, staring into the distance. "Grady, I'm sorry. Delia passed away."

Grady closed his eyes. He didn't care if Fuller or anyone else saw the tears that rolled slowly down his cheeks.

❧

Grady sat on the lumpy bed with his face in his hands, the cornstalks crunching beneath his weight. "Anna, I'm sorry. I didn't want you to ever have to live like this—"

"It ain't your fault," she said. "Every slave in South Carolina's in the same mess we're in. At least we have each other. Some folks probably never will find their husbands and wives and children."

He lifted his head to look at her. She was so beautiful that he forgot to breathe sometimes when he gazed at her. And so strong. She'd become a strong, courageous woman while he'd been gone. He took her hands in his and pulled her down on the bed beside him. "I love you," he said.

"I know. And it ain't the end of the world if we have to live above the stable for a while."

He felt the seed of panic begin to grow and send out shoots again. "We might only be able to stay here for a night or two. Massa Fuller has to sell the house. I been hoping we'd have more time to figure out what we're gonna do, but—"

"You've only been home two days," she said, caressing his face. "And we've both been wanting to spend every minute in each other's arms."

Grady leaned forward to kiss her, but she shook her head, smiling playfully. "First we're gonna make some plans. If you could have any job in the whole world, Grady, what would you like to do?"

"I been thinking about that, all the while I been away at war," he said, "but I don't know how I can ever make it happen: I'd like to have my own stable and some horses. I'd like to start a livery business."

"Then let's do it, Grady. We might have to work for other people at first, but if we save all our money, then maybe we'll be able to buy that stable, someday."

He looked into her dark eyes and believed that anything was possible. He leaned forward to kiss her, but she stopped him again.

"Not yet," she said, smiling. "I been thinking, too, and remembering how much you were always wanting to go back home to Richmond."

"Anna, I don't have any money for that."

"I know. But I do. I been saving this for a surprise." She stood and rummaged through the little bundle of possessions that she'd carried over from Massa's town house. "Hold out your hands," she ordered.

Grady's jaw dropped when she poured a small pile of silver dollars into his cupped hands. "What . . . ? Where did you get this?"

"Miss Ada at the mission helped me sell some drawings to a newspaper up north. I been saving this money for your boat fare. It probably ain't enough for all of us, but I want you to go, Grady."

"I can't be taking your money. We'll need this to live on."

"It's *our* money. We're husband and wife. You been telling me to think like a free woman, and you been saying that free women get paid for the work they do—well, that's my pay. And a free wife can help her husband go to Richmond, if she wants to."

"But what will you do while I'm gone?"

"I been thinking about that while I been packing. Miss Ada and Miss Helen already offered me a place to stay at the mission. They want me to keep on teaching. We'll be okay, Grady. Honest we will."

He stood and pulled her into his arms, holding her tightly, unwilling to let her go. It would be hard to be apart again, but they'd weathered much longer separations before. "I know," he said. "From now on we'll all be okay."

She pulled him down on the bed again and said, "Now, I want you to tell me about all the people you'll see up in Richmond, starting with your mama. I'm gonna draw pictures of George for all of them, so they'll know what he looks like."

"Let's see, there's Mama . . . and Eli . . . and Esther . . ." he said, kissing her between each name. "And I have some unfinished business with Massa Fletcher."

"What?" she said, pushing him away. "What kind of business?"

He hesitated, afraid to tell her. Her look of surprise changed to one of understanding—then horror.

"Oh, Grady, no. I thought you were all done with hating people. I thought you were wanting to see your mother and Eli—"

"I am. But I have to see Massa Fletcher, too. I been waiting all these years to face him."

"But why? What difference will it make after all this time?" When he didn't reply she began to cry. "You're still wanting revenge, aren't you? You're gonna kill him! Don't try and deny it, Grady. I can see all the hatred that's still in your heart for that man, and it scares me. Please don't do it, Grady. Please, just forget about him."

"He deserves to die!" Grady heard the deadly chill in his own voice.

"And what about us?" she asked, swiping at her tears. "When they arrest you and hang you for murdering him, what's gonna happen to George and me?"

"I didn't get caught when I killed Coop."

She closed her eyes. "Please don't do it, Grady."

"Do you want your money back?" he asked, holding it out to her. "Are you changing your mind about giving it to me?"

"No. I want *you* back—the free Grady who isn't storing up a big load of bitterness in his heart anymore."

Grady understood why she was upset, but he was no less determined. "I have to see him, Anna. I don't think I'll ever be right with myself until I do."

She gazed at him for a long moment, love and sorrow shining in her dark eyes. She turned away from him again. "Then go," she said softly.

"I'll come back to you, Anna. I promise."

❦

RICHMOND, VIRGINIA

Anxiety gripped Grady as he stood in the bow of the ship and gazed at the charred wreckage of Richmond. He barely recognized the city that had once been his home. All that remained of the bridges that had once spanned the James River were stone pilings. Block after block of buildings in Richmond's downtown area had all been destroyed, reduced to skeletons of toppling bricks with vacant, empty window frames. Piles of rubble lay everywhere, from the river's edge to the hill where the soot-covered capitol building still stood. And everywhere that Grady looked, he saw white women clothed in black and the now-familiar sight of ragged, homeless slaves. As they sifted through the debris, they wore the haunted, frightened expressions of castaways adrift on a rudderless ship.

Clearly, Richmond's inhabitants had suffered greatly. The scars that the burned and broken city bore were proof enough. Grady could only imagine what his mother and other loved ones must have suffered. The thought filled him with dread.

He began the long, circuitous walk through the rubble-clogged streets with deep foreboding, the stench of burning still thick in the air, even after all these months. But his panic began to ease as he turned onto Broad Street and hurried up the hill. The area of Richmond where he had once lived looked unkempt but relatively undamaged. He passed St. John's church and turned down the familiar street where Eli had always turned. Massa Fletcher's house still stood on the corner at the end of the block.

Grady paused and drew a deep breath when he saw it. Then he quickened his pace, jogging around to the rear where his family lived. The wrought-iron gate stood open, and he hurried through it and into the stable.

And there was Eli.

Grady's eyes filled with tears at the sight of him. Eli didn't hear him or see him, and Grady stood watching for a long moment as Eli adjusted the bridle on one of the horses. His every gesture was so familiar, so beloved, that it seemed as though Grady had left only yesterday. But Eli's movements were slower and stiffer now, and his hair and beard pure white. He had once seemed so tall and powerful, but now Grady was taller than Eli was.

When he could speak, Grady called out his name. "Eli . . ."

He turned, and recognition lit Eli's eyes the moment he saw him. "Praise God," he murmured as he walked toward him. "Praise Massa Jesus; He brought our Grady home."

They hugged each other fiercely, clinging to one another for a long, long time. At last, Eli pulled back to face him. "You still hiding God's Word in your heart?" he asked.

Grady remembered Joe's warning not to let the devil tell him that he wasn't forgiven. He smiled and tapped his chest. "It's in there, Eli. God's Word is still hiding in there, just like you taught me."

"Praise God . . . thank you, Massa Jesus," Eli said as he embraced him again.

Grady drew a deep breath, afraid to hope. "Is my mama here? Is she okay?"

"Tessie's doing just fine," Eli said with a broad grin. "She's married to my son, Josiah, now, and they're living in a little house of their own not too far from here. I'll take you there. But we better go see Esther first, or she'll have my hide for sure."

Eli led the way down the path from the stable to the kitchen. The yard where Grady used to play with Caroline looked different, the boxwood hedges and flower gardens plowed up and replaced by a vegetable patch. The magnolia tree in the rear of the yard was still there, but it seemed not to have grown in the twelve years Grady had been gone—or was it because he had grown taller himself?

"Esther, look who's here!" Eli called, pushing open the kitchen door. "Grady's home!"

"Grady? *Our* Grady?" she cried. "Oh, bless the Good Lord in heaven!" Esther flew at him, hugging him so tightly that Grady thought his spine would snap. It felt wonderful. "Look at you!" she murmured. "All growed up into a man. A fine, handsome man, too!"

"Don't break all his bones, Esther," Eli warned. "Tessie's gonna want a piece of him, too. I'm gonna take him right on over there to see her as soon as you're letting go of him."

Grady longed to see his mother, but he needed to go to the Big House first. As he steeled himself to confront Massa Fletcher, Grady felt every muscle and nerve ending grow tense and alert, the way he used to feel as he'd marched toward an enemy encampment, his rifle loaded and ready.

"Before we go, Eli . . . is . . . um . . . is Massa Fletcher around?"

Eli studied him for a long moment, as if trying to read his thoughts. He nodded slowly. "Yeah, he's here. Been gone to the islands for a couple of months, but he's back home now."

"I need to see him." Grady turned and walked quickly toward the house before he could lose his nerve or change his mind. He'd never been inside the Big House before, but he walked through the back door without knocking, as if he belonged there. He peered into several small, deserted rooms off the rear hallway, then followed the aroma of cigar smoke to the front foyer and to an office near the door.

George Fletcher sat behind his desk, reading a newspaper. He looked thinner and older, more gray-haired than Grady remembered. When Fletcher looked up and saw Grady in the doorway, he dropped the paper and rose to his feet.

"Who are you? What are you doing in my house?" His voice was stern, commanding, but Grady didn't flinch. He had learned how to look a man in the eye—even a white man.

"I'm Tessie's boy, Grady. . . . Your son."

Fletcher slowly sank down in his chair as if the strength had drained out of him. Grady continued to stare defiantly, face to face, refusing to lower his eyes. The embers of twelve years of simmering anger and hatred stirred to a roaring blaze at the sight of the man who had caused him so much suffering. He waited for Fletcher to speak first.

"So. You've come back."

Grady nodded. "I've been in the Union Army for the past three years, the Thirty-third United States Colored Troops. They promoted me to sergeant." He walked into the room and stood in front of his father. He was just a man, a defeated man, in spite of his attempts to act stern. "I helped kill Rebels like you and bring an end to your precious Confederacy," Grady said. "And I helped Abraham Lincoln set all your slaves free."

Fletcher's hand trembled as he laid his cigar in the ashtray. "What do you want?"

"Justice," Grady said quietly. "And I want to know why you sold your own son to a slave trader."

Fletcher looked away for the first time. Grady was surprised to see his jaw tremble with emotion. "I didn't want to do it," Fletcher said hoarsely. "My wife—Caroline's mother—was very ill. She knew that you were . . . She knew who you were, and it upset her to see you every day. She wasn't able to give me a son. I thought it might help her get well if I . . ." His voice trailed away. He cleared his throat. "I'm sorry."

Fletcher spoke the words so softly that Grady wasn't really sure he'd heard them. He stared in disbelief. Fletcher finally met his gaze again and repeated it. "I'm sorry for selling you."

Now it was Grady who had to look away. He had expected anger, resentment, even contempt, but not regret.

"Well, it's too late for apologies," Grady said, exhaling. "I been dreaming of this day, planning for it all these years. First I want to hear you beg for your life the same way my mama and I begged you the day you sold me. I want to make you suffer just a little of what I been suffering all this time—the beatings, the whippings, the weeks spent in filthy slave cells without a soul who cared if I lived or died. And after you beg and plead and feel some of the fear I been feeling day after day for all these years . . . then I plan to blow your brains out. Right here in your big fancy house. The house I was never good enough to step inside, even though half of the blood in my veins is the same as yours—white man's blood."

Fletcher closed his eyes. Grady expected to see fear in them when he opened them again, but instead he saw resignation. His father looked old and tired, the fight all gone out of him. "I know some of what you suffered," Fletcher said quietly. "I spent time in a Union prison camp. But I won't beg for my life."

"You deserve to die!"

Fletcher shrugged. "We all do."

Grady thought of Edward Coop's lifeless body—of the guilt that had haunted him after he'd murdered Coop. Grady knew that he deserved to die for killing him. But Jesus had taken the death penalty for him so that he could live.

For some reason, as Grady gazed at his father, he saw his own son. And he realized that if Fletcher hadn't sold him all those years ago, he never would have met Anna, never would have had a son.

"I've dreamed of killing you," Grady repeated. "But I'm not going to. I have a son of my own, now. I want to live as a free man, not hang for giving you what you deserve. I want to be a father to him. I want to show him what a real father is like."

Fletcher's jaw trembled with emotion. "What's his name?"

"It's . . . it's George. But—" Grady started to tell him that it was just a coincidence, that his son wasn't named after him, but Fletcher gripped the arms of his chair and suddenly pulled himself to his feet. Grady was stunned to see tears in his eyes. His father walked over to a bookshelf, pulled down a volume, and opened it. It was hollow inside and hid a drawstring bag. He tossed the bag to Grady. He felt the jangling weight of coins.

"What's this?" Grady asked.

"Open it."

Grady loosened the strings enough to see dozens of large, gold coins inside. He glared at his father. "Why are you giving me this? Are you trying to soothe your guilty conscience by buying me off?"

"I know you won't believe me . . . but I loved your mother. Tessie was—" He paused, clearing his throat. "I'm giving it to you because you're a Fletcher."

451

"I don't want your money," he said, holding out the bag. "I ain't gonna help ease your guilt."

Fletcher shoved his hands in his pockets. "Then give the money to your son. He's a Fletcher, too."

Grady studied his father for a long moment, surprised to find that he felt only pity, not hatred. George Fletcher would have to give an accounting to God for what he had done—and hadn't done. The way Edward Coop had. The way Grady himself would, someday.

Grady knew there had been a time in his life when he would have thrown the money in Fletcher's face, too bitter to take anything from a white man. There had been a time when he would have taken the gold and demanded even more in payment for a lifetime of slavery. But he didn't do either of those things. His father was asking for forgiveness in the only way he knew how—and if Grady wanted God's forgiveness, then he had to forgive his father, as well.

Grady put the bag of coins in his pocket and slowly turned away— a free man at last.

Bestselling author **Lynn Austin** has sold more than one million copies of her books worldwide. She is an eight-time Christy Award winner for her historical novels, as well as a popular speaker at retreats and conventions. Lynn and her husband have raised three children and live near Chicago. Learn more at www.lynnaustin.org.

More From Lynn Austin

To learn more about Lynn and her books, visit lynnaustin.org.

Bringing to life the biblical books of Ezra and Nehemiah, *Return to Me* is the compelling story of Babylonian exiles Iddo and Zechariah, the women who love them, and the faithful followers who struggle to rebuild their lives in obedience to the God who beckons them home.

Return to Me
THE RESTORATION CHRONICLES #1

For the first time, beloved author Lynn Austin offers a glimpse into her private life as she shares the inspiring, deeply personal story of her search for spiritual renewal in the Holy Land. With gripping honesty, Lynn seamlessly weaves personal events with insights from Scripture as she finds hope, renewed faith, and a new sense of direction in her journey throughout Israel.

Pilgrimage

You May Also Enjoy...

After a devastating fire destroys her city, Mollie Knox struggles to rebuild her business while two men vie for her affections. Can Mollie rise from the ashes with both her company and her heart intact?

Into the Whirlwind by Elizabeth Camden
elizabethcamden.com

Melanie and Caleb thought their mutual claims to the mercantile were a problem, but there's deeper trouble in store when a body is discovered on their doorstep.

Trouble in Store by Carol Cox
authorcarolcox.com

When an abandoned child brings Nick Lovelace and Anne Tillerton together, is Nick prepared to risk his future plans for an unexpected chance at love?

Caught in the Middle by Regina Jennings
reginajennings.com